MW01166113

"A shocking yet warmly human story. Very much worth reading."
—Marion Zimmer Bradley,
author of *The Mists of Avalon*

"To those who read [*Child of the Light*] it will be a powerful, perhaps unforgettable experience."
—Orson Scott Card,
author of *Ender's Game*

"...Disturbing and lyrical...spellbinding and haunting."
—*Affair de coeur*

"Unflinchingly confronts its subject head-on while tempering the onslaught of emotion with an otherworldness."
—*Anchorage Daily News*

Child
OF THE JOURNEY

JANET

BERLINER

AND

GEORGE

GUTHRIDGE

Child of the Journey is
a product of White Wolf Publishing.

Copyright © 1996 by Janet Berliner and George Guthridge.
All rights reserved. This book may not be reproduced, in
whole or in part, without the written permission of the
publisher, except for the purpose of reviews.

This is a work of fiction. The principal characters described
in this book are products of the authors' imagination.
Although some historical figures do appear, the events and
circumstances described herein are entirely fictional, and any
resemblance to events or persons, living or dead, is purely
coincidental.

The mention of or reference to any companies or products
in these pages is not a challenge to the trademarks or
copyrights concerned.

Because of the mature themes presented within, reader
discretion is advised.

White Wolf is committed to reducing waste in publishing.
For this reason, we do not permit our covers to be "stripped"
in exchange for credit. Instead we require that the book be
returned, allowing us to resell it.

Cover Illustration: Matt Manley
Cover Design: Michelle Prahler

White Wolf Publishing
780 Park North Boulevard, Suite 100
Clarkston, GA 30021
World Wide Web Page: www.white-wolf.com

Printed in Canada

ACKNOWLEDGMENTS

The authors wish to thank Laurie Harper of Sebastian Agency, Rob Hatch, our in-House editor supreme, and Staley Krause and everyone else at White Wolf for their support and enthusiasm, including Stephe Pagel who makes sure the books are visible.

Janet and George thank Dave Smeds for his excellent eye. Special thanks go to "Cowboy Bob," Robert L. Fleck, without whose patience, help, and good nature the sky would tumble.

Both writers thank Janet's mother, Thea Cowan, for her oral history and research, and for her willingness to relive it all at eighty-something. *Ich liebe dich, Mutti.*

George extends his special thanks to Noi and to Keith Dunn, Katie Hardesty, Karen Pletnikoff, and Carmen Watkins for their assistance.

Janet wishes to thank Sam Draper, Michael Gluckman, and her daughter, Stefanie, for their longterm encouragement, and Laurie Harper for her unflagging friendship through the insanity of the years; may we continue to share the laughter and the tears.

to the survivors

PART I

"What is the price of five sparrows? A couple of pennies? Not much more than that. Yet God does not forget a single one of them."

— Luke 12:6

W

Chapter one

BERLIN
April 1938

Was there any vestige left of the girl-woman who had enchanted the boys that night in Kaverne, Miriam wondered, or had the shadow of these last years erased it all?

Tilting her head, she inspected herself in the ornate mirror of her childhood. She had twisted her hair into a dancer's chignon and decorated it with a sprig of lilac, as she had done the night she first met Erich and Solomon. Leaning closer to the mirror, she inspected the inevitable fine lines that proved the passage of the years. She was more than twice the age now that she had been then. How was that possible, when only yesterday she had been fresh and young and fifteen?

Yesterday, and forever ago.

Time was a vagabond, at once a memory saboteur and a comforter, like an eiderdown that keeps you cozy and warm while it makes you weep and your skin itch.

Here, alone in her old room at what had once been her family estate, Miriam felt relatively safe. She was aware of the comings and goings of Erich's Abwehr colleagues, and of occasional visits by Hermann Göring and Paul Joseph Goebbels, but when she stood on her balcony and stared out across the gardens, she saw only the quietly suburban, upper-crust veneer of the Grünewald. Erich kept to his own quarters, rarely intruding upon her privacy except by invitation, and she had plenty of time for solitude.

An excess of time, probably, judging by how often she caught herself avoiding the present and dwelling on a past that was, at least for the moment, lost to her, and a future that had become increasingly inaccessible.

As if venting her anger on it would somehow help, she picked up her hairbrush and flung it across the room. The futility of the gesture served only to increase her misery. The last thing in the world she wanted to do was attend a party honoring Adolph Hitler, she thought, contemplating her partially dressed image in the mirror. It would be delusional to believe that the Führer's birthday celebration would be anything but a stiff and formal dinner party, with nary a guest on the list who could provide her with either entertainment or intellectual stimulation.

So she had dallied too long. Now she was sure to be late, which would infuriate Erich, and cause the evening to turn out more unpleasant yet.

JANET BERLINER AND GEORGE GUTHRIDGE

She retrieved her brush from the carpet and sat back down in front of the mirror, but instead of busying herself with the business of dressing, she allowed herself to drift sixteen years into the past, to a dinner party which had been anything but dull.

"*Wenn der weisse Flieder wieder Blüht,*" she sang softly, reprising the song from her memories of that night at Kaverne, the cabaret her grandmother had built in the converted basement beneath a fur shop. It was an unusual place for a nightclub, across the street from the block of flats where Erich Weisser and Solomon Freund lived, and next door to their parents' cigar shop. Only she had not known any of that at the time. Nor would she have cared if she *had* known. They were around twelve, going on thirteen. Mere *boys*. She, on the other hand, had been fifteen, just back from dance training in America, her head filled with visions of stardom. Still, she knew enough to be grateful to her grandmother, Oma Rathenau, and to what the social gossips called her grandmother's crusade to bring respectability to Berlin's entertainment industry. Nor did she resent the suggestion that the real purpose of the cabaret was to showcase her talents. Why not? She was the old lady's granddaughter and the niece of Germany's newly appointed Foreign Minister, not to speak of being the heir to the Rathenau fortune.

What would her life have been like now, Miriam wondered, had she not performed at Kaverne's preopening dinner party? There might have been no Solomon in her life. There certainly would have been no Erich, for it was there that she had met both of them: Solomon, clutching his cello and dressed as if for his own bar mitzvah; and Erich, hair slicked back, wearing pressed trousers, a white shirt with starched, rounded collar, and his father's silk paisley cravat.

From strangers to acquaintances, from friends to intimates. It was a strange, wonderful, and terrifying progression, fraught with the best and the worst that human nature had to offer.

Enduring the customary pain that accompanied even the most fleeting reminder of Sol, she opened one of the drawers of the tiny porcelain music box he had won for her in the ring-toss booth at Luna Park.

"*Glühwürmchen, Glühwürmchen, glimm're....* Shine little glowworm, glimmer, glimmer...." The Paul Lincke song was one of Solomon's favorites, the first of the two songs she sang at Kaverne. There, for the first time, she met Erich. It was not until later that night that she actually met Solomon, Erich's brother-in-blood and, now, her dearest husband-of-the-heart.

How disappointed she had felt at the tepid applause of the audience that night, though it was what she had learned to expect from the Germans, disciplined, and so unlike the Americans, with their wild enthusiasms and their appreciation for youth and beauty.

Smiling at her instantaneous fifteen-year-old rebellion against the self-control of her audience, *she remembered....*

...Tossing aside her shawl, she erupted into a cancan, whirling, kicking, repeating the routine until, with a suddenness calculated to send an ache through the

groin of the shy-looking bespectacled young man who
had just crept into the cabaret, and to shock the other
boy who had risen to his feet and was clapping wildly,
she dropped into a split. She was playing to him and
to Solomon, and they both repaid her with naked
adoration, staring at her as if she were the beautiful film
star, Lilian Harvey, in the flesh.

Her diminutive uncle raised a black eyebrow and
blew a perfect smoke ring into the air before applauding
his favorite niece's performance. She smiled prettily at
him and at her bejeweled old grandmother as the band
began to play and couples gravitated toward the dance
floor.

She approached her uncle's table. Having introduced
herself to Erich's parents and exchanged a few
pleasantries with them—the woman looked a little too
nervous; the man, at best, uncomfortable, his nose red,
as if he had been drinking too much, and his eyes
hard—she glanced sideways at the boy. He was good-
looking, not like either of his parents, yet he had his
father's square jaw and his mother's light hair.

Miriam turned her attention to Solomon's family. His
sister Recha looked like Goldilocks with a nose-cold.
Her father looked nervous but proud, as did her mother,
who had leaned over and whispered something in her
husband's ear. His eyes flashed angrily behind his thick
lenses as he turned toward Sol, who had finally stepped
all the way into the room.

She looked from one boy to the other. How very
different they seemed. She liked Erich's Aryan good

looks but there was something about Solomon that appealed to the gentlest side of her. He looked sensitive. And *forlorn.*

Too late, she rose to speak to him, for he was following his father through the doorway.

Curious, Miriam followed them. Herr Freund had left the door slightly ajar. She pushed at it gently, let herself through, and found herself standing in the shadows at the top of a flight of stairs which led to a subbasement.

She went down just far enough to be able to see Solomon and his father, who stood arguing under a dangling naked light bulb.

Herr Freund clicked open an engraved gold watchcase that hung from a chain across his waist, wiped dust from his shoes with a Reichsbanner handkerchief he removed from the breast pocket of his pinstriped *Shabbas* suit, and reprimanded Solomon for keeping an important man like her uncle waiting. "Herr Rathenau is not merely an important man," Herr Freund said. "He is an important Jew."

"You are an important Jew, Papa." Solomon looked up. "You won the Iron Cross, First Class…."

She touched the Iron Cross that lay inside her music box, remembering how—a dozen years later—Solomon had removed it from the body of his dead father. Even now she gagged at the memory of the gentle and generous Jacob Freund, hanging by the neck in his own shop. Dead. Blue. Hanged by the neck with the war medal's cord…and her uncle also dead, victim of an assassin's grenade. Why were men of peace always targeted!

She clutched the Iron Cross in her palm, letting its sharp edges dig into her skin, the way Sol had done before he had handed it to her to keep in trust. For Sol it was an instrument of pride, of terror, of death. For her it was a reminder of Solomon and of all that she held most dear.

She shut that drawer of the music box and opened a second one. Carefully, as if it were made of butterfly wings, she took out her cigar-band wedding ring and slipped it onto her finger next to the ostentatious diamond Erich had given her. On an absolute basis she supposed it was quite extraordinary, but to her it was as synthetic as their mockery of a marriage.

If anything ever happens to me, go to Erich, Sol had told her. *It is tradition that a man take care of his brother's wife.*

She remembered the expression on Erich's face that childhood night in Kaverne, when she returned from eavesdropping on Solomon and his father. Strange, like a swimmer on the verge of diving into icy water. Stammering as he begged her to take a walk with him on the darkened streets outside. She had wondered if he always stammered under pressure, when he did not feel in control.

Her decision to do as he asked had been colored by the knowledge that Konnie, her chauffeur, was out next to the limousine, and would protect her.

Dear Konnie. After so many years of driving her uncle—driving her—around, he was at the beck and call of the boy she had teased that night.

That boy was a man now. A potent force in the Party—or so he told her. Still stammering when he lost control. But alive. As Konnie was alive. Not dead like her uncle and her grandmother, or half-alive, like her.

Like Sol.

She wound up the music box. "*Glühwürmchen, Glühwürmchen...*"

The barrel-organ man had played the song that night in the street, as if it were her theme song. She had executed a few dance steps and grabbed Erich's hand. "Listen. He's playing 'Glowworm.' I never get enough of that song."

She had lifted Erich's hand to see it more clearly in the lamplight, kissed the red scars she had noticed earlier, and asked what had happened to cause them.

"M-my badge of courage?" He was blushing, though whether from pleasure at the touch of her or out of embarrassment, she could not tell. "L-long time ago. An accident..."

Whatever else he had said was submerged in the sound of her own voice. "*Glühwürmchen, Glühwürmchen, glimm're—*"

She had not realized she was singing aloud that night. People stared at her—not that she cared, but it wasn't exactly smart to draw attention to herself like that, in the middle of the street. Still she had danced toward the music.

Someone started to applaud and others joined in.

"More!" a man yelled. "More!"

"Play, barrel-organ man!" another shouted. "Bring out the beer. We're going to have a real Saturday night party!"

The barrel-organ man grinned widely and patted the

head of his monkey; it seemed to be grinning too. The stiff-necked upper crust could keep their genteel appreciation, she thought as she curtsied and began to sing. This was more like it, she had thought; this was the real thing.

But that night wasn't real. Not anymore. So far in her past that it was like another life. Make-believe.

Tonight...was real.

"I made a deal with Erich, Sol," she whispered, holding her ring finger close to her cheek. "He may share my bed when he pleases, but I decide who shares my heart."

Erich's terms had been clear; he would make sure Solomon stayed alive in the camp if she publicly renounced Judaism and became Frau Erich Alois...in the eyes of the world, his loving wife.

Be alive, Solomon, she prayed. Oh God, be alive. I'm doing my part. Do yours, and we'll make it out of this God-forsaken country.

She replaced the cigar band in the music box and bent over to smell the roses from the Argentinean emissary, Juan Perón.

"He still sends them to you every time he is in Berlin, doesn't he?" Erich came up behind her. He sounded peeved.

"Yes, he does." He had since before Uncle Walther's death. She pictured Perón's face the last time she had seen him, watching her place a wreath under the plaque commemorating her uncle's assassins.

They had the courage of their convictions, the plaque read.

Men and women do what they must to survive, Perón's card told her, as if he felt the need to rationalize her actions for her. This, all the ugly things, were for Sol. Always for Sol. She was his protector, carrying his spirit, and the three of them—she, Erich, Solomon— were a triumvirate still, as they had been from the start. Only now Sol was in a camp and she was in a different kind of prison, wearing a traitor's hat.

"An Argentinean custom—courting another man's wife?"

Miriam stared at Erich in the mirror as he strolled out onto the balcony. Seeing him out there never failed to remind her of the time, eons ago, when he had climbed the rose trellis and watched her in her peignoir in front of this same mirror. And Solomon somewhere out there in the darkness, Erich's constant friend and support system. There—but too embarrassed to show himself, even when Erich made her the gift of a puppy.

Watching Erich kiss her.

Watching her let him.

She had insisted on having this bedroom before agreeing to move back to the estate. The move, he had said, would prove her sincerity to Hitler and Goebbels. Perhaps he secretly hoped that the move would placate her. The estate, hers by birthright after her uncle's and grandmother's death, had been stolen by the Nazis…and now, ironically, was hers again. To use, but not to own. And for a price.

She had allowed Erich to apply to have her status changed from Jew to Aryan.

To further placate her, he had indulged her trivial

request for the bedroom. That was the trick to getting what she wanted: convince him an issue was trivial.

"Do I look beautiful enough for your precious Führer's party?"

"Almost perfect, my darling." Erich came inside.

"Almost perfect?" she said as flippantly as she could.

"Wear this and you'll look absolutely perfect." He put his hand in his pocket and took out a necklace. "Here."

He reached in front of her and centered a large sapphire above her décolletage. "It matches your eyes." He bent to kiss the back of her neck before fastening the delicate gold chain beneath her hair. "My God!" He stood back to look at her reflection. "You just get more lovely."

Heart thumping, she fingered the necklace. "Where did you find this? It belonged to…"

"Your Oma."

She clamped down on her rising rage and fought with the clasp, trying to open it. "I can't wear it!" she said, momentarily losing control. "I can't go tonight. You'll have to say I'm ill—"

"Don't be hysterical," he said coolly. "The necklace looks magnificent, and I've already made excuses for you once too often. It was an honor to be invited. This is important to me. To us."

To me and us, only a different us, she thought, knowing she had to pull herself together in case someone at the party had a message for her from the underground.

"I suppose I can't let my dressmaker down." She forced a half smile. "She would never forgive me if I didn't show off her creation. She tells me it's going to be polka dots for the opera season, if Berlin still has an opera house by then."

"I've been meaning to ask why you go to Baden-Baden for your dresses. Are there no seamstresses here, in Berlin?"

"Of course there are. But I like Madame Pérrault. I've known her since I was a young girl." She stopped. She must be careful to say just enough and not too much. When Konnie drove her to Baden-Baden, they spent only minutes with the seamstress; the rest of the time was devoted to meeting with various members of the underground, for whom she acted as liaison here in Berlin.

"Remember Nabokov, my tennis instructor?" she asked him.

He nodded, his expression telling her that he had not forgotten his childish jealousy of what he took to be the man's obvious desire for young Miss Rathenau.

"This woman was his mistress," Miriam went on. "He deserted her when his first book came out, and she came to me for help. As you see, she is good at what she does."

She got up and showed off the full effect of the dress.

"You'll be the belle of the ball."

"The belly of the ball's more like it! I'm getting fat. I'm getting fat without my dancing. Maybe I should have had her make the dress in some simple fabric and fashion—something more suitable for a matron of the Reich."

Erich laughed. "You'll never look matronly, *Prinzessin*. Not even if you were…pregnant."

Miriam met his gaze in the mirror. Such an event was unlikely. They had not had intercourse for a couple of months, and it had been a fortnight since he had even slept with her, preferring his own bedroom for reasons she could not fathom. Whatever the cause, she was thankful.

Unable to pass up the opportunity for sarcasm, however, she added, "And if I were? How would you feel about that, Erich? After all, my blood is tainted no matter how many times I renounce my faith. Could you dare love a child that would be a *Mischling*—half-breed?"

The color rose in his cheeks, and she thought she had gone too far, but he simply shrugged and said quietly, "If you were carrying my child, I'd strut around like a Pfaueninsel peacock, and the hell with anyone worried about genealogy."

Miriam chuckled. "Peacock strutting is conduct unbecoming of an officer of the Reich." She wished there were more moments like this. He generally took himself and his damn Party so seriously, it was hard for her to recall if he had the capacity for anything else.

"It's good to hear you laugh," he said.

He reached for his cigarette case, clicked it open, and automatically offered her a smoke. When she shook her head, he took out one of the fashionable flat cigarettes he smoked on formal occasions, and lit it with the engraved lighter his parents had given him when they reopened the shop. He inhaled and blew several smoke rings. She watched them drift toward the ceiling.

"Time to go." He removed his formal jacket from the wardrobe.

Miriam stared at the armband, as if its white circle and red-and-black emblem were an adder about to strike.

"Our dear Gauleiter has already grown impatient and gone on without us," he said.

"Don't worry. As long as he had his schnapps, he won't care. Why on earth did you ask him to come here before the party anyway?"

"He keeps making such a point of telling me how much he misses living here at the estate. " He paused and glanced down at his arm. "I have to wear it," he said coldly.

She had not realized that she was still staring at the armband. "You like to wear it."

"Let's not start that again."

She turned back to the mirror and removed Oma's necklace. Fiddling with the row of minute pearl buttons that ran from her lace-edged décolletage to her waistline, she said, "I'm sorry, Erich. The necklace holds too many memories." She picked up the double pearl choker he had given her for her birthday and struggled with the clasp.

"Women! I give up." Erich sighed and helped her with the necklace. "Now we really do have to go."

CHAPTER TWO

Less than half an hour later, Konrad pulled up outside Schloss Gehrhus. Two cars were ahead of them. Miriam watched as men in evening dress and women in gowns and furs stepped out. They wore the somber colors that were reputedly the Führer's preference, all but one, an ambassador's wife who had—or so Erich had told her—graced his bed upon more than one occasion. She was tall and angular, quite beautiful. A silver mink dangled from her arm. Her gown was midnight blue, beaded across the right shoulder in silver bugle beads and black sequins.

A little dressmaker in Baden-Baden, no doubt, Miriam thought cynically. Turning her head, she looked at the castle's façade. No sequins there. The architecture was severe, if not dull—more like Jagdschloss Grünewald, the famous hunting lodge, than a castle.

Inside, as she recalled from the visits of her youth, opulence gave the lie to the exterior. The castle, built by one Dr. Pannwitz, personal attorney to his Majesty Kaiser Wilhelm II, had long been a gathering place for important people. Politicians, artists, scientists and diplomats from all over the world had met there, striding across its oriental carpets, exchanging confidences under its crystal chandeliers, dancing across the parquet floor of its two-storied mirrored ballroom. The Kaiser himself had been the first guest to enter the house, shortly before the outbreak of the Great War.

Konrad opened the car door.

"How long do we have to stay?" Miriam asked.

"As long as seems expedient," Erich said curtly. Apparently immediately regretting the brusqueness of his answer, he reached for her gloved hand. She pulled it away. "I'm sorry, *Prinzessin*," he said. "I have much on my mind. And this is, after all, the Führer's birthday celebration."

On his actual birthday, on the twentieth of April, Hitler was at Berchtesgaden with Eva and his cronies. By his order, the streets of Berlin had been filled with open crates of oranges; the crates would be replenished all week.

Tonight, three days later, the leaders of his "master race" were gathering at Schloss Gehrhus to eat caviar and pheasant and drink champagne to his continued good health.

"How many celebrations does that madman need!" she asked.

Hoping that someone from the underground would be here with a message for her to pass along so she could rationalize her presence to herself, she allowed Konnie to help her from the car. She pulled her cape around her shoulders and followed Erich up the stone steps and into the entry hall. It was filled with people. Champagne flowed freely and flowers streamed over the balustrades, fresh roses and carnations from the estate which ranged across more than twelve thousand square meters.

"Doesn't such extravagance make you at all uncomfortable?" She tugged at her gloves.

"I can never walk in here without wanting to touch everything." He looked as excited as a sailor confronted by the infinite variety of Amsterdam's red-light district.

He lusts after the oriental carpets and mahogany balustrades, she thought. She took in the gilt-edged chairs and matching tapestry-covered walls, the vaulted ceilings carved with inlaid wood, the giant arrangements of agapanthus and gladioli in the entryway. From the dining hall she could hear *"Für Elise,"* one of Hitler's favorites, and the buzz of conversation.

"So you two lovebirds finally decided to grace us with your presence," Goebbels called out from across the foyer. Short and spare, he leaned toward them as he hoisted the inevitable glass of schnapps in a mock toast. "Perhaps now we can eat."

As he moved toward them, the chandelier caught the movement of the silver-haired man who had been standing against the wall in the shadows, behind the

Gauleiter. Heart pounding, she thought she recognized the man responsible for giving orders outside the cigar shop, on the day of Jacob's death.

"We shall talk more later, Otto," Goebbels said, over his shoulder.

The tall man clicked his heels. "Certainly, Gauleiter. It will be my pleasure."

Hearing the voice, Miriam was certain that she was right. "Erich, that's—?" she began.

Goebbels was already at her side and she could say no more. She gave him the closest approximation she could manage of a smile, and instantly wished she had not when he offered her his arm. Erich was forced to escort Magda. Miriam could feel him watching her, feel his ridiculous jealousy. Apparently he could not help himself, no matter who the man was. He had even flinched when she so much as mentioned Nabokov with the least bit of affection in her voice.

The four of them wandered into the dining hall. According to Erich, there were fifty invited couples— one for each year of the Führer's life, plus one for the coming year. They seemed all to be here, examining place cards at eight small tables set for ten people apiece. The rest, including the Goebbels, who quickly excused themselves, floated toward the head table, where one seat remained conspicuously empty, waiting for a host who seldom arrived until the meal was well under way.

As drums rolled, a group of boys from the Adolph Hitler school, apprentices for the Hitler Elite Guard, entered the dining hall. Seven years in training, culminating in the honor of service to their Führer, Miriam thought, first as waiters at his birthday party, later in the SS or at some foreign Front.

The youths were assisted by pigtailed girls from the RAD—*the new human beings*, they were called—wearing white pinafores, orange kerchiefs and the royal blue shirts that marked them as new members. They were supervised by graduate black-uniformed Elite Guard members while the female graduates, distinguishable by their white shirts and ties, navy skirts and aprons, were relegated to the kitchen and the reception area.

The orchestra switched to Strauss.

"*Prosit!*" Erich lifted his glass and addressed the officer across from him, but his gaze was on Miriam.

Lift your glass, she told herself. Respond to the music. Smile. Eat. Look as if you want to be here. But though the meal was exquisitely prepared, she barely picked at her food. Even the dessert of raspberries and *crème fraiche* held no appeal.

"Champagne?"

"Thank you. Pour it for me. I'll be right back."

"Feeling all right, my dear? Like me to accompany you?" The officer's wife gave her an emphatic *You must be in the family way* glance.

Miriam dabbed at her lips with the linen serviette. "No thank you. Most kind of you, but I'm fine."

She left the room and was headed to the garden when she spotted a narrow staircase barred with a chain and a sign that warned her not to go beyond it. Picking up the candle lantern that stood on the bottom step, she unhooked the chain and made her way up the stairs to the grand ballroom.

This was not her first visit to Schloss Gehrhus. She had been here before with her uncle at a diplomatic function honoring a group of visitors from South America. What a fuss they had made of her—the exquisite Miriam Rathenau! She had danced all night, up here, mostly with a handsome young diplomat in training, a South American attached to the Italian Embassy. Of course he was too old for her, but for a few days she had walked around with the glassy-eyed look of young love while her uncle teased her unmercifully, especially when roses arrived for her the following morning.

A week later, her uncle had informed her with mock sadness that Juan Perón had left for Rome. In the throes of her first "desertion," she had sworn never to come back to the Schloss—especially not up here.

She placed the lantern on the floor and gave herself up to a harmless memory of a time long gone, and then to a time more recent. A time of hope for a safe future, when for a moment she had believed Erich's assurances, believed that he would be able to provide Sol with safe transit to Amsterdam.

Surrounded by mirrors and haunted by a harmonica, she closed her eyes and slowly waltzed, remembering the last bittersweet hours she had spent with Sol in the dust-covered remains of what had once been Kaverne.

Sol had put his finger to her lips and picked up a candle. Taking her hand, he had led her up the stairs and into the cabaret. On the dusty dance floor, amid the pallor of greenish light beaming down through one of the few small, stained-glass windows that remained unbroken, he lifted her knuckles to his lips and closed his eyes.

"There is a season for all things, Miri," she remembered him saying. "They have turned this into a season of endings. Let us defy them and make it one of beginnings. Marry me."

"Here? Tonight? And who will be the rabbi?"

"God."

They had stood among dusty muslin sheets, thrown carelessly over once-new tables and chairs surrounding an abandoned dance floor in a closed cabaret in a world seemingly without hope, and uttered words that denied Berlin, the Reich, Erich, and hopelessness. They spoke of ultimately finding freedom and a life together in South America.

They spoke of marriage, and of enduring love.

She squeezed his hands, and smiled. "Make two stacks of three tables each. I'll be right back." By the time Sol had the tables piled up in the center of the dance floor, Miriam had returned, the rose-colored shawl that she had worn that first night in the cabaret retrieved from the costume trunk.

"We have to have a canopy, don't we? It wouldn't be a wedding without one."

Before he could say anything else she had left again, this time to retrieve a hidden bottle of burgundy and three dusty glasses.

Wriggling out of her slip, she wrapped it around one of the glasses, placed it under the canopy, and twirled around to show him the spray of lavender silk lilac she had twisted into her hair.

Now, standing in the Grand Ballroom of Schloss Gehrhus, she touched the fresh sprig of lilac in her hair. Her eyes misted with tears. In her mind's eye, she watched Solomon pull a harmonica from his pocket and blow into it to clear it of dust. She saw him cup the instrument lovingly in his hands, and felt him watch her sway as he softly played one of her favorite Schubert melodies.

When he had finished, he fished in his pocket, pulled out two cigars, and removed their gold bands—the ones she now kept hidden in her music box, among the gaudy jewelry she wore to impress Erich's fellow officers.

That night, as dusk faded and shadows lengthened, she and Solomon had held fast to each other and to their dream of a tomorrow. When night came, so did Konrad.

"The train for Amsterdam leaves in just over half an hour, and you are expected at the flat," Konnie had told her, glancing at the wristwatch she had brought him from America.

"One dance, my love."

She whispered the words to the walls of the empty ballroom, as she had to Solomon then.

Back then, warmed by wine and passion, she and Sol had danced to imaginary violins playing Schubert and Strauss and Brahms. Now she danced alone, not for want of a partner, but because the only partner she wanted was lost to her, perhaps forever, except in memory.

"May I have this dance?"

She looked up at Erich and graced him with one of her rare, open smiles. "You caught me," she said.

He bowed and took her in his arms. "Do you have any idea how beautiful you are, Miriam?"

"It's this room," she said softly. With a graceful sweep of her arm, she guided his gaze to the ballroom ceiling, two stories high, to the twenty floor-to-ceiling mirrors, each reflecting the soft glow of the lantern, to the moon, shining through the beveled French doors and adding its shadows to the fairy-tale glow.

"It's not simply the room, Fräulein," another voice said.

Miriam's sweeping gesture faltered and froze in midair as Erich whirled around to face the Führer, who stood at the top of the forbidden stairway, arms crossed in the familiar pose.

"Forgive me. You must be Frau Alois. Herr Rittmeister, where have you been hiding this extraordinary creature? May I have the pleasure?" He stepped toward them. "You don't mind, do you, Alois? After all, it is my birthday. It is only fair that I be allowed to dance with the most beautiful woman at my celebration."

Erich nodded and let go of Miriam's waist. He watched as Hitler pushed her stiffly around the floor to the strains of Strauss.

Somehow, she thought, I will get through this moment.

"I saw the light from outside and came up here first." The Führer wiped her sweat from his palms as the notes faded. "How fortunate that I did. You are a wonderful dancer. Now, however, we should join my other guests."

Asking forgiveness of Sol, Miriam held onto Hitler's arm and allowed herself to be ushered downstairs and into the dining hall. The band switched to *"Deutschland über Alles,"* and Erich saluted with the others.

"Hoch soll sie leben!" They toasted their Führer. "May he live well."

Smiling a pinched smile, Hitler acknowledged the repeated good wishes as he made his way to the main table. When he was seated, the orchestra renewed its evening of Strauss with "The Blue Danube."

"Why didn't anybody ever tell Strauss that the Danube is gray and dirty, not blue?" Miriam said irritably.

Erich was too busy watching Hitler to respond. The Führer was going through his ritual of consuming a quantity of tablets, probably Dr. Koster's strychnine and atropine antigas pills, which he took constantly to reduce the flatulence that reputedly plagued him.

Wishing he would choke on them, Miriam also watched the ritual. When it was over, Hitler leaned across the table and spoke to his Gauleiter, who, face red with fury, whispered something to his wife and stood up.

After making his way to Erich's table, Goebbels said in an icy tone, "The Führer wishes to have you and your wife dine with him."

"No, Erich," Miriam whispered. She had done enough for him tonight, dancing with Hitler, smiling at the rest of his sick ménage, and not even a message from the underground to make her feel useful. "I—" She looked at his face and gave up.

This was not going to be one of the times to expect indulgences.

CHAPTER THREE

"Please...be seated." Hitler waved at the chairs vacated by Dr. and Frau Goebbels. "Tell me more about this beautiful woman." His tone was genial. Expansive. "Can she really be the niece of that traitor Rathenau?"

"Walther Rathenau was—"

"Her adopted uncle," Erich said, finishing Miriam's sentence. "She was adopted by his sister and brother-in-law, mein Führer."

"Where are they, these people?"

"Dead, mein Führer."

"Just as well." Hitler scrutinized Miriam as if she were a piece of fruit and he a prospective customer making sure there were no bruises. "With your grace and beauty, you could be a wonderful tool for the Reich. I have been assured that you believe in our cause and reject that Jew's philosophies."

He turned to Erich. "Pity she is so dark, although they tell me that can be easily remedied these days—"

A drum roll announced the presentation of Hitler's birthday gift, a globe whose uneven surface outlined the world's topography. Erich was grateful for the interruption; he could feel the heat of Miriam's wrath rising from her like steam from a radiator. He held onto the hope that the distraction would remove the Führer's attention from her, but no sooner had the orchestra resumed playing than Hitler returned to the same topic.

"We must let the newspeople ascertain that she was adopted. Exposed to Jewish blood, but not possessed of any. I will make the necessary arrangements."

"Thank you, mein Führer, but we have already applied to the Reichs Department for Genealogical Research to invoke the 1934 edict you yourself wrote," Erich said.

"Good!" Hitler turned to Miriam. "I will contact Leni Riefenstahl and make sure she puts you in her next propaganda film."

There was only one way he was going to get Miriam to do this, Erich knew. Again he would have to use Solomon's safety as a bargaining tool. He would even offer to try again to "find" Sol. Good thing he had mailed that letter to Amsterdam, effectively stopping the flood of correspondence to Miriam. It had been tiresome intercepting everything, and even more tiresome having to change the telephone number at the old place. It was better now that they had moved to the estate; even if Sol forgave her, he would not attempt to contact Miriam there.

"What a pity she is not expecting a child." Hitler's voice had become shrill. Excited. People around them looked up and listened. "You are a Nazirite, the true Biblical figurehead of commitment."

The man was beginning to ramble, something he did frequently. His five-minute audiences were notorious for lasting hours; people left them exhausted and confused.

"Even the Christian God, you know, though spineless, ordained our triumphs." Hitler laughed, pleased with himself. "Ordained," he repeated. "Like my departure from art into politics. Have I ever told you, Alois, how that came to pass?"

His voice turned soft. Dreamy. "I was in a hospital, having been overcome by mustard gas fumes on a train. While recovering from my ordeal, I heard voices, Alois. They told me what to do."

Mustard fumes! Voices! The man's as crazy as Solomon, Erich thought.

Another drum roll saved him from further speculation.

"It is time for the entertainment." Goebbels stood up to make the announcement. "Let us proceed outdoors."

"I must talk to you," Miriam whispered.

"Later."

"Now!"

"Talk, then." Erich dawdled behind the others, who were hurrying into the garden. He knew what had been planned. He had seen it all before, had taken part in a similar ceremony usually reserved for Midsummer Night.

"You must promise me something," Miriam said urgently. "I cannot make such a film!"

"Miriam." He was pleading with her. "How can I promise you that? You heard what he said."

"Who is he—God? I can't! I won't!"

"Think of Solomon if you will not think of me," Erich said.

"Is that a threat?"

"It's a statement of fact."

"What will happen if I refuse to do this thing? Will you let them take your *friend* from your Führer's precious camp and hang your *friend* in public?"

Erich searched for a lie by omission to pacify her, if only for the moment. Lies by omission were easier, less likely to ricochet.

"I must see for myself that Sol is all right," she said.

"We have been over this a thousand times." He spoke as patiently as he could. "You cannot go to Solomon. The danger to both of you is worse now."

"You mean danger to you," she said flatly.

"You're no fool, Miriam. The Führer's attention is on you—"

"*There* you are, Herr Rittmeister," Goebbels said. For once Erich was grateful for the Gauleiter's appearance on the scene. "I wish to speak to you for a minute."

"Certainly, Herr Minister."

The two men moved ahead of Miriam as they walked toward the lawns at the back of the Schloss Gehrhus estate.

"The Führer has told me to contact Riefenstahl

regarding Miriam." Goebbels' voice remained icy. "I will, of course, do his bidding, but—"

"But what?" Erich sensed he was not going to like what was coming; he would have to watch his back more closely than ever.

"In my opinion, your wife's reformation needs something more. A doctor at the Sachsenhausen camp, Schmidt by name, has some interesting ideas. She is conducting experiments...." He paused, then quickly added, "I have suggested to the Führer that Miriam take part in those experiments."

"Experiments?" Erich tried not to sound afraid, but his voice was gravelly.

"Total blood transfusions." Goebbels smiled. "Don't look so shocked. After all, if Miriam were to be transfused with Aryan blood, no one would dispute her place beside you in the New Order."

"Isn't such an operation...dangerous?"

"We must all take risks for the Fatherland, Herr Rittmeister."

Goebbels veered to the right and the conversation ended.

Drawing on deep reserves of self-discipline, Erich set his face in a smile and waited for Miriam to catch up. He would have to worry about this new issue later, he decided, as, arm around her waist, he guided her toward a group of RAD girls and students from the Adolph Hitler School. They had gathered in a circle around a blazing fire.

To one side of them stood a woman dressed in the uniform of the RAD graduates. "The young people before you have formed a magic circle around the sacred flames. They have been taught that the highest honor they can receive is to lay down their lives for the Fatherland." Her voice was deep as a man's.

"From Rhineland Hills blaze upward and ascend," she said in a chant. "Let those of you with dreams of a heroic future dedicated to our Fatherland take hands and leap over the flames to prove your love for our Führer and for our cause."

Two by two, holding hands and laughing, the new human beings and students of the Adolph Hitler School leapt over the flames and ran into the woods.

"Could we please leave now, Erich?" Miriam asked, when only the flames and the adults remained.

Erich looked at her face. She had her eyes shut and looked as if she were about to faint. "Let us say our farewells," he said, leading her over to the Führer.

"Yes. Good night." Hitler waved his hand arbitrarily, as if he had already forgotten both of them.

"What will happen if I refuse to make the film?" Miriam asked on the way home.

"To whom?"

"To all of us. Me, you, Solomon?"

Omission, Erich reminded himself. But because he could not find a half truth that would serve the purpose, he said nothing.

As they drove along Brahmstrasse, away from Schloss Gehrhus and toward the Rathenau estate, he kept wanting to touch her hand. When he finally did, at least for the few minutes that it took to get to their destination, she did not pull away. Usually his displays of affection were met with neutrality, if not coldness. He was grateful for even so small a concession. Neither of them spoke again until she stood in the doorway of her bedroom.

"What about Solomon and your conscience?" she asked then, as if the conversation had not been broken.

There was no answer he could give her, so he simply kissed her lightly and retired to his quarters. He was barely in bed when a knock sounded on the door downstairs. Grumbling, he climbed from bed and drew on his robe, a garment given him by a youthful whore Goebbels had brought home for a week after his trip to Lisbon. The girl's name was *Toy*. He could recall that much because he had not heard the name before or since, but he hardly remembered the girl herself. He did, however, love the black silk robe with its red fire-breathing dragon embroidered on the back. Most of all he loved it because it reminded him of Goebbels' anger upon discovering that Erich had bedded her. The man had threatened to chop her into dog meat for the kennels and had, in fact, given her to his guards...all twenty of them. Rumor had it she now was working the Elbe waterfront.

The knock came again, louder this time. Knotting the robe's sash, Erich descended the steps with a certain sense of urgency. Even now, after midnight, his men were putting the shepherds through obedience drills. At this hour, it could only be a trainer having problems with one of the dogs.

He glanced up at the crossed Nazi flags above the front door. The midnight sky peered in the tall front window; the mace-wielding suit of armor that stood in the corner, beside the aquarium he had recently acquired for Miriam's amusement, seemed to be waiting for him to open the door.

The knock came a third time.

"All right, all right! I'm coming!"

He opened the door a crack, then threw it wide open. A soldier stood there, a messenger. He saluted and handed Erich a sealed envelope. The letter had Hitler's personal blue seal.

Erich felt his blood run cold. Trembling, he slit open the envelope with his finger. What if Goebbels had talked Hitler into demanding that Miriam have the transfusion? What would he do? Hide her, promise again to send her away? What a waste that would be! Instead of using her talents, the Reich would lose out again. That seemed to be the leitmotif of the Reich: abuse talent, beat out the brains of people who had so much to give, drive others into exile. If only Hitler, or that fat imbecile Göring, would wise up. The Führer had said in Erich's presence that the Jews and Gypsies would ultimately serve the state.

But as what? Fuel?

As long as Goebbels keeps seeing to it that I'm excluded from all important discussions with the Führer, he thought angrily, I will never know the answer.

"The Führer feels you're too emotionally tied to the situation," Goebbels had explained on one of his many returns to the mansion that had been his private brothel. "He's afraid you could not examine the issue with enough dispassion. But you can be sure we will keep your ideas concerning reeducation of the Jews at the forefront of our discussions."

The soldier cleared his throat. Erich opened the envelope and focused on the paper with its official letterhead. He laughed. A promotion to major! Immediate, and at the Führer's personal behest.

It all was too good to be true. His moving from being in charge of security at the estate to running the place...that goddamn Otto Hempel out of his hair, transferred to helping run the detention camp outside Oranienburg...and now this!

"Happy birthday to you," he said. Paper in one hand and envelope in the other, he danced around the foyer. *Hoch soll er leben—*

As if they had heard him, the dogs began to bark.

"Do you hear them? My dogs?" he asked the soldier. "It seems the Führer has finally understood that they could be a major force in a blitzkrieg operation. Think of it! A canine commando unit, trained to infiltrate and neutralize enemy advance units!"

The young man stared at him with a dazed expression. Erich smiled pleasantly at him. "It's late, soldier. Go home to bed."

The soldier saluted and half ran toward his motorcycle, as if anxious to get away from this strange man who danced around hallways in a silk kimono.

Not ready to go back upstairs, Erich went outside. Though it was not yet May, an early warm spell had fooled the chestnut trees into blossoming. The scent

JANET BERLINER AND GEORGE GUTHRIDGE

was sweet, like a woman perfumed to please her man. If only Miriam…

He discarded the thought.

They had lived together at the estate for well over a year, and not once had she indicated even the slightest softening in her attitude toward him. Small wonder he could become erect with her only when he gave himself over to his anger…*to baser instincts*, he forced himself to admit. How had the Führer worded the edict? When it came to Jewish women, "the soldiers' baser instincts are not to be denied." It disgusted him. Potent only when he imagined himself raping her—what kind of lovemaking was that, even if he thought for a moment she was truly his? Was there no circumventing the reality of whom she belonged to, at least while Solomon was alive?

Nothing but a poor substitute for a sparrow such as Solomon Freund. What a price to pay for the love of one woman! He had no such problems with the rental ladies he brought to the apartment to service his needs, so, clearly, the fault lay with Miriam. Her bedroom seemed almost an arena for trial by combat, one he could win only by trampling down the sanctity of his beliefs like so much clover. The pride he felt in denying himself the God-given right as her husband, of taking her as often and as thoroughly as he pleased, brought him some satisfaction, but nothing, he was certain, to equal what he would feel when she eventually came to him of her own free will.

Some night she would be his. Completely. Without

his having to degrade her in his mind while he took her. And without thought of what she or Solomon could gain by it. *Then* he would show her the lovemaking of which he was capable! Had not his capacity for multiple orgasms earned him the name Javelin Man among Frau Goebbels' socialite friends? Meanwhile, he would keep Miriam guessing, wondering why he was sleeping apart from her. For most women, rejection was an aphrodisiac. Why not for her?

Determined to continue in his current mode, he hurried toward the kennels. At least his dogs gave him what he needed—unqualified love and respect.

He wondered if dogs had a conscience, and then laughed at the absurdity of questioning a dog's morality. Such a thing could not possibly exist within their framework. They would not care if one of their fellows was in a place like Sachsenhausen, or even if their master were a human cur like Otto Hempel. What might it feel like to be truly amoral, to live only for obedience and food, for sleep and the praise of your master?

"Kinemann," he called out as he approached the kennels. "Could I see you for a moment?"

The trainer, a pudgy corporal, was kneeling next to Aries, holding her firmly by her collar. Though the dog appeared to be calm, Erich could sense the fury that rippled beneath her fur.

"The dogs are restless tonight," the trainer said.

"Any special reason?"

Kinemann looked at Erich strangely, as if he was not

quite sure if he or the dog were being addressed. "I'm not certain, sir."

As he had been able to do since early childhood, Erich tuned in to the dog's consciousness. She growled softly, a visceral rumble like an instrument tuning up for an overture.

Erich felt his anger mount. "The motorcycle disturbed her. This one's always been extremely sensitive," he said.

Erich knew that there was not enough space, even on this large estate, for the kind of kennels he would prefer—where the comings and goings of motorcars and bikes would not disturb trainer-shepherd concentration. He had performed miracles with the dogs, glad that Hitler himself knew enough to insist that each dog respond to the command of its individual trainer *and* to Erich, the officer in charge. That way, order could be maintained if the trainer were killed during a military action.

But that was not enough.

Given the right place, isolated, tall trees and meadows, the right combination of love and discipline, his shepherds could be trained to do almost anything.

Chapter four

Miriam glanced around Friedrich Ebert Strasse at the aftermath of *Kristallnacht*.

Seven months ago, she thought, *moonlight shone through the glass of Schloss Gehrhus. Now all windows everywhere are shattered*.

The sun shone on remnants of broken glass, still unswept after gangs of young Nazis, many of them driving cars, went on a rampage. *Cars*, for God's sake, she thought. They actually *drove* during the riot. Leaned out of motorcar windows to smash thousands of store fronts belonging to Jewish merchants and destroy hundreds of Jewish homes. Looting, robbing, killing. When would such carnage end!

How ironic that a young Polish Jew, Herschel

Grynspan, had inadvertently sparked this recent night of so-called retribution. Distraught over the treatment his parents had received in Germany and intent on assassinating the German ambassador, Grynspan had murdered Ernst von Rath, a minor German official living at the Parisian consulate—only to find out, Konnie had told her, that von Rath was been under Gestapo scrutiny for *opposing* anti-Semitism.

According to news reports, Grynspan, under arrest in Paris, said, "Being a Jew is not a crime. I am not a dog. I have a right to live and the Jewish people have a right to exist on this earth. Wherever I have been, I have been chased like an animal."

"What a goddamn mess. About time you got here." Erich's father unlocked the door of the shop and signaled her inside. "I'll be leaving right away." He adjusted his tie and buttoned the waistcoat of his Sunday suit. "And you can tell your chauffeur this will be the last time you'll need him here. After what happened earlier this week, I've requested a security guard for the shop at night, and for Sundays."

At least the synagogue in her suburb, Grünewald, had not been desecrated, not yet. Still, with so many synagogues stoned and Berlin's main synagogue burned to the ground, she was worried about her friend, Beadle Cohen, the custodian-scholar who had taught Solomon so much about religion and about life.

"You don't need anyone else here on Sundays," she told Herr Weisser, afraid that acceptance on her part would endanger the already tenuous safe house of the ancient sewer that ran beneath the tobacco shop and what had been the cabaret, below the furrier's next door. In the seven months that had passed since Hitler's birthday party at Schloss Gehrhus, she had provided sanctuary for an ever-increasing number of people.

Konnie was essential for her to continue such work. He was the only one she could trust to guard the shop while she guided transients through the deserted cabaret and into the sewer. After last Wednesday's terrors, there was sure to be increased demand for a place to hide until night claimed the streets.

Needing access to the sewer, she had traded on the fact that the Weissers also accorded her, their son's wife, no more status than an animal. She was right. They had jumped at her offer to be their unpaid Sunday Jew, to keep the shop open while they went to Mass and cleansed their souls. They equally readily agreed to let her stay on for the rest of the day while Friedrich played poker with the other newly affluent merchants of Friedrich Ebert Strasse, whose poker stakes also came from tills conveniently "neglected" by Jews.

As she had known it would be, her offer was irresistible: free labor from someone who knew the shop, someone it pleased them to denigrate. Six days a week she moved in the same circles as Goebbels and even the Führer; on Sunday she stepped down from her high-and-mighty pedestal and assumed her true identity—a Jew dancer turned shop girl after she had frittered away her fortune; the seducer of their beloved son and the reason he never visited, ashamed to face their disapproval for his poor matrimonial choice.

Miriam turned on the lights and readied herself for another ten hours at the shop. She glanced at herself in the counter glass as she removed the two crossed diamond hatpins she had placed in her hat as carefully as if she were going to a garden party. It was a navy-blue picture hat. The soft waves of her hair were visible in front. The rest—more auburn than chocolate now that she had given in to the vanity of repeated henna washings—had been pulled into a severe bun from which only tiny wisps escaped. The heron feathers that decorated the hat were the latest fashion, and the hue made her eyes look the color of iodine. Her dress was a low-cut navy woolen affair with a white lace collar and a fitted waist. Where her décolletage ended, she had clipped a lavender shell cameo; each of her high-heeled boots was decorated with a dozen tiny buttons. The boots, long out of fashion, reminded her of her grandmother.

She had told Erich she'd found the boots on the estate and the hat and dress on a pile of discarded clothes and furniture outside the home of the Weintraub family, who had been transported from the apartments across the street the previous Saturday. The truth was, the clothing was a gift directly from Frau Weintraub in gratitude for being hidden downstairs in the sewer one Sunday. She had waited there to be spirited out through Kaverne in the early hours of the following morning. Where she was now was anybody's guess.

"I'm hungry," she told Konrad, who stood at the door staring impassively out on the street.

He nodded at the code and went to the car. When he returned, he carried a large shopping bag which held their food for the day. Without further discussion, he went downstairs to add that to the supplies they had already secreted in the sewer.

"I really am hungry," she said, when he came back upstairs.

"Me too. Should I go back down and bring up something for us?"

She shook her head. "There's little enough in the way of supplies. Whoever's there next will need it more than we do. You know what I'd really like? A Berliner *Bulette!*" Unlike many other Germans, who derided Americans for calling the beefsteak *ham*burger, Miriam knew that the sandwich had originated in Hamburg, New York. She had lived in the United States, touring the country and learning American dances, for four years following the Great War.

Reaching into her own shopping bag, she pulled out a bar of chocolate and a package that contained one of the new so-called unbreakable gramophone records. She had bought the old kind first and clumsily dropped it on the sidewalk; the record had shattered like a Jewish windowpane.

"How long should I go on believing Erich wants to protect Sol, Konnie?" She split the chocolate bar and handed him half. "Sometimes I think his protestations are about as solid as that record I dropped yesterday. For all I know, Solomon's dead...."

It had been two years since Erich learned that Sol had not made it out of Germany, that he was in a camp.

JANET BERLINER AND GEORGE GUTHRIDGE

Two years since, to protect Sol, she had consented to a marriage ceremony and moved into the estate with Erich. At first, thinking Sol safely in Amsterdam and believing that Erich was working on getting her out of the country, she had lived as a virtual prisoner in his apartment.

That was better, she thought; being at the estate hurt too much. At least at the flat they had made one person happy: Erich's landlady. She had been delighted with the extra money he had given her to keep her mouth shut.

"Don't worry, mein Herr," the landlady had said. "For my part, Satan can hump the Virgin Mary in this house, as long as the authorities stay away. I have nothing against Jews—only against *poor* Jews."

What might she have said had she known Erich was housing Walther Rathenau's only living relative!

Two figures approaching the shop distracted Miriam from her thoughts. When they got close, she saw that one of them was Beadle Cohen. He carried a satchel and held a boy by the hand, a gamin of about nine who wore black pants and a gray shirt, and whose eyes looked glassy. Blank. The look, she fearfully realized, of shock.

"We need help, Miriam," the beadle whispered without preamble. "This is Misha Czisça." Leaning forward, he whispered, "His parents, Rabbi Czisça and his wife…transported."

The beadle stopped and released the boy's hand. He bent down. Looking into the child's eyes, he said, "Listen to me, Misha. We do not know where your parents are, or if they are. You must do whatever Miriam and I tell you. Now go and sit on the linoleum behind the counter, where you will not be seen, and practice your Hebrew lettering. Before you know it, you will be thirteen. You cannot neglect your bar mitzvah studies."

The boy did not answer, nor did he move. He stood in the middle of the shop, dry-eyed, a picture of stoicism. In one hand he held a notebook and a pencil.

"The main temple has been destroyed. Mine will probably be next," the beadle said, standing up. "The boy and I must get out of Germany. I have papers that, with luck, will get me to Copenhagen." He lowered his voice. "Somehow I'll get the boy through, too."

"And then?"

The beadle smiled. *"L'shanah haba-a b'Yerushalayim."*

"Next year in Jerusalem." Miriam repeated the ancient words that symbolized the Jews' hope for a safe harbor where they would always be welcome.

"Perhaps the following year." The old twinkle momentarily returned to the beadle's eyes. "Via New York, I hope. I intend to get to Holland first—I'll have the best chance of a berth from the Port of Amsterdam. While I wait, I'll find Sol's mother and sister."

"Don't tell them about Sol," Miriam said, "not even Recha. She might let it slip."

The beadle looked puzzled. "Surely you correspond with them—?"

"I did, while Sol was with me. When Erich told me that Sol was captured...his mother has been in such a precarious state, I thought the truth might—" She stopped.

What *was* the truth? At first she had rationalized that the news of Sol's internment would kill his mother, that Sol would be out soon, that they had not known Sol was en route to Amsterdam in the first place. And there was Erich. Her life with him was so public. She had crumpled page after page of attempts to explain why she was with Erich. No matter what she wrote, her words sounded like a hollow series of excuses for choosing a soft life. She had finally dashed off a note, saying simply that Sol was safe and that they should not expect to hear from him until, with God's help, they saw him. Her letter had crossed with one from Recha, his sister. She had seen Miriam on the Movietone News, flanked by Erich and Hitler, laying a wreath at the foot of the memorial to her uncle's assassins. Further correspondence from Miriam, Recha said, would be returned unopened.

She had written back twice. Recha remained good as her word. She had not written again. And telephoning? Out of the question. She couldn't. She simply couldn't.

"Come with us to Amsterdam," the beadle said. "I am sure it can be arranged."

Miriam shook her head and thought about another letter, the one Erich had agreed to have delivered to Sol at the camp. He had censored it, made her phrase it so it would seem that she had chosen to be with Erich because she loved him. By the time she had determined to find a way to send an uncensored letter to Sol, someone—according to Erich, it was probably Goebbels or Hempel—had arranged for Sol's transfer to another camp. Erich said he had been unable to ferret out which one, and she had tried, too, with equally fruitless results. Since Sol had no way to communicate with her, she might never know if she had succeeded in her attempt to convey the truth between the heartless lines Erich had forced her to write.

"I'm sorry, Beadle," she said. "If I stay, Sol has a chance."

The beadle took her arm. "I understand. We must each be true to ourselves." Unexpectedly, he kissed her cheek. "Now, to the business at hand. You said that if I ever needed help, to come to you. You said you could hide me." He looked at the boy. "I must ask you to hide *us*."

Miriam was happy to replace words with action. "Of course," she said. "At once. But you must leave the safe house before first light, through the empty cabaret next door. We jimmied the cabaret door, so you can slip in or out if need be. The sewer is not exactly the Hotel Kemp—"

She saw the boy stiffen and stopped in midword, mentally slapping herself on the wrist for her own thoughtlessness. The Kempinski was practically next door to the temple the ruffians had destroyed, and to the boy's home. Any mention of it would naturally cause him more pain.

"Ah yes, the Kempinski," the beadle said, as if by saying the word out loud he was removing her guilt at her tactlessness. Or if not removing it, making it a shared guilt. "The price and the service are better here."

"You are right on both counts," Miriam said. "I'm forced to breakfast there tomorrow, my once-a-week concession to Erich's insistence that we be seen out regularly together in public, *like any other married couple*." She was struck, as always, by life's inequities. Where was it written that this good man and this innocent child had to hide like rats underground, while she, by accident of a somewhat skewed birth, lived out her social exile in physical comfort? "You'll be safe here for one night," she said.

"One night it is." The beadle smiled sadly, and tapped a fingernail against a tattered manuscript he drew out from under his coat. "I will make it as worthwhile a night as possible. And you and I, Miss Rathenau…will meet again."

Miriam also smiled, picturing the beadle and his charge huddled beneath candlelight over Hebrew lettering; even now, the learning would go on.

She leaned toward him and kissed him on the cheek. "Yes, Beadle Cohen," she said. Though she knew the beadle's words had been said mostly for the boy, out of reassurance rather than conviction, she played along and mouthed the standard Jewish refrain. "We will meet again. Next year, in Jerusalem."

Chapter five

Misha huddled under the train-station bench and occupied himself by squinting upward through the slats at the lights hanging from the high roof overhead. He cupped a grubby hand over one eye and then the other, noting the way the lights appeared to be moving when he did that, even though he knew they were not.

It was the only thing he could think of with which to occupy himself until the train left with the beadle on it. He had to consider what he was going to do next.

His course had seemed perfectly clear and simple to him sitting in the sewer, awake while the beadle slept: stay in Berlin and find Mama and Papa. Exactly how he was going to find them, or how he was going to stay warm and fed during his search had seemed irrelevant then. Now that his stomach was rumbling and he was shivering from the cold November draft blowing across him from the open railroad tracks, he was less sure of himself. It was not that he was any less determined to keep his promise to himself to find his parents, he told himself; it was just that, like Mama and Papa always told him, it was a big world out here and he was only a small boy.

Forgetting his game, he flattened himself on his belly and looked up and down the platform. Though the ticket inspector was on the steps, a whistle in his mouth, the beadle continued to rush up and down the platform, with complete disregard for his own safety, looking for the boy. In his hand he held the satchel that Misha knew contained what food had been left in the sewer, minus the few pieces of bread and chocolate he had secreted away in his pocket.

Misha took out the chocolate, smelled it, felt himself salivate, but resisted the temptation to nibble. He allowed himself a corner crust of bread, and replaced that, too, in his pocket. His hunger could wait to be appeased. It wasn't going anywhere. It would sit there like something alive, making noises inside his stomach, and eventually he would have to eat. But not now. Not yet.

"Misha," the beadle yelled. "Mishele. *Nu, komm schon.* Come already. Do not do this foolhardy thing."

It was cold and draughty so low down near the cement of the station platform. Misha wrapped himself up with his own arms and determined that, no matter what happened, he would not cry. Not now or ever again.

Dry-eyed and feeling like a traitor, he watched the

beadle give up the search and, holding his hands palms-up in exasperation, board the train. "Goodbye, Beadle Cohen," he whispered. "I'm sorry to be a trouble to you."

The inspector gave three long blasts on his whistle. The train rattled its own warning, chugged forward a hiccup, and stopped. A swirl of steam rolled down the platform. Misha watched it hopefully. If it reached him, it would improve the look of his wrinkled black pants and gray shirt, and warm him up a little.

Three short blasts on the whistle, and the beadle was gone.

There's no time to panic, Misha told himself, pushing away the feeling of total isolation that threatened immobility. What he needed now was a plan. That much he had to have. He could not just wander around Berlin. For one thing, by tonight the robbers and destroyers could own the streets again; for another, it would be cold and probably raining. Maybe even snowing.

He stood up and dusted himself off. He would run, if he knew in what direction. As he reached the cherub clock, someone called his name.

"Papa?"

Heart beating wildly, Misha turned around. Herr Becker, the owner of the bakery around the corner from the temple, waved from across the platform. He was a gentle man who used to put old bread out at the back for people to take to the Zoo Gardens to feed the ducks and the swans. Misha's hunger tempted him to answer, but then he remembered that Herr Becker didn't feed the birds anymore. Now, even when the bread was old and hard, he *sold* it. Ready-made toast, Mama used to joke.

Misha waved back and turned to run, as if he were late for an appointment.

"Why is a cute little boy like you running around this place on his own?" A fat man held Misha by the arm and spun him around. He had a nasty glint in his eye and stank roundly of herring and beer. "If you don't have any place to go, you can always come with me. I know someone who would love to take a bite out of you." He smiled, showing a row of rotting teeth.

Stories about Georg Haarmann, murderer and cannibal, rose to the surface of Misha's memory. A fat, no-neck, heavy-jowled man like this, Misha was sure, ugly as a bulldog. Bet this one kidnapped boys and girls, too, and cut them up, and cooked them and ate them. And it was all true. Twenty years ago, Papa said, but true. He thought his papa had said the man was dead, but—

He shook himself loose, stumbled, fell, got up and ran on, feet automatically running in the direction of home.

Several blocks from the station, he finally slowed down. He looked into the shattered glass of a Jewish shop window and caught his fractured image. He had to look pretty closely to see even a glimpse of Rabbi Czisça's neat young son. For the first time, he noticed the hole in his pants his falling onto the pavement had caused. Such a klutz, Papa used to say. Other people wish they had a third eye in their heads to improve their psychic abilities, or in their chests to add to their understanding. Not our son. He needs a third eye underfoot.

Less afraid now of being recognized, but feeling no less hungry or helpless, he continued in the direction of home. Or what used to be home. He was almost at the Kempinski corner before he admitted to himself that he was being followed. He glanced back over his shoulder.

The no-neck man grinned, making no secret of being in pursuit.

Less afraid now that he was out in the open, in the streets, Misha crossed the street at Kempinski corner, and hovered at a gap in the hedge that separated the building from the people who walked the sidewalk. Between the glass windows of Kempinski Café and the hedge lay an outdoor dining area. Stacks of square green iron tables and chairs stood unusably wet from the early morning rain that lay in puddles in the narrow corridor.

Suddenly he heard the echo of Miriam's voice: *I'm forced to breakfast there tomorrow.*

There was the Kempinski, and today was yesterday's tomorrow. Misha walked quickly through the break in the foliage. Perhaps God had sent him a piece of luck because he was doing what Papa always told him, and helping himself.

Sure enough, as he neared the café's plate-glass window he saw Fräulein Miriam and a uniformed man

seated at the table nearest the light. She must have
been cold, for her coat was thrown around her
shoulders. With one hand she toyed with a bowl of fresh
strawberries; her other hand lay ungloved on her lap,
beneath the table. The man's uniform was different
from the ones the men who had taken his parents away
had worn, but it still succeeded in reminding him of
them. A covered wicker basket of bread lay untouched
between them, and a pot of what he assumed must be
coffee.

As if she felt his presence, Miriam looked up and
turned her head. She seemed to be looking straight at
him, yet she did not react. Perhaps the glare of sunlight
on the glass was distorting her view, he thought,
moving to a different position.

He waved at her, and pointed at the table, expecting
to be beckoned inside. Miriam started slightly, looked
straight at him briefly, and shook her head. She made
a similar gesture with the hand that was out of sight,
pointed down the street, indicating that he should
leave, and clenched her fist.

Shocked, he walked on, past the entrance to the
hotel. He glanced into the lobby, at the huge displays
of flowers, the knots of tourists and businessmen in pinstriped suits, the uniformed, black-booted officers with
their Gestapo leathers.

He was at the corner when the same fat male hand
spun him around.

He kicked out and felt his toes connect. No-neck
yelped and momentarily released the boy.

Giving no thought to direction, Misha took off at high speed—and barreled straight into a tall man in black.

"Hey, there, young man," Konrad said, his hand lightly but firmly on Misha's shoulder. "Where's the fire?"

Misha glanced quickly around. He was standing between the entrance to the Kempinski and the street where Miriam was seated half-in half-out of the back of a shiny limousine. No-neck had disappeared, as had the uniformed man. Was the uniformed man, Misha wondered, the one called Erich, of whom Fräulein Miriam had spoken when she talked to Beadle Cohen?

"Get him into the car and let's go, Konnie," Miriam said. She slid across the back seat of the car and patted the seat beside her. "Get in, Misha. Quickly. I'm late for the shop. We can talk on the way and you can tell me why you aren't on the train." She paled. "Did something happen to the beadle?"

"He's fine, Fräulein Miriam," he said. "I ran away and he looked for me but I hid, and—"

"Thank God. Now get in the car."

"But...but—"

"No buts. Get in."

Totally confused by her mixed message, Misha copied the gesture she had made earlier. "You shooed me away," he said, "like the son of Rabbi Czisça was a...a street beggar."

"I'm sorry, child. I did what I had to do. I'll explain later, I promise."

Shaking his head, not knowing whether to be grateful

or terrified, Misha climbed into the car. As Konrad started the car and pulled away from the curb, Misha knelt on the seat and looked out of the back window. At once, Miriam's hand came up to steady him. Its warmth comforted him almost as much as the fact that the fat, no-neck man was nowhere in sight.

CHAPTER SIX

Kosher or not, Solomon had grown to like Amsterdam's Javanese food. He liked the variety, and the manner in which it was served—in many small bowls, and with condiments as varied as raw fish and sliced bananas. Except he was tired of eating alone.

Tonight, he decided, his mother and Recha would join him at the little restaurant he frequented when he sought diversion from teaching and his own studies, which currently centered on the relationship between present mystical thought and that of the ancients. His latest obsession was with the Lost Tribe, and with the Falashas—Ethiopian Jews who lacked knowledge of Hebrew and the Talmud, and who had priests rather than rabbis.

He chose the long route home from the temple where he taught Hebrew school. As always, on his *Spaziergang,* he mulled over the latest news from Berlin. It had been a month since *Kristallnacht*; the temple buzzed with talk of an underground, of German rabbis transported to camps, of cantors and beadles whose services, should the men escape, might become available to Dutch congregations.

After his two years in Amsterdam, Berlin seemed at last to be losing its hold on him. He had spent the first year mourning his father, the second growing to think of Holland as home. He still mourned the loss of Miriam. At first, each minute was tinged with the anticipation of hearing from her, seeing her, especially after Hitler declared Holland to be neutral territory. When the letter he had been waiting for finally had arrived, his hands shook so much he could not open it.

Recha had no such reluctance. As if without thinking, she had read Miriam's letter aloud. "...I have come to realize that I love him."

"I don't believe it," Sol said. "I *won't* believe it."

"You had better believe it, Sol." Recha had handed him the letter.

How vigorously he had charged to Miriam's defense, refusing the evidence of his own eyes, insisting Erich had dictated the words.

Recha's counterargument was irrefutable. She took him to see the Movietone News clip of Miriam honoring her uncle's assassins.

He went home and tore up the letter he had started to write, affirming his love. If he were to write at all, it must be to break the ties between them. He could not do it, not while the hope existed that she would change her mind. She had let go of him, but he was not ready to let go of her. Recently, to his amazement, though the ache remained, the pain had begun to lessen.

Then, three months later, her face stared up at him from the pages of the Sunday tabloid. She was dancing in Hitler's arms, "and not for the first time," the text said. Erich stood proudly by. The paper also reported that the niece of Walther Rathenau had renounced her heritage and married Major Erich Alois, "her childhood love."

After the tears, after the sorrowing, Sol no longer had any choices to make. In the beginning there had seemed to be a need for decision: run to her and pull her out of Erich's embrace, or stay here and wait for her to come to him. Slowly, surely, he had begun to realize that *he* had no choice because she had already made it. If she wanted to be in Berlin, with Erich, then she must have what she had chosen. There would always be times when he would wonder what she was feeling, if she had thought of him when she danced with Adolph Hitler, if she had buried him when she buried her heritage...just as there would be times, like now, when he wondered about Erich.

Had Erich really risen to such dizzying heights in the Party? Did he ever remember that he once had a brother in blood?

Turning away from the grassy walk along the canal, Sol descended the steps to a concrete platform, built next to the water. He sat down next to a narrow culvert opening, balanced Joseph Halévy's study of the Falashas on the inside of its curved edge, and leaned back.

At once he found himself bothered by the sunlight reflecting off the water. He took off his glasses, closed one eye, and tested his peripheral vision. His eyesight was definitely worsening. Ultimately he would learn to accept that, the way he had learned to accept all of the other inescapable things in his life, even the presence of the dybbuk, the wandering soul that had possessed him since that terrible day when he witnessed Walther Rathenau's assassination.

Eyes closed, Solomon recalled Beadle Cohen's words: *sometimes those souls seek refuge in the bodies of living persons, causing instability, speaking foreign words through their mouths.* Such lost souls, the beadle had maintained, were unable to transmigrate to a higher world because they had sinned against humanity.

But what sin had so absorbed Judith, the nurse whom the grenade had also killed, that her soul had sought a new vessel?

A flash of light exploded out of the water, and then another—cerebral fireworks, come to warn him that he should pay heed. A cobalt-blue glow followed. He shut his eyes and waited, feeling the sun warm his cheeks. Soon, he thought, letting his mind drift, it will be dusk and another day will be over. Meanwhile, in his mind's eye, he decided, he would watch another vision the voices brought. Some, at first, had been fascinating. Then many had turned ugly...because of his losing Miriam?

He watched, waited, like someone fearing an execution but anxious for the finality to begin.

He saw a cobalt-blue dusk, and an orange sun setting

above the domed keep of a ruined castle. It was the Ethiopian vision again, the one that had sparked his interest in the Falashas——

A black man, lanky, rawboned, bald but for a bowl of hair at the crown of his skull, leans crouched against a castle wall. His left shoulder is draped with a white cloak, caked with dust; a brown stallion grazes beside him, amid waist-high daisies. He seems so weary that only his spear shaft holds him up.

At the bottom of a grassy slope, a short distance below, is an elderly woman wearing bifocals and a safari hat wrapped and tied under her chin with a bright blue chiffon sash. She sits crossways in a motorcycle sidecar, her boots up on the main seat. As she watches him with the quick-eyed appreciation women usually reserve for new lovers, she makes quick, easy strokes on the pages of a combination sketch pad and graph-paper notebook balanced awkwardly across her lap. She draws him rapidly, not looking at the paper. Her wrinkled hands are the same hue as her khaki jacket and pants.

"Don't change your mind now, Zaehev Emanuel," she says in English, talking softly to herself. "This old girl's come too far for that."

A bee buzzes in front of her face. She swishes it away. When another lands on her lapel, she flicks it off with forefinger and thumb and, frowning, glances back over her shoulder. Thirty meters behind her, a dozen two-meter-high man-made beehives resembling banded sheaves of straw stand as if in formation. Smoke plumes from two of them, mixing with that of a campfire built between two stones. A small black man wrapped from head to ankles in a tattered robe squats beside the fire, pouring batter in a spiral onto a ceramic griddle. On the matted grass beside him sit an ebony jug and two bowls, plus several wicker baskets decorated with chevrons. Set into an hourglass-shaped basket is a metal dish holding bread rounds. They look like enormous uncooked *latkes*...potato pancakes.

"Can't you just *cook* instead of fiddling with your bees, Malifu?" she asks.

The man beside the griddle lifts a hand in acquiescence. He removes smoking torches from the base of each of the two pluming hives and shoves the sticks, base down, into the ground.

Suddenly it is night. A horse and rider, silhouetted by a full moon, amble down the hill. Stones click beneath the horse's hooves. The rider is carrying a spear perpendicular to the ground, as if he is a standard-bearer.

"It just might happen tonight." She sits up straighter, holding the pencil poised above the paper. "Just might happen."

The rider reaches the motorcycle. Slackening the reins, he rises to sniff the air. "Sandalwood incense and *injera*. Bread." He speaks in a strange, musical Hebrew. "Such odors could domesticate a man." He smiles wanly, obviously exhausted. "Hopefully, the smoke will attract a swarm to the hive. They do say it charms the bees." He looks around tentatively, as though seeing the scalloped, verdant valley for the first time.

"Malifu indicated that it doesn't look promising," she replies, also in Hebrew. "Getting more bees, I mean."

She grunts as, with forearms and elbows, she pushes herself up from the sidecar and extends him a hand.

Leaning down, he clumsily kisses her knuckles. "I am honored you have journeyed so far to see one so lowly as I."

"The honor is all mine, Zaehev Emanuel."

"You know *my* name, while I—"

"Judith Bielman-O'Hearn. Judy." Having extricated herself from the sidecar, she brushes dust from her jacket.

"I trust your travels were pleasant, Miss Judith."

"Malifu guided me. He sat in the sidecar with his head down, gesturing wildly the whole way. I think he had his eyes shut most of the time. The trip was..." She grins, shrugs, opens her hands in supplication.

"Mountainous?"

"Eventful. One I shan't soon forget."

He laughs, swings a leg over the pommel, dismounts. "You were not," he ties the reins to a bush and lifts his eyes toward her, "followed?"

She answers with a shake of her head.

"Not even..." He undulates his hand in the air and makes a motor sound deep in his throat.

"I saw no airplanes, if that's what you mean."

"The beekeeper is a friend of yours?"

"Not exactly. He heard I was looking for someone from your village and offered to guide me here. He seems harmless enough."

"Doesn't everything? Even the airplanes, the first time we saw them." He moves toward the fire, swatting hard at the bees in front of his face, as if to rile them.

"I hardly imagine you journeyed to Gojjam, the province of honey, to talk of innocence and insects...or even of airplanes."

Notebook in hand, she follows him to the fire.

"I have questions," she says, "but I also have *injera*. You must be terribly hungry." Her voice is sharp, as if in rebuke. "Honey wine, too. And coffee rich enough to melt the soul."

"You've driven all the way from Addis Ababa to feed me?"

He kneels beside Malifu, who has placed a black lid over the pan. The smaller man appears to stiffen. Shooing away flies, the horseman opens the lid of a vase-shaped wicker, reaches in, and withdraws a slab of honey translucent as amber. He wraps it in one of the breads as though in bunting.

"You want me to take a bite?" the woman asks. "To prove the food is not poisoned?"

He shakes his head and bites off a huge hunk. Strands of honey cling to his lips and chin. His sinewy muscles seem to slacken while he eats. As he devours half the sandwich, he sits on his haunches, arms draped across knees, eyes blank.

She brings a gray woolen blanket from the sidecar and spreads it out before him. He appears to take no notice. When she moves the black jug and one of the bowls onto the blanket, he ceases eating and, holding the honey-and-bread, removes a tiny golden spoon from his broad belt. Eagerly he plunges it into the bowl, scooping up a dollop of dark honey. This he places beneath his tongue. Then he withdraws the spoon, slowly and upside down, cleans it with his lips, and puts it back in his belt.

"I've never seen a man carry around a spoon before, especially one like that." She sets down her sketchpad and pours coffee into two small cups painted with silver leafwork on a blue field. "Does each man in your village carry one?"

His eyes shift to her. His smile holds neither humor nor suspicion.

"I'm sorry," she says. "I shouldn't pry. When I'm excited I sometimes overstep. I meant no harm."

"The spoon *is* very beautiful." He touches it as if to assure himself of its presence. Taking the cup she offers him, he says, "Perhaps it is all right to tell you that I am *not* the only man in my village to wear such a thing."

She curls two fingers into the bowl, scoops out a glob of honey, and places it beneath her tongue. "Would it be something a village boy might wear?"

He lifts his cup in a toast; she responds in kind. "*L'Chaim.*"

"*L'Chaim.*" She slurps, sets down the cup and picks up her sketch pad.

"They say the trick is not to swallow—but to *savor*," he tells her in a voice devoid of inflection. "But they are wrong. It is not a trick. It merely mixes the black," he bows slightly, then points his glass at her, "with the sweet." He nods toward her, makes as if to toast again, and drinks half the cup's contents. After several moments, during which she continues her work, he smacks his lips.

"My compliments to your gentle man," he says.

"He likes your coffee," she tells Malifu in English, raising her voice like someone speaking to a deaf person.

His back to her, Malifu lifts an index finger in answer and peeks under the griddle lid. He replaces it with a clang of metal against ceramic and blows mightily on his fingertips.

Emanuel chews off another chunk of bread and lays it down on the blanket; the honey—melting from the warmth of the *injera*—spreads among the fibers.

She has resumed sketching. "I understand you've fought the Italians for seven years," she says without looking at him.

"And will seven more, if necessary. And seven thereafter."

"Were you the only person in your village to go off to war?"

"This time." He sounds despondent.

"Malifu tells me you call yourself a *dejasmatch*—one who, in war, camps near the door of the Emperor's tent."

"I prefer to think of it as 'one who will not surrender.'"

"But surely you've no love for Selassie! What did he ever do for any of the Black Jews? Not even allow you to own land! Persecutions at every turn! Not that I don't admire you for fighting the Fascists, you understand."

"Am I to understand that you have come all this way to steal the worth of those seven years?"

"Fighting Mussolini—that makes sense! But vowing devotion to the monarchy that held Black Jews in servitude for fourteen centuries? Even the title—*dejasmatch*—is that not limited only to the Coptic aristocrat...the legendary Christian warrior-prince?"

After a moment he says quietly, "Perhaps when we Ethiopians found ourselves fighting tanks with ancient rifles and machine guns with spears, the slaughter was so great that most of the legendary Christian *dejasmatch* were cut down like Maskal daisies gathered with a scythe. Perhaps when my country capitulated to the Fascists, a list was drawn up of the surviving *dejasmatch*, or at least those willing to go on fighting. Perhaps—"

He pauses, as if gauging her response. When she remains silent he smiles as if to concede her a minor victory and finishes his thought. "Perhaps," he says, "the scarcity of remaining *dejasmatch* left room at the bottom of the list for a *dejasmatch* who imagines he is also a Jew."——

"Is there room for an old Jew to sit down?"

The familiar voice came from behind Sol. He withdrew from the vision and turned around. Hoping. "My God—can it be?" He jumped to his feet and took the beadle in his arms. "You still smell like old books, you old Jew," he said. "What are you doing here?"

"Mostly looking for a place to rest my weary bones." The beadle grinned widely. "Your sister told me I would find you here. May I join you?" Groaning slightly, he lowered himself to the concrete. "As Miriam said of the sewer, it's not exactly the Hotel Kempinski, but it is cheap."

Heart pounding, Solomon sat down next to the beadle. What he really wanted was news of Miriam, but he could not bear even to speak her name. "Was your temple destroyed?" he asked.

The beadle shook his head. "Not yet, but I could see no reason to stay." He took a breath, as if he were about to say something more, then shut his mouth.

"Say it, Beadle Cohen. You were never a man to go out of your way for a mere exchange of pleasantries."

"When I arrived in Amsterdam a few hours ago, I went straight to the temple. I asked if anyone had heard of Ella and Recha Freund—"

"Did you not ask after me?"

"I did not, and for very good reason. Until I spoke to your mother and sister, I thought you had been transported—"

Once again Sol jumped to his feet. "To a camp? What made you think that!"

"You are shouting, Solomon. Calm down—sit down! I am too old for this much excitement."

Obediently, Sol sat down.

"Erich has convinced Miriam that you are in a camp, Sol. She has no idea you ever reached Amsterdam—"

"But my letters!"

"Did you address them to the estate?"

"Of course not! I wrote almost daily, in care of Erich's apartment, until—" He stopped. "The estate?"

"They moved there soon after you left."

"And disconnected the phone at the flat," Sol said quietly, beginning to understand. Small wonder he had not been able to get in touch with her. Erich had seen to that—disconnected the phone, waylaid the letters. "So that is why she has done all those things—married Erich, renounced our faith."

"She thinks she is protecting you, Solomon."

"That son of a bitch," Sol said slowly. "That Nazi bastard."

He was pacing up and down the narrow concrete platform. He would call the estate at once. No. Erich might answer or find out about the call, which could endanger her life. The man was obviously capable of anything. He would go to her. On the next train. Pluck her out of the hands of that lying son of a—

"If you're thinking of going back, think it through again. Except for her work with the underground, she is quite safe—"

"The underground?"

Laboriously the beadle rose to his feet. "Erich's parents have reopened the shop. Miriam works there every Sunday—their Sunday Jew, she calls herself. The sewer is being used as a safe house. I myself hid there for one night."

A sadness passed over his face, as of a memory he would rather forget.

"I must go there!" Sol said. "I should have known!"

"You could not have known," the beadle said. "If you must go, you must, but see to it that you arrive there on a Sunday. It will be the easiest way, perhaps the only way, to make contact. Except when she is with Konrad, Erich keeps her pretty well confined to the estate."

Taking the beadle's arm, Sol led him up the steps,

away from the water. "You'll stay with us for awhile?" he asked.

The beadle nodded.

"And perhaps you will take over my teaching duties?"

The beadle nodded again.

"That is good," Sol said. "Because, God willing, I intend to be at that shop on Sunday—and I intend to come back...this time, with Miriam."

Chapter Seven

Astonished at how easy it was to get into Berlin, at how little notice anyone took of him, Sol walked from the station to Friedrich Ebert Strasse. Getting out should only be that easy, he thought, but then getting into *prison* is easy too.

Getting out—getting to Amsterdam—he'd had phony letters and affidavits from Erich. Erich had provided everything, down to actual train tickets. He had even included a time-table in the package, and a book to read on the train.

Now, two years later, getting out would be much harder. This time he had real affidavits, but papers from a Hebrew School would carry little if any weight if there were trouble. He had brought affidavits for Miri, too, but she would need more than that. She was too visible a personality to be able to leave quietly.

It was ten o'clock in the morning. He had no intention of being in Germany any longer than he had to—a day at most—so he had brought nothing with him save what he could fit in the pockets of the heavy winter coat he had bought at a secondhand store before leaving Amsterdam. He was determined that, no matter what, by tomorrow morning he and Miriam would be on a train, headed back to the tenuous safety of Holland.

Everything else, the question of Erich, the problem of getting all of them out of the country—to South America or South Africa or South Australia, he did not care where—could wait until later.

Before he knew it, he was within sight of the shop. Herr Weisser stood alone in front of the door. Seeing him filled Sol with a burning hatred that almost—but not quite—equaled what Sol felt for their son. He tugged at the Homburg he had purchased along with the coat, crossed the street, and walked on.

He had forgotten how dreary Berlin was at this time of year.

The sky was gray. The wind whistled around the corners of the buildings, and the air smelled of soot from chimney smoke held in by the low clouds. People en route to church walked with their heads down against the wind. Every now and then, a man or a woman with a dog stopped to let the animal do what it must. The occasional motorcar passed by, and once in a while a man with heavy black boots and a long woolen coat strode by, smelling of Gestapo as strongly as the air was scented with the threat of a late-November snowfall.

He circled the block several times, alert for the Rathenau limousine. It passed him at last. Konnie was at the wheel, alone in front. The back was too dark for him to see who sat there.

Don't let Erich be in that car, he prayed as the limousine slowed to a halt in front of the shop and Miriam stepped out. Despite his increased pulse rate, Sol tried to look at her dispassionately. Her movements were graceful and fluid; her coat was trimmed in white fur, to match her hat, and her boots were the latest fashion. As she leaned back into the car to get something she had apparently left on the seat, her coat pulled up and he could see her legs—trim as a girl's though without the slight muscularity of a dancer's calf.

She's thirty-two, he reminded himself. I have missed so much!

He watched her talk to Herr Weisser, watched him unlock the door and let her inside. Knowing he dared not go in until Weisser had left, and that he had probably already stood in one spot long enough to have aroused suspicion for loitering, he walked in the direction of the Tiergarten. He forced himself to keep moving away from the shop. When he could stand it no longer, he turned back. He walked faster and faster until he was running, and did not slow down until the shop came into view.

Konnie stood at the door, staring out into the street. Sol followed the direction of the chauffeur's gaze. He could see two people walking in the opposite direction.

JANET BERLINER AND GEORGE GUTHRIDGE

Squinting, he thought he recognized Frau Weisser's movements.

Konnie disappeared into the shop, reappeared, and went to the car. Moments later, he went back inside, this time carrying a shopping bag.

At the end of his patience, Sol approached the tobacco shop, *Die Ziggarrenkiste*.

The familiar jangle of the bell over the door made his stomach tighten. Miriam stood with her back to him, reaching for something on a shelf high above her head.

Konrad saw him at once. "Herr—" He turned pale, then beamed as Sol put a finger to his lips.

Walking up to the counter, Sol pulled his hat down low and bent his head as if to examine the cigars that lay beneath the glass. *"Kan ek yets kopen, Mejevrou?"* he asked softly in Dutch. "Could I buy something, Miss?"

She turned around, startled in the way of someone whose thoughts have been a million kilometers away.

"Forgive me, sir, I don't speak—" she began.

He lifted his head. She stopped, grew so pale he thought she would faint, and began to cry.

At once he was behind the counter, his arm around her waist. Tightening the heel of his hand against the base of her spine, he arched her toward him and bent to kiss her. Her mouth tasted warm and moist. He kissed her face, drinking in her salty tears.

"You're alive...free!"

"I've been in Amsterdam all this time."

Miriam touched his face as if to assure herself that

he was flesh and blood. She could not seem to stem the flow of tears down her cheeks. "Erich," she managed between sobs. "He...said you'd been arrested. Put in a camp." She took a deep breath. "He said the only hope I had of protecting you was to stay with him and do everything he said!"

Sol's thoughts must have been written on his face; as if she could read them, she looked at him seriously. "He could not force me to love him the way I love you."

"I know what happened," he said gently. "Beadle Cohen made it to Amsterdam. He told me."

"Why didn't you write? What you must have thought before you knew..."

"I did write...at first. Erich must have intercepted the letters. Later, I decided you had made a choice. You do have that right, you know."

"I am your *wife*, Sol. I made my choice a long time ago."

"We'll get out—this time together." Sol lowered his voice. "Can we talk here? Is it safe?"

As if in answer to his question, the doorbell jangled. He glanced at the curtain that separated the shop from the cellar stairs, and she nodded. "I'll be down as soon as I can."

He went down into the cellar and opened the grate that led to the sewer. A child again, climbing down into the hideaway that had been his and Erich's secret place.

The sewer was cold and damp. He took off his coat and put it over his knees like a blanket. He waited.

There was a flash of light. A cobalt-blue glow infused

the sewer. Let it be the Ethiopian vision, he thought. On the train from Amsterdam, he had decided that the woman, Judith, represented the dybbuk. Knowing that, he would watch more closely, listen more carefully. He had experienced visions since childhood. At first he had thought them disjointed, random, but slowly there had emerged common themes. Each had a person who might, like himself, be possessed by a dybbuk. Mention of a Jewish homeland on the African island of Madagascar—an idea similar, Herr Rathenau had once told him, to what the Nazis had long considered.

Eventually, Sol thought, giving himself over to the light, I will understand the visions' lessons…if indeed they have anything to teach——

Stars sprinkle the cobalt-blue heavens. They shine on beehives rising up like ancient columns and on a black man and a white woman who sit on a blanket spread out among daisies and wisps of smoke. The woman lies down on her side, props herself up on one arm and begins to sketch. The man remains on his haunches, forearms across knees—hands turned palms up; anguish etches his face.

"I want to be considered a *whole* Jew!" His voice is strained with emotion. "Can't they understand that?"

"You *are* a whole Jew." She sounds more clinical than concerned. "Only the Falasha think differently."

"They treat my people like lepers! Because of them, we have been forced to live in the honeycomb caves for a hundred generations. It is neither right nor fair!"

"Prejudice exists everywhere." She shakes her head

sadly, folds the overleaves of her sketch pad down flat, and drops her pencil. "What *is* the name of your tribe, Emanuel?"

"*L'Am*—The People. Do not ask me where they are. As for *why* they are, if I knew, I would tell you that!" He covers his head with his hands. "When I was young, my nights were full of such questions, but I did not ask my elders for fear they did not know the answers." His voice has taken on a hollow, haunted tone. "One day a group of Falasha nomads camped near our caves, come to graze their goats. At night I could hear them praying. One night, when I could not sleep, I stole in among their tents. Their *kohamin*—the priest—spotted me. They threw me into a thornbush. As I lay crying and bleeding, the priest spat on me. 'Hydra-headed Jew!' he shouted. 'Go home to your pagan gods!'"

"No doubt he was referring to the First Commandment—'Thou shalt have no other gods before Me'," the woman says.

"Does that Commandment not prove there are other, lesser gods? Yet they pretend otherwise! And our language—"

"What about your language, Emanuel?"

He stares at the cocoon of bread with its melting honey.

She leans toward him. "Tell me."

"The Falasha...they laugh at it. They call it 'The Language of the Bee.'"

"Yours is the language of the Song of Deborah."

"De-bo-rah." He pronounces the word as if it were music.

She places a loving hand on his arm. "Deborah means 'bee' in Old Hebrew," she says. "She was a prophetess— a judge who was instrumental in freeing the ancient Israelites from the Canaanites."

"I do not understand." He looks at her curiously, as though she is saying words he has never heard before.

"The Cushitic Falashas—we call them Black Jews— don't speak your language," she says. "Only musty scholars like myself and your people know Old Hebrew. The true language of liturgy, I call it, for it is free of the Aramaic influences that changed Hebrew forever." She gives him a gentle shake as if to break him from his mood. "Your tribe is blessed, Emanuel. Your...your *agony*, if you will, has preserved the past. Soon the whole world will know of your suffering and be grateful to you."

He furrows his forehead, then looks down at the ground as Malifu pads forward. The smaller man holds a huge dish quilted with *injera* layered with chunks of meat and light broth. The two men do not look at each other.

"The *wat*—stew—looks lovely," the woman tells Malifu, taking the dish from him. "Fetch the wine, please. Then tend to your bees. The hives *farthest away* need the most attention."

He bows; understood. He has not once looked at Emanuel. After he brings the wine, he wanders off amid the hives.

"*Tej*—honey wine...nectar of the gods." The woman grins and drinks deeply. "If nothing else, *this* proves the whole universe isn't monotheistic!"

Emanuel too drinks deeply, thoughtfully. "I prayed, after the Falasha threw me into the thornbush like so much excrement. I wanted to understand why they had treated me in that manner. But Jehovah would not answer. At dawn, the goddess Anuket spoke to me out of the sun as I sat looking at the mountains and the hills lush with flowers. I knew it was she, for she wore a crown of feathers and carried her scepter and *ankh*."

"Anuket—goddess of the Nile, nourisher of the fields." The woman takes notes in small, impeccably neat handwriting. "What other gods are important to you?"

"Her sister, Sati. Their husband, Khnum, god of the cataract."

"Anuket, Sati, Khnum." Her voice is breathless. "The Elephantine Triad. Does your tribe believe in any other Egyptian gods?"

"*Egyptian?*" He frowns and leans forward to peer over the top of her notebook.

"Any other *gods*." She tears off a piece of bread, wraps it around a morsel of meat and, after popping it into her mouth, readies the pencil above the graph paper.

He puts his arms around a bent knee and looks toward the far horizon. "There is, of course, Ra, god of the sun."

"Is Ra greater than Jehovah?"

"Jehovah made the heavens and the earth. Therefore He created Ra. At least, as a child I thought so. That is what I was taught to believe. Now…I'm not sure."

For awhile there is silence. In the tension silence can cause, the woman's face seems to lose its look of aged innocence. She stops writing and presses the pencil hard against the page; the tip breaks.

"Tell me, Emanuel," she says quietly, "do you believe that the gods are punishing you for leaving your village…that they have taken away your heritage, only to replace it with doubts?"

"I cannot understand why Jehovah sits by and winks at war. Had I not left home I would not have known the meaning of war and—"

"I, too, have doubts." The woman removes her hat and sets it down with trembling hands. She watches him eat more of the stew, jiggling the hot bread in his hand; there is a deep sadness in her eyes. "All these years of searching, Emanuel, and now that I have found you, I am no longer sure I should ever have begun the quest," she says finally.

"Quest? Explain, please." He leans close.

"Seventy-five years ago, a French professor named Joseph Halévy discovered the Falashas—African Jews who lacked knowledge of Hebrew and the Talmud, and who had priests rather than rabbis. The Lost Tribe, he called them. Probably descended from—"

"Menelik the First, son of Sheba. They all say so."

She nods. "All those centuries, living by the dictates and dreams of the Jewish people, yet unaware other Jews existed!" As if in an effort to calm herself, she selects and wraps another morsel, which she holds before Emanuel's mouth. "The finest portion, to honor the favored guest."

He opens his mouth for it like a bird.

"After the Italians invaded Ethiopia," she says, "we

heard rumors of a tiny enclave of Jews who were *not* Falashas. A people who spoke Hebrew but did not follow Levite law concerning monotheism. Perhaps descended from Jews who were driven out of their colony at Elephantine, the Nile's southernmost cataract in Egypt, and never heard of again. Four *hundred* years," she looks at him soberly, "before the Christians' Messiah, and a century before the Hebrew language began to change." She starts to roll another bread-and-meat, then stops. "The destruction of the Jewish temple and the slaughter at Elephantine occurred," she says quietly, no longer looking at him, "when Khnum priests realized they were losing power and therefore bribed the commander of the Egyptian garrison."

She holds out the morsel, dangling it between forefinger and thumb. He cranes his neck around in order to take it between his lips. As he eats, he eyes her steadily. "So you wish to study us and make yourself as famous as the Frenchman."

She looks away. "I come from a country called Ireland, but I am a Jew with an African heart," she tells him. Her shoulders sag, and she runs her fingers through thinning hair. "I spent years among the Bushmen. Now I'm not sure who I am. Like you, in a way," she adds softly. "If I expose you to the world you will suffer less—but it will change you. Your people will never be the same. Having found you, I could fulfill *my* dream." She lifts her gaze and looks directly into his eyes; her expression is intense, searching, caring. "It would be better if that were your wish, too."

"I am most confused," he says.

She turns a page of the sketch pad to reveal an excellently rendered drawing of Emanuel squatted peasant-style beside the blanket. "This is *real*." She holds up the sketch pad. "*This…you…*you are the living essence of my Jewish heritage. My needs are only a part of this. Everywhere, Jews are being forced to deny their heritage if they wish to survive."——

"You can come out now, Sol."

Miriam's voice pulled Sol out of the vision. He hoped it would not be one of the fragmentary ones that never returned. The people intrigued him—the woman with her sketch pad, the princely black man.

"It's safe for a little while," Miriam said. "You remember—the customers always seem to come in waves. I left Konrad up there. He will call me the moment someone approaches the shop."

Sol took a few seconds to allow the blue glow of the vision to dissipate. "I…fell asleep," he said. There would be time later to talk of the visions, he told himself, clambering out of the sewer to take Miriam in his arms.

They dared not turn on a light. He wanted to look at her, to drink her in as he might a good wine. Instead, he traced her features with his fingers—the slant of her eyes, the curve of her lips, the high cheekbones. He buried his face in her hair, inhaling its sweet, clean smell as if it were a field of freesias. "God, how I missed you," he whispered.

"We may only have minutes," she said, drawing away from his embrace. "We have plans to make."

"Let's just leave. Now. Walk away from here. Better

yet, drive away in the limousine until we're close to the border."

"And go where?" she asked.

"Amsterdam. We'll make it there, somehow."

"*If* we do, we'll have to keep running."

"From Erich?"

She held fast to his hand. "From Hitler. Eventually Holland will be as unsafe as Germany."

"By then we—"

"No, Sol." She had a new firmness in her voice. "This time we are going to South America...together. I have my own contacts now, in the underground, and Juan Perón has become a good friend. I will go to him myself. When we're safe, hopefully in Buenos Aires, then I'm sure he'll help us send for your mother and Recha."

They sat side by side at the bottom of the staircase, bodies touching, but not embracing. "You seem so sure of this friend's help," he said. "Are you and he—"

"We stand with one foot in the grave, and you cast innuendoes!"

"I'm sorry. There has been so much pain...."

Tears glistened on her face. "You're right," she said more quietly, relaxing the stiff set of her shoulders. "I've worked very hard to wrap Perón around my little finger." She lowered her voice. "Berlin is a perilous city, and I have been playing a perilous game. If I weren't such a good player, I could not be here talking to you. As it is, I'll be holding my breath the whole week. One word to Erich that I know you are free, and it's all over. He would guess at once where you are, and that we are making plans. We would lose our safe house—and each other."

"What would he do? Have me killed?"

"I don't know. He's rising in the Party, but the way he hates them—"

She stopped, cocked her head, and listened. Sol heard the soft echo of a whistle.

"That's Konnie!" She stood up. "I have to go upstairs. I'll come down again before I close the shop. After that, I can't return until next Sunday, by which time I should have been able to contact Perón." She was talking fast, her voice insistent. "If I don't come, it means there's something I have to do with Erich, or that—"

He cut her short. "What about food?" he asked.

"There are supplies down there—enough for a week, if you're careful."

"Fraülein Miriam!"

"You see how things have changed." She snuffed the candle. Her voice held a hint of laughter. "Konnie is part of us now, so he allows himself to be much less formal…he no longer calls me Fraülein *Rathenau!*"

Afraid he might never see her again once he returned to the stinking brick crypt, Sol stood too, and took her in his arms. How he wanted to keep her there, to make plans, laugh, make love.

"I *must* go," she said, her voice strained.

He released her and listened to her footsteps until they faded. Back in the sewer, he thought about all she had said. Her reasoning was sensible—but sensible was not what he had wanted. She could have agreed to stay with him, he told himself peevishly. There *was* the alternative of slipping out after dark to contact Perón while he waited here for her.

Fool! He berated himself for thinking like a child. For the next seven days, he would be alone with his memories and his doubts. Such thoughts would not help him find the strength to live through the hours she was gone. He must manage as he had in Amsterdam, by reliving their lovemaking, pretending they were together with all the time in the world. Sometimes he had tried to understand why a makeshift marriage ceremony in a deserted cabaret, with God as their only witness, made him feel so tied to her, so hopeful that life would ultimately reward him for being a good man.

Exhausted, he closed his eyes. Instead of sleep, the vision returned——

"What does your Hitler propose to do with the Jews of Europe?" Emanuel asks.

The woman bristles. "He is not *my* anything," she says angrily. There is an awkward silence between them. "He proposes to rid the world of them," she adds in a quiet voice, having apparently calmed herself.

"How? By killing them all?"

"If necessary."

Emanuel turns his face to one side and spits into the sand. He rubs his arms, as if his flesh has suddenly become cold.

"There is a ray of hope," the woman says. "A physician named Schmidt, under a doctor named Mengele, has developed a theory concerning the genetic passing of cultural attributes from one generation to the next. Hitler has offered a reward for each piece of tangible new evidence that furthers her research."

"And what might that reward be?" Emanuel looks skeptical.

"He has sworn to create a homeland for the Jews—in Madagascar. Each addition to Schmidt's research means a shipload of our people is sent to the Jewish homeland."

"This Hitler is like the god Apepi, who tried to stop the progress of the solar barque. They who trust in him, trust a serpent." He rises from the blanket and towers over her. "You have come here to provide their Schmidt with subjects for research." He pronounces each syllable with knifelike clarity. "Perhaps you can get the serpent to agree to one shipload per body!"

"With subjects as unique as your tribe, I think Mengele could get Hitler to agree to one shipload per person."

"Per *body*," he says.

"The researchers want to examine the bodies of your ancestors, Emanuel. From the living, they want only blood samples. Blood. Nothing more. Your tribal whereabouts will remain a secret. Our meeting places will remain discreet."

He looks down at her, his face a study in contempt. "For over two millennia no one knew or cared that we existed. We were better off." He takes the meat from his mouth and drops it onto the plate. "I will relay your request to my people. The decision must be theirs."——

The vision faded. Sol covered himself with his coat

and slept. He woke to the sound of Miriam's voice. Responding more quickly this time, he climbed from the sewer.

"We only have a little while," Miriam said. "The shop is closed. Konnie has some errands to run. He'll be back in an hour."

Without saying a word, Sol took her hand and led her to Kaverne. There, on the carpet, they made love. Concentrating, Sol experienced each place where they joined. He wanted to imprint the sensations on his consciousness so that he could savor them later. Instead, he flowed into her and they floated in a magical space and time where nothing existed except the rainbow of love that once had been two people.

Afterward, when he touched her, his love and desire for her seemed contained in a sheath of pride and of wonder that God had seen fit to bless him with such good fortune. He held her close, trying to understand why the fog of self-doubt that he had lived with since Walter Rathenau's death was gone. Later would be time enough to examine that, he decided, pretending to be asleep so that Miriam would continue to lie quietly in his arms.

"I love you, Solomon. I am *your* wife, and no one else's," she said at last, as if in answer to his earlier doubts.

The words reverberated inside him, then etched themselves onto the deepest part of his soul.

Your wife, they echoed.

Your wife…

Chapter Eight

Erich opened the long velvet box and examined the diamond bracelet he had bought for Miriam more than a week before, for no particular reason except that he thought it belonged around her wrist. He had been carrying it around ever since, hoping for a moment when she would seem receptive.

For the last few days, she had been more distant, more preoccupied than ever. The longer he waited, the less benign he felt toward her—and the less inclined to give her something bought in a fit of tenderness and longing. He was sure she would find a way to denigrate his gift. Not crassly sarcastic, but subtly and, thus, more emotionally devastating. He had no way to fight her verbal choreographies, except to play the stoic soldier and swallow his rage.

Worse yet, like a mother offering strudel because

one's blocks were picked up, she would invite him to his reward between her legs—reminding him all the while that her hatred of anything Nazi or even vaguely military was being fueled by his weakness for her.

What would happen then? Doubtless another erectile failure and the pretense that her satisfaction was all he wanted this night. Small wonder that the act which he had in the past anticipated with pleasure now revolted him, as it had done ever since the business with Hempel and that poor prostitute. What had her name been? *Toy.*

There was only one female with whom he could truly share his feelings, Erich thought. The one who had loved him unconditionally.

Taurus.

Slipping into his black silk robe, he poured himself a cognac against the November dawn, pocketed the bracelet, and went outside. By the time he reached the kennels, he had disposed of the brandy. He was about to set the glass under a tree, where he could find it later, when he saw that the duty officer was Krayller—a loner who would certainly not find the need for a cognac unbecoming of the conduct of his superior officer.

"You weren't scheduled for duty tonight," Erich said.

Though Erich's tone was conversational, Krayller reddened. "One of the other men." His reluctance to name the man stemmed, Erich knew, from an effort to avoid getting the other trainer in trouble. "I'm filling in."

Erich tried to rearrange his features to reflect a stern demeanor in the face of the trainers again changing the duty roster without permission, but secretly the *esprit de corps* and self-sufficiency the trainers exhibited pleased him. He took pride in the fact that his men were different from so many German soldiers, with their rigidity and blind insistences. While his men certainly knew the value of following orders, he encouraged them to question. To think for themselves, unlike some of the so-called finest units, who reminded him of the Communist insurgents of his childhood whose takeover had failed because they'd lacked proper tickets to board the train. One conductor, armed with nothing but a ticket punch, had stopped a coup.

As a member of the Abwehr, the security branch of the armed forces, he had visited many units and often been on assessment teams. What others applauded made him shudder. He had asked himself: what would become of those units if the officers were killed, or if the commander were a Judas goat? What would become of the country?

"I've no problem with changes. Just make sure the paperwork's proper," Erich said, nodding at Krayller. "Oberschütze Müller visiting his sister again?"

The man hesitated, then nodded. "Yes, sir," he said. "And thank you, sir." He adjusted his carbine on his shoulder.

Erich thought about Ursula Müller, remembering the time when, both of them barely into puberty, she had tried to goad him into probing her with his *damaged* fingers. She was ready for something new and different, she had said. His fearful refusal had triggered her sarcastic laughter and made him so angry that he had lied to the other boys—Solomon among them—bragging about something he hadn't done.

Now where was she, with her weak IQ and strong libido? A depressive, institutionalized by the New Order and forced to service the officers under threat of involuntary sterilization. "You're forever filling in," Erich said. "Volunteering in an emergency I can understand. But you seem to make a career of it."

The corporal scooped up the affenpinscher, his constant companion, and held the black monkey terrier against his huge chest, playing with the forelegs. "The other men have families, sir. Me...I'm a loner, a sort of...clown."

"Clown?"

"Like Grog, sir." Krayller puffed up his corpulent cheeks, as if expecting Erich to join him in *Sch-ö-ö-n*, the clown routine the real Grog had made famous. When Erich did not respond, Krayller said, somewhat awkwardly, "Always smiling—always alone." He quickly added, "Except for Grog Junior, here." He patted the terrier.

"Fine, but don't let your generosity interfere with your regular duties," Erich said, ambling down the ramp that led to the garage underneath the mansion. "I don't want anyone falling asleep during drills."

"No, sir. I'll sleep after I'm dead. Nothing to do then but lie around anyway," Krayller called after him. "Just so they bury me with my smile painted on—sir."

Until he pulled the chain of the dangling bulb, Erich was unsure why he had entered the garage, with its two rows of army and civilian vehicles lined up like troops awaiting inspection. Then he noticed Hawk, his bicycle since childhood, and thanked the impulse that had brought him down here. Someone—Konnie, perhaps— had washed the bike and polished its considerable chrome to a high shine.

Sch-ö-ö-n, he thought. *Beautiful*.

Pulling off his robe, he exchanged it and his empty glass for the military blouse he kept in his garage locker. Without thinking, he transferred the bracelet from the pocket of his robe to the pocket of his shirt. Then he snapped off the light and walked Hawk clear of the garage and up into the breaking dawn, aware that the feeling of oppression was draining from him.

Some of the shepherds whined or whimpered pitifully when he unchained Taurus from her dog-run. Others performed a retinue of tricks or simply, shamelessly begged. To no avail. Tonight, he wanted no other companion than Taurus. He hooked up her leash and led dog and bike past Krayller's post.

Older than any of the other dogs by half a dozen years, Taurus lifted her head like a princess and pranced along, basking in her master's affections. The corporal saluted smartly, and Erich returned it left-handed, a bit of occasional military irreverence the men seemed to enjoy.

Then he was off, dawn flooding the streets, Taurus' claws clicking against pavement as she trotted alongside. He rode slowly, both to savor the moment and in respect for the dysplasia that had invaded Taurus' hips and likely would eventually cripple her. She moved easily this morning; her pain seemed far away, no more than a dark cloud on a horizon. He opened his mind to her, exulting in her sense of smell and purpose. Her happiness at roaming and being beside him beat against his consciousness as colorfully as the wings of a luna moth against a window screen. He was a boy again. He wondered if he had ever, really, grown up. Everyone else seemed so much older, so much more mature. Did they feel like boys, too, or was he the only one who felt forever boy, his dog beside him, clothespinned-on playing cards fluttering against his spokes?

They went up the Kurfurstendamm and down Mauerstrasse. When they reached Ananas, to which he realized he had unconsciously been heading the whole time, he was inordinately thirsty—and hungry for human camaraderie. He chained the bike to a pole outside the nightclub and threaded the leash around the handlebars. Almost paradoxically, in contrast to its wilder, cabaret days, the place was now an officers' club and never closed.

He glanced up at the spread-winged Nazi eagle on the marquee, remembering with nostalgic regret how the nightclub had once flown on wings of creativity and artistic verve. Once, when Miriam was the star; once, when Werner Fink's deadly humor was applauded even by those who feared its edge, and the likes of Bertoldt Brecht drank nightly at their regular tables.

Once, when there was hope.

Guard the bike, he mentally told Taurus, almost in afterthought as his depression returned.

Inside, in the foyer, a stolidly bosomed hat-check girl

wearing a severe suit took Erich's officer's cap, eyeing him appreciatively. He wished she were one of the chorines from the old days, dressed only in feathers and flesh, then hoped she wasn't. Some changes he could not abide.

The atmosphere in the cabaret proper was subdued and smoky, not the usual gaiety and toasting by men coming off duty. Soldiers of all ranks meandered among the tables, beer mugs in hand, but conversations were quiet. There was a tension in the air in counterpoint to the atmosphere of *Gemütlichkeit* he had sought. Many men just sat and stared at the pineapples that served as table centerpieces. Someone had painted them green, so that they looked like grenades—hardly the exotic, erotic symbols that once could buy a man a night between almost any woman's legs, if not a lifetime in her heart.

But that change was not new, not since his last visit. There was something else odd, something he could not determine, much less name. He looked around, trying to figure out what had changed.

The stage was darkened except for a tiny light above a drum set and a tuba cradled on a stand. It seemed almost funereal, the antithesis of the delightful exhibitionism of just a half-dozen years ago. Gone were acts like kohl-eyed Mimi de Rue—Miriam's stage name; she had dropped "Rathenau" in the hope of obtaining work—the professionally trained dancer who sang like a seductress. Gone too, though who knew where—Erich had heard that, miraculously, Fink had not been arrested—were *conferenciers* like Werner Fink, whose outrageous comedy had been like a Hitler salute right up the nearest Nazi's ass. Now, when there was a revue, Nazi comics about as interesting as beer left in a mug for a week introduced the acts.

Abruptly, Erich realized what had changed since his last visit. Except for one woman near the bar, clad in expensive black nylons and what looked like a pink houserobe, all the waitresses were gone. He was about to ask the nearest soldier about the change, when he noticed one of the trainers, Corporal Hans Müller, sitting in the corner, smoking, the back of his head against the wall.

"I heard you had gone to the, um, hospital," Erich said, ambling over to him.

The corporal nodded for Erich to sit down but did not in any way acknowledge his rank. "I went to the *nuthouse*," Hans said. "You can say it, Herr Major. It doesn't bother me."

Müller thumped out his cigarette against the ashtray, swirled the wrong end in his mouth to make sure it was dead, and replaced it in his pack. Habit, Erich knew, borne of the Depression days that Hitler's military regime had ended.

"They released her," Müller said. "She was gone by the time I got there. Left. On her own. No money. No family with her. The doctor told me they needed the bed for someone *useful*. Someone who might return to society and produce strong Nazi babies." He looked around as if to make sure that they were not being overheard. "Nazi *bastards*," he added in a low voice.

"There's no room left in the Reich for old-fashioned sentimentalism, for compassion."

"I'm sorry," Erich said, at a loss for words. "Where is she now?"

Müller shrugged. "Your guess is as good as mine. Probably at the bottom of the Elbe. I wouldn't know where to begin to look. Aren't we all siblings in the eyes of the State? I'll just find another sister."

Erich stared at the grain lines in the table top. Had he contributed to her downfall by refusing her, he wondered? *Getting as bad as Solomon,* he thought. *Shrouding myself in conscience. Only real difference between a goddamn Jew and a goddamn Catholic is the degree of guilt. Has little to do with Jesus.*

In an attempt to lift a corner of his gloom, he listened to the conversation of the soldiers at the next table, heads together like chuckling conspirators, and then wished he hadn't. They were describing their latest sojourn with a Jewish prostitute. "Big-nosed bronco busting," one called it, trying for an American cowboy inflection. "They can't get enough of it. Not when *we* start poking them."

The conversation sickened Erich, though he knew he should be used to it. The Jewesses who worked the alleys had no other choice. Those who did not do it for food, did it in a desperate attempt to help rescue loved ones from work camps—begging for something as simple as a letter forwarded to the right authority. *Like Miriam with me,* Erich thought, annoyed with himself for making the comparison. *Except Solomon really isn't incarcerated.*

"I left her tied up, back there," the soldier went on. "Ready for the next one." His laughter, ringing hollow in the otherwise quiet cabaret, chilled Erich. *Back there.* There were prostitutes in here now? Not that there hadn't always been a working girl or two among the tables, but this was different. These were...*Slaves.*

Back there, beat within his brain.

They had a Jewish woman, perhaps several, tied up in the back rooms. Maybe even in Miriam's former dressing room, the one with the tawdry, half-peeled star on the door. Is that what it had stood for all these years...a Star of David?

His throat felt parched, and his heart thudded. He rose, quivering with rage, turned to face the soldiers, and saw the ratty high heels sticking up from beneath the tablecloth as a woman serviced the service man.

A pressure burrowed up his spine and hit the base of his skull. His head jerked back. "I—I'm sorr-sorry about Urs-ula," he said over his shoulder. In some part of his mind, unaffected by the lightning seizure that held him, the illogic of it all pulsed like a heavy Latin beat. Sexual union between Germans and Jews was forbidden, but rape of Jewesses and Jewish boys was condoned, if not encouraged.

He stood, everything off-kilter. He watched the grins of the soldiers drain and the glazed eyes of the one receiving fellatio change from glassy to fearful.

"W-what is an arm-army without hon...without honor," Erich stammered, knowing that they would think him drunk. "J-ust l-look at you. W-what have we be-become."

In a single movement, he approached the table, bent down, and tugged at the legs of the woman underneath. She allowed herself to be drawn forth, but made no attempt to stand.

"Get out of here," Erich said softly. "And don't ever come back."

On impulse, he dug into his shirt pocket, pulled out the diamond bracelet, and dropped it onto the woman. Then, trembling, unable to catch his breath, he stumbled backward toward the door, careful not to turn his back on the young soldiers.

He yanked his cap from the hat-check girl's extended hands, and shouldered his way outside into a gloomy, overcast winter morning. Taurus gained her feet awkwardly, wagging her tail despite the pain of her dysplasia. He wanted to sag to his knees and wrap his arms around her neck but felt unworthy of her affection. Against the pole, Hawk too seemed apart from him, as though leaning away from his attention, a prize he did not deserve.

The door opened behind him. When Müller put a tentative hand on his shoulder, he did not pull away or otherwise resist the familiarity, though the corporal clearly was over the limits of military protocol. "Are you all right, Herr Major? You went white as a ghost."

Erich took a deep breath to slow his pounding heart. "I-I'm fine. Thanks for asking, Oberschütze M-Müller."

"Do you need to go back inside?"

"I'll never g-go back inside."

"Nor I." Müller held the bike while Erich unchained it. "And to think," he said, face flushed with the knowledge that he was out of line, "that I used to be proud to call myself a soldier," he finished.

"I understand. Only too well," Erich said, grateful that he had stopped stammering. He looked up at the marquee. "We need a nightclub without...without women."

"Where we can be ourselves," Müller finished, a look of finality and defeat on his face. "I think I need to walk," he said. "A long walk. Somewhere beyond the sun." He stuck his hands in his pockets and, softly whistling "Mack the Knife," walked away.

Erich lit a cheroot and dragged deeply. He knew he had to do something to slough off his anger over Ananas and his anguish about Ursula, though what he was not sure. He mounted the bike and pedaled around the corner into the early morning traffic, Taurus close beside him. Drivers, perhaps seeing his uniform, cautiously veered around him.

He steered down a sidestreet—his old neighborhood—and the answer stared right at him. Visiting the butcher shop had always been a favorite part of his times with Taurus—a simple enough pleasure, and one that would certainly cheer him up now.

He stopped before the butcher's, chained his bicycle to a pole, and mentally commanded Taurus to "*Stay.*" Taurus lay on the stoop, her head on the doorway threshold, eyeing the meat hanging behind the crescent-shaped counter. Half a pig, complete with snout and tail, dangled from a hook in the corner in full view of the customers because Faussan, the butcher, liked to perform his artistry as much as possible in public. His meat was, he claimed, the best in Berlin, and the show was good for business.

Good for his ego, Erich thought, standing before the counter and studying the meat beneath the fingerprint-smeared glass. He had rescued his first dog, Bull, from the alley behind the shop—rescue being the operative word, since Bull had clearly been slated for someone's dinner table...not an unusual event in the lean times following the Great War. The rescue grew more noble, and his frustration greater, with each retelling.

That had been the dog his father drowned. For Erich, father and butcher had become one. He hated them equally, and suspected that he returned to this particular shop so often to torment the owner.

Their encounter was always the same:

"Something I can get for you, Herr Major?" A tired voice, for surely the butcher knew what the answer would be.

"No dogs or cats today, no human flesh?"

"That's not funny, Herr Major." Followed by a whack of the cleaver. The man's paunch—so evident twenty years before—was gone, but the inevitable cigarette still peeked out from behind one ear. It was balanced with a pencil behind the other, announcing him to be a man of revenue. "That's not funny at all."

No Berlin butcher liked being reminded that Carl Grossman, who specialized in picking up peasant girls from the train station, or Georg Haarmann, who specialized in picking up orphan boys wandering around the station, had both been city butchers—and in more than one sense of the word. Grossman maintained he had not killed and cannibalized over two dozen women, until detectives agreed to let him confess the murders to his pet bird, which seemed not at all ill at ease sitting on his shoulder. Haarmann was mild-mannered, soft-spoken; during rape, he would tear out his victim's throat with his teeth, then boil and neatly package the result. Both men did a brisk wholesale business: Grossman in several local shops, Haarmann on the black market. After their confessions, there was, according to the papers, furtive inspections of larders and meat jars, furtive vomiting.

Today, as usual, the shop smelled of blood—the sawdust that covered the floor was clumped where droplets had fallen—but Faussan was not present.

"Your papa visiting the abattoir?" Erich asked the butcher's daughter, a pigtailed blonde with rounded shoulders who emerged from the back rooms, wiping her hands on a rag. She wore a bloodied apron and, surprisingly, a perfectly white blouse cut low across the bodice and gathered at the shoulders. Seeing him, her whole demeanor changed. The worn-out, bedraggled shop girl look vanished as with her wrist she pushed back a curl from her forehead.

"Papa's at his telephone. We finally got one. I think he's called most of Berlin." She leaned over to wipe off the fingerprints, her weight against the side of the counter so that her cleavage was better exposed. She smiled when she saw Erich looking. "I'd be happy to help you, Herr Major," she offered in a sing-song,

admiring his uniform, "any way I can. He will probably
be tied up—for hours."

"Sausage. Smoked." He had half a mind to run a hand
down the blouse. Would she object, or merely thrust
out that wonderful chest even further? "A dozen links,"
he added, pleased that he felt less revolted by the idea
of sex than he had in a long time.

"These big ones?" she asked, pointing. "I *love*
sausage."

What she loved, Erich knew, had little to do with
him personally. What the Führer had called an honor
and a duty had given young women the moral license
to sleep with soldiers. Officers were, as in the butcher-
shop parlance, prime. Married or not, a young blonde
pregnant by an Aryan officer was lauded and pampered.
Once the child surpassed infancy, the State institutions
gradually relieved her of her maternal responsibilities
and eased her out the door. He wondered if she was
aware of that.

"I've seen you with your dog before," she said. "I've
watched the little game you play with her. Looks like
fun."

"It is," he said. How often had he sat on the shop
stoop, letting Taurus take a sausage from his mouth, so
delighted by his dog's trust in him that he had hardly
noticed this enchanting creature?

He glanced toward Taurus, paternally sentimental,
and felt a surge of dismay. She was slowly bellying across
the sawdust, heading for the pig. "*Back,*" he mentally
commanded.

Perhaps it was the pride in his mind, perhaps the absence of the shop's owner. Whatever the reason, Taurus did not obey. She put her head down and looked up at him dolefully. When he repeated the command to back up, she rose and reluctantly moved back half a meter, until her hips were within the doorway. Then she lay down, and no number of repeated commands made her move. He knew that if he mentally scolded her harshly enough, she would obey, but she was old and almost always in pain. He let her lie.

The shop girl put a hand on his forearm. When he did not resist, she slipped around the counter with a dancer's dexterity and slid her arm through his. "I've been thinking about closing up for a while, while Papa's on the phone. You think I should?"

She was—what? Fifteen? Sixteen? Was she right now calculating the days since her last period, considering her chances...? He let the back of his hand rest against her side, then shifted to cup a fleshy buttock. She murmured throatily.

"Do you have a place?" she asked. "Or do we need to sneak upstairs?"

Why couldn't Miriam be so unsophisticated, so loving and willing? He steered himself from answering, *Why not here on the sawdust* and was about to say, "I have an apartment overlooking the Landwehr," when he again saw Taurus sneaking forward.

This time when she gazed up at him, she growled. *Jealous.*

Erich let go of the sweet, rounded buttock.

"What's going on here!"

Erich glanced toward the back rooms, expecting her father, but the voice came from a figure, a boy, really, standing in the front door, just behind Taurus. He wore a Hitler Youth uniform with the sash indicating *Block Warden*, which made him responsible for political correctness in the neighborhood. A pistol was holstered at his side. Erich had never heard of the Hitler Youth carrying pistols, not officially anyway, but he was happy when he did not hear about that organization at all.

"Bertel!" the boy said, as if unsure he had been heard before.

"Oh, Gregor." She clucked in disappointment and went back around the counter, working again at the fingerprints in passing.

Eyes narrowed, a hand on the pistol grip, the youth maneuvered around Erich and leaned over the counter. She backed up; he clutched her by the wrist. "I thought you said there would never be a next time."

"We were just talking, Gregor. Besides, you hardly ever come around anymore." She was pouting.

"You think it's easy being a Block Warden? We cannot put the individual above the State."

Parroting, Erich knew. *Just like I used to....*

He lifted up the sack of sausage, wishing he'd had time to take her before her boyfriend arrived, so he might have handed her over, wet sex and all. *Like Hempel using Goebbels' castoffs*, he thought with a strange combination of delight and disgust. *Sharing the seed.*

The direction of his thoughts caused a disconnect from Taurus. Seizing the moment, she leapt for the pig.

It was not the power-ballet leap of which she had been capable just a year ago. More a standing take-off from pain-filled legs. But it was accurate. She grabbed the pig by the forelegs and, though probably intending only to yank off a mouthful, brought it down with a twist of her powerful head.

"Stop that!" Forgetting her boyfriend, Bertel clutched at the pig's wired-together hind legs.

Taurus growled, backing away, refusing to release her grip.

For several moments, dog and shop-girl pulled in opposite directions, like the two women, it occurred to Erich, fighting over the baby in the Solomon legend. Then the Hitler Youth stepped away from the counter, legs spread and weight balanced, like a gunfighter in a cowboy film.

Erich took out a cheroot. "If you shoot, you'd better hit your girlfriend," he said calmly. "Because if you hurt the dog, I'll break both your arms. *Then* I'll break your legs."

The young gunman turned his attention toward Erich.

Erich lit the cheroot.

"Kill," he told Taurus matter-of-factly. "Kill the little bastard."

Taurus was scrambling across sawdust and in the air before Erich finished speaking. Her whole weight crashed into the youth, who cried out as he was knocked against the counter. Almost miraculously, the glass did not break.

The boy sat on the sawdust, mouth open, arms and

legs splayed out like a rag doll, while Taurus licked his face.

"Kill him harder," Erich said, laughing with Taurus at their private joke and dragging on the cheroot.

The boy sputtered, but appeared to be afraid to move away. Taurus licked the youth's lips and all but stuck her tongue up his nose.

"Good girl." Erich bent beside her as she backed off. He could sense the fury that rippled beneath her fur at not being allowed to do real damage, feel it as she growled softly. "Would you like her to *kill* you too?" he asked Bertel.

"No, *thank* you." The words dropped like icicles from her lips, but the light in her eyes danced with amusement.

He paid for the sausages with a banknote and backed out the door. That was twice in one morning that he had been loath to expose his back, he thought. Suddenly he wished Hitler's war would come—almost a foregone conclusion these days. A battlefield where one could recognize the enemy might prove less dangerous than Berlin.

C HAPTER NINE

Erich mounted Hawk and rode off, thinking about the girl, Bertel, about Miriam, about the woman beneath the table at Ananas. How different the world would be without women! Not better, but less...complicated.

Müller's comment came back to him. *We need a place without women. Where we can be ourselves.*

With that in mind, Erich abruptly steered across traffic and headed for Friedrich Ebert Strasse. He usually avoided his home-street, especially now that his parents had returned to the apartment they had abandoned, and taken over the tobacco shop again. That thieves such as his parents could be gifted the business they had previously ransacked was indicative of the moral penury of the times. It sickened him—but whether because of the immorality or because he hated his father, he wasn't sure.

Today was Sunday, and his father had not yet opened the shop. Probably gone to Mass, now that he was wealthy; celebrating not the bread and wine, but the roast duckling and vintage sherry he and Erich's mother would later enjoy.

The idea Corporal Müller had given him overpowered Erich's scorn for everything the tobacco shop represented. He passed the place, its shades halfway down, the tall windows looking sleepy-eyed, and parked his bike next door, against the gold-plated guardrail above what was once Kaverne, Granddame Rathenau's cabaret for the upper crust. He looped Taurus' leash through the rail and descended the stairs. Like regressing into a past life, he thought, letting the cool, moist shadows invade him.

Shaking, he removed his lock picks, a memento from childhood, from the small leather pouch at the end of his keychain. He willed the shaking to stop, and was thankful, regardless of the trembling, when he was able to open the door.

He slipped in quickly, like a boy afraid the bogeyman was coming, and shut the door quietly and firmly behind him. The basement nightclub awaited him at the bottom of the metal spiral stairs, dust dancing in the light streaming through the green, sidewalk-level windows.

The place smelled old and musty. Disused. The chairs were upended on the tables, and everything was covered with dusty muslin. He assumed, for lack of specific knowledge, that the ownership of the place had reverted to the furriers upstairs from whom the Granddame had purchased it, though perhaps it belonged to Miriam and she did not know it. Had Goebbels confiscated all her property, or just the Grünewald estate? It was worth looking into.

He went slowly down the steps, the metal ringing, his eyes on the empty dance floor. *There* he—and Solomon—had first seen *her*, a sylph in white tights, form-fitting tunic, swirl of pale pink ninon. Her singing once again hummed in his ears, her subsequent cancan—with his first look at her leotarded thighs— danced before his eyes. She had been fifteen or sixteen then, probably the same age as the girl today at the butcher shop, he thought with a slight shame; he and Sol two years younger. *"Wenn der weisse Flieder wieder blüht,"* she had sung, with the voice of an angel. "When the white lilac blooms again."

Someone had stacked two sets of two tables each close to the dance floor and canopied the creation with a shawl, as though to form an archway through which dancers might pass. Kids, he thought; probably partying. He wondered if they had gotten in as he and Sol used to, with lock picks. They could not have come up through the ancient sewer that ran beneath the cabaret and the tobacco shop, because his father had welded the grate shut at the shop, and he assumed the padlock had been replaced at this end. Not that he was about to go down into the cellar to find out. The place held too many bitter memories.

His fingers, injured when the grate came down, throbbed. As though needing something physical to alleviate the memory, he pulled down the shawl.

Remembering when he had last seen it, that night of the cabaret's pre-opening celebration, he buried his face in the cloth. The effect of its scent, of Miriam's perfume even after all these years, was immediate: he was instantly aroused.

Her thighs, her armpits, the line of her jaw—each place her colognes and perfumes touched—had its separate scent which lingered with him long after it should have dissipated. Of the senses, his sense of smell and hearing were the keenest.

He put the shawl over his shoulder like a beach towel and ascended the stairs, thinking about how the place would make a wonderful club for soldiers stationed in Berlin. Where officers and enlisted could mingle and drink without the distraction of women and with only minimal talk of the Party and the Führer. He would have to find out who owned the place and get permission for such an establishment without inviting suspicion that he was seeking to rescue Rathenau assets. But stopping now and again on the stairs and drinking in the smell of the shawl, he vowed not only to attempt the endeavor, but to succeed.

As he reached the top of the stairs, barking began, then a frenzied growling.

Seized with fear for Taurus' safety, he slammed through the door, locked it, and raced up to the sidewalk, almost in one motion.

Gregor stood in the street, both hands on the pistol,

which was aimed at the dog. The youth's eyes were engorged, the veins in his neck corded from anger. "She's a danger to the Reich," he said, not taking his gaze off the animal.

Gall rose from within Erich as though Satan's hand had reached into his intestines and squeezed, bringing forth his bitterest, most terrifying memory: Hitler forcing him to shoot Achilles, Taurus' mother, for chasing a prized peacock.

"Put the gun down," he said, "and I will forget you were ever here."

He would acquiesce to anything, *anything*, but knew better than to attempt to bargain with the young crazies the Hitler Youth attracted.

"Do you know what this bitch took from me?" The boy's voice was shrill. "Do you think I'll be able to perform my duties, once word gets out? The whole neighborhood will laugh! Bertel will never stop laughing!"

Erich moved forward so stealthily and smoothly the boy probably did not realize he was advancing. Years learning woodsman's skills and two months with Otto Braun, the German martial arts expert who had fought alongside Mao Tse Tung, had taught him well.

"The next time you fuck your Bertel, your face will be in the pillow and you'll think she's coming," he said, seeking to dull the youth's mental edge. "But she'll just be laughing at you. *Laughing*."

The boy swung the pistol, and fired.

But he was too late. Erich had already launched feet-first into a baseball slide. The bullet zinged over his head, knocked a shard of glass from a window, and then his right foot snapped up, connecting with the youth's groin. Years of training and a lifetime of anger went into the kick. Air whooshed from the boy's mouth. He dropped the gun, doubled over, and collapsed to his knees as he fought for breath.

Erich lifted himself up, calmly brushed off his pants— his knee was scraped and bleeding, but he pretended not to notice—and picked up the pistol. He unloaded it and, after holding a cartridge between forefinger and thumb, dropped the bullets down the sidewalk drain. They clinked as they hit. Lovely as church chimes, he thought.

He knelt beside the boy, clenched the youth's chin in his hand, and jerked the face his way. "Which do you want me to break first, your arms or your legs?" he asked, carefully modulating his voice. "Or would you rather I let Taurus loose so she can chew off your balls?"

The face, already bedsheet-white with shock, whitened still more.

"Answer me," Erich said, "or both Taurus *and* I will go to work on you. We're a team, you know."

The boy's tongue worked spastically, but no sound emerged.

Erich threw the pistol down the street. It hit asphalt with a clatter.

"You tell your girlfriend that the next time I stop for sausages, she better be ready for me. I'm going to have her every way I can think of. Right there in the sawdust, if I feel like it, with her butt propped up on a flank roast." He pressed an index finger against the youth's nose as though pushing a button. "You don't tell her that, I'm coming after you and…" A phrase occurred to him, part of a hit song the Georg Haarmann scandal had inspired. *"Mach ich Pökelfleisch aus dir,"* he paraphrased to the boy. "I'll make smoked meat out of you."

Chapter Ten

Sol extracted a brown egg from his pocket. He held it up to the moonlight filtering through the cigar shop's plate-glass window and turned it this way and that, wondering at God's artistry for having made something so simple, so perfect. "If I sat on you long enough, would God turn you into a chicken?" he asked aloud.

The egg was the last of a dozen he had found in the sewer—together with cheese and bratwurst, a box of chocolates, candles, a pencil and notebook, and a supply of books—*his*.

He patted his coat pocket. The biography of Isaac ben Solomon Luria, the mystic, was there, as always; he carried it around like a symbol of life, as if having it on his person ensured his survival.

Aside from the small supply of food, the sewer contained a canteen and two bottles filled with water, plus a bottle of cognac which, judging by the quality, had been lifted from the wine cellar of the estate. There was also a blanket, a pillow, and a box of first-aid items—including, to his initial amusement, a snakebite kit. He had felt less amused when he realized the kit was probably meant to be used in the event of a bite by a sewer rat seeking food and warmth.

Cracking the egg, he lifted it to his mouth and sucked out the insides. It slid easily down his throat. He crunched the shell in the palm of his hand, looked around for somewhere to discard it, then put it in his pocket. "Bless you, Miriam Freund," he said, feeling a surge of energy.

One more night, Sol thought, looking around—one more long, damp night, and we will be out of here. For six days and nights he had lived a reverse existence. During the day, so as to make as little noise as possible, he slept. At night—like a vampire bat—he emerged from the sewer to wander around the basement and the deserted cabaret. Sometimes, like now, he came up to the shop, but mostly the memories here were too painful.

Once, a few hours before dawn, he actually had the temerity to go into the street. Hat pulled down low like that of an American film gangster, he wandered the streets. But he did not look enough like a derelict to fit in with the alleyway vagrants, and he was certainly not elegant enough to blend with the wealthy nightclub set; he was neither SS nor Wehrmacht, and the middle-class—scholars and merchants alike—were tucked safely in bed.

He pulled a pencil stub out of his pocket, licked the point, and crossed Saturday off his calendar. He had found the calendar that night, on the sidewalk, after watching the owners of the furrier shop above the cabaret throw what remained of their inventory into a beat-up lorry and leave as if the very devils of hell were chasing them. Doubtless they feared an SS witch-burning for their former Communist sympathies. The calendar had blown from the heap of litter they had left behind. From what he had seen in his brief wanderings, it was the same all over the city: piles of discarded belongings defied the image of flawless organization and a perfect society.

He stared at the picture of a leggy blonde in a white bathing suit. She stood on a balcony that overlooked Lake Geneva, leaning against the railing to support herself and displaying an ermine coat which hung casually from one of her tanned shoulders, its silk lining exposed. The Alps lay behind her.

FURS BY HELVETIA
SURROUND HER WITH SILVER LININGS

He imagined Miriam wearing the fur; imagined the two of them strolling together along the shore of the lake. He had found himself smiling. The sooner he could leave the claustrophobic atmosphere of the sewer forever, the better he would feel. He felt trapped down there, panicked, obsessed with ticking off the minutes, the seconds, till Sunday.

He ran a hand over his scraggly beard and grimaced at his image in the teak-framed mirror that had miraculously remained intact on the cigar-shop wall.

His beard had grown in patches and was mottled underneath with scaly brown blemishes. He was gaunt and haggard. There was no heat during the night. Though he wore his coat all the time, he had developed a dry hacking cough which could well be symptomatic of TB or something equally deadly. Typhoid perhaps?

Angry at himself for being so morbid, he thrust the calendar and a fist into a pocket of his coat and surveyed the shop. The windows and door had been replaced or repaired, but the store still had a dark, oppressive quality that could not be explained away merely because the lights were off. The sewer held its terrors, but the shop depressed him—and in a large way that was worse, much worse, for in here he had known love and happiness and his father's bright eyes and bad jokes.

How much better, he thought, if *Die Ziggarrenkiste* were still like the other Jewish shops he had passed on his night of wandering, the exterior walls grimed with swastikas and excrement. At least then it would still *belong*. To his people. And thus to him.

Standing with his forehead pressed against the wall, he cursed the whole Weisser family—and himself, for ever having believed in them. He found himself wishing that the goon who had started the fire in the cellar would return and finish the job. Only the memory of his father kept him from dousing the shop in gasoline and putting a match to it himself.

How secure he had once felt in his beliefs! Secure and...virtuous. That was it! As if being part of Walther

Rathenau's dream of God and good government made him better than he would have been as just Solomon Freund, a Jew with a yen for scholarship.

The New Order had taken care of that, all right. Stripped him of his virtue. Now Hitler's followers were the ones who felt purposeful and fired with moral rectitude.

He envied them.

Even in a Berlin given way to penury and pain, he coveted their sense of conviction...those beautiful couples, glad to give up their strolls through the Tiergarten. They knew—*knew!*—that devil-may-care lives were evil and there was beauty only in Nazi law and order. Now, Hitler Youth used sawed-off boards to practice maneuvers between manicured shrubs where the wealthy had walked. Today felt good to them and they believed in an even better tomorrow. Trivia did not trouble them; it meant nothing to them that theirs was a world where the premium on good cigars had been replaced by so pressing a demand for weapons that Berlin's stores had run out of toy guns.

From the Zoo Station came the rumble of the night train from Frankfurt, as always exactly on time, running with Teutonic precision. Now *there* was true virtue.

The sound of running footsteps outside cut through his thoughts. Instinctively he stepped into the shadows.

"Herr Freund?"

A small pair of hands planted themselves on the outside of the lowest window pane.

"Herr Freund?"

A boy's cap and dirty face poked into view. Feeling silly for his fear, Sol saw it was a youth eight or nine years old.

He made his way across the shop; the gaslight outside revealed the child, standing in filthy tweed cap, ill-fitting coat, and woolen knickers, while snow lightly swirled around him. One sock was down around a skinny ankle.

"I bring word from Miriam Rathenau!" The boy's mouth was so close to the pane that his breath made a small ragged circle.

Fearing to open the door, Solomon tugged at the window, trying unsuccessfully to open it a crack. "Tell me!"

The boy glanced anxiously up and down the street, then reached inside his coat. "You are Solomon Freund?"

"I am."

The boy drew in his cheeks as if he were biting the inside of them to lend him courage.

"You need food?" Sol set caution aside and inched open the door. "Shelter? I'd be glad to share what I have."

The child shoved a thick envelope toward him. "I have to go."

Sol moved closer and took the letter. Word from Miriam! His emigration papers? *Their* papers? He stared down at the envelope.

By the time he looked up, the boy had dashed across the street.

"Wait!" Sol waved frantically. "Come back!"

The boy reached the alley beside the apartment building that had been Sol's former residence. Stopping in the shadow created by a cornice, he turned around.

Sol stepped into the swirling snowfall, concerned more for the child than for his own safety. The beadle had told him of a boy he had tried to take out of Berlin, the son of a rabbi whose parents were transported. The youth, determined to remain in the city to search for his mama and papa, had slipped away in the confusion and crowds at the train station, too quick and too late for Beadle Cohen to find him. Could this be that boy?

Looking petulantly at the ground, the youth shuffled toward Solomon, pigeon-toed and tentative. A blast from the station stopped him. The ground shook. There was a *chug-whoosh* of the engine and of airbrakes releasing as the night train pulled away.

"Come quickly!" Solomon shouted above the din.

Suddenly the unmistakable wail of a police car shattered the night. A Mercedes squealed around a corner, fishtailing on the icy asphalt. Like a roach surprised by light, the boy scurried down the alley.

Run! Sol screamed at himself. Into the shop! Hide in the darkness and pray they aren't looking for you—

What kind of man was he becoming, he thought as he reached the door, that he could hope they were after anyone but him...even a boy—a child?

Asking forgiveness from the boy and from God, he closed the door of the shop and pushed the letter into his coat pocket. Reentering at this time of night could draw attention to himself, and running would be sheer stupidity. He must be like any merchant shutting up his place of business and strolling away—careful to hear and see nothing he was not supposed to.

Head down as though against the snow, he walked slowly but steadily toward the cabaret. When he could stand the tension no longer, he pretended to look at the watch he did not have, and tilted his head like any curious-but-respectful passerby.

Overhead light flashing, siren blaring, the car had skidded to a halt in front of the apartment house. Two Gestapo agents in long black overcoats leapt out, pistols in hand. One of them, small and wizened—his hat had fallen off and Sol could see that he was bald—jumped the blue-spruce hedge and flattened himself against the wall of the apartment house like a combat soldier storming a pillbox.

"Halt where you are!"

The second agent, more youth than man, squatted at the alley entrance, pistol braced against his uplifted forearm as he aimed.

Paralyzed by the drama being played out before him, Sol stared through snowflakes gathering on his glasses.

The snap and whine of the bullet raged above the siren's scream. Sol tried to move, but his legs felt thick and heavy. His stomach heaved as he relived that moment he had witnessed Walther Rathenau's assassination...grenade spinning on the street...death shots hanging in the air.

Clutching his stomach, he forced himself toward the

cabaret's stairs, gripped the handrail and swung himself down, slamming against the stairwell wall. Mustering what strength he still possessed, he peered over the edge of the sidewalk.

The men had disappeared down the alley.

He used his penknife to draw back the cabaret's jimmied deadbolt from its metal casing and eased himself inside. Standing on the wrought-iron landing, he rebolted the door. Sweating and shaking, he leaned against the wall.

Safe! Thank God!

He congratulated Miriam for having had the good sense to adjust the tumblers so the club would only *seem* to be locked. She had learned well from Erich and his lock picks.

What am I thinking? A child's life was being threatened, perhaps for the very crime of having delivered him Miriam's message. He should be overcome with grief—and gratitude. But what if they captured the boy alive? Dragged him from the alley, what would he tell them? What *could* he tell them?

Slowly, as if the self-inflicted delay were punishment for his emotions, Sol took the letter from his coat's inner pocket. Using his penknife, he slit the edge of the envelope and, trembling, took out the single sheet of paper, folded many times. He recognized the handwriting at once as Miriam's:

DEAREST, *THEY* MOVE INTO K TOMORROW— A PERFECT PLACE TO WARM THEMSELVES, PLAY CARDS, DRINK. STAY OUT OF SIGHT

UNTIL I COME—WHICH MAY NOT BE AS PLANNED. LOOK AFTER THE BOY.

All my love.

MRF

Sol let the paper slip from his hands. It floated down among the tables, catching the dusty moonlight that slanted through the stained-glass windows.

K—*Kaverne*; MRF—Miriam Rathenau *Freund*.

If only he had insisted Miriam leave with him at once! Surely they could have bribed their way out of the country...but with what? *Erich's* money?

Outside, the siren stopped. On tiptoes, Sol peered through a hole made by a rock tossed at the window. The Gestapo emerged empty-handed from the alley. "Thank you, God," Sol whispered, with renewed shame and relief. "Now please send them away."

The men crossed the street and stood outside the cigar store. The bald one lit a cigarette, exhaled a mix of smoke and steaming breath. He said something to his companion, laughed loudly, and took hold of the door as if to check its security.

My God, I forgot to lock it! How could I have been so stupid!

Looking concerned, the man ground out his cigarette on the sidewalk and went inside, the other man surveying the street suspiciously. The lights went on. Sol cursed himself for his stupidity in dallying at the window; the cabaret was bound to be next. He must hurry, silently, to the sewer's comparative safety.

He started down into darkness. The first step squeaked and the metal spiral staircase echoed, amplifying the sound. He backstepped onto the landing and checked outside. Mopping sweat from his brow, he picked up the note from Miriam and descended the stairs with catlike caution. He crept across the dance floor and down into the subbasement. Remembering the light, he felt around for the chain and pulled it on. The bulb popped and died.

He dropped to his knees, found and lifted the sewer grate.

After the night's crisp air, the sewer's stench billowed up like a tangible force. He held his breath, lowered himself onto the two-by-twelve and stretched upward to pull down the grate. It clanged shut. He groped for the boxes of provisions, wanting to touch them not so much for reassurance as for a focal point of existence. They were the immediate essentials of life, though how long a life was anyone's guess. He felt certain only that, for now, the sewer was the one refuge left to him in Berlin.

CHAPTER ELEVEN

Miriam had thought of Sol incarcerated in a camp for so long that it had become habit, like a bitter pill she'd had to swallow daily. Now that he was here, beneath her feet, she found herself tiptoeing around the shop. It was as if she were walking on his head and feared that she was causing him physical pain.

Every now and then she would forget for a moment and return to the images she had called forth over the years: Sol being beaten, starved, worked like a laborer. Then a board would creak beneath her soles, or the wind would whistle through the space between the shop door and the floor, and she would start guiltily, as if by forgetting she had somehow let him down. Again.

She had much to think about. She would have to be careful not to let Erich see a change in her. She would have to contact Perón. Most importantly, she would have to find a way to go down into the sewer and see Sol. By now, he would need food, water, possibly even medicines if the dampness down there had made him ill. She had been trying to think of some way to induce both of the Weissers to take the day off, but had come up with nothing. Now, miraculously, she was halfway there. She had been instructed to come and work at the shop today because, Herr Weisser had said, a friend was unexpectedly coming into town and he wanted to be free to spend some time with him. With any luck, his wife, Inge, would develop a headache, or remember a commitment to play cards, and Miriam would be left alone.

Whatever it took, Miriam thought, she had to persuade Sol to go back to safety, to Amsterdam. And, if possible, she would send young Misha there with him. Though he might not agree with her at this moment, outside of finding his parents—a next-to-impossible task—reuniting the boy with the beadle would be the best thing she could do for him. She had been happy to find him a temporary haven with the underground group led by the furrier's son, but that was over now. She felt guilty about having been the person whose message had placed him in danger. On the other hand, they had already made Misha a message runner by then, and it had been only a matter of time before he would have taken it into his head to begin once more the futile search for his parents. All in all, he was better off where he was now, in Baden-Baden.

"Why are you staring into space? Is there no work to be done?"

The bell signaling her entry into the shop coincided with Inge Weisser's first criticism of the day. She had determined from the start to turn Miriam into *Aschenbrödel*, and Cinderella Miriam stayed. No matter what she did—not so much to please the woman but to keep the peace—Erich's mother felt obliged to spew venom whenever her husband was in earshot. Since he had entered behind her, this was one of those times.

She shed her fur, threw it at Miriam with a brusque instruction to handle it carefully and hang it up, and emplaced herself at the end of the counter. Her husband entered behind her, followed closely by none other than Deputy Commandant Otto Hempel.

"Sit, sit," Herr Weisser said, pulling out one of the chairs at the corner table. He pushed a box of cigars toward the man. "Help yourself. How about a schnapps to go with it? You are, after all, on holiday."

Hempel shrugged off his coat and smiled a feral smile. "A schnapps? In the morning? Why not. It's cold enough out there to freeze a nun's tits."

Weisser brought forth the bottle of cognac—his second best, Miriam noted. "How are things at the camp?"

"Tiring. Tiring. Those stinking Jews will never learn their place. I, for one, will be delighted when we have rid ourselves of all of them. And here? How is business?"

"Wonderful, Hauptsturmführer. We are most comfortable, Inge and I—thanks in great part to your...assistance. I have often wondered why God selected me for such good fortune."

"God? Perhaps." Hempel sipped at his cognac, put

down his glass, lifted his cigar. "I suppose that makes me His instrument. Pity. I had hoped to take the credit. As I told you, I have great admiration for your son. When I came to you, it was because I wanted to ingratiate myself, shall we say, with his beloved family." He waved airily with the other hand. "I wish getting rid of the rest of them were as simple as that one. I regret not having kept the Iron Cross as a memento. You don't happen to have it, do you?"

Miriam froze. Though she knew that Sol could not possibly hear what these two disgusting excuses for human beings were saying, she almost expected him to intuit the scene and come flying up the stairs from the sewer, hands outstretched to grab Hempel by the throat—if she could restrain herself from doing it first.

Perhaps fortunately for her, the shop was invaded by a noisy group of officers. Stomping their feet to shake off the rain that had begun to fall, they entered the shop to buy supplies to take to Kaverne. The disarray, the noise and dust of refurbishing, did not seem to bother these officers of the Reich who gathered there at all times of the day or night—to play cards, drink, smoke cigars, and exchange stories about their conquests.

On the one hand, Miriam thought, their presence made Sol's hiding place a more dangerous choice; on the other, the combination of their noise, and that of sawing and hammering, served to cover whatever mishaps he might have in the darkness of the sewer.

Like everything in life, it was a toss-up.

She picked up the leather dice-cup from the end of

the counter, shook it, and turned it over. Naturally, she thought, looking at her impossibly high score. When there are no stakes, I win.

CHAPTER TWELVE

Someone, probably the beadle, had enriched the sewer with one of Sol's favorite treatises on the Kabbalah. The text was written in an ornate and frustrating style by an anonymous sixteenth-century physician accused of initiating impotence through sorcery. The man was found guilty of ligature, a necromancer's term that would later be incorporated into medicine.

The treatise appeared to touch upon such peripheral aspects of the Kabbalah that, at first reading, Solomon had thought the doctor lacked the acuity to dig deeper. Later, he had come to believe that the author had been afraid to go beyond the edges. Each rereading confirmed the clarity *behind* the words.

Our familiar, physical world, the author concluded, was only one part of a vast system of worlds, most of which were spiritual in their essence. That did not mean the spiritual realms existed somewhere else, but rather that they existed in different dimensions of being and that they interacted so much with physical reality that they could be considered counterparts of one another.

After six or seven rereadings by guttering candlelight, the physician's interpretation took on an increasing ring of truth.

"Spiritual realms exist in different dimensions of being," Sol summarized aloud. "They interact with physical reality. Thus, the spiritual and physical worlds must be counterparts of one another."

If gradation of *being* overlapped, he thought, could it not be possible that time did also?

By Wednesday he wished the visions *would* come—to offset the loneliness. If they came, he would try to place them within the context of his new theory. The visions did not come. To slow his bodily functions and to preserve his supplies, he ate and drank as little as possible. Thirst plagued him, but by the fourth or fifth day, he lost his appetite. What little he ate, he consumed out of boredom.

Boisterous commands erupted in the cabaret. Every now and then he heard hammering and the sound of furniture being scooted. Kaverne, he guessed with deepening fear, was being renovated. When the racket stopped, light laughter, men's voices, and military songs filtered down at all hours. He figured that meant that those who frequented the new club, SS or Gestapo, or

Wehrmacht assigned to political roundups, pulled duty at odd times.

Even during the rare silences, he feared venturing up into the cabaret. Someone might come in unexpectedly, or he might leave evidence behind. An accidentally moved object might bring down Gestapo vultures.

Once, he stole up into the tobacco shop, amazed to find it empty after having heard people moving around up there at all hours. He had his hand on the door latch when he saw the sentry outside, patrolling the sidewalk between the shop and the cabaret. Keeping watch while those inside drank and sang. And, as likely, pretending to guard against Jewish assassins eager to murder good German soldiers.

Descending, Sol occupied himself with removing bricks at the sewer's east end, hoping to squirm into the major system, if need be. He succeeded only in substantially increasing the seepage.

On Sunday the tobacco shop, like the cabaret, was filled with rowdy laughter and the tromp of boots. Once, soft footfalls descended the tobacco-cellar stairs; Sol rose to his feet, certain it must be Miriam, only to have his hopes dashed when Frau Weisser curtly called her upstairs. Miriam did not come down again.

The night brought greater laughter above, greater depression below. By the next Tuesday, he cared only about the candles. Once they were gone and he was in darkness…what madness might set in?

He had read about experiments conducted in France's Chateau Caverns. Researchers discovered that subjects in dark isolation experienced metabolic changes. Biological time-clocks malfunctioned, approximating a forty-eight rather than twenty-four-hour cycle. People slept fourteen hours and stayed awake thirty-four, though their minds insisted their bodies underwent no changes.

Given the endless partying in the cabaret and the fact that the shop was staying open later and later to serve the new clientele, calculating time became impossible. The longer he was down in the sewer, the less he was able to tell how closely his mental time-count resembled reality. He grew more lethargic, less able to follow thoughts through to logical conclusions.

Have to keep moving, keep thinking, he told himself.

Chin against chest, he shambled back and forth, back and forth across the disassembled crates, through the sewer slosh that with maddening regularity raised or lowered around his shoes like part of an undercity tide—sixty steps there and sixty steps back, ducking under the boards below the grates at each end of the sewer, the distance seemingly preordained. Concentrating on parts he had memorized from the treatise, while his brain ticked off sixty steps...turn, duck...another sixty. A minute's slow walk...one and two and three—regular as a metronome in a sitting room where proper children performed Mozart and Mendelsohn and knew nothing of Nazis and the notion of world domination. Fifty-eight, fifty-nine, duck and, sixty, turn.

The seepage dripped as if playing counterpoint,

forcing him to remember other music—most especially the Brahms Sonata he had heard Beadle Cohen play that first afternoon in the music room of the Judaica library on Behrenstrasse. The man was a violinist, a pianist, a wizard at setting Victrolas at precisely the right speed. "I am responsible for the upkeep of the temple," he had told Sol, "but I am equally responsible for the upkeep of my own wits and soul."

Aside from his duties at the temple, and his love of influencing the minds of children, only three things in his life mattered—books, music, and the study of the Kabbalah. Yet, except for sporadic gifts like *The Life of Luria*, the beadle had not spoken with Sol in any depth about Jewish mysticism until after the deaths of Rathenau and Grace and their discussion about dybbuks and lost souls and prophesies.

Searching for balance, Sol had gone to the library seeking something to help him overcome his sense of loss and inadequacy. Too short to reach a top bookshelf and too impatient to retrieve the library ladder, he had looked around for help—and there was the beadle.

Within that seemingly simple act of having discovered him in time of need, the beadle said, lay the first lesson of the ten *Sefirot*: the existence of fundamental forces of divine flow. The beadle's interpretation of the Jewish mystics, Solomon was later to realize, was tempered by his appreciation of the science of Einstein and Planck. Before God created light, and time therefore began, the beadle told him, the universe was random...but no longer; God did not roll dice. The aisles and avenues the free will can walk were divinely mapped, the journey preordained but not predestined. Beadle Cohen's being in the library was no accident, he argued, for God had known since before time began that he would be there.

The universe according to the beadle...as orderly as the number of steps in the sewer.

At their next meeting, the beadle talked of the Zohar, which he considered the foundation of the Kabbalah and the metaphysical basis of Judaism; he also gave Sol more books, dustier than usual.

Sensing his parents would disapprove, Sol had confined his reading to the old man's drafty garret above the library, with its two tiny windows shaped like a dove's wings. He had said little to his parents about his discussions with the beadle, even when his school marks dropped and Papa's questions and anger surfaced.

After a year's study, he had understood only that the Kabbalah encompassed a wealth of thinking one could not comprehend fully even in several lifetimes....

The last candle guttered and died.

He stretched out his arms as if to keep the walls from closing in, and stumbled onward. The muck again broke over his shoes. When he pulled off his shoes and wet socks, his flesh seemed puffy and slick. Something slimy was attached to his ankle. A leech.

He shuddered, and felt like hurling the treatise into the sewage. What use was it to him now! What use had his obsession with the printed page ever been! Erich had been right all along: in a world spinning out of control—a *dreidel* with blanks instead of letters—

learning for which there was no immediate and practical application was effete snobbery.

The muck continued to rise.

He rolled up his trousers and paced on. Fifty-nine...duck...sixty...turn.

A rat, mewling, scuttled between his legs.

He threw crate parts atop one another, climbed on the makeshift island. How many days, he wondered, since he had seen Miriam? Made love to her? She knew the extent of his provisions and the health risk of staying in the sewer. She would get him out.

Something nuzzled his ankle.

He cried out, drew up his knees. The rat scurried off, but soon padded back through the slosh. Sol imagined it up on hind legs, nose twitching, sniffing the air, watching him for signs of weakness. He hoisted himself onto the two-by-twelve.

A canteen and a seaman's bag containing what little food was left hung near him. At least that was out of reach of the rodent! Digging into the bag, he found cheese stuck to the brandy bottle.

He peeled it off, ate most of it, threw the rest toward the other end of the tunnel, and immediately regretted the action. Knowing food was near would make the rat more aggressive.

The rat scampered, and he laughed. Like one of Erich's dogs gone to fetch! A wheezing seized him; he doubled over, coughing.

Trembling, he climbed down to the rickety island, trying to catch his breath. His lungs sounded as if they were filled with fluid. Sweat stung his eyes, and spectral motes of light danced before him in the darkness. In his desire to hear something living, he listened for the rat—imagining it fat and furry and asleep, dreaming of cheese and human flesh.

The coughing began again, pain piercing his lungs.

"Hear that, Doctor Rat? What do you think? Pneumonia?" He fought to keep his breathing steady, but the slightest inhalation sent a cartilaginous crackling through his ears and chest.

"This keeps up—you'll have a real meal to remember!"

For a long time he tried desperately to hold onto the vestiges of consciousness despite his feverish sweating and shivering. In the dark, only the rat and the sweat that ran in rivulets down his forehead and back seemed tangible.

The rodent stopped running when he fed it—bread, cheese, nearly a kilo of rancid corned beef that he found in the bottom of the seaman's bag, wrapped in a necktie.

A necktie, in a crypt! Sol chuckled—coughed—went on with the game. He sent the rat scurrying for food. He placed morsels in a circle around himself, as if he and the food were a ritualistic offering. He slept, sensing the rat running across his legs, sniffing his armpits and crotch, licking salt from his hands and hair. He began to welcome the possibility of being bitten. Pain was reality, was it not?

He shook the canteen. Precious little left. Seepage dripped onto his shoulders. He tried to stand, but his senses were awry. Which were the walls—what was the floor? A paroxysm of coughing shook him. His head pounded. Tottering like an old man, he reached for the walls or the plank to steady himself, unsure if they would be there, then sat back down, cradling the canteen like an infant.

"*As the result of the liberation of Ethiopia by our Italian friends,*" a gravelly voice said in German, "*we have been given a unique opportunity.*"

"Go to hell!" Sol waved his hands, pleased at being able to muster the strength to react. The canteen, its cap unscrewed, slipped from him. He lunged...clutched darkness, fell into the muck, struggled to right himself.

"Pardon me," he gasped as he crawled back onto the wood. "My mistake. *Welcome* to Hell!"

Chapter Thirteen

"Welcome to the world of the dead!" the voice replied. A stench like that of Limburger cheese. A burst of light. A round of soft applause.

Sol lost interest in the canteen and turned toward the sound, for a blue glow told him a vision had come to divert him——

A bulb in a metal collar hangs garishly from a slatted-board ceiling. A tall man dressed in a surgical gown and gloves hits his head on the bulb and sets it in motion. The increased circle of light reveals Emanuel, legs spread, naked, strapped into a chair.

"Let us hope the world of death will place us on the path to immortality," the tall man says. He reaches up to stop the motion. Then he bows slightly, in deference to the applause of a semicircle of SS officers wearing white gloves and dress swords, their faces made amorphous by the shadows.

"I apologize for the odor." He looks amused. "We doctors are immune to it, but some of you, those who are not physicians, may be less used to the smell of death than others. It is not always quite this putrid, gentlemen...*lady!*"

He emphasizes the last word and holds out a hand— a magician introducing his assistant. Judith Bielmann-O'Hearn, wearing an apron similar to the doctor's, emerges from the shadows. She is pushing a cart laden with surgical equipment. She does not look at him as she rolls a gurney from the corner, over beside Emanuel. The gurney is rigged with gutters on both sides, and at its foot is a large sink with a faucet, to which Judith attaches a long rubber hose.

The doctor adjusts the light so it shines down directly on the table and the mummified body that lies on it. "Take a look, gentlemen. A century of lying entombed, and the elder-of-elders you see here—disinterred by kind permission of that man in the chair—is more alive than many of my patients. Jews, you know, are forbidden to embalm their dead, a religious law the Elephantine Jews chose to ignore." He wrinkles up his nose. "If you think he smells bad now, you should have been around yesterday when he was exhumed!"

His humor is rewarded by uncomfortable chuckles. Though the body on the table is slippery with gravewax and the limbs look like sweet-potato tubers, the head is graced with a full head of hair.

"In a moment," the doctor goes on, "we will begin the autopsy. Keep in mind that embalming does not preserve the organs, so to examine *those* we must use our living specimen."

Emanuel strains against the straps that hold him down; Judith begins to cry audibly.

"Stop sniveling," the doctor tells her. "You got what you wanted. Your boatload of Jews is en route to the new homeland of Madagascar. However, the ship *can* be turned back. I suggest you cooperate."

"But, Herr Doktor Mengele, I did not know—"

"Nor, they say, did Judas. Did you think we carried the latest scientific equipment all the way here to Addis Abbaba merely to see Ethiopia?" In an aside to the officers he says, "With the help of X-ray crystallography, we will be able to examine the unique, recently discovered subspecies of Jew, the Elephantines, and compare an ancient, though remarkably preserved, specimen to its modern counterpart—a living black prince!" He makes a sweeping gesture toward Emanuel as though introducing a trapeze artist.

"Please," Judith begs. "If this—this *demonstration*—must be performed, use me."

Mengele frowns. "Of what possible use could a flabby flat-chested Irish Jewess be to the cause of science? You have your boatloads. I suggest you adhere to your promise."

"But you said you would only need the Elephantines' *blood*!"

"And what good is blood if the vessel is not taken into account as a major variable? Be serious, woman!

I'll vivisect every member of the tribe if need be! Now, silence! I will have silence!"

Judith steps back into the shadows, her face dark with pain.

"Herr Doktor Mengele." A voice from the crowd. "Why do you feel this subspecies of Black Jew is such a good candidate for your experiment?"

Mengele smiles. "Black Jews represent two races rather than one. We considered that alone to be worthy of study, which is why we turned our attention to the Cushitic Falashas. Now, thanks to the efforts of Frau O'Hearn here, we found the perfect subjects, the Elephantines, as they've come to be called."

Obviously conscious of his stage presence, he moves around the gurney to be closer to the audience. "Analysis reveals that even though they have been separated from the mainstream of the Jewish species for twenty-four hundred years, these Elephantines have a genetic anomaly corresponding to similar anomalies observed among various other relatively isolated Jew-subsects. After identifying that gene and placing it in mice, we found that, regardless of overcrowding in the cages, those mice carrying the gene appeared to experience *far* less distress when subjected to such living conditions, as compared to our control mice. In fact, some of the genetically altered mice appeared to *thrive* in such an atmosphere."

"Ghetto conditions?" the voice asks.

"Exactly." Mengele adjusts his monocle, thrusts out his hand.

Eyes filled with hate, Judith steps into the light,

holding a scalpel. It looks as if she might stab the doctor, but instead she slaps the instrument into his glove.

"Any further questions before we begin?" he asks the audience.

"Yes, Herr Doktor," a squat SS colonel says. "Do you really believe it possible to isolate the enzyme—or gene, or whatever you call it—which contains this...this *collective unconscious* we've heard about? The *thing* that supposedly could enable you scientists to combine the natural cunning of the panther with the conniving of the Jew?"

"Anything the mind can conceive is possible, Standartenführer."

The doctor casually slices around the corpse's head and pulls the scalp down, opening it like a coconut shell. Judith turns her head and looks away.

"We have been working with dried blood serum for a decade," Mengele continues. "Now we are beginning to make rapid progress. Recently, for instance, Americans isolated the pituitary hormone. The real question is, how many ancient Elephantines will we have to exhume and compare with their living relatives before our results prove conclusive or the hypothesis proves false."

Straining slightly, he slices the body from the base of the throat down. Judith removes disintegrated gray matter from inside the corpse. A wavery vapor seems to arise, as if the spirit of the man has cried out against the violation. Emanuel moans softly but does not avert his eyes.

"These Elephantine Black Jews are remarkably resourceful and tenacious," Mengele says, "particularly when one considers the cowardice and physical ineptitude of other Jews. The specimen in the chair, for example, fought the Italians for years even after the liberation was formally declared. We could have used a few more like him when we marched on Cairo."

The testy murmuring his last comment provokes apparently pleases Mengele, for he smiles wryly before continuing.

"Enough conjecture. Let's begin at the beginning. Following the performance of the athlete Jesse Owens, the Führer personally instructed the scientific community to undertake a study of the musculature of African athletes. It seemed to the Führer that each subspecies might have physical characteristics which in some way could enhance the superior characteristics of our German youth."

The colonel again raises his hand. "We are here because your work, and that of Doktor Schmidt at Sachsenhausen, has enormous potential for bolstering performance on the *battlefield*, not the athletic field. I wish to know about morale. Would not surgically realigned soldiers, as you have called them, feel racially impure? Grafting musculature from Negroid subspecies onto our brave boys...I don't know, Herr Doktor." The colonel shakes his head uncertainly. "I doubt the men would stand for it...or if I could bring myself to lead troops that are not one hundred percent...*German*. It would seem an affront to..."

"God?" Mengele gives the officer a patronizing smile.

"To create the perfect Aryan, we are forced to contemplate the idea that perhaps we have been too narrow-minded. We might consider the possibility of creating, by combining natural selection and modern science, men and women of *inferior* mental, moral, and racial stock who nonetheless possess enhanced strength, speed, and endurance. These traits would enable them to serve the Fatherland equally well on the battlefield…or in the barnyard."

He lifts his hands palms out, silently begging forbearance. "I am the first to agree that this poses a moral question. Is it in our best interest to transform inferior humans into soldier-workers—non-Aryan *drones*—in order to reduce the loss of German blood on the battlefield and loss of time spent performing menial tasks?"

Mengele eyes the audience with a look of satisfaction, then turns to Emanuel and pushes aside the swatch of torn blanket that covers the naked man's groin.

"I remind you that I am a physician, not a philosopher. I leave moral choices to gods and dogs." A ripple of relieved laughter answers him. "Please, observe closely." He holds up the scalpel, glinting in the light. "The muscle fiber of most Negroes uses oxygen inefficiently. This results in explosive bursts of speed—witness Jesse Owens—but poor endurance. In other words, natural selection produced Africans that ran *away from* large animals, not ran them down." More chuckles. "In other parts of the world—Europe for instance, among some North American Indians, and in a few places here in Africa, such as among the

Ethiopians," he lays the side of the scalpel on Emanuel's inner left thigh; the black man quivers and squeezes shut his eyes, "conditions were such that long-distance running was required."

Replacing the monocle, Mengele bends over his subject and cuts a careful incision from the groin to the knee. Sweat shines on Emanuel's blue-black skin and his body arches. Mengele cuts perpendicularly at each end of the incision and carefully peels back the epidermis, exposing tissue. Blood wells in the wound and streams down the leg. Emanuel twists his head from side to side and his features scream silently with pain, but he does not utter a sound. Judith stands immobilized. When Mengele orders her to sponge the area, her hand trembles convulsively.

"They say sprinters are born, not made. This is because sprinters' muscles, unlike those of distance runners, cannot be developed regardless of the amount of athletic training." Mengele draws the scalpel toward himself through the tissue as though exquisitely filleting a trout. The black man's mouth, turned toward the ceiling, opens. He still makes no sound. "However, we have found that a few select runners, a very select few," Mengele lifts an index finger for emphasis, "have a high proportion of muscle similar to those of sprinters...*but still maintain the efficient use of oxygen characteristic of the long-distance runner.* Put another way: they can run very fast—very far. Or vice versa." He breaks into a boyish grin.

Rising, he drops the monocle expertly into his free hand and, balancing the reddish-pink tissue across the scalpel, transfers it to the gurney. He skins off a tiny slice and, using tweezers, places it in a specimen jar.

"We have found evidence of all this in many Ethiopians—also in Kenyans, I might add, though subjects available for analysis have been harder to obtain in that nation. Here we can rely on our Italian friends. So! Many Ethiopians possess this rare combination of sprinters' muscle and oxygen efficiency. They are slender, from a high-altitude country, and raised in a culture where long-distance running for communication and hunting was necessitated. Mark my words, gentlemen—even without the benefit of modern training methods, an Ethiopian such as Prinz Zaehev Emanuel here could win," sarcasm surfaced in his voice, "an Olympic marathon."

With a showman's skill he gestures toward his star performer. Everyone laughs. Emanuel is unconscious, his head tipped against his left shoulder, blood meandering down his leg and pooling on the floor. Judith is on her knees, sponging the linoleum.

Mengele scrapes tissue from the mummified corpse into a second jar. "Imagine a future," he tells the officers, "in which human drones who thrive in extremely crowded conditions are capable of working at great speed and with tremendous endurance! Imagine how well we could use the assets and abilities of the lesser races, for the benefit of the Fatherland...and with minimal impact upon German *Lebensraum!*"

The officers look at one another. Heads nod; eyebrows raise in affirmation.

"Frau *Doktor*." Mengele labels the specimen jars and

places them in a box. "Take these to the laboratory. When the film has been developed, bring it back."

Judith gets up from her knees, takes the box with a distasteful look. She almost drops it, and makes a sound. What emerges is a gurgle——

Solomon awakened into the sound, but it was not Judith's; it was his own. He tried to shift an arm. A leg.

I'm just dreaming I'm awake, just dreaming! he told himself, but he knew his eyes were open. As was his mouth. *If I can just say something!*

No sound issued through his lips. He could not move even his tongue. Then, relieved, he felt movement, only to have his relief turn to horror. His tongue had not moved. Something else—

—a spider.

He felt its velvety pads claim purchase on his chin and cheek as it struggled to extricate itself—legs, head, thorax—from his mouth. He could see nothing in the pitch darkness, could not brush it away as it crept up his face and passed across his left eye, hairs twitching against his pupil.

Wake up! he screamed at himself. *Wake up!*

The spider climbed his upper eyelashes and tested his brow. Taking its time, it spun a web…crossing and recrossing the left side of his face…drawing sticky gossamer from his brow to his mouth. Still he could not move. Could not scream. Could feel only the spider—and tears spawned by fear rolling down his cheeks.

Time passed, how much he had no way of measuring

save for the racing of his heartbeats, until the blue came, flickering, changing from hyacinth to cerulean and finally, to cobalt——

Dusk. The sky is deeply blue and refractive, as if a bowl of colored crystal has been turned upside down. Angry clouds skewer the horizon. Mengele, scalpel in hand as though it is a cigarette, leans against a waist-high semi-circular balcony wall of whitewashed masonry carved with arabesques. The SS officers stand beside him and in the portal of shadow created by the open balcony doors.

On the ground far below, black men, women, and children—most dressed in white muslin tunics or colorful sateen robes—raise their voices in a litany sung in a strange tongue. Their skin appears darkly chestnut in the light, a sea of bronze faces.

"They call this event 'Maskal,'" Mengele tells his audience. "It honors Queen Helena's supposedly finding Christ's Cross. To give thanks, she lit a bonfire in Palestine so big her son Constantine saw its glow back in Constantinople. Christians never have been known for choosing verisimilitude over hyperbole."

The officers chuckle. Below, the sea of spectators parts; a procession of priests carrying tasseled ceremonial umbrellas, and laymen and boys robed in embroidered satins and carrying incense and elaborately molded golden crosses, serpentine in stately rhythm toward the tallest of three towers of piled wood.

"Time to show our respect for the newest subjects of our Italian friends," Mengele says. He and the other officers snap to a Nazi salute as the procession winds below, followed by a parade of white-gowned men holding straw torches aloft. Next come brass bands and then floats, heavy with flowers, sporting flaming crosses.

The trailing celebrants, more than a thousand strong, carry wicker baskets filled with bread and daisies.

"Perhaps in another two thousand years the Ethiopians will celebrate a much more lasting and meaningful cross," Mengele says in a low, impassioned voice, "the swastika!"

"*Sieg heil!*" his listeners say quietly but earnestly.

Judith appears in the doorway behind them. She slips a scalpel and a piece of cut surgical tape into her lab coat, then clears her throat. "Herr *Doktor*," she says, "the X-ray films are ready."

The priests below begin to circle the towers, bowing, blessing what the flames will consume, swinging incense burners like pendulums and filling the air with the scent of jasmine and sandalwood. Mengele breathes deeply, appreciatively. "Let us go inside—committed with new purpose," he says.

The other officers stand aside respectfully as he enters the room. Brows furrowing, he pauses and covers his nose. "Our prince has emptied his bowels. He apparently has no respect for medical history or for our sensibilities."

Emanuel, seemingly still bound to the chair, has fallen sideways onto the floor. When the doctor starts to nudge him with the toe of a shoe, the black man leaps up. Shrieking, babbling, he reaches for the doctor's neck. Pulls it close. Bites.

Mengele squeals. Gargles. Chokes. His thick flesh bulges against the black man's fury, and a bone snaps——

The scene dissolved. The voices stilled. Solomon felt warm blood on his hands and, in them, the movement of a furred thing.

Grimacing, he dropped the rat into the seepage. Without pity, he listened to it flop and cough in its death throes. If the Kabbalistic tradition of the transmigration of souls were truly part of the order of the universe, he reasoned, then transmogrification must also be possible: man becomes animal; and animal, man.

He forced himself to become calm. Had he not just now placated whatever spirit had pervaded the sewer, Berlin, and his life? The rat was Mengele. He—Solomon—was Emanuel…and free at last.

CHAPTER FOURTEEN

No matter what he did, the sadness in Misha would not go away. It so enshrouded his thoughts that he was hardly aware of the passage of the days.

When he had literally bumped into Fräulein Miriam after the beadle's departure from Berlin, he'd still had hope. He had waved farewell to her from the limousine when Konrad dropped her off at the tobacco shop, believing her when she promised to do everything she could to get news of his parents.

"It could take time, Misha. And the news will probably be bad," she said, holding him close. "Do you understand what that means?"

He understood. But understanding and acceptance were not the same thing.

Konnie drove him to a block of flats at the dark end of Kantstrasse. There he was taken in by a rough-looking group of young people who, he quickly learned, were part of the underground. The flats, Konnie told him, had belonged to the furriers who had owned the shop next door to *Die Ziggarrenkiste*—above the sewer where he and the beadle had taken refuge. This was confirmed when one of the young men gave him a fur coat to use as a blanket and identified himself as the son of the owners of *Das Ostleute Haus*. He was given enough food to survive, a blanket on the floor, a few books, and instructions to stay out of the way.

He was not sure how long he had been there when he ran his first message, perhaps about a week. He was given a tweed cap, a coat of sorts, and a pair of warm knickers, and sent out into the snow. Two days and half-a-dozen deliveries later, he was handed a note from Miriam to Solomon Freund. What he knew he would never forget was creeping uncertainly across the street to the tobacco shop and seeing Herr Freund's gaunt, bearded face appear behind the plate-glass window. He had scaly brown stuff on his face, and was coughing as if he had pneumonia or something.

And suddenly there were sirens, and a Mercedes with Gestapo and guns and shots, and he was racing down an alleyway like a hunted animal.

The next morning, one of his companions awoke him before dawn.

"The Gestapo know what you look like," the youth said. "It is too dangerous for us—and for you—to stay here. Go to the corner of Kant and Niebuhrstrasse. Konnie will be waiting for you there. Don't say anything. Just get into the car."

Misha did what he was told. By the end of the day he was ensconced at the home of Fräulein Miriam's dressmaker in Baden-Baden, where Konnie had driven him on the pretext of taking her several bolts of fabric to make into dresses for Miriam for the upcoming holiday season. The trip across the country and south was a long one, but the car was comfortable and warm, and he slept most of the way. It was dark when they got there and he was hungry.

Madame Pérrault fed him at once. She was a pretty woman, bright, cheerful, and practical. He liked her.

The next morning, she put him to work at the button-covering machine to earn his keep. To his surprise, he enjoyed the work.

The machine looked something like the microscope at school, except that the top was hinged. There was an indentation on the ledge for a metal shell, and another in the lever.

Madame Pérrault would hand him scraps of fabric that matched the outfits she was sewing. He laid a scrap on the ledge, pressed in a shell, and covered it over with the fabric. Then he inserted a smaller shell into the lever and pressed down.

The top fitted into the bottom and became a covered button which she could trim and attach to the clothing of her wealthy customers.

He quickly developed a rhythm and produced, she said, more buttons each hour than she could make in a day.

He expected to be hidden away, in a place like the sewer. To his surprise, Madame Pérrault simply told him to be careful not to talk to strangers, bedded him down in a small attic room where she stored her supplies, and introduced him as her cousin's son, come to visit from the city. He was well fed and reasonably well clothed. She patched his trousers, kept his shirt clean, and treated him with kindness.

Still, she was not his mama.

When Fräulein Miriam returned with Konnie, she returned the bolts of cloth, had a brief discussion with the seamstress about patterns, and took him into the garden.

"I have no news for you," she said, kneeling before him. "You must be patient."

"I want to come back to Berlin with you."

"You are safe here, Mishele." She stroked his head. "Is Madame not treating you well?"

"That's not it at all," he said, staring her down. "I want to be there when you find my mama and papa."

She sighed heavily. "I thought you understood, Misha. The chances are we will not find them. Berlin is a dangerous place. You are better off right here."

"Then I will walk to Berlin. I will. Truly. I want to go...home."

"But I can't take care of you," Miriam said. "Herr Freund, the man to whom you delivered my message, is in the sewer."

"I can stay with him in the sewer. Please."

"I cannot get him out, let alone get you in," she said.

"Please."

She looked as if she were about to say something more, but remained silent. He took that to mean yes.

Remembering his manners, he went indoors to say farewell and thank you to his hostess who looked shocked, kissed him, and said he could return any time he wished.

He went outside to the car. It was gone. Only his earlier resolve kept him from bursting into tears.

"Sometime around Christmas I will have to go to Berlin myself for fabrics and threads, and to visit family," Madame Pérrault said. "If you still want to return, I will take you with me."

Reassured, but still angry at what he saw as Miriam's betrayal, Misha settled back into the routine of the household. Days passed, then more than a week, not unpleasantly, and as it did, so did his anger. He remembered how Miriam signaled him away on the day the beadle left, and then rescued him. He remembered her explanation and her kindnesses. When the time came for Madame Pérrault to make her trip, he had almost forgotten his anger.

But he had not forgotten why he had to return to Berlin.

"I cannot take you to Fräulein Miriam," she said, when he reiterated his wish to go with her. "She has more than enough worries. I will have to take you back to the underground. They will take you in if you are willing to be a messenger for them again."

"But the Gestapo…?"

"By now, hopefully, they have forgotten you."

"Do the others know that I am coming back?" Misha asked.

"Perhaps yes, perhaps no. I sent word, but I have not

had confirmation. You will have to take your chances."

"Will you tell *her* where I am?"

"Of course. She would want to know."

At the end of the day, with a quick kiss, a hug, and a wish for his safety, Madame Pérrault pressed a bag of food into his hands and deposited him on the sidewalk, two blocks from the flats on Kantstrasse. Behind him he heard her say quietly, "Merry Christmas, boy. Happy Hanukkah."

Suddenly afraid, remembering no-neck and the sound of jackboots and gunshots, Misha ran the two blocks in the darkness of what he now realized was Christmas Eve. Though he slunk into the building and tried to be quiet, his footsteps echoed hollowly in the deserted stairwell.

When he reached the flat, he found the door ajar. The place had been ransacked and there was no one there. Terrified, careless of his own safety, he charged down the stairs and away from the building. When he stopped running, he found himself at the fence of a small, concrete school playground on Niebuhrstrasse. At the back of the playground, he could see a large tree, beneath which stood a cluster of garbage cans. He scooted over the fence and headed straight for them.

Upending one of them, which happened to be empty because, he supposed, of school holidays, he crawled inside and, despite the freezing cold, fell into a sleep filled with nightmares of fat men with boots and guns and no neck. He awoke at dawn to the sound of Christmas churchbells. Shivering and stiff with cold, and silently thanking Madame Pérrault, he opened the bag of food and ate a roll and a piece of sausage and tried to plan his next move.

All he could think of was Fräulein Miriam and the sewer safe house. He waited as long as he was able, hoping some other idea would come to him. Finally, driven by the cold, he crawled from his hiding place, scaled the fence, and started toward the tobacco shop. When he got there, the lights were on and the door was ajar.

Thank God, he thought, bursting into the shop. "Fräulein Miriam," he said. "Help me. Please. You must hide me in the sewer with Herr Freu—"

Hands gripped him from behind and turned him around. He had not noticed the two men sitting at the table in the corner, a miniature Christmas tree and two brandy snifters between them on the table. The one leaning forward to hold him looked like an older version of the uniformed man with whom Fräulein Miriam had breakfasted that morning at the Kempinski Café; the other wore the uniform of the men who had chased him down the alley. Misha stared at his hair, which shone as brightly silver as the tinsel on the miniature tree.

"So that's where he is," the man who held him said. "I might have known."

"What a charming looking youth," the silver-haired man said, smiling. He motioned for the older man to release the boy and, taking hold of Misha's wrist with one hand, tussled Misha's hair. "And how fortuitous that he should bring us this information. I will leave you to take care of him for me, Friedrich, while we take care of our morning business."

Misha struggled against the grip of the man who held him.

"Don't be afraid," the silver-haired soldier said. "We're here to help."

"He is a handful," the other man said.

Misha craned his neck to look outside and prayed desperately that he would see Fräulein Miriam headed toward the shop. His view was blocked by the ugly, no-neck man, who was leaning casually against the plate-glass storefront, smoking a fat cigar.

He stopped struggling.

Chapter Fifteen

Thirst. The faucet in the subbasement beckoned like a mirage. He lay on the crating, lost in vertigo, suffocating in the stench, listening to his own panting. The darkness wheezed with each breath. His mouth worked spasmodically, like that of a sleeping infant searching for the breast. Sometimes he ran a hand along the slick wall so contact with physical reality outside himself would tell him he was still alive. His muscles, lacking water, ached; his scalp itched with lice or fleas. He had clawed, scratched, torn at his clothes, but the insects continued feasting.

Finally he crawled from the drain to the antique sinks in the subbasement corner beneath the stairs. One of the tap handles had rusted off; the other, though loose, was intact. He used a packing-crate endboard for a pry bar. The handle turned, protesting and squealing.

Belching, groaning, the tap dribbled—then gushed.

The water, rusty, burned his parched throat. He retched, spat, cursed the plumbing as he let the tap run, then cupped his hands and slurped. The metallic taste was still present. Though he knew what drinking rust might cause, he filled his canteen and tried shutting off the tap. The handle spun loosely in its collar.

Putting a thumbnail in the headscrew to secure it, he pressed down on the handle. A major victory—the only casualty one-half of a thumbnail. Now the tap fizzed like weak soda water.

For a moment he felt like sneaking up the stairs and peering under the cabaret door as he had as a child, when he had first seen Miriam—the featured performer at a private party her grandmother had thrown in the cabaret—but common sense won out, and he lowered himself back into the drain.

He slept fitfully and awoke feverish, his guts gripped by a steel hand. He drew up his legs and pushed his fists against his stomach, praying that the cramps would leave him.

Warm wetness suddenly flowed between his thighs. Diarrhea. He might as well have filled the canteen with seawater.

He picked himself up, his movements jerky, uncoordinated, a marionette with an unskilled master. What transcendence, he wondered bitterly, did the Kabbalah prescribe for lifting body rather than soul? How fortunate the composer who'd spent his life creating music in honor of Judaism, only to be killed by a Torah scroll which fell from its cabinet and struck him on the head. That seemed fitting for a scholar; rotting and dying in a sewer did not.

He boosted himself onto the plank, lay dizzied and panting, then groped for the seabag. At the bottom were two crackers. He put one in his mouth, chewed, massaged his throat to get it down. Like force-feeding a reptile, he thought angrily.

Faces shimmered in the blackness. His father, in the rocker, floating above Friedrick Ebert Strasse by holding himself up by the Iron Cross ribbon around his neck. Then appeared Mutti and Recha, waving good-bye as a train streamed beyond the end of its tracks and sank with a hiss into the North Sea. Miriam, eyes smiling as she fellated Erich, who leaned nonchalantly against a tree, a German shepherd beside him on a choke chain.

Rathenau. Shattered bone and flesh blackened by powder burns, a Reichsbanner handkerchief pinned to his cheek.

Stop! Sol reached to squeeze the apparition into nothingness. Pinwheels of light exploded inside his head. Above him, boot heels clattered on concrete. He seized Rathenau by the throat.

And lost his balance. Clutched the plank, upside-down like a sloth, he fell with a splash.

He tried to climb from the seepage, but his hands slid down the wet wall and he toppled backward. When he arose, sputtering, he heard a hinge squeal. Light lanced into the blackness. He raised his hands to shield his eyes, begging a vision to come erase the nightmare of whatever new reality had invaded his awful domain.

"You are right, Herr Weisser," someone said in a northern dialect. "There *is* a Jew in here—and he stinks like a pig!"

Sol pawed at the light.

"Merry Christmas, Jew," the man continued in *Plattdeutsch*. "Climb from your sty!"

Delirium followed. He felt himself crawl onto the board and was yanked by the arms through the drain, then sent hurtling up the stairs. He staggered into the cabaret and collapsed. Someone said, "Jew football!" and kicked him in the ribs. He lay weeping on the floor. Before him lay shards of a wineglass, like the one he had crushed underfoot at the end of his and Miriam's marriage ceremony. He took hold of a shard, gripping it so tightly that it dug into his palm. Through his fog of pain and humiliation, he saw blood rise between his fingers. The sight of it brought a peculiar sense of relief: the pain felt sharp and clear. *Clean.* Self-inflicted, and returning to him a bit of dignity he had thought gone forever.

The fog lifted from his eyes.

"What day is it?" he gasped. "What date?"

"Stinking Jew doesn't even know when Christmas is celebrated!"

Again he was kicked. He doubled over in agony. *So many days in the sewer. Weeks.* The darkness had worked its black magic on his senses all too well.

He looked up, saw Miriam's shawl draped around an autographed picture of Hitler.

"Herr Freund?"

A child in a ratty coat entered Sol's sight. Where had he seen the boy before? When?

Blood trickled from the boy's nose. He was crying quietly. "I'm sorry, Herr Freund," he whispered. "I didn't mean to...Those people in the tobacco shop...I thought they were your friends. I thought they would hide me down *there* again."

"Whatever happened, it's all right," Sol whispered back as he struggled to stand. A soldier shoved him with a rifle and he went pitching up the metal stairs, but he reached back and took the boy by the hand before he stepped out of Kaverne and into the street.

CHAPTER SIXTEEN

If I don't get out of the car right now, I'll be sick.

Miriam tapped Konnie on the shoulder. "Let me off. *Here.* I'll walk the rest of the way to the shop."

By the set of his back, Miriam knew he disapproved. That made two disapproving males in the last hour; Erich had insisted she did not look well and should stay home.

Climbing from the car, she pulled her coat closed against the biting cold. Sick, all right; but not from the weather. Sick with worry. Sol—down there two weeks, with too little food and drink.

Not that she had good news for him. Perón was apparently not in Germany. Last Sunday, she had tried to get down to the cellar, but the shop was never emptied of its beer-happy customers popping in from Kaverne. With the shop that busy, the Weissers had not gone to Mass. They had watched her every move, calling her back if she were out of sight even for seconds.

Today would be equally busy, but it was Christmas. Surely the Weissers would go to Mass. It was only a matter of time until some soldier wandered down to the subbasement, perhaps to sleep off a drunk, saw a candle within the sewer or heard a noise. Someone coughing. The shuffling of feet.

She quickened her pace.

"Merry Christmas!" a barrel-organ man called to her.

"Merry Christmas." She slowed down and dug for a coin to deposit in his hat. On impulse, she said, "Come to the shop later. I'll find you a good cigar."

He grinned and ground out the beginning notes of "*O Tannenbaum.*" She walked on, head lowered against the wind.

From a block away a siren blasted, drowning out the carol.

She looked up.

Konrad, disobeying her instructions to go home to his family and spend Christmas Day with them, had parked the touring-car up against the curb in front of the shop. He seemed to be signaling her to stay back.

She stepped into the shelter of a doorway and waited as a car with the SS insignia pulled up in front of Kaverne and three men got out. Two of them, rifles in hand, hurried down the cabaret steps. The third loitered at the sidewalk. She recognized him from the estate. She frowned, puzzled.

Hadn't Erich said that Otto Hempel was now deputy

commandant of the Sachsenhausen detention center? Had he flown that little plane of his back to Berlin to personally oversee an arrest?

Oh my God, she thought. Sol. Flattening herself against the wall, she pressed her hand to her mouth to stifle a scream. Friedrich Weisser burst from the shop, dragging Misha by the hand. He and Hempel exchanged looks. He prodded Misha toward the steps, and the three of them disappeared.

Frozen with fear and cold and nausea, she watched as a silent column of men, women and children, flanked by guards with shepherds, rounded the far corner.

She had seen such lines before—emerging from side streets and alleys—guards and shepherds herding them along the avenue. Quiet Jews. Heads down. Men carrying satchels; women with babies bundled in lovingly crocheted shawls and patchwork blankets, as if El Greco, ordered to paint a tragedy in somber hues, had carelessly splashed his canvas with bright colors. They moved with the steady step of people headed for a train they knew would not leave without them. Some had children tagging along like exiles from a classroom. Others were murmuring thanks to God for giving them the foresight to have put their sons and daughters on the special trains to Amsterdam and Zurich.

When the column stopped in front of Kaverne, not a person moved. No one murmured, or looked toward the cabaret. *They know why they're stopping,* she thought desperately. *They've seen it too many times.* They were in a funeral march, mourning themselves.

Moments later Sol and Misha stumbled up the steps

that led down to Kaverne and sprawled headlong into the street. Misha stood up first and stooped to help Sol. A guard shoved the boy aside and ordered the column to move on.

Miriam bit into her gloved hand as Sol staggered to his feet. The child looked terrified. Sol, painfully thin and apparently more humiliated than frightened, seemed to be concentrating on the physical act of walking.

Keeping a fair distance behind them, Miriam followed. Once in a while, a face appeared at a window, pulling aside a lace curtain to stare out. On every corner, Nazi flags snapped in the breeze. The snow had stopped and, as the procession passed the first corner of the Tiergarten, the sun filtered through the clouds. Passersby standing among dried and dead shrubs stopped to stare.

The column reached the Zoo Station and paused beneath the huge clock, its horn-blowing cherubs decorated with holly.

At the far side of the station, a dirty steam engine stood in front of three boxcars and a caboose. The train had apparently been conscripted from a tourist run; wilted streamers and deflated balloons dangled from the cab.

The guards released the pins of the boxcar locks and pushed the doors open with a clang. "Get in!" One motioned with his carbine.

No one moved.

"In!"

A heavy-set woman with a baby in her arms

approached a guard cradling a submachine gun. The shepherd heeled beside him rose. Growling. Hackles raised. The woman detoured around the dog, unknotted her scarf and shook out her curly hair, as though doing so would improve her looks and her bargaining power. "They have made a mistake. I have done nothing."

The man gave her a fatherly smile. "You're not a Jew, eh? Just born to the wrong parents?"

"I've done nothing," she repeated.

His smile broadened. "If you've done nothing, you're a non-contributor to the State and should be eliminated."

"I don't mean I've done *nothing*. I mean I've done nothing wrong." She uncovered the infant's head. "Nor has my little one."

"Are you Jews?"

"Yes."

"Then you are criminals."

"Don't you understand?" She grabbed his sleeve. "I am a German."

The man's smile froze. He issued a soft command, and the dog at his feet growled again and leapt. The woman fell beneath its attack, one arm raised in a feeble effort to ward off the animal, the other tightened around her child. The dog sank its teeth into her cheek, ripped out a hunk of flesh and bit down again. She shrieked. Her curls bounced obscenely as the dog shook her head side to side. Blood pooled on the asphalt.

Miriam saw that Sol was not watching the terror, but rather the guard. *Do nothing*, she silently begged him. *Nothing*.

The baby rolled from her arms and lay kicking, too young to know its danger as the animal backed off and shook itself as though after a swim. Blood from its jowls showered the street.

Lying on her side, the mother reached for the child. Her legs just moved anxiously while her upper body remained in place, like a live insect pinned through the head.

The dog padded over to the child, poked its nose beneath the blanket, and opened its huge jaws.

Miriam could not move. She felt cast in amber.

"Down, Prince," the soldier said softly. "Good boy."

The dog backed away from the baby and the guard knelt to feed it a treat. As he petted the dog, he leaned his submachine gun against his leg, calmly unholstered his pistol, and shot the woman between the eyes. The roar echoed inside Miriam's bones, turning marrow into flame. Blood and gray matter sprayed the street.

"Anyone else done nothing wrong?" The guard looked around. Several people were vomiting. Others cried softly and covered the eyes of their children.

"You two!" He pointed at two prisoners. "Remove that mess."

One man, trembling and white-faced, obeyed. The other paid for his hesitation with his life.

"All right, you!"

The third man obeyed at once. The first man had already scooped up the child in a massive arm and handed it to the nearest female prisoner. Now the two men carried the dead woman up the ridged plank and into the nearest car.

"Everyone in!" the guard commanded.

As if seeking shelter from a city gone mad—or sure that what awaited them could not be worse—the people crowded into the boxcars. A horn blasted, like the animate sound of Miriam's conscience. She too had done nothing. *Nothing!* Not one move to help the woman. Nor could she attempt to help Sol and Misha without endangering them and herself. If only she had fled with Sol either of the two times he had begged her to! *It's my fault. My fault,* she cried inwardly in despair.

"Come, Miriam." Konrad appeared behind her and took her arm.

Like a little girl—perhaps because he finally called her *Miriam*—she did as she was told.

"Oh, God, Konnie! Why?" she whispered as she slid onto the front seat and, needing his strength, clung to his arm and put her head against his shoulder. Her sobbing made her whole body heave. "I don't understand. They killed that woman and then the man—"

"I saw," he said quietly.

"It was cold-blooded murder! All she did was ask a question. She wasn't even resisting arrest. She had a baby in her arms....How do they justify it?"

"The records will show that the man disobeyed orders and the woman resisted arrest...or tried to escape."

"Escape the SS, and rifles, and dogs? Risk retribution—to their families, their friends?" Would she, she wondered? "Where will they take them?" she asked, feeling stupid. They always said the same things: *A holding facility—a resettlement camp—until emigration or vocational relocation can be arranged.* Meanwhile, their houses, land, possessions were confiscated. They called *that* redistribution of wealth. *All Germans must share evenly*, the rhetoric explained.

Damn the rhetoric, she thought, and damn them all to Hell. What had happened, what was continuing to happen, was as fathomless as Solomon's concept of an infinite nothingness at the center of the universe. By ridding the society of its Jews, the Reich was creating a moral void; those who insisted on the laws of justice instead of the jungle were being driven out.

"Where do you want to go?" Konrad asked.

"Take me to Erich's flat."

She needed to be alone—and *not* at the estate. Alone to think, to plan, to examine her Jewishness. And she was Jewish, wasn't she? *Wasn't she?*

If Erich is behind this I will kill him, she thought feverishly. *Poison, I'll do it with poison and watch him die.*

After sending Konnie home to Christmas dinner, she let herself into the apartment, kicked off her shoes, and lay down on the bed without bothering to draw the curtain that separated it from the rest of the room.

There had to be something she could do to help Sol! Gripping the pillow, she fought to keep the panic dammed that brimmed along the edge of her consciousness. Perón was not around. There had to be someone influential who could find out where Sol and Misha had been taken. That would be the first step. *Find them.*

She brewed coffee and began to pace around the flat. She was on her third cup when she thought of Werner

Fink, the outrageous *conferencier* with whom she had worked when she had been the star attraction at the Ananas cabaret.

He was certain to have connections; otherwise how would he have avoided arrest for so long, especially since, as he had told her, he had a twin brother incarcerated in Sachsenhausen? What hold might he have on the Nazis that had kept him free for so long? Photographs, perhaps, of orgies in after-hours cabarets, to be made available should he disappear? He was a survivor, that one.

Her own underground connections, with which she had helped save a dozen desperate lives, were of no use to her now that she needed them; the network had been compromised. Erich had told her that the furriers had been arrested.

What else did he know? There was no point in asking him. If Erich could tell her that Sol was in camp, knowing that he was safe in Amsterdam, he was capable of any lie. A better question was, how influential was he? The Gestapo knew about the safe house. Did they know about her, too? Was Erich the reason she had not been arrested as well?

Had he found out about Sol's return, and was he responsible for—

No, she decided, forcing herself to calm down. Even Himmler could not have interceded had the Gestapo found out about her. Her cover remained intact because she had insisted that communications be double-blinded. No one knew the others' identities. The day after Erich had told her about the Lubovs, her last communique had arrived, telling her the network was dissolved until further notice.

Sol's arrest probably had nothing to do with the use of the hideout as a safe house. Yes, he had been discovered hiding down there, but that did not link him to the underground. After all, he had been using the sewer as a refuge since childhood.

Perhaps, then, Erich knew nothing about today's happenings. Wait, she told herself. Reserve judgment.

Coffee cup in hand, she wandered around the small flat. Though she had a key and was often in the area, she hadn't been here since moving into the estate with Erich. Doubtless he had, she thought, noting the remains of a meal on the table.

The place had never been a typical bachelor refuge, barren except for beer and bratwurst and the hope of feminine conquests, but now there had been changes that stirred her to even deeper anger—a candelabra, probably "liberated" from Jews, a four-poster brass bed, exquisite Danish linens, the Dresden china. She opened the pantry. It was stocked with canned venison marinated in sour cream, Norwegian salt herring, assorted sausages, and fine French mustards. She wondered if the prostitutes Erich brought here were women who reminded him in some way of her, or if he specialized in officer's wives, whose precoital and postcoital whispers might serve him in the Party.

For all she knew, they had even furnished the place for him. She ran a hand along the small claw-footed bathtub that sat before the balcony doors and doubled as a base for Erich's desk. According to Erich, it had been the darling of Friedrich the Great's personal physician, and it had taken three strong men half a day to maneuver the tub up the stairs.

She lay back down on the bed, finally exhausted.

Had Erich forged Goebbels' cramped handwriting to waylay prize pieces of furniture from Jewish inventory? Had he lied to her about Sol because he loved her that much, or because what one did to a Jew didn't matter? Either way, maybe his guilt about the lies had caused him to leave her bed and spend most of his nights in the room that once had been her uncle's. Perhaps Erich's need to prove himself with other women was tied to her and, therefore, to Solomon.

Should she tell him about Sol—offer forgiveness for his lies in exchange for help—or would she simply get more lies?

No, she thought. Take vengeance. Use him. Match him lie for lie.

She buried her head in the pillow. "God, what am I becoming!"

She closed her eyes.

The sound of a key turning in the lock awakened her. The flat was dark. She could hear a woman's laughter—low, sensual—and Erich, fumbling with the door. She slid off the bed and stepped behind the corner of the wardrobe.

"Make yourself at home, Anneliese," Erich said. "Pour a bath, for both of us. I'll go down and arrange for dinner." He put a flame to two candles, set them on the table, and transferred the dirty dishes to the sink. "Be right back. Make yourself beautiful for me."

Erich sounded inebriated. Not drunk, but well on the way. The woman heated water, filled the tub, added bath oil, and stripped, flinging her clothes onto the carpet. By the time Miriam knew what she had to do, Anneliese had raised one leg to climb into the tub.

Miriam stepped into the room.

"A threesome!" The woman seemed unperturbed by Miriam's appearance. "Erich said I'm his birthday surprise—but this *is* pleasant! What fun!" She was pretty, in her late thirties, long dark hair, high cheekbones. They could almost have been sisters.

"Leave." Miriam handed the woman her clothes. "I'm his wife."

Anneliese shrugged. "All the same to me," she said. "He promised me two hundred marks. I'll leave, but I want my money."

Miriam rummaged in Erich's dresser. She found a stack of notes under his shirts and gave some to the woman. "Now dress," she said, "and get out."

CHAPTER SEVENTEEN

"Anneliese?"

Must be on the toilet, Erich thought, touching her tub water. It was warm and silky with oil. He heard the chain being pulled and the subsequent flush.

Undressing, he slipped into the tub, anticipating how relaxed she and the water would make him and thinking about the dinner he had selected. Trout *au bleu*, garnished with spring peas, pineapple, and wild mushrooms. Dilled potatoes sautéed in butter and surrounded by sweetmeats. A natural-state May wine from a Rhein-Hessen vineyard.

For dessert he had chosen one of his favorites, cream cheese tucked in a peach and flamed with kirsch, accompanied by a bottle of Rothschild he had tucked away in the Bierstube wine cellar for just such a special occasion as a birthday. Followed by Viennese coffee with whipped cream and a generous helping of sherry.

What on earth was she doing in there? "Anneliese!"

"In a minute," she said softly and sweetly from the bathroom.

He lay back in the tub. He was not so drunk yet that he could stop wondering why every whore he brought here looked like Miriam, spoke like her, walked with her particular grace.

Close to sleep, he allowed himself to drift, the tepid water seducing him. He dreamed that a sheath encapsulated him. On a white beach, a shepherd bayed, its howling a river of sound cutting into the furred, spiked foliage that lined the shore. With each howl the placenta around him breathed, but he could not cry out for help lest the film that clung to his lips suffocate him. He was an infant, helpless, drowning in amniotic fluid. What he could not understand was why he liked it, why it felt warm, comfortable, secure.

He awoke pleasantly to a line of warm red liquid curling down from his shoulder and across his chest, just visible in the candlelight. For a second he thought he had been knifed and, strangely, it hardly mattered.

"Wine massage?" The voice was soft and female.

Erich swiped at the red liquid, tasted it, and laughed. Without turning his head, he secured a cheroot from among his clothes on the chair, lit it, and lay back, still half asleep. In the flickering candlelight he saw her silhouette on the wall above the bed as, continuing to kneel behind him, she began working the warm wine into his shoulders and scalp.

At last, a woman who knew how to please. A satisfied

murmur passed through his lips. No quick hump and head for the door, this one. He would invite her back.

"*Sich verwöhnen lassen,*" she whispered huskily. "Let yourself be pampered."

Pampered? An understatement. He felt the beginning of an erection.

Her hands stopped moving and she shifted position. He could see her, but not well, at the edge of his peripheral vision. With one hand she unbuttoned and opened the robe she was wearing—his robe, revealing a silk slip. He was unsure if her slight smile reflected amusement or contempt. My God, he thought, this one really does look like Miriam. Yes, she would definitely be a rehire. For many nights.

Happy birthday, Erich, he told himself.

"Your hand has fed me well, but I can no longer accept your charity." She let the robe slide to the floor. "You really haven't had your money's worth, Erich Alois!"

"Miriam!" Was he still having a nightmare? He lurched upright in the tub, the bitterness in her voice instantly sobering him. "Where's—"

"I paid her the two hundred marks and sent her home."

"I never said I was a monk." Annoyed at himself for sounding defensive, he shrugged and lay back in the tub, relaxing, as if to show her her being there did not upset him. "I have asked you for nothing. Why can't we forget—"

"Forget!"

He regretted having opened his mouth. When he was a boy, after a fight with Solomon about something insignificant, he had overheard Frau Freund say of Sol, "My son's words go from the lung to the tongue." The underpinnings of his self-anger took hold.

"I don't mean forget the larger picture," he said. "Nothing can right the wrongs done you years ago." He reached up and touched her hand. She pulled away.

"Life isn't real to you, Erich. Just one big hall of mirrors."

"You and your Jewish sense of the dramatic." He stared at her body in the soft candlelight. "I won't be taunted," he said suddenly. "Especially not by you."

"Is that your limit? When Uncle was alive I used to think the world was without limits because I was a Rathenau. I didn't realize that even he had me on a leash. The older I got, the more freedom I thought I had acquired, the more limits were secretly being imposed."

"What has that to do with us!"

"It has to do with me, and with what I wanted then."

"You still want what you want, when you want it."

"I'm still a Rathenau."

He wondered why her statement did not bother him. "What was your uncle really grooming you for? Not to be a dancer, I think. Marriage? To some foreign blueblood? An old-fashioned marriage of alliance?"

"Politics."

"Politics! I don't believe it!" He laughed derisively. "Did he hope to get you a seat in the Reichstag?"

"He found politics depressing and ugly. He had no intention of marrying, so *I* was to be politics' antithesis. His canvas."

"Purity on a pedestal, while he toiled in the mud of political trenches!" He motioned with thumb and index finger as if indicating a headline. "Miriam Madonna Rathenau, Virgin of the Grünewald."

"Not virginal, but at least not vile."

He blew cigar smoke toward the ceiling. "The man was an anachronism," he said, feeling suddenly small despite his lean muscularity. Turning abruptly, he pulled her down to him and kissed her hard, sliding his tongue into her mouth and along her palate, and then releasing her just as abruptly. "If only we had lived in another time," he said hoarsely, "maybe things would have worked out differently."

She raised her hand as if to slap him, then let it drop. "We did live in another time." Glaring at him, she stood up, put her hands beneath the slip's straps as if to slide them off her shoulders. "It's late and I'm tired. God forbid I should *upset* you, so either have me or have me leave."

Beneath the silk, her back and buttocks looked like tawny shadows. How could one so beautiful talk so cavalierly about sexual pleasure?

"Well, make up your mind," she said coldly.

"That's enough!"

She leaned down toward him. "And if I go on talking? What'll you do? Punish me? Take away my family estate?"

Furious, he stabbed out his cheroot in the water and,

reaching up, gripped her by the throat. He tightened his grip on her neck and put his other hand on her breast, not caressing her so much as clutching it, clinging to her. But the pent-up rage of all his hatreds had not left him. Pulling her toward him, he again kissed her hard on the lips, put his arms around her waist and drew her awkwardly onto the rim of the tub.

She nuzzled her mouth down against his shoulder and, without warning, sank her teeth into his flesh.

Immediately, insistently aroused, he pulled her further onto the tub rim, forcing her knees apart, rising up in the water and pressing his hips against hers, unmindful of her angry squirming.

"You bastard!" Suspended unnaturally, she cried out in pain and anger. "I hate you."

Fighting as if for her life, she twisted from his grasp and climbed awkwardly off the rim of the tub. She picked up his jacket and began tearing off the Nazi insignia as if it were alive. Then she hurled it across the room and limped over to the bed.

"What's your game, Miriam?" He touched his cheek where she had hit him. "Tell me the rules so I can play too!"

"I want you not to be a Nazi. I want Solomon. I—"

"I can't change things no matter how much I'd like to turn back the calendar. I sit at my desk, intent on mapping out security, and instead find myself staring out the window for hours, thinking about the people out there I'd like to know, whose lives I would like to share. You're not the only one who *wants*, Miriam. I *want* too! Not possessions, not even power. Just to be part of others' lives." His emotion expended itself. So did his erection. "But I don't know how," he said quietly and bitterly.

He sat up and, elbows on his knees, put his head in his hands. On my birthday! he thought. Why is she torturing me like this on my goddamn birthday! Still, he could not stop himself from talking and—*telling her*. Maybe, he thought, he was rambling *because* it was his birthday, the day he had hated for so long. "So much is happening out there, so much we can never know," he went on. "I feel locked inside myself…isolated from everything, everyone, that could have had real meaning for me."

He felt ashamed. He had never spoken like this to anyone before, not even Solomon. "I've no right to tell you my troubles," he said, staring at the rose-colored water. "Especially after the pain you've been through."

"Save the poetics for your Hitler Youth virgins." She lay down on the featherbed, face buried in the silver-tasseled pillow that homely Magda Goebbels had given him in remembrance of the time she had stayed the night with him.

He said nothing, waiting for her to do something. Anything. He felt too embarrassed and weak to fight any longer.

"I never credited you with the capacity for honesty," she said finally, in an emotionless voice. She lifted her head. "Everyone has the right to burden others with their despair, at least sometimes."

"Would things have been better between us if—"

"Had things been better, would you have lived differently?"

"You mean, would I have divorced myself from the Party? Would I hate Hitler more than I do? Probably not."

He rose from the tub and toweled himself. "Miriam? Miri? I'm sorry if I hurt you just now."

His mind in tumult, he knelt at the foot of the bed and massaged her feet. He had wronged her again, but was it, he wondered, really his fault? Was any of it? He could not have saved her estate, not even if she hadn't been off in her precious world of Parisian art and ballet. As for her taunting, she should know better than to treat him like some insentient being; he was a man, with a man's needs.

Yes, he had lied to her about Solomon. Intercepted the letters to her. Pretended regularly to be checking on Sol's condition, mostly to make certain that she would not take matters into her own hands and try to find him, but at least he had never truly planned the lie.

And the things he had done to keep her from learning the truth—things for which he had hated himself—he had done for her. Why else would he so degrade himself, except to hold on to her regardless of the price? Besides, he had lived that lie in the full knowledge that the man was safe in Amsterdam with his mother and sister. He had even broken a vow to never speak to his parents again. After they had ransacked the tobacco shop, he had phoned, reprimanding them. They swore they had stolen nothing; knowing they would be accused of a theft of which they were innocent, they had simply left town for a while—until, they had said, the real culprits were found.

Though he wanted to pretend that the lie was truth—the past could not be changed, after all—the discussion had grown heated, and he had ended up slamming down the receiver, angry with himself for bothering with them again.

"I really am sorry I hurt you, Miriam," he said. "But God knows I've waited so long for you—"

"God? What do you know of God!" Hugging the pillow, she turned onto her back. She narrowed her eyes and glared at him with an expression of hatred. "Save your sorrow for the virgins with swastikas on their wings. That's what you're good at!"

"I'll show you what I'm good at."

Standing at the foot of the bed, he had the fleeting thought that perhaps the nickname Javelin Man had reached Miriam. Had she, not knowing his reasons for staying away from her bed, laughed at him on those many nights he had slept away from her? He looked at his penis. She wouldn't laugh at him after tonight.

Roughly, he pulled her forward until he was between her legs.

"Stop it, Erich! God*damn* you, let me go!"

Tightening his grasp, he entered her.

"You'll pay for this." She gasped. "I promise you'll pay!"

He concentrated, pushing deeply inside her. "I

already did," he said. "You gave Anneliese two hundred marks. Now earn them."

Squirming and kicking, she tried to fend him off. Then, releasing the pillow, she gripped the rods of the brass headboard and let him slam into her with orderly, methodical strokes.

He gripped her hair. Turned her head to the side so that she faced the wall. "Count the money, as if I just gave it to you."

"You're crazy!"

"Now!"

"One...two...three..."

He reveled in the hatred in her voice. "Slower!"

"Four..."

"Again! From the beginning!"

"One..."

Hoping to delay orgasm, he closed his eyes and thought of his shepherds, seeing each with the clarity of a delirium dream. But he soon lost all control. Covered with sweat and unable to delay any longer, he came and crumpled on top of her, continuing to thrust—while she continued, tonelessly, to count—until sleep enfolded him.

He dreamed of a ship buffeted by the sea and of the beach where shepherds howled. When he awoke, the sun had broken through the clouds and he was alone, cold and uncovered yet strangely fulfilled. He climbed out of bed and padded across the carpet to the mirror. Contemplating his image, he decided he was better looking than ever.

Behind him, he saw the meal he had ordered the

night before. It lay untouched, browning around the edges. They must have delivered it after he was asleep, after Miriam left, he thought. What a waste!

He walked over to the table, poured himself a glass of wine and nibbled at the dessert, a little astonished that he felt absolutely no contrition. If he owed Miriam an apology, she owed him one too for her lack of gratitude. He had taken her in. Kept her safe. As for Sol, he was safe in Amsterdam. *He* knew that, even if Miriam did not.

Chapter Eighteen

April 1939

"Why don't you get up, get dressed and come with me, Miriam? An outing will do you good. You've hardly left the estate since…since Christmas."

Erich avoided looking into Miriam's eyes and allowed his gaze to rest on the slight swell of her belly. In the past he had avoided pregnant women. They had appeared clumsy to him, repulsive, their eyes filled with a secret awareness that excluded him and the rest of the male world. Yet the idea of this child—his child—conceived though it was in anger, continued to excite him.

"You really want me to get up before dawn and come with you to Abwehr headquarters?" Miriam's voice was laced with sarcasm. "To do what, pray tell—enlist in the military? Today's Easter, Erich. You should go to Mass. You and all your Nazi friends. I'm having lunch with Werner."

"Never mind," he said bitterly.

Annoyed with himself for having made the suggestion, Erich swung his legs out of the bed they again shared. Women were peculiar...Miriam no less than the rest. He had expected fury when he demanded to return to her bedroom, but she had simply shrugged, saying she did not care where he slept or with whom. She did not refuse him when he touched her, though he sensed that she knew he was sustaining his erection by reliving what he had come to think of as the Christmas Rape.

Not that she showed any real interest in him, or anyone else except Werner Fink. Erich indulged her need to spend time with that troublemaker because it got her out of the house—

He stopped himself.

The truth was that she had asked for little since Christmas, except to be left alone. Unnerved by her long silences, he had gone on his knees to ask her forgiveness. His apologies, profound and constant, were met with disinterest: a cold stare, a cold shoulder.

"Why do you stay with me, Miriam?" he asked quietly.

She answered simply, giving him the same reason she had always given him. "You are your brother's keeper."

He stood up and looked down at her. She was anything but a fool, this niece of Walther Rathenau: a permanent reminder to him of Solomon and of his own weakness. She knew what was best for her own well-being and that of the child.

"Miri, it's Easter," he said, determining to try one more time. "All I have to do is pick up some papers at headquarters and then slip out for the day. It's too late to get to Oberammergau, but we could drive into the country, perhaps to the Harz."

"I told you—" She doubled up suddenly, as if in severe pain.

Erich struggled to find the lamp chain. By the time he had the light on, she was lying with her back arched, pressing her fists into her silk-gowned belly.

"What's the matter? What is it!"

"How should I know! I've never been pregnant before."

"What does it feel like?"

"Like pain."

His rudimentary medical training in the military had not included childbirth. He felt helpless. Grappling for the telephone to call for help, he knocked her photograph off his nightstand. "I'll have the car brought around."

Her features contorted. Struggling, she rolled onto her side and pulled up her legs. "It's only the fourth month!" She was gasping. "I must be losing the baby!"

Grabbing a handful of crumpled silk, Erich pulled himself toward her. He thrust his lips close to her ear. "You can't lose the baby—our son! You hear? Please, Miriam!"

In his anxiety, he thought he heard Goebbels'

laughter. He stopped to listen. Fool! Probably a radio broadcast coming from downstairs or, at worst, the Gauleiter with another hopeful starlet.

"I think I'm okay now," Miriam said after a time, her face to the wall.

"You *think* you're okay?"

She took a deep breath. "Lately I'm sure of nothing."

He dropped the telephone in its cradle as if it were a megaphone threatening to announce his incompetence to the world. "Can you sleep?" he asked as gently as he could. Hoping to soften her attitude, he reached over her and placed his hand on her belly. "Let me feel him, Miriam."

"Stop it!" She batted his hand away. "You're like an old horse trader gloating over his prize mare." After a moment she relented and took his hand in hers. She placed it on the slightly mounded flesh of what had once been a dancer's slender belly, to the right of center.

He had learned how to listen through his fingers to the tiny intermittent flutters.

His son!

She moved away and turned to stare at the velvet-flocked wallpaper. It's normal for her to emotionally distance herself in preparation for motherhood, he told himself. Animals do it, so why not humans? She would redirect her attention to him after the birth. For now, the boy was rightly her main concern—

What nonsense! he thought. The truth was, she hated him, and for good reason. Given time, and the birth of their child, she would forgive him. He could not expect her to forget, but surely forgiveness was possible.

Meanwhile, given her physical changes and the larger ones to come, her attitude was actually something of a relief; it excused his occasional desire for other women—like Leni Riefenstahl, the film director. Trim body. So sure of herself. She was said to prefer women, but that only made her all the more exciting. Not that he intended to do anything about his desire for her— those days were over—just that it was natural to contemplate…

While Miriam dozed, he dressed. By first light he was outside. The day smelled of spring and he felt good despite Miriam's surliness; on impulse, he chose to ride his motorcycle to headquarters. There would be no going to Mass this day or any other in the new Germany. More and more people—like the woman at the Passion Play in Oberammergau during his bivouac in the Black Forest—confused Hitler with God. He felt no such confusion, but he had long since lost his taste for the overt trappings of Catholicism. Besides, Mass was not exactly part of the Party platform; all officers made it a point to show up for duty—and punctually!— on this day, or face possible reprimand.

Still, policy and his own angers could not keep him from celebrating the Earth—God's creation. The breaking dawn was beautiful, and he thoroughly enjoyed the ride to Oranienburg, home of Abwehr headquarters and once home of his glory on the athletic field.

After reporting in and collecting the papers he needed, he wandered into the officers' club. He downed three large rolls with cheese and liverwurst, and half a pot of coffee.

Tomorrow, he thought, he would make sure Miriam and the child were all right. He would take them to see Doctor Morell. He congratulated himself for being important enough to have Miriam taken care of by Hitler's personal physician. Perhaps he would have a check-up himself; he had been getting far too little exercise of late.

With that in mind, he decided to leave the cycle in front of headquarters, where it would be seen, and enjoy an Easter stroll before sitting down to the paperwork that, as usual, he had allowed to pile up. A Sunday morning hike—just like in the Wandervögel days. Whistling softly, he headed down the main road and toward the mortuary, which lay about two kilometers out of town. He would turn around there.

However, he soon abandoned his plan and cut through the woods. Pines, beeches, and hemlock rose into an orange Easter dawn; mushrooms had proliferated from the spring rains, and their smell permeated the air. He stopped to examine one of them, wondering if he could still tell the difference between mushrooms and toadstools. He was crouching near the ground when voices claimed his attention. Curious, he followed them out to the road and found the good people of Oranienburg, released from work by the holy day, gathered along the Waldstrasse.

"An Easter parade?" he asked one of them pleasantly.

"Might call it that." The man grinned and pointed at a column of men just coming into view.

"Who are they?" Erich asked.

"As if you don't know!" The man stared at Erich's uniform.

"Haven't been around this area for a long time."

The man shrugged. "Whatever you say. It's the labor detail from Sachsenhausen on their three-kilometer stroll to the quarry. Mostly political prisoners—but enough Jews to make it worthwhile!"

Erich's stomach clenched as the sorry group headed toward him, herded by rifle butts and billyclubs. They looked beaten and starved. As the head of the column passed him by, he saw those who appeared to be the oldest of the men—though it was hard to tell—squeeze to the center of the human cage without breaking rank. Their comrades supported them as best they could.

"*Blüt für Blüt!*—blood for blood!" shouted a townsman in lederhosen and a green felt hat decorated with a red feather.

Next to him, a woman in a tight-bodiced dirndl took up the chant. She smiled companionably as she raised her Brownie to photograph the Easter entertainment

I didn't know, he wanted to shout at the ragged column. The prisoners looked half alive—skeletons staring out of skulls whose eyes had seen too much death.

God! I didn't know.

The woman with the camera hurled a stone into the ranks.

Soon everyone was claiming the right to kill a Jew

for Jesus before sunrise Services. Blows were rendered with clubs and broomsticks, with fireplace pokers hurriedly gathered from neat little houses, with stones plucked from gardens seeded with berries and beans. Young children hurled eggs and insults, their obscenities drowned by the shrieks of the prisoners as their rifle-bearing masters beat and shot them into submission.

The men along the outside of the column peeled off like old paint, skeletons performing a ghastly dance; they fell and were trampled by others fighting inward in their battle to survive.

"No," Erich whispered. The rumors about the detention centers, the abuses, the humiliations—true. All of it. Holy Mother of God, they were true.

Could Hell be any worse?

An elderly man next to Erich spat in a laborer's face and shook his fist. "It was because of *you* that our Lord was crucified!"

The inmate straightened his shoulders and wiped off the spittle on the striped sleeve of his prison uniform. A rock bounced off the temple of the man next to him. He swayed. His friend held him up and they staggered on.

Erich looked around. At least Sol was not here, facing the good people of Oranienburg—so blind to all but hatred. Their tile and shoe factories loomed unmanned, the machinery silent—and why? To commemorate Easter in a Germany that had officially declared the Christian god a manifestation of the Jewish disease. Yet the claptrap continued about Jews killing and bleeding

Aryan infants for Passover rituals…and they went on blaming the Jews for the death of Christ. Were they stupid, bloodthirsty, or simply naïve?

He did not know; all he was sure of was, when the truth of this surfaced, not one of them—neither man, woman, nor child—would admit to having been here this day.

Nor, he thought sadly, feeling sick, would he.

CHAPTER NINETEEN

At the rear of the column, Sol wiped the residue of an Easter egg off his face. The good people of Oranienburg must have run out of stones, he thought. How fortunate.

He bent and offered his fingers to Misha, who licked them clean. Sol smiled gently, but the boy did not smile back. He seemed to have forgotten how. And no small wonder. Yesterday it was Christmas, now it was Easter. From Chanukah to Passover, they had been living in a Panoptikum, a house of mirrors called Sachsenhausen.

Abruptly, the Oranienburg gauntlet was behind them...the morning "Running of the Bull," his new friend Hans Hannes called it.

Turning his head, he glanced back toward the camp. It was a nightmare, a zoetrope filled with slides of the black and white pain of Dadaism and filled with savage, sinister people turned inside-out by despair. Caricatures George Grosz may have rendered—only the camp artist was not Grosz or Van Gogh. He was SS Captain Hempel.

His whip was the brush, the flesh of men his canvas. His favorite subject lay inherent in his introductory speech to new arrivals: "This is not a penitentiary or a prison. It is a place of instruction. Order and discipline are its highest law. If you hope to see freedom again, you must submit to severe training. You must convince us that our methods of training have borne fruit. You must deny your old way of life. Our methods are thorough...."

Translated, that meant, "...you will not go hungry. Not if you will eat ruthlessness for dessert after your entree of cruelty."

Each step toward the quarry sent pains shooting through Sol's stomach and spine. Beside him, around him, fellow inmates with torn flesh and broken bones stumbled on through fields black from spring plowing. He remembered other days in these grain fields. Athletic festivals. Erich-the-Teuton practicing his javelin; or he, Erich, and Miriam walking through the woods, talking, listening to birds.

It troubled him when birds sang here now. Their freedom and the beauty of their songs mocked him.

The column reached the quarry. By now, for some, standing took too much effort. They collapsed onto the marly ground.

"Boy!"

Hempel dismounted from his stallion. His silver hair

shone in the early morning light, and his eyes brightened with pleasure as Misha came running to him. Using the tip of the barrel of his pistol, Hempel caressed the boy's cheek. He moved the pistol to the other cheek, and repeated the gesture.

Misha whimpered but did not cry. Far too small to carry out the work of the hard labor detail, he had to march with them. The order had come directly from Hempel, whose penchant for boys—the younger the better—was no secret.

"Eyes front!" Hans whispered to Sol. "You won't help the child by getting yourself killed."

"You were out of step back there, you little bastard!" Hempel said.

"Ja, Hauptsturmführer!" Misha said. "Forgive me, Hauptsturmführer! I am a wretched Jew, unworthy to lick your boots."

Sol glanced quickly at Hempel. The captain was smiling.

"Fifteen on the stock might make you worthy," Hempel said conversationally. "What do you think?"

"Ja. Thank you, Hauptsturmführer."

Remounting, Hempel spurred his horse. His wolfhound, busy and bloodied from the roundup of straggling inmates, joined horse and rider.

"Be strong, Misha," Sol whispered to the boy when he returned to the ranks. The child was so terribly young! He did not deserve the ugly lessons he would learn from that master of the grotesque, Otto Hempel.

Misha stared as man, horse, and dog ran into and onto and over prisoners—who screamed as bones, brittle from dietary deficiencies, broke like twigs.

Dear God, let the boy stay conscious throughout the whipping, Sol prayed. As long as he counted the lashes aloud, he would get no more than those assigned. Would it be the cane whip or the horse whip? The length of flex-steel, perhaps? The immediate agony was all that differed. Whatever was used, his buttocks would become raw mincemeat. Later, Hempel would doubtlessly abuse him or, worse yet, hand him over to the guards who had a taste for gang rape. Camp gallows-humor insisted they raped because they believed that by doing so they spread the seed of National Socialism.

Sol shut his eyes.

A Kapo's stick pushed into the small of his back. "You! Filth! Into the pit with the rest of them!"

The column broke into rows and snaked downward into the cold shadows that filled the limestone quarry. Sol descended the steep steps that had been carved into the pitside, trying to imagine himself entering Persepolis or one of the Egyptian digs that had so seized the world's imagination a decade before.

"All right, you lazy Jew. Get those hods rolling." The slap of Pleshdimer's stick across his ribs reminded him that this was no archaeological dig. The Kapo raised his voice. "The rest of you—move yesterday's stones up the hill!" He shouted loudly enough to be heard by the guards who stood at the top of the pit, holding dogs and machine-pistols at the ready. "On with it, or tomorrow I'll be gone and someone who really knows how to teach you the value of industry will stand here in my place!"

Sol joined the rush to secure a stone that could be balanced on his back with one hand, leaving the other free in case he stumbled or fell. Stumble, and he would be forced to pitch himself sideways into a long and possibly fatal tumble down the jagged rubble that banked the steps. Fall, and he would receive an immediate beating and twenty-five lashes; fall backward—knock down other prisoners and halt progress—and death would be the easiest punishment.

Prisoners were grouped by the color of the patches sewn onto their sleeves. Each group worked a different part of the pit.

The red-triangled politicals and green-triangled criminals usually got the best of it, breaking and shaping stones; the violet-triangled Jehovah's Witnesses and black-triangled work-dodgers and anti-socials were next in the caste system.

The prisoners the Nazis labeled the worst degenerates in the Reich, the Jews and homosexuals, were lumped together. The homosexuals wore pink triangles, the Jews yellow ones. Solomon's was crossed with a green one. His crime: defiling a German sewer.

Together, his two triangles formed a Star of David.

Like beasts of burden, the Jews and the homosexuals carried rocks to the top of the quarry, a double-dozen steps up an almost perpendicular incline. Denied medical attention during illness or following an accident, deliberate or provoked, and on half rations, the sick and the starving hauled the boulders. Up; and run down. Up; and run down—

Sol shouldered his first burden of the day. The best

he could find was a shapeless rock that weighed at least forty kilos. He had become a connoisseur of weights, able to judge them with a kind of sick precision. There was a time he had weighed eighty kilos, a time his mother had bragged, "God should only make a bull's haunch so lean and tough as my Sol's." Now he guessed his weight was about fifty-five kilos. Driven by fear, he found he could carry rocks all day he would have had trouble lifting when he was in good health.

He pictured himself balanced on a scale being held not by Justice but by the Angel of Death. On the other side of the scale was a different kind of boulder, heavier and much more important: the burden every Jew had to carry.

"Move!"

The guard amused himself by hitting Sol across the shoulders with his gun—his "fat squirter," as the prisoners called the weapons—and waited impatiently, eagerly, for someone else to slow down.

Sol wavered, sucking air to replace the breath stolen from him by the unexpected blow. Only those guards circling the top of the pit around the limestone crusher occasionally missed an opportunity for cruelty, because they had the distraction of their shepherds straining against their leashes and slavering as they eyed the inmates they had been trained to hate.

Sol wondered if any of them had been bred in Erich's kennels.

Bent double by the rock, he staggered up the steps. His eardrums felt ready to burst from the interminable shouting, and his joints, not yet warmed to the task, felt cemented. Soon his bones would feel ready to crumble, and the pit's shadows would invade his lungs like a cold dark hand.

The hours passed in a blur of pain and fatigue.

"Sing!" Hempel ordered.

His comrades, grinning, took up the command for the camp song. "Sing, you scum!"

The column twisted, going down alongside itself like an indecisive caterpillar. The inmates running down the steps, mindful of the guards' demands, kept their knees lifted as though for a soccer drill.

"*Dear old Moses, come again,*" they sang. "*Lead your Jewish fellowmen…once more to their promised land.*"

Sol stopped singing and put down the rock. Eyes rigidly forward, he prepared himself for the dash down the hill.

"Sing!" A guard kicked him in the shin. He reeled— and sang:

"*Split once more for them the sea…*"

Beyond exhaustion, he fell onto his side. Arms and legs moving spastically, he murmured the rest of the song.

"*When the Jews are all inside*
On their pathway, long and wide,
Shut the trap, Lord, do your best!
Give us the world its lasting rest!"

Arms enfolded him. Like a dying spider, he continued to move. Finally his limbs slowed and he sagged in Hans' arms. His head lolled, his mouth opened, closed. Spittle drooled down his chin.

"It's over." Hans' voice. "We're dismissed to the barracks."

Sol realized he was no longer at the quarry. "Hot roll call"—exercising until the weak collapsed from exhaustion, and were shot—had just ended.

Later, wedged into his "Olympic" bunk, the top of five wooden tiers and so narrow that he could only slide in and remain in one position, he could not sleep. The barracks, designed for eighty and filled with three hundred, stank of the sweat and vomit of men too crammed together to rise and relieve themselves. The prisoners who had chosen to lie on the avenues of dirt floor below became receptacles for the urine and excrement that fell from above, but—too tired and weak to awaken—they did not know it until morning.

With only about forty centimeters between his bunk and the ceiling, Sol's bunk was too high up, too inaccessible to be subject to inspection like the one Misha shared with Hans Hannes—a "trap" bottom bunk. What he would give for half an hour of rest in a soft bed! Thirty minutes. The time it took to make love or put together a noodle pudding, or to kill—how many?

He thought about Misha.

The boy had not marched back with them; he had not yet come back to the barracks. Sleep, Sol told himself, knowing he would need strength when Misha returned...if he returned.

"I can't sleep either," Hans whispered, standing up.

Though not a Jew, he had requested and been granted

quarters in the Jewish barracks. He wore the pink triangle of a homosexual; the guards loathed him perhaps even more than they hated the Jews and the Gypsies. He reminded the guards too much of many of their own.

Whispering so as not to disturb the others, Sol asked, "What happened to the Gypsies who arrived yesterday from Burgenland?"

"They had some kind of infectious eye disease. I heard they were taken to the hospital in Jena. You should tell them about your eyes, Solomon. It might be your way out of here."

"The politicals occasionally get emigration papers," Sol said. "The only way out for the rest of us is feet first." He thought about Carl von Ossetzky, released when he won the Nobel Prize for literature. What good had freedom done him? He had died anyway as the result of the torture and inhumanity he suffered here.

"At least ask them for spectacles," Hans insisted.

"I did. Before I knew what went on in the sick ward."

"Apply to the Chief Security Office in Berlin for a visitor. If they allow one, your visitor can bring you spectacles."

"Sometimes," Sol answered, "it is better not to see."

"Shssh!" Hans silenced him. "They are bringing the boy back."

He disappeared. Sol scooted to the edge of his bunk. He had barely enough room to turn his head and look down.

"Did they not tell you, Misha Czisça, that death through sorrow is forbidden here?" Hans whispered. He

lifted the boy in his arms and carried him to his bunk.
The boy lay with his back to Hans, staring at the far
wall. Now and again, despite Hans' whispered protests,
he scraped his fingers along the filthy floor to take a
handful of dirt and transfer it to his mouth.

Hans bent over him. He was weeping quietly. A tear,
dripping from his chin, fell into Misha's hair.

"Son of a bitch!" He looked up at Solomon, his face
white, his eyes red-rimmed but suddenly clear and
intensely blue, as if hatred had lent them new life.

Staring at Hans, Solomon saw a fragile, empty vessel.
The face of death lay beneath the mask of the man who
had seemed always to possess greater stamina than any
other person in the barracks.

Hans Hannes, with his humor and humanity,
reminded him of Grog, the clown, for whom the world
was no longer "Schö-ö-ön."

"He can have my daily ration of bread and soup," Sol
whispered, his own eyes filling with tears. "I would give
him my life, if it would stop him from blaming himself
for my imprisonment."

"To stop him you must live, not die," Hans said. "He
told me our beloved Hauptsturmführer found it too
distasteful to do the beating himself. He handed Misha
over to Pleshdimer. Then Hempel salted his wounds
and licked them. Licked them! The man should be
locked up in the kennels with the rest of
Standartenführer Koch's dogs!"

The boy's dry-eyed sobs quieted. "Is he asleep?"
Solomon asked.

The actor nodded and covered Misha's limp body

with a threadbare blanket. The boy awakened and tried to sit up, but fell back in pain. "The leather strap. He soaked it in brine, Hans. There were holes in it."

Gently, Hans turned the boy over. Blisters were forming where the flesh had come through the holes in the leather strap.

After Misha fell back into an exhausted sleep, Sol descended from his bunk. Together, he and Hans walked over to one of the barrack's two tiny windows.

"Punishing someone that way—for being out of step, for God's sake!" Sol asked. *"Why!"*

"Why ask a fool's question, Solomon? Go to sleep. Tomorrow we go back to the quarry. You will need all your strength." He turned his back on Sol, leaned against the windowsill, and looked out.

Sol returned to his bunk and passed into a fitful sleep filled with dreams of the past months. He was on the train from Berlin, coughing and feverish from the fetid damp of the sewer. Tramping down Karacho Way into the "camp for protective custody." Stumbling through gates inscribed, "My Fatherland—right or wrong." He dreamed of a hospital bed, Dr. Schmidt bending over him, saying, "You will serve us yet for many years." And he heard laughter—not human—as the visions and the voices intruded, mocking him.

"I thought I'd be killing lice," he heard a voice say from one of his childhood visions.

Then another: *"Give me your axe!...You've hurt me enough, you've hurt me."*

He blinked. He was in the quarry. Such an indulgence, the voices and visions, compared to what he now must endure! The weight upon his back displaced them. There was only the next step to climb, the bent back of the wretch before him, the sweat runneling down his face...and the rock. Always the rock.

Up.

Deposit the rock.

Down, singing of Jewish destruction. Up, a skin-and-bone machine whose only reality was pain so great it congealed within the flesh like pus. Certain each trip up the quarry steps would be his last, that he would drop dead and slide down the rubble to stare through vacant eyes at those too foolish to embrace the long sweet sleep of eternity.

He put down his tenth rock—or was it his ten-thousandth?—and raised his head. The other prisoners were sitting or lying about. He lay down where he had stood, savoring the cold stony ground and the feathery clouds chasing each other across the sky.

They brought sleep, and he dreamed he was dreaming...a dream within a dream....

He was a bulldog. Stocky, large, jaw square, eyes red with anger. When he awoke within the dream, the anger was still in him. He growled up at the edge of the pit, at the circle of shepherds. They disappeared. A wall of blood rose to a crescent. Curled at the edges. Began to trickle, then to pour down the hillside, meandering among the rubble, branching again and again until it reddened the limestone talus.

At the top of the pit, the shepherds returned, lifted their heads, howled at an ice-white moon.

In the pit, the blood became a torrent. Engulfing him. Red-black and gelatinous, and as stinking as the pheasant he'd shot during his family's one vacation in the Black Forest and had left too long in the sun....

Streaming into the pit, the blood turned blue. Blue as the veins beneath the skin of living skeletons. He felt a vision coming, and could not keep it from engulfing him. He was too tired. The light was big, and blue as cobalt——

A lamp pours light onto two women on cots set in an alcove of a crumbling brick wall, under an unframed picture of the Führer.

The older woman, wearing a pink slip, is sitting up, smoking, reading a letter, a dirty sheet draped over her legs. "Doktor Hahn must have written this in the lab. See how cramped the handwriting is?" She shows the letter to the younger woman. "He writes that way when he's excited, otherwise he has the most beautiful penmanship. And see this smear?" She taps the paper with a fingernail. "Graphite...and not from a pencil, that's for certain." She nods conclusively. "Definitely written in the lab."

Nightgowned in ragged flannel, the other woman looks dolefully into a shard of mirror she holds, and checks her hair. "I don't know how you can constantly read and reread those love letters. You even make notes in the margins, as though they were some kind of grammar exercise. How can you be so stoic? Your Otto wrote those two years ago! Don't you wonder where he is...*if* he is?"

Her eyes fill with remorse and she puts down the

mirror. "I'm sorry, Lise...*Doktor* Meitner. You must think me morbid."

"Nonsense, Judith!" Lise mashes her cigarette in an ashtray on the cot. "You've husband and child. Your concern for their safety suffuses your every thought and breath, as well it should. But just because they incarcerated Otto Hahn doesn't mean he's come to harm. He isn't Jewish, after all. Besides, even Hitler would think twice about exterminating a Nobel Laureate, no matter how outspoken. How ironic! They detain him for practicing the Jewish science of Bohr and Einstein, then as punishment demand that he go on practicing."

She carefully folds the yellowed pages of the letter and places it among others in a tin, removes a brick from the wall, inserts the tin, and replaces the brick. "Otto Hahn is with me every moment. His love guides me in every experiment we perform."

"And if we achieve critical mass?"

"He'll be there too. Especially then."

"Even if it means giving the Nazis—"

"The power of the atom? In exchange for guaranteed freedom for our people? Yes, Doktor Hahn will be there should that happen, even if only in spirit."

The younger woman stretches out on her cot, her head upon her extended arm, and looks at Lise with loving admiration. "You never expect to see him again, and yet you go on...."

Lise chuckles sadly. "When the Nazis split us, they split our atom. If you and I and Professor Heisenberg split the real atom, Doktor Hahn and I will remain forever split. They'll see to that. A female, Jewish Nobel candidate working alongside a Gentile Nobel Laureate who preaches the Jewish science he practices? That smacks of miscegenation, even though I was raised Protestant. The Nazis wouldn't hear of our being together again. But while we're apart...well, there is always hope. So we continue working."

The younger woman sighs. Despite lines of worry and overwork that crease her forehead, she now seems at ease. "Will I ever be as wise as you? My Franz may only be a laborer, but he's more knowledgeable about life than I'll ever be. And you with your—"

"My hopes—dead hopes—for a Nobel?"

"Yes. Being your lab assistant is an honor, Doktor Meitner. Sometimes, though, I wish you'd been my mother."

Lise frowns petulantly. "So you could have begun studying radium as a toddler? I would have made a terrible parent. I can see you now, a two-year-old worrying about nuclear properties and chain reactions." She reaches for another cigarette.

"And about your chain smoking." Judith takes the cigarette and wags a finger of admonition at Lise, who snatches at the cigarette and laughs when she misses.

Her laughter dissipates as the resonant chords of a Bach fugue played on a pipe organ fill the room.

"He's at it again," Judith says, suddenly sullen. "They only give us four or five hours' rest, yet every night Heisenberg plays—"

"He's a very good musician. Sometimes I think he'd rather devote his life to Bach's theories than to Bohr's."

221

"I hate him," Judith says bitterly. "He sold out to the Nazis. He's worse than Göring. Werner Heisenberg has the capacity to take a moral stand. The world respects him. Instead he simply gave in. At least he could have emigrated! Einstein did, and Fermi, and Slizard…who knows how many others? Now, with Bohr gone as well—"

"Heisenberg has no love for Hitler."

"He lectured in Switzerland and visited America." Judith says. "He didn't have to return."

"Should he have left his family behind?"

"Others did."

"Others did not have the weight of the scientific community on their shoulders."

"They bore the weight of the *Jewish* community," Judith says. "That's why they're helping the Allies."

Lise looks pained. "And who is helping European Jews while the United States chases the atom's Holy Grail? Has so much as a single conventional bomb been dropped on a death camp? The Allies surely know of the camps by now, yet nothing is done."

"Our people would die if the camps were bombed!"

"They'll die anyway, except those you and I manage to save." Lise's hand trembles as she lights a cigarette. "Why not destroy the slaughterhouses and slow down the killing?"

"*Everyone* will die, if we give Hitler what he wants," Judith says morosely. "I don't know why you agreed to this insanity! And me a part of it! A scientific breakthrough here…ten thousand saved." She moves her hand around on the cot as if picking up and setting down chessmen. "Another breakthrough there...ten thousand more. What happens when we run out of breakthroughs and must deliver the real thing? What good will have become of all this! Are you so naïve as to think Hitler will keep his promise to send all Jews to that homeland he's creating in Madagascar?"

Bending closely, Lise says in a low voice, "We pray to Jehovah that the war will end before the bomb is born."

"And in the meantime?"

"In the meantime...as long as the Nazis remain divided about Jewish science, they will continue to dole out to a dozen research facilities what little heavy water there is available, instead of concentrating efforts and supplies. The bomb could be delayed for a decade."

Lise's voice has risen earnestly. Judith puts a finger to her lips.

"The music drowns out our whispers," she says. "Why else do you think Heisenberg plays the pipes for half an hour every night, rather than immediately returning to his family in Hechingen? Even he isn't that much of a music enthusiast. He gives us time to talk—to assess—to plan."

"Doktor Heisenberg knows of our deal with Hitler?"

"Of course he knows," the older woman says impatiently. "Is he a part of it? I'm not sure. He's very complex, especially morally. He feels that if Germany doesn't have the bomb, we won't be able to stop the Allies from using theirs, should they create one. And yet...give the Luftwaffe the bomb? Who can say what

Heisenberg thinks! You think he wasn't upset when the papers called him a White Jew?"

"The usual Nazi logic. Destroy the best."

"That's why there's hope! You bash in the brains of a wolf and it may go on snapping, but not for long."

Judith curls into a ball, to sleep; the cot has no blanket. Lise reaches to turn off the light, but the door opens and an obese man with a pink and white complexion enters. Judith jerks upright, crossing her arms protectively across her bosom.

"I have two lion cubs at my home in Berlin," the man says. "They remind me of you ladies. Cuddly but dangerous."

Lise stands and, with an air of arrogance, leans against the wall and drags on the cigarette. "Is this your idea of a surprise inspection, Feldmarschall Göring?" She blows smoke in his direction. "Play games with *this* physicist and you can bet your jackboots that her mind goes blank in the lab tomorrow!"

"Someday, Doktor," he says genially, "that mouth of yours is going to get your tongue torn out."

"Someday I will be eliminated like the troublesome burr that I am. Until then, you need me. I know it. You know it."

"That day might come sooner than you think." Göring licks a palm and smooths back his hair. "In the meantime, let us not forget that uncooperative laboratory assistants arrive in Auschwitz by the boxcar load...as do their families."

Her face anguished, Judith puts her head against her fists.

"You promised—we work without provocation," Lise says.

He looks at her with disdain. "And you promised delivery. Until then, promises are just...promises."——

Sol awoke panting from the stuffiness of the room. He was not in the quarry, as he expected, but back in the barracks. Had he ever left? The sky was dark and the moon, framed in the window, filled the barracks with liquid silver. Hans was standing with one hand gripping the barrack's noose. He gazed toward the sentry tower.

Taking hold of the next bunk edge, Sol once again slid from the cramped space and crept among the sleepers to stand beside his friend. The camp's gate was open, and people were being herded inside. "Another pogrom," Sol said. "If only they knew how much easier it would be for them if they died now." He took the noose from Hans and tugged at it.

Hans laughed bitterly. "I've heard the dead are taken to the crematoria in Gotha and Eisenback. Also Weimar. That's where my father has his farm. The soil there is being spread with a new fertilizer. Gray-white. They sell human ashes to the farmers, Solomon. They are mad, all of them."

"Shhh. You'll bring the Kapo down on us."

Hans turned back to the window. "Know why I was imprisoned? For watching a couple copulate in a city park outside of Stuttgart. *For watching!* The man was a Party official. I thought they would let me go...you know, like the man who goes to the Kaiserhof with his secretary and meets his brother-in-law having a night on the town. They are silenced by mutual guilt."

Solomon put an arm across Hans' shoulder and gave his friend's upper arm an affectionate squeeze. The boy moaned in his sleep.

"I love that boy, Solomon." Hans' eyes welled with tears. "He has dignity far beyond his years, but they're taking it from him."

"He is young and strong."

"Young enough to believe in God and good men of government?"

"He will survive. You and I will see to that."

"You will have to do it alone, Solomon." Hans gripped a bunk post, his face wracked with anguish. "Sooner or later, they will get me. Ten years ago some sociologist decided there were over a million homosexual men in Germany. Himmler rounded the number up to *two* million and swore to rid the Reich of them all. In the so-called Dark Ages, homosexuals were drowned in bogs or rolled in blankets for use as faggots during witch burnings."

"I heard talk that you pink-triangles are to be marched to the camp brothel. If you perform with a woman, you'll be released into the civilian labor force."

"Perform!" Hans grabbed his groin with such hatred, it seemed he wanted to tear off his genitals.

"If you refuse, they'll kill you," Sol said.

"They'll kill us anyway." Forehead against the post, Hans said quietly, "When I was making movies one after another, working literally night and day, UFA put me on antidepressants. For my mental health, they said. They had me working seven days a week. I was so tired, and always afraid for my brother. Their damned antidepressants gave me priapism. Know what that is, my friend?"

Solomon shook his head.

"An eternal erection." He looked at Sol through eyes filled with agony. "The pain—you cannot believe the pain, Solomon. The beatings we endure are nothing compared to it." He released a slow breath. "Priapism results in a form of gangrene," he said.

"Your name will become a part of medical history," the voice in the Ethiopian vision echoed. "The hospital's a death trap for both of us," Sol said.

A movement outside caught his eye. He watched Pleshdimer cross the yard, a thick-necked murderer who, as Hempel's human watchdog, had found his calling in Sachsenhausen. To him, passion and cruelty were synonymous, but the fear he inspired in all of the prisoners was multiplied tenfold for Misha, who had several times seen the man outside the camp.

"HEIL HITLER!" the loudspeakers boomed. "PRISONERS ARISE!"

Less than ten minutes till roll call. Sol had to hurry in order to have precious seconds in which to relieve himself in the holes in the floor of the room that adjoined the barracks.

"I'd sell my soul to see Hempel dead," Hans said. He lumbered over to the sleeping boy and shook him gently to arouse him.

"You'd sell your soul for a bowl of semolina soup," a voice from Sol's childhood whispered in his head.

As quickly as he could, he straightened his bunk,

collected his bag with its dry piece of bread—remnant of the previous day's rations—and relieved himself. Still, he and Hans and Misha only just made it outside in time for roll call. Holding a roster on a clipboard, Pleshdimer made his morning announcements, his huge forehead furrowed in concentration.

"Three, sev-en, sev-en, ze-ro four. Hos-spit-tal." He used a forefinger as a pointer. Gap-toothed, he looked up and grinned. "Today you work in the quarry. When you get back they will examine you, Jew."

Sol felt a sick, sinking feeling in his gut. *"Your name will become a part of medical history."*

"Nine, sev-en..." Pleshdimer stopped and pointed at Misha. "The Hauptsturmführer wants you in his quarters when you get back."

Sol saw raw fear in the boy's eyes.

"Is this your season of sadness, Solomon Freund?" a voice in Sol's head asked.

"The *world's* season of sadness," he answered, joining the column headed for the gate and the quarry.

CHAPTER TWENTY

Terrified of what the day would bring, Misha dawdled alongside Hans. He knew that eventually he would have to join the line of shuffling humans leaving for the quarry, but every minute he stayed behind seemed like a gift of time, delaying what lay at the day's end.

"I was watching. Listening," a man in a corpsman's uniform said, emerging from the closest building to address Misha. "Do whatever you must to survive. Someone has to tell them about this when it's over. You are young and strong. You can make it."

As quickly as the man had appeared, he was gone.

Hans held onto Misha's shoulder. "Bite off the bastard's cock if he tries anything," he whispered into the boy's ear.

"How can I do it, Uncle Hans?" Misha asked.

"You bite down, like this—"

229

"No. Don't make jokes." The boy shook his head impatiently. "I meant, how can I survive?"

"You can because you must," Hans said. He prodded Misha into the line before he continued talking, very softly, so as not to be overheard by the Kapo. "You must think of yourself as a soldier, defending yourself against the enemy."

"But I have no weapons."

"Yes, you do." Hans paused. "Listen carefully. You have weapons, but they are hidden. It is simply a question of finding them."

Pleshdimer was heading toward them down the line. Automatically, they stopped whispering.

"Let me give you some suggestions," Hans went on when the Kapo had passed. "The first thing you must learn to do is cry."

Misha shook his head, remembering his promise to himself.

"It washes out the eyes and is good for the soul. If you think you have forgotten how, I can teach you. I am a great actor. I can cry on command."

"What else?"

"You must think about something you were going to do, something you were struggling for before all of this—"

"Like my bar mitzvah?"

"Precisely. Remember your lessons and repeat them to yourself as if you know with absolute certainty that your bar mitzvah will come to pass. I have been to a bar mitzvah. I know that it requires much work, much planning. You must plan every detail, down to the shine on your shoes. Debate the menu with yourself, day after day. Month after month if need be. Wake up with it in your mind. Go to sleep thinking about it."

None of that made sense to Misha, but he stored it away in his head so that he could think about it later.

"One more thing," Hans said. "I met a man once, from Poland. He told me something I will never forget. He said that life is nothing more or less than a huge ledger. On one side, there is a list of all of the good things that have happened to you, and all of the good things that you have done. On the other, a list of all of the bad things that have happened to you, and," he smiled gently down at Misha, "the bad things you have done—even if they were not done on purpose. If you have any luck at all, the good side will always be longer than the bad side. Only when that is not true is life no longer worth living."

"I don't understand."

"You must keep such a ledger, Misha. It will become one of your best weapons."

"But I have no paper, Uncle Hans. No pencil. Even if I did, they would take it away from me."

Hans chuckled. "And you told me not to joke," he said. "I had forgotten that children were so literal. You must keep the ledger in your mind, Misha. That way you will never run out of pages or lead."

He stopped talking and left Misha to his thoughts. What nonsense, Misha thought. Ledgers and bar mitzvahs and tears. Those were not weapons. Guns were weapons. Hateful things, like guns and whips and—

Pleshdimer returned down the line. "Good thing you stopped your chit-chat," he said, jabbing Misha in the thigh with his stick. "I was about to stop it myself by stuffing this in your mouth." He waved the stick in front of Misha's face.

Misha shrunk from it. *I hate you*, he thought. *Hate you, hate you, hate you.*

That was it, he knew suddenly. There was an event he could plan down to the last detail, and he did have a weapon after all. In fact if hatred was, as he suspected, the most powerful weapon he owned, he had just discovered within himself an entire arsenal.

Misha picked up his feet and squared his shoulders. As soon as he could, he would tell Sol about this, he thought, watching the line snake around a bend in the road. Uncle Hans, too. Then the three of them could become warriors together against the enemy.

With that in mind, he opened a page in his thought-ledger and began to make his first list: enemies on one side, friends on the other.

Without knowing why, he included amongst his friends the man in the corpsman's uniform, the one who had stepped out of the shadows to tell him that he had to survive.

CHAPTER TWENTY-ONE

How long was it since he and Misha and Hans had been reassigned from the quarry? Sol wondered. He was beginning to lose track of time again, the way he had done in the sewer. Here, it felt worse. In the sewer there had been hope…and darkness to keep him from seeing his own physical degeneration.

Here, he not only saw his own, he saw others'.

Misha worked in the morgue next door to *Pathologie*, where prisoners were experimented upon—vivisection and dissection on a stainless-steel table with sloped troughs for collecting blood. The boy's job was to pry out gold teeth and search for gemstones in the rectums of corpses awaiting transport in Oranienburg garbage trucks to the city's crematorium. He said he did not mind it too much because of his new friend, Franz, a corpsman who had apparently dared question the huge casualty list at the camp and earned himself an assignment as *Pathologie* guard. He was the same man who, Misha said, had spoken to the boy kindly on the last morning of his quarry duty, a German of apparent compassion who, upon occasion, sneaked Misha a chocolate bar, which Misha shared with Sol and Hans.

The choice, he insisted, was his.

Hans had been reassigned to the brickworks, then to the Klinker factory's ships in the Oranienburg Kanal, to the holds and the heat and the dust. His job was to shovel coal and rubble up onto sloped platforms. More often than not, he said, it fell back on him.

His multiple injuries had been compounded by a hacking cough. Judging by the color and particles in his sputum, he was already a victim of the early stages of black lung disease. His skin was becoming permanently discolored; any attempt at a smile caused his lips to crack into ridges of blood and dust. He was also forced to perform in the brothel twice a day and often several times on Sundays, when the Klinker factory closed to give management a rest.

Instead of effecting his release, his priapism had brought him under Schmidt's scrutiny. He was made to move from woman to woman while Kapos whipped him, used electro-shock, or shoved numbing suppositories up his rectum...all in the name of science.

"Sooner or later they'll neuter me," he told Solomon. "Then I will kill Schmidt and myself."

The choice, he insisted, was his.

They were given a choice, all right, Sol thought

bitterly. Cooperate and survive; fight and die...if you're lucky.

He thought back to the first day of his own reassignment, the day he became Doctor Schmidt's prime guinea pig in her eye experiments...an attempt to reduce the problem of night blindness in pilots. She had injected dye at the outer edge of each of his eyes. When it took effect, there was an hour of photographing and peering and examination through various lenses. He had to lie still and keep his blinking to a minimum, or suffer Schmidt's syringe in his stomach.

The choice, she insisted, was his.

The process was repeated once or twice a week. Each time she repeated the same questions. Was your father sensitive to light? As a child, did you prefer dark places?

After the sessions in the laboratory, he was free until roll call—not out of compassion, but because Schmidt wanted him nearby in case she wished to repeat some part of her experiment. He was to have no food or water until dinner—why, he did not know. His was not to question, but to accept and survive.

That was his mandate.

Meanwhile, he could not ignore the fact that Schmidt's dyes were accelerating the deterioration of his eyesight; he was beginning to perceive colors differently, like the gray pebbles beneath his feet, which were beginning to look purple. But as his peripheral vision deteriorated, the clarity of his central vision improved. He wanted to see less, not more. Blindness would spare him the sight of all the horrors; with luck, it might even induce the SS to bless him with a bullet in the neck.

Until then, life would continue to be made up of eye days and, when Schmidt did not send for him, foot days.

Today was a foot day.

He looked down at his shoes. Inside, his feet were slimed with blood and dirt, and crammed so tightly into the too-small shoes that he made macabre jokes to himself about being a Chinese princess.

At the request of local shoe manufacturers looking for "a true test of durability," a walkway was built along the edge of the roll call area. The walkway's *raison d'être* was the provision of superior footwear for Germans to more comfortably carry the banners of truth and racial purity to the ends of the earth.

Sol picked up a sandbag and began to walk. As he did at the beginning of each foot day, he read the signs along the edge of the walkway, hand-lettered, blooming like large white flowers: Give Sacrifice and Glory to the Fatherland! Obedience. Industry. Honesty. Cleanliness.

For the rest of the day, the track would define his universe. Each path-length averaged six thousand steps. He was required to walk it—back and forth—seven times. Even wearing good, firm shoes, negotiating forty kilometers of stretches of cement, cinders, crushed stones, and broken glass embedded in tar, gravel, and sand would have been difficult and painful; in shoes a full size too small, carrying increasingly heavy sandbags, the foot days added a new color to the fresco that was Sol's life: the color of blood.

He smelled it everywhere, tasted it. Saw it in the wake left by the line of feet walking the shoe track. Up and down—

Familiar with every hazard on the track, his only defense against the deadly combination of pain and boredom was to resort to the same tactic he had used in the sewer: counting his steps.

Seven hundred twenty-six...seven hundred twenty-seven....

He continued walking and counting until he reached the far end of the walkway, the one nearest *Pathologie*. A scream interrupted his counting.

In the brief silence between screams, Sol turned and started back toward the beginning of the crescent-shaped walkway.

...six thousand and one...

Like a flagellant, he had learned to relish the pain. Dragging his feet, feeling the blood ooze, he gritted his teeth in a kind of pleasure as a matching pain pulsed behind his eyes. There was a flash of light, and then another. A blue glow grew out of the walkway and enveloped him.

Grateful that the universe defined by the track was about to be expanded, he did not try to shut out the vision——

Lise Meitner and her assistant sit on the edges of their cots, staring hopelessly at the floor. Göring stands over them.

"Our lab...shut down!" Lise utters in disbelief. Now she peers up, her face strained. "But we were making such progress."

Göring chuckles haughtily. "We have no need of parasites like you, now that we'll soon have," he pauses for effect, "the bomb."

"Impossible!"

"The Copenhagen plant has made certain breakthroughs—"

"So Bohr did give you heavy water before he escaped."

"Before he was kidnapped!" Göring snaps.

"But the partisans—they blew up the Norsk-Hydro power plant!"

"Those inept traitors?" The Feldmarschall tilts his face toward the ceiling and laughs so hard that he takes out a handkerchief and wipes tears from his eyes. "We let the British jellyfish *think* they had succeeded. We hadn't counted on the Americans having Bohr as well as Einstein, so we circulated the sabotage story so people would think we were still using heavy water as a neutron moderator instead of...graphite."

"You're lying." Suddenly pale, she speaks without conviction.

"We no longer need your cooperation *or* your brilliance, Doktor Meitner. We have everything we need in the notes that *Doktor* Hahn coded into your love letters. We've had your material for months."

Lise goes white.

"That's right, Doktor. Critical mass. We've had your notes, Copenhagen's success, and now we're tooling up at the Mauthausen camp at Ebensee. The bomb's to be built in a cavern carved out of granite by Jewish halfwits and whores just like you two."

"My letters. My notes. How!" Lise asks desperately, of no one.

"Oh my God." Sobbing, Judith reaches for her. "You said the letters were just reminiscences, and I believed you. I thought I was tricking them…protecting you.…"

"Perhaps we'll keep you alive, Doktor, until the weapon is finished and field tested. You will love the site we've picked. A second-rate military target, but ideologically perfect." Bending with difficulty, he lifts Lise's head by the chin, as if to kiss her. "The heart of the land of milk and honey. Jerusalem."

"My soul is dirty," Lise whimpers. "Let me die."——

"Get on with it!"

The crack of a whip, Captain Hempel's personal gift to Kapo Pleshdimer, punctuated the order and dissipated the vision. Sol stooped to pick up a heavier sandbag. He squeezed his feet into a pair of shoes yet another size too small and began, again, to walk—and to count—

Five thousand, six hundred twelve…five thousand six hundred thirteen…

The usual screams filled his imaginings as he tottered toward his milestone. *Pathologie*, directly in his line of vision, expanded and contracted like a creature alive, its brick belly filled with shrieking death. How he longed to suck at that breast. Sol slowed down. Leaned his body toward her.

"Walk, Professor!"

The Kapo's stick cracked against Sol's ribs. He doubled over, straightened up, counted, turned, pushed himself forward. Five thousand and…. Had it been days since he had seen Hans? Weeks?…Five thousand and…

"Walk!"

Let me die, Lord! Sol's thoughts echoed the voice from the vision. It contained all of the elements of the others. Again it showed the abuse of Jewish talents; again it talked of a Jewish homeland in Madagascar. If only he understood what it all meant—not that it mattered anymore. Still, he would rather go to his death knowing than unknowing. He was almost happy when he saw a blue glow——

Gossamer veils of blue, dust-moted light filter through a stained-glass window onto a man seated at a pipe organ. He is blond and broad shouldered, and looks as athletic as he is musically talented. The Bach concerto he plays reverberates throughout the tall reaches of a rococo church that was obviously once a castle.

Göring enters the nave, pushing a stumbling Lise before him.

The man at the organ continues to play feverishly, his arched fingers pounding the huge, tiered, ivory-inlaid keys. His head is lifted as though he sees something reverent in the tall brass pipes.

Göring opens the door. The organist does not turn around. Outside there is a bell tower and a flagstone landing. A long, very steep flight of stone stairs serpentines down the thumb-shaped limestone ledge on which the *Schlosskirche* perches. Beyond the castle-church lies farming country and half-timbered houses with gingerbread roofs.

"At least let Judith go," Lise pleads.

"As soon as my bodyguards finish with her, we'll let her go—to Auschwitz." Göring grabs her by the hair and drags her down the steps.

"I didn't deceive you about the graphite, Herr Feldmarschall! I swear I didn't."

He hits her—twice. She staggers back, then rocks forward and…pushes. He fights to keep his balance, but is too heavy. Fat arms flailing, screaming, he tumbles down the stone steps——

The vision faded. Sol twisted uneasily on his bunk. Dawn filtered through the barracks window. There was movement in the barracks as others who had not slept prepared for a new day.

CHAPTER TWENTY-TWO

Lately, the Rathenau rose garden had become Miriam's place for private and often dangerous thoughts. No one interfered with her inside the house, but that did not diminish her feeling that somehow her mental plotting and scheming could be overheard.

It was, she knew, a monumental foolishness. The only person who could possibly know what she was thinking was the baby, if, in fact, fetuses, embryos— whatever it was at this stage—could *know* anything.

Sitting in the rose garden at sundown on the day of summer solstice, she contemplated her future. She could see herself, with Erich; in her more optimistic moments she could see herself with Sol. But she found it almost impossible to place a child, her child, in the picture.

If by now, almost six months into her pregnancy, she was supposed to be feeling maternal, something had gone wrong. If she were master of the universe, she decided, the first thing she would do would be to make men's bodies capable of childbearing.

Even feeling the way she did, she could not help but smile at the very idea. Husband, home, children—weren't those what *women* were supposed to want? When this was over, this black period in German history, there would surely be those who would tell her that she should have been satisfied with what she had. It was, after all, so much more than what most had.

Maybe so, but she wanted more.

Had she fought against the flow, and failed, she might have been content. Or maybe she was just being optimistic and naïve, the inveterate performer thinking that life was going to work out with the form and balance of a play. Poverty did not appeal to her, but it had never frightened her either. At least, having tried and failed, her failure would have been of her own volition. But the Nazis had come, and taken away her will. They tore her mansion from her womb, and tore her from her mansion. Her birthright. She was back again, but it was not the same, for it was no longer hers. Its walls did not enclose and protect her, they were her cage—as her body was the child's.

One thing she did know: men would surely be more careful about making babies if there were no way to know before the fact who had to go through nine months of physical changes and emotional instability.

"What you're feeling is perfectly normal," the doctor kept saying. "Your body chemistry is not the same as it was; why would you expect to feel like yourself? Get out more, Frau Alois. Walk in the rose garden. Occupy yourself. Knit baby clothes."

Frau Alois.

There was never a time that she could hear herself called that without cringing. She kept telling herself that a rose was rose was a rose, but it didn't work.

Knit baby clothes! She should sit and knit when her world was falling—had long since fallen—apart.

Well, at least one thing had gone right. Erich had managed to remove the threat of the blood transfusion. Never in her life would she forget that conversation between the two men, walking ahead of her on the night of Hitler's birthday party. A beautiful spring evening, the air still, allowing snatches of their discussion to be easily overheard as she walked behind them. *"In my opinion, your wife's reformation needs something more. A doctor at Sachsenhausen…conducting experiments…Total blood transfusions…if Miriam were to be transfused with Aryan blood, no one would dispute her place beside you in the New Order."*

She stared at the blood-red profusion of roses around her and, lulled by the warmth of the day, fell into a state between sleeping and waking. She felt her head nod and saw a figure with a watering can, spraying roses with water that ran the color of blood. The roses fell to the ground, but on the bushes, here and there a petal remained, dangling between thorns like pieces of torn flesh.

She jerked herself fully awake. She could not allow herself to become morbid. It was not healthy for her or for the baby. She had asked the doctor about that, whether her thoughts could transfer themselves to the child she was carrying.

"We're not sure how much transfer there is between mother and embryo," he'd said. "Or, for that matter, the other way around."

She hadn't really thought about that until now. Perhaps she was being influenced by whatever was growing inside her. Was it a boy or girl, normal or shaped by her past and its father's? Bonded to her, and yet a stranger. Stretching her, she feeding it, blood and food intermingled, one with the other.

"I thought I might find you out here, Señora."

Miriam jerked herself fully awake. "Domingo," she said happily.

"You sound pleased to see me. How pleasant," the South American said, bowing with mock formality. He plucked a rose from the closest bush. "Why do all beautiful things have thorns," he said, sucking a drop of blood from his finger where a thorn had scraped it. He breathed in the scent of the rose. "It smells almost as lovely as you," he said, presenting it to her. "I had no time to purchase flowers for you before coming here, though why I would continue to do that when you are surrounded by the best I do not know."

Miriam smiled. "Don't ever change," she said. "I would be lost without your flattery. I *am* happy to see you."

"I just returned to Berlin and was told that you had been trying to get in touch with me. And I have news for you besides."

"Of Solomon?" She started to rise from the small bench upon which she had been resting.

"Mostly of Erich."

She sat back down. "Tell me," she said listlessly, as if the conversation no longer held her interest.

"May I sit down? I have not slept in many hours and I am more weary than usual."

She felt immediately apologetic. "I'm sorry, Domingo. I am not always polite of late."

He sat down next to her and took her hand. "You must not speak to anyone of what I am going to tell you. It is the reason I returned to Berlin sooner than expected, but for now it must remain a private matter between us. Soon, very soon, the Herr Major will be called in to headquarters. He is to be given a double promotion—"

"A *double* promotion?"

"It is not quite what it sounds. There are strings attached. I am not sure how to phrase this. The words sound so ridiculous."

He looked at her, as if to be sure he had her full attention. Apparently satisfied that he did, he continued. "I won't go into the history of all of this," he said. "You may even be aware of some of it. Certainly you must have heard that there has been much debate about what the Führer calls 'the Jewish question.' Part of that debate has included suggestions for the deportation of all Jews to a homeland far away from Germany. It appears that a location has been settled upon. Madagascar."

"Madagascar?" Miriam said the word slowly, but her mind was racing, remembering. There were two people who had spoken to her of Madagascar. One of them was Sol. Over and over, he had told her about his visions, and about the single link between them: the creation of a Jewish homeland in Madagascar. The other was her Uncle Walther.

"He told my Uncle that all Jews should be penned like animals in Madagascar."

"He?"

"The Führer. I remember Uncle Walther telling me about it. And Sol…" She stopped. She would think about that connection later. "No matter," she said. "What does this have to do with Erich and his promotion?"

"I suppose the only way to say this is to say it. Erich—and his canine unit—are to lead the first resettlement effort."

Miriam frowned. "Erich and his dogs? I don't understand."

"Before the end of the summer, a ship will leave for Africa. He and his dogs and trainers will be on it. There are military reasons that I cannot discuss which require my presence on board, and—"

"Am I to stay here?" Miriam asked slowly.

Perón shook his head.

Miriam stood up and began to pace agitatedly. Perón simply watched her. "There's more to this than you're telling me," she said, stopping to stare down at him. "Who else is to go? Which Jews?" She sat back down heavily beside him. "Which Jews?" she repeated.

"I am not sure, Miriam. Rumor has it that they will be—perhaps have already been—hand-picked from one of the camps. They will be artisans, mostly. Builders, carpenters. Farmers, too. People logically suited to be part of such an advance party. Fewer than two hundred in all, but enough to use for a major international propaganda effort."

Miriam started to shake. "Solomon," she said. She gripped Perón's arm. "You must do it for me. You must arrange for Solomon to be on that ship."

"Erich would never allow it," Perón said.

"Then," Miriam said quietly, "he must not know until it is too late."

"You cannot get your hopes up, Miriam," Perón said. "This may not be possible. Besides, from what you have told me your Solomon is hardly an artisan. Did you not say that he is a scholar by avocation and a bookkeeper by trade?"

"He has the heart and mind of a professor. He is also a linguist. There will surely be a need for someone able to speak…what is the native language?"

"Sad to say, my education is lacking. I admit, I do not know the answer." He thought for a moment. "How good is his French? I do know that the French influence is enormous in that part of the world."

"He speaks excellent French," Miriam said, "As do I."

"I am not sure how much I can influence the choice of settlers," Perón said. "This much I promise you. I will do what I can."

"And I," Miriam said, "will do what I must."

PART II

"Never shall I forget these things, even if I am condemned to live as long as God Himself."

— Elie Wiesel

Chapter Twenty-Three

June 1939

The dying sun cast an orange glow across a sky feathered by clouds and painted a web of intricate shadows on the concrete at Solomon's feet. He laughed bitterly at God's sense of the absurd.

Why provide such beauty to watch over a concentration camp?

Sol stood at the hub of Sachsenhausen, one of Germany's monuments to Hell. Within the pyramid of the outer fences, the camp's eighty-six barracks, hospital, and guards' quarters spread out behind him in an enormous semicircle. As he looked at the barbed, electrified wire and at the sentry towers placed at one hundred and eighty meter intervals, a seductive thought occurred to him: one false move—a single motion toward freedom—would set the whole barbaric machine into motion. For a split second...before they mowed him down...he would be in control.

A surge of power infused him. His heartbeat increased. Contemplating death, he pulsed with new life. It was a heady sensation, meaningless to anyone not in his position, probably beyond their comprehension. With a single, casual pace beyond the boundaries set for him and his fellow prisoners, he could impel a small army into action, disrupt its mealtime, create disorder. Best of all, he could add to the mound of paperwork with which the ever-so-meticulous Nazis documented their days and nights.

Then the crack of the Kapo's whip announced evening roll. As Sol turned to stare at the barracks guard, his sense of hopelessness returned to ask, "And so?" He discarded the urge for martyrdom and began to search the faces of the gathering inmates for his friends, Hans Hannes and Misha, who had been missing for two days—they and that damned pederast, Captain Hempel.

Instinctively Sol glanced in the direction of *Pathologie*. The hospital's windows winked obscenely at him in the sunset, like the ten diamond-fruits of the Kabbalah's Tree of Life. Inside lay the face of death, eyes shiny and open and eager...promising, finally, a surfeit of terror.

Roll call began and ended, and still he stared at the building, certain that it held the answers to his friends' disappearance. Yet he hoped. Always hoped...and prayed.

Two screams came from *Pathologie*.

The Kapo, a convicted murderer elevated to the status of barracks guard, turned toward the building and smiled. He intoned the daily litany: "You must make ever greater efforts to honor the Reich and throw off the burden of the Jewish yoke—dismissed!"

The prisoners moved toward the barracks, all but Sol who set out grimly in the direction of *Pathologie*. Before he reached it, the clopping of a horse's hooves rang through the yard, and Captain Otto Hempel emerged from between the hospital and another barracks. He rode easily atop his mount and, as always, his black-muzzled wolfhound loped alongside. The boy, Misha Czisça, staggered in the lead, his movements impaired by a lidded, army-green watering can attached to a strap across his shoulder. The can hung awkwardly beneath his armpit.

The horse snorted and shook its head, as if bothered by the presence of youth.

Sol whipped off his cap and snapped to attention. "Good evening, Hauptsturmführer Hempel!" Give the required greeting. Do not look at the deputy commandant. "May the Teutonic gods and the spirit of our Messiah Adolph Hitler go with you this night!" Sol added, trusting in Hempel to misread the sarcasm.

"A beautiful evening."

His tone benign, Hempel reined up beside Solomon. Leather creaking, he rose in the saddle like a handsome lord-overseer—lean, without appearing hard-muscled, silver-haired without appearing elderly. Except for a red and black scarf around his neck, his uniform was without decoration: the quintessential captain. "Some day the Reich will be so far-reaching, there will always be such a sky beaming over it." The captain gestured upward with his bone-handled riding crop. His other hand rested lightly on his pistol. "Such weather makes a man feel truly alive—eh, prisoner?"

"Ja, Hauptsturmführer!"

"Good! We are in agreement." He relaxed into the saddle and thrust out his boots in wordless command.

It is our duty to survive and tell the world, Sol reminded himself. *Do whatever the captain wants. Lick his boots. Shine them with your cap. Pay special attention to the instep. Say, "Ja, Hauptsturmführer."*

The horse urinated, splashing Solomon. He kept at his job.

"You are the one they call Professor, not so?"

"Ja, Hauptsturmführer."

"Your name?"

Sol held up his arm. Prisoner number 37704.

"And they call you Professor! You have the mind of a sparrow." The riding crop rose. "Your *name!*"

"Freund, Hauptsturmführer. Solomon Freund."

"I thought so." Hempel smiled as if at some private joke. "Long-time friend of Major Erich Alois."

He touched Sol between the eyes with the butt of the crop. "You will keep yourself alive. You will remain healthy in mind and body. One day you will have the privilege of testifying in a court of law about your *friend!*" Using his whip, he pointed at the puddle the horse had left. "Clean that up, then follow us."

He spurred the mount. Misha, who had not once met

Solomon's gaze, hurried to stay ahead of the animal as they headed in the direction of the *Gärtnerei*, site of the commandant's hothouses, huge flower and vegetable gardens, and—source of his greatest pride—his hog farm. Sol quickly joined them. It was dusk, and sentry spotlights swept the area. There is a world, Sol thought, where dusk is the time for drama and love.

"Take care of the roses," Hempel told the child.

Misha nodded. Dazed, he lifted the lid of his watering can, then raised on tiptoes to kiss the tip of Hempel's riding crop.

Turning to Solomon, the captain said amiably, one gentleman addressing another, "Those are the Kommandant's prize hybrids. His 'Centurians,' he calls them. They've won several awards at the Reichsblume Konkurenz in Hamburg." He drooled his expensive Indian chewing tobacco into the can. "Go with the boy. Help him tamp the soil—get a little German earth under your nails."

Misha moved to the rose beds, keening softly. Sol backed down the row and crouched beside him. The blooms smelled almost obscenely sweet after the sour odors of the camp. He glanced in Hempel's direction, wondering what lay behind his being allowed to linger here.

Hempel waved pleasantly.

Sol buried his face in a cluster of roses. Assailed by a memory he could not quite touch, he closed his eyes and placed the petals, warm and velvety, against his skin. His mother's nightgown had smelled like this, fresh out of the dresser drawer with its sachets of dried rose petals, but it was Miriam's spirit that suffused him. Miriam, the love who once...still...embodied for him all that was beautiful.

He opened his eyes and reveled in the rose's color, red as a sailor's sunset.

"Miriam," he murmured, caressing the blossom gently with his lips, as if its petals were her womanhood and he a free man making love to her for the first time, drinking in her softness.

A drop of warm liquid touched his skin. Thinking it to be one of Misha's tears and pleased that the boy had at last been able to allow himself the solace of tears, Sol looked up at him.

"I'm sorry," Misha said.

"It's nothing." Sol smiled. "If a drop of water on my arm is the worst crime you ever commit against me—"

"I'm sorry, Uncle Hans." The boy tilted the watering can. Talking to it and not to Solomon, he said, "I'm sorry. I'm sorry."

The searchlight moved and returned, capturing the child like a player on a stage. Sol stared at the fine spray of burgundy liquid. He felt another droplet on his skin. When the spotlight returned, he stared at it lying on his flesh like a perfect garnet.

"The Kommandant insists there is no better fertilizer," Hempel called out.

Sol looked from the watering can toward the captain, who nodded and laughed. A sudden urgency started Sol's heart pounding like a jackhammer. "Misha? What have you been saying!"

"They d-drained him," the boy stammered. "Like all

the others." Dry heaves caused his back to rise and fall with each exhalation as though he were an ancient pump. "Mama!" he called out. "Mama!"

"Put the can down, Misha. God of our Fathers! Put it down!" Sol took the boy by the shoulders. "Listen to me! That's not our friend in there. He's here with us. His spirit is in us both."

The boy's face tightened into a bud of hatred. He flailed his arms, hitting Solomon's chest, scratching his cheeks as he tried to break free, and spilling the remainder of the blood from the watering can as it flew from his grasp.

"One day I'll kill him." He looked up at the captain, who had dismounted and was ambling toward them. "I'll kill all of them!"

"Misha, listen to me—"

Sol stopped. The wolfhound, gliding like a phantom between the rosebushes and gardenias, had joined his master. They were now within a meter of the boy.

"Kiss it!" Hempel held out his riding crop.

Misha leaned forward and Hempel instantly twisted the handle hard against the boy's lips. "The Professor and I have business to attend to," he said. "Remain here at attention until I return."

He looked at the dog and snapped his fingers. "Guard!" Hackles raised and teeth bared, the dog moved in front of the boy, watching him with shiny eyes. Hempel shifted his gaze to Solomon. "If the boy moves so much as an eyelid, the dog will kill him. You come with me!"

They went along the west wall and cut in at

Pathologie. Sol wanted to run from the place. Beneath the harsh lights of the outer room were rows of neatly labeled jars filled with formaldehyde and human organs. Eyeballs floating in fluid watched his fear.

The captain knocked at the slightly open door of the examining room.

Doctor Schmidt looked up. "I see you found him. Well, don't just stand there. Come in, come in, both of you."

Sol blinked against the fluorescent desk lamp that turned the doctor's face into a serene blend of light and shadow. She had removed her surgical cap. Her dark, well-brushed hair cascaded across her shoulders and her eyes were soft, with expressive brows and lids set off by just the right touch of make-up.

"I didn't have to go far to find him, *Medizinalrat.*"

"Today we had a fruitful session with a friend of yours," the physician told Solomon. "His name was…" She ran a slim finger down a long list. "Ah, yes. Here it is. Hans Hannes. Original name Hans Fink." Smiling sweetly, she added, "He called out your name several times."

"What do you want with me, *Medizinalrat?*"

"All in good time," the woman said. "We try to observe the niceties around here whenever possible, don't we, Otto?" She looked up at the captain. They exchanged a confidential nod.

Hempel picked up a folder from the desk. Opening it, he drew out a paper rimmed with a logo of golden wreathwork. "Why we have to go through these formalities is beyond my understanding."

"It is the law," Schmidt said.

Fighting to keep calm, Solomon squinted at the tiny print. He could read the line in bold and the signature beneath it:

IN ORDER TO RID MYSELF OF MY PERVERTED SEXUAL INSTINCTS, I HEREBY APPLY FOR CASTRATION.

Hans Hannes Fink

A wave of helplessness weakened Sol's knees and he sagged against the wall. Some twisted logic dictated that castration needed the written permission of the victim. Mere sterilization—a privilege generally reserved for the handicapped, the retarded, and Jews who'd had intercourse with Aryans—could be carried out without consent. In truth, homosexuals were rarely castrated, but Hannes had suffered fiercely from priapism. That made him different...just as Sol's eye disease set him apart. He knew Schmidt must be longing to scoop out his eyeballs and add them to her collection.

"I won't sign anything," he said. "Not now. Not ever."

Hempel raised a fist and took a step forward.

"Now, Otto, you told me you needed him alive and, besides, you know how easily your blood vessels tend to break at the knuckles." Schmidt picked up what looked like a list of names printed beneath an official letterhead. "We have another reason to keep him reasonably fit, which is why I asked you to find him for me. My old friend Eichmann is taking another stab at immortality. This prisoner is on the list of those selected. See for yourself."

She handed Hempel the sheet of paper, and turned to Sol.

"In a few days you will be issued new spectacles," she said. "Meanwhile, take care of your eyes." She looked up at Hempel. "Pity. This case interested me. Freak diseases always do."

She lifted a canning jar from atop a black filing cabinet that stood behind her. Within floated testicles and a purplish penis. Holding the jar before her face, she studied the contents. The jar magnified her face like a mirror at the Panoptikum. "Did I tell you, Otto, I have you to thank for this wonderful specimen? You were the one who first talked to me of tabun. Though your interest in it has, of course, a different base than mine, your enthusiasm led me to acquire a small supply of it in liquid form."

She set the jar at the desk edge nearest Hempel and went on speaking as if she had forgotten Sol's presence.

"Have you any idea how effective tabun is?" she asked.

"I just know the nerve gas works," he said.

"*How* it works, that's the wonder!…inhibits the action of the enzyme cholinesterase…causes uncontrolled muscular contractions, followed by paralysis…and, finally, death." Her eyes were bright. "I placed a few drops on Hannes' spine during coitus, while he was performing in our brothel. You should've seen how it affected him—even with his special, shall we say, equipment." She put her hand on the jar and leaned forward confidentially. "When I was young, I read how Darwin cut off the legs of a frog engaged in coitus, and the frog continued to perform." She tapped the jar lid with a fingernail. "*This* rivals...no, *eclipses* Darwin's experiment." She gave Hempel a warm smile, then turned to Solomon. "Otto has arranged for this specimen to be shipped to Berlin via his mother in Strasbourg. She is fascinated with our work here."

"How can you, a doctor, do this?" Sol asked. Despite feeling weak with fear, he wanted to take hold of her neck and wring it like a chicken from his uncle's barnyard.

Schmidt patted the jar. "You think me a monster? You are wrong. I admire you Jews. You gave the world its first judicial system, its first efficient society, its first schools, some of its first doctors. The list of your achievements is endless."

She leaned closer. Perhaps realizing that the tops of her breasts were showing, she spread a hand across her lapels. Sol pulled back, as if she were diseased. He looked around for Otto Hempel. The captain had gone.

Relieved, Sol told himself that he had imagined it all. Misha and Hans were safely back at the barracks. He must take care to reconnect with reality.

"Listen to me," Schmidt said. Her voice held a lover's caress. Sol's gaze rested on the jar at the edge of her desk, the momentary flare of hope extinguished. "Though science and medicine interest me above all else," she said, "you would be hard pressed to find a better humanitarian."

CHAPTER TWENTY-four

Crouched against the barracks wall opposite Hans' empty bunk, Solomon watched those fellow inmates who were awake mill about the area. They were skeletal. Stuporous. Compliant. Gray, amorphous figures in striped pajamas.

May their souls find rest, he thought, trying one more time to pray for Hans. One more time, he could not find the words. No matter how deeply inside he reached, all he found was pain. He could not even pray for the living anymore; the prayers stuck in his throat. He just kept seeing that jar in *Pathologie* and hearing Schmidt's last words: *"You'd be hard pressed to find a better humanitarian."* And something else…he could not quite remember what…about Eichmann, and spectacles, and some absurdity about taking care of himself!

JANET BERLINER AND GEORGE GUTHRIDGE

Not that anything Schmidt had said mattered. He did not care what diabolical scheme she and her colleagues were cooking up. He did not need new glasses. He needed to be left alone, to do nothing. Think nothing. To reach the state of *ayin ha'gamur*, that complete nothingness which the Kabbalah described as the last obstacle facing rational thought when it has reached the limits of its capacity.

He had imagined that when he reached that limit, that place where human understanding would be insufficient to make sense of the world, his consciousness would explode into nothingness.

But *ayin* was still denied him.

"*Oh God, let me die*," a woman pleaded, her voice filling the void inside his head. "*Let me die.*" An infant mewled and something laughed, something at best partly human.

Cradling himself with bony arms, Solomon began to rock. Back and forth, back and forth.

Remembering.

…He saw himself as a boy Misha's age, being battered by disembodied voices and sounds that only he could hear. Painfully, he recalled the day that brought shape and form to those voices and sounds, bringing him a series of visions that terrified him beyond measure. He heard the squeal of brakes and the explosions that shattered the sun and gentle silence of a Sabbath afternoon. He saw his friend's car careen to the side of the road and looked at the face of death through cobalt-blue eyes filled with tears. He swam inside them, defenseless and drawn into the dying; he felt again the thing take residence in his body....

The thing—that was how he had thought of it then, before he learned about dybbuks and ghosts, before his secret voices gave way to visions. A *thing*—bringing black moods, long silences, the easy tears and dark circles that came from sleepless nights spent agonizing over what sin he might unknowingly have committed to warrant such punishment.

He still did not know the source of the visions, but he had come to understand that the dybbuk inside him had given substance to the voices. It was the key to the visions. Strange, he thought, how repetition brought mundanity in its wake, no matter how fearsome or bizarre the experience. He had long since moved away from his childhood fear, through acceptance and curiosity, and on to a hunger for interpretation and understanding.

Some visions came to him in their entirety, but came only once; others began slowly, building over years like serial stories. And there were fragments, too, that came and went so quickly they might have been dreams had they not contained the common strains that appeared in each one: each had its hero, its victim, its dybbuk; each spoke of a Jewish homeland in, of all places, Madagascar.

Sitting there, he catalogued the visions: Jews forced to work for National Socialism, building bombs, fighting on the Russian Front, helping with medical experiments. Jews assassinating politicians, gathering huge sums of money for the Nazi cause, operating a death squad from a unique type of airplane they called a helicopter. There was even a Jew who taught others to counterfeit foreign currency, thereby ruining enemy economies.

Ultimately, each had a single, overriding theme: Nazi abuse of Jewish assets and abilities.

He would distract Schmidt by telling her some of the stories, he decided. She could study his flawed second sight to find out why he could not apply his powers to something as simple as knowing what was going to happen to his friends. Better yet, to preventing it from happening. That would surely be more entertaining than diseased eyeballs.

The flashes of light that inevitably heralded a vision interrupted what was becoming a bitter discourse with himself. "*Dayenu*—enough!" he said out loud. "Oh Lord of the Universe, grant me *ayin.*"

But the flashes of light came again, followed this time by the cobalt-blue glow that also presaged every vision. God is apparently not listening, he thought wryly, or perhaps the patent on the concept of nothingness applied only to realms of theosophy—to His universe and not the devil's. Even for God, it must be difficult to distinguish a single voice in an outcry from Hell.

Since there was no escape, Sol gave himself up to a potpourri of scenes from a past and future as familiar to him now as a series of old films many times revisited ——

A full moon shines down on the domed keep of a ruined castle and on a dozen beehives rising up like ancient columns behind a black man. He is lanky and rawboned, bald except for a bowl of hair at the crown of his skull. His left shoulder is draped with a white cloak. He sits on his haunches, forearms across knees—hands turned palms up, fingers crabbed. "I want to be considered a *whole* Jew!" His face is etched with anguish, his voice strained with emotion. "Can't they understand that?"——

The scene faded. Another replaced it. Sol repositioned his body and watched——

A bulb in a blue metal collar hangs garishly from a slatted-board ceiling. The bulb swings to and fro, to and fro, over the head of the tall, aproned doctor who has bumped into it and set it in motion. The room is awash in the cobalt reflection of the bulb's collar. The stench that fills the air is like that of aged Limburger cheese.

"Welcome to the world of the dead!"——

A hand shook Sol's shoulder. "Herr Freund," Misha whispered. "They are taking some of us somewhere tomorrow. I heard them talking about an experiment, and I saw trucks."

Sol saw an image of an Opel Blitz, its canvas back open like a carnival crier's mouth. "I prefer to die right here."

"Come to bed. Please!" The boy shook him harder. "You need to be rested."

Sol's unresisting head snapped back and forth against the boards. His lids were heavy, his eyes listless, his energy so sapped he had not enough left to curse the guards. He could see the boy, but the child's face had a gauzy, pointillist quality. He thought of Hans. He is drinking honey wine with Emanuel, he told himself, deliberately confusing reality with the vision of Ethiopia.

"Don't you know what's happening to you!" the boy screamed. "You're willing yourself to die."

Yes, Sol thought. He was becoming *Schmuckstück*— costume jewelry—an ornament bejeweled by sores.

"Please be Herr Freund again," Misha begged. "Please don't die! I don't want the ghost inside you to jump into me!"

With slowly mounting resolve, Sol pulled himself away from the opiate of introspection. "What could you know of ghosts?" he asked Misha.

"Everything."

Misha's gesture took in the world. Solomon smiled. Even here, now, lost among the forgotten souls of Sachsenhausen, childhood encompassed enviable absolutes. "Why would my…*ghost* choose to go to you?"

"If I were right next to you and you were dying," the boy said, "it would come to me. I know about dybbuks. They're evil dead people, ones whose dreams we live in."

"If you believe in such things, Misha, you must stay away from me."

Though clearly terrified, the boy shook his head.

Even in his state of apathy, Solomon knew the urgency of the boy's fear of dybbuks—those souls unable to transmigrate to a higher world because of the enormity of their sins; souls that sought refuge in the bodies of living persons, causing instability, speaking foreign words through their mouths. He remembered begging his mentor, Beadle Cohen, to help him exorcise the dybbuk. The beadle had led him, instead, to the Kabbalah.

"You are strong, Solomon," the beadle insisted. *"The dybbuk has opened doors for you to see what other men cannot. Continue to be strong and it will leave as it came. Meanwhile, try to understand its message."*

Why had that alien and separate personality cloven to him! If he were guilty of some secret sin that had created an opening for the unquiet soul to enter his own, it was one committed without knowledge or malice. Now, at nearly thirty, he believed that goodness rested in a single tenet of life—in treating your fellow man as you would be treated. Had that been his sin? Had he, at not quite thirteen, neglected to live by that creed?

Taking pity on the child, Sol let himself be led to Hans' bunk. They lay down together. Misha put his head on Sol's shoulder. A tear pressed out of his right eye and trickled down his cheek. He swiped at it angrily, as if it had no right to be there and prove him human.

Sol wanted to cry with him, but who was he to allow himself that luxury? He was nothing special, nor was his suffering. He closed his eyes and held them shut. He wanted nothing more of this world. "Tell me exactly what you meant just now," he whispered.

"My papa is…was a rabbi. One time a man came to the house so Papa could get rid of the ghost-thing inside him. Papa called it a dybbuk."

"What makes you think I have a dybbuk inside *me?*"

"Your eyes are strange, like his," the child said. "Papa said the man saw things we could not see. Heard them too. You know. Inside his head. Things from the past and from the future."

Sol thought again about the recurring figures in his visions: the Ethiopian Jew, his black head bald but for the crown of hair that looked like a *yarmulke;* an old man and a woman, robed in tattered blankets and bent over a steaming teapot; an infant held up to a horned totem by a disembodied brown hand. He knew of no such men, no such baby, no such realities. And the other visions, like Göring talking about something called critical mass, or experiments on the mummified corpse of an ancient Hebrew.

How tired he was of it all—of visions of people in a past and future that made no sense.

"Do you know what legends are, Misha? Myths?" he asked.

The boy nodded. "Papa called them stories based on a grain of truth."

"Did your papa rid the man of his dybbuk?"

Misha disentangled himself and turned on his side. "When the ghost came out of the man, I thought it went into me," he said in a whisper. "Papa laughed and said he had made sure the closest thing to the man was a big black cat. That was right before…"

"Before what?" Sol asked.

"Before they took Mama and Papa away. Papa put me outside on the fire-landing. He said, 'Mishele, now *you* must be quiet as a ghost.' I heard noise. Shouting. I stayed out there all night. When I went back in, the front door had been knocked down. Mama and Papa were gone. Sometimes..."

The boy hesitated. "Sometimes," he went on, "I think I turned into a ghost and that's why the Nazis punished Mama and Papa." He was trembling, weak with memories. "Maybe the Hauptsturmführer is my real papa, as he says...."

"Stop that!" Sol insisted. The child must have an aunt, an uncle, someone who could attempt his release. Such miracles did happen. Money. Someone knew someone willing to...

Sol stopped himself. There were dreams and there were dreams. Better to be *Schmuckstück* than to hope falsely, for that could just bring deeper despair. Especially to Misha. Hempel would never let the child go. Not alive.

"Listen to me, Misha. I cannot, will not, return to that hospital alive."

He lay on Hans' bunk, listening to the echo of his own words inside his head. Hempel had recently ordered the windows and doors kept closed for "security." Sweat, breath, and body effluvia mingled in a heat as oppressive as a steam bath. With less than a foot of sleeping space per person, the inmates slept spoon-style, arms thrown about each other like caricatures of connubial bliss. He could not so much as lift an arm. In his own bunk, no more than a hand's width separated his face from the roof joist. Searching for air in the stifling barracks, he had worked free a composition tile. By lifting a bit of the roofing, he could breathe in the night.

Whatever this was, it was not living.

When sleep had claimed the boy, Sol made himself a promise. He would have no more of this. Head twisted toward the moonlight, he planned his own execution. He would carry no more stones, hobble no more with bleeding feet along the shoe-track designed to test footwear for good German soldiers. Above all, he would not lie alive beneath Schmidt's instrument.

If they wanted his eyes or his testicles, they could remove them from a corpse.

Gripping the edge of the bunk, he wriggled out of it. Below and beside him were the sweat-slicked faces of over three hundred wretches hacking and choking in their sleep...swaddled in striped bunting, asleep in the Führer's arms.

Sol moved among them, careful to awaken no one. Oddly calm, he made his way toward the far corner of the barracks, where the inmates had hung a tattered blanket to provide suicides with a triangle of privacy. As he reached out to pull aside the blanket, it occurred to him that he might not find the noose empty. There were not too many days or nights that it went unused.

The noose dangled empty and alluring.

As if wanting a witness to his act, he shuffled to the window and wiped away the accumulation of breath with his sleeve. The sentry tower was silhouetted by a new moon, and he could see a helmeted guard bending his head to light a cigarette. A good German soldier, smoking on duty? Shame!

He turned to face the noose and bumped into Misha. "Herr Freund, you mustn't." The boy tugged at Sol.

"You should not be here," Sol said sternly.

The boy let go and took a step backward. "I *am* here," he said, "and I will stay. You're in this camp because of me. The Nazis would never have found you if I hadn't led them to you. Only I didn't know it was going to happen. It will be your fault if your dybbuk finds me—but you will *know*...."

The sentry light swept across the window, highlighting the expression of raw fear—and courage—on the young face. The child was right, Sol thought, relinquishing the moment. He must alleviate Misha's fear.

Then he would be free to do this for himself.

Chapter Twenty-five

Under cover of night, the religious among the almost-dead gathered outside Barracks 18 to pray for themselves. Sometimes they were led by a rabbi. More often than not, the task of leading the prayers fell to the physically strongest among them. The bodies of those who died during prayers simply lay there until the morning detail carried them away, along with the others who had died in their bunks during the night. For the time being, the Nazis found this piling of corpses convenient and chose not to interfere.

Tonight was *Shabbas*—Sabbath. Rumor had it that a rabbi known for the depth and breadth of his studies had recently been brought into the camp. If the reb, whose name Sol had not been able to ascertain, remained among the living, Sol thought, he would be conducting the Service. When he had first come to the camp, Sol had tried, for Misha's sake, to find out whether the boy's parents had ended up here. Often, people were sent to Oranienburg first from Berlin, so he had asked everyone who had been there if they had met Rabbi Czisça and his wife. He discovered only, from someone who had shared the journey with them, that they had indeed been transported to Oranienburg. Whether or not one or both of them were still there, alive, was a question that remained unanswered. Since men and women were separated upon arrival, here at Sachsenhausen and at the holding camp in Oranienburg, he was unlikely to learn more about Misha's mama. As for the rabbi, Misha's papa, he would ask that again tonight. Perhaps this new rabbi would turn out to be Rabbi Czisça himself; such coincidences abounded in the strange subculture of the camp.

"Go back to sleep, Misha," Sol whispered, saying nothing of this to the boy for fear of raising his hopes in vain. "I will find the rabbi and he will get rid of the dybbuk so that you need not be afraid."

He led the boy to the bunk and made it out to Barracks 18 without incident. In the quadrangle separating the barracks from Nazi quarters, thirty men hung from a crossbar. Each time the searchlights swept the area, he could see them jerking and convulsing. Earlier that evening, they had been hooked onto the crossbar by the same rope that cuffed their wrists together behind their backs. Though they would be dead by morning, in their present pain they begged for death now. Huddled against the wall, in the blackness of the night, Sol listened to their wails and to the chanting of the congregation of the dying.

Almost at once, as if their lament had drawn it to him, the strains of a Bach concerto began inside Sol's head— —

Gossamer veils of blue dust-moted light filter through a stained-glass window and onto a man seated at a pipe organ. Blond and broad-shouldered, he is obviously as athletic as he is musically talented. His outward appearance is that of the idealized German farm boy.

The Bach concerto he is playing reverberates throughout the tall reaches of a rococo church that looks as if it were once a castle. Pale blue Grecian designs and rectangular moldings trimmed with gilt separate the walls from the ceilings. Everywhere there are frescoes with Biblical themes—

"Who is there?"

The words, heavy with Spanish accent, dissipated the vision and the music and the blue light. Sol turned toward the voice. A searchlight swept the area and he caught a glimpse of dark skin.

"Solomon Freund."

"Welcome. I'm Reb Nathanson."

Sol felt a deep sense of disappointment and realized how much he had been hoping to be able to bring the boy good news. "I need help, Reb," he said without further preamble.

"Who among us does not?"

Despite himself, Sol chuckled softly at the hint of humor in the rabbi's voice. "I have long believed there is a dybbuk in me," he said, feeling more at ease. "The time has come to have it removed so that I can—"

"I understand," the rabbi said. "I have dealt with such matters before. If you are right, God willing I can make it disappear. At worst, I will persuade it to leave you for one of those wretches on the crossbar. It can cause no harm in that labyrinth of the dying."

"Can that be done?"

"Anything is possible. Now be quiet. It is enough to risk our lives for a purpose. For idle chatter it is stupidity."

"Is there…?" Sol restrained himself from laughing aloud. He had been about to ask if there were danger in the ritual. What could be more dangerous than being out here after roll call, shrouded only by the night and threatened by the constant sweep of the searchlights? If the Nazis so much as suspected the performance of a Kabbalistic ritual inside Sachsenhausen….

"I'm ready," he whispered, though for what he could not imagine. "What do you want me to do?"

"Lie flat on your belly. That way, if you must cry out, the ground will muffle the noise. I will put my hands on your head and keep them there until I have removed the demon."

If there is one, Sol thought, lying down.

The searchlights passed again and he waited for the rabbi to begin…what? An exorcism in a charnel house! The incongruity of it was absurd. "Aren't you afraid it will enter *you?*" he asked.

"It wouldn't dare." Moving soundlessly, the rabbi

straddled Solomon's back. "I'm sorry there is no time for niceties." His face was so close that his warm breath raised the hairs on Solomon's neck.

"You are named after Solomon, the wise king and arch magician of the Hebrews." The rabbi was panting, bearing down hard. "He created the incantation I am about to use. When you are ready, repeat it with me until I tell you to stop: *Lofaham, Solomon, Iyouel, Iyisebaiyu*—Leave this man and give yourself to…"

"*Lofaham, Solomon, Iyouel, Iyisebaiyu*…"

"Don't stop! When I feel the dybbuk coming, I am going to use an ancient Hebraic incantation. Take no notice. You keep repeating those four words."

The taste of bile filled Sol's mouth and a wave of nausea engulfed him. He saw, again, some of the people in his visions—a woman, eyes anguished, begging to die. A blanket-robed old man, lashes and brows furred with frost, kneeling in the snow beside the frozen body of a young soldier. The Ethiopian, staring unmoving at the disemboweled body of his ancestor.

"Prepare yourself," the rabbi said softly. "If it is in you, it will fight to stay there."

More than anything else in the world, Sol wanted to put an end to this. Then he thought of Hans Hannes Fink lying mutilated on a stainless steel table, and he chanted the words of that other Solomon over and over, until he could hear only the ragged sound of his own voice, feel nothing but the throbbing in his head, see nothing but the sweep of the searchlight.

"*Shabriri*—Diminish!" the rabbi commanded.

Silence. The soft pad of a prisoner's bare feet.

"Are you in pain?" the rabbi whispered, his voice gentle.

Sol felt the dirt beneath his cheek…and nothing else.

The searchlights swept by, catching the crossbar where the hanging men had ceased their movements. He stared at their bodies.

"Say the words again."

"Lofaham, Solomon—"

"Stop." The rabbi removed his hands. "All I can do for you, Solomon Freund, is ask for God's blessing. You had a dybbuk in you once. It is no longer there, but I believe it remains flesh of your flesh and blood of your blood. Whatever is in you *now* was always yours—and always will be." Very softly he said, "Let us pray together."

Holding his hands above Solomon's head, he began the traditional blessing: "*Boruch Ato Adonoy, Elohaynoo Melech Hoolom.* Blessed art Thou, O Lord our God, King of the Universe…"

Flooded with memories, Sol heard little more until the final words of the prayer. *May the Lord make His countenance to shine upon you and bring you peace. Amen.*

More at peace with himself than he had been in a long time, Sol returned to his barracks. He went straight to the corner that held the noose and unhooked it from its nail. Holding it firmly, he mounted the stool. With his head touching the rafter, he looked out across the camp. The other barracks lay like a series of crypts in a moonlit cemetery. Would God forgive him this act?—and what, he wondered, lay beyond the moon's gray-gold shroud? Some other reality? Or would he at last attain that state of complete nothingness that called to him like a teat to a baby lamb?

Certainly the act of dying no longer held any great mystery. A body was a body—nothing more. He would be stacked in the morgue, and Misha and the other boys who were put to work there would search his orifices for valuables. The Nazis allowed a noose per barracks out of expedience, not mercy. Each dead Jew made the Führer's task easier. Nevertheless, suicide was not popular on camp reports; Schmidt would certify "death due to accidental strangulation" or "suffocation as the result of pneumonia."

He closed the curtain and tested the rope. It held firm. Pulse racing, he put the noose over his head. The knot cuddled against the back of his neck. He fondled it. Where best to place it? he wondered. Where it lay now, it might cause him to twist and struggle several more seconds than necessary.

Cupping the knot in his palm, he turned it to the left and drew the rope tight. Gazing at the moonlight ribbed among the rafters, he took a deliberate, calming breath and shut his eyes. The stench of the blankets wafted into his sinuses. Around him the sound of snoring rose in crescendo. His pulse pounded behind his eardrums and the muscles along his calves tensed. He wondered if the Nazis would take his teeth; those of hanged men were supposed to be important in sorcery. Far away, he heard the mocking laughter of

Erich Alois Weisser. He thought he heard the old man of his visions speak longingly of the taste of ginger tea.

"Yiskadal..." he began. But mourning for himself seemed blasphemous. Perhaps Miriam would

Miriam.

"I'm so tired, Miri," he whispered. "So very tired."

Stepping from the stool, he kicked it gratefully aside. The noose around his neck held tight. His legs dangled. His body turned beneath the rope.

"*You must live, Solomon. Live!*" said Emanuel, the Ethiopian Jew. "*You have not yet fulfilled your destiny.*"

Could the voices not leave him in peace even now, at the moment of dying?

"*Survival, Solomon! Therein lies your duty!*" said Margabrook, the old man wrapped in the blanket. "*There are things to be done that only you can do.*"

"*How dare you, Solomon!*" said Lise Meitner, raising her voice to be heard above the organ strains of the Bach Concerto he had heard earlier. "*Only God has the right to order the Universe.*"

Sol tried to respond. He could not. His own voice was no more his than his body, and the dark that surrounded him was an emollient, amniotic and safe.

"Don't you dare die, Herr Freund!"

Misha's voice reached out from the other side of death and Solomon opened his eyes. Moon-bathed rafters wavered and wheeled above him, and the sounds of his own gasping and choking roared in his ears. Shadows exploded before his eyes. A dry fire seared his throat. He clawed at the rope around his neck, tearing at flesh he knew to be his own.

"I've got your legs! Grab the joist!"

Through retinas that threatened to burst, Sol saw a hand groping at the air in slow motion, as if its fingers had a separate existence. He was a puppet, dangling, his strings intact, watching his hand—the puppeteer—relearn the art of manipulating its toy.

Grab the joist, he tried to tell the hand.

His fingers clutched the wood. His vision cleared. It became intense, precise. He saw his fingers grip the wood, watched the splinters peel off and pierce his flesh. The pain was sweet. He leaned into it, accepting it with gratitude as, suddenly, he knew he was not ready to die.

With God-given strength, the child bolstered Sol's weight, suspending him like an upended log. For an instant, a window in time, gravity abandoned its grip upon Sol. It was time enough for him to loosen and open the noose.

Collapsing to the floor on top of Misha, he clutched his throat and struggled for breath. Stale barracks air passed in and out of his throat, cool and sweet as late-blooming lilac. The voices of the other prisoners demanding quiet greeted him like a symphony. He wanted to embrace them all. Then their voices stilled, and he was faced with the certain knowledge that he would never again have the passing courage to put an end to his life.

Cradling his face in the crook of his arm, he wept for himself and for all of the others without choices.

"You're...squishing...me!"

An elbow poked Solomon's ribs. Still weeping, he rolled aside.

"Why did you do it, Misha?" he asked, his voice hoarse from its recent battle with the rope.

"I owed you your life."

"So we are even," Sol said seriously. "Now go to your bunk. There is little enough time left for rest."

"You, too, Freund," someone said. "Hang yourself or go to sleep!"

Shaking, Sol arose and climbed up into his own bunk. Death had been denied him; as for sleep, there was little chance of that tonight. Some things, he thought, were a matter of choice, while others....

Just how much of life, he wondered, was truly a matter of choice? How much inevitable, given the impact of the collective unconscious of the past on man's actions?

A new idea came to him.

What if there were another collective unconscious, a storehouse that contained *future* knowledge? Imagine how *that* would impact man's present behavior!

The concept exhilarated him. Was *this* what he was meant to learn from the voices and visions that had plagued him through life and tried to keep him from dying? Nothing happened without reason, of that he was convinced. Yet was not what had happened to him and to his people insane?

Willing, for the first time, to try to induce the second sight with which he had been blessed—or damned— he lifted his secret place of roofing and closed his eyes. Perhaps the answers to his questions lay somewhere in his past. He would journey there through his own memories and through those of the two people with whom his life had been inextricably bound.

For what was left of the night, he journeyed through his own past...and Erich's...and Miriam's, but the answers to his questions still eluded him. All that was clear was that yesterday he and Misha had watered the commandant's roses with Hans' blood. That yesterday, he had tried to take his own life. And that the moment had passed. He could not give in now. He had to survive, if not for his own sake then for Misha's. For all of the Mishas, and for his mother and Recha, if they were alive.

For Miriam, if she still cared.

She had no place here, so he must not think of her except in the small dark hours when he could not help himself. Then, listening to the weeping and hacking, smelling the odor of death in the barracks, he would balance his love for her with his hatred of Erich, and wonder which was stronger.

C HAPTER TWENTY-SIX

As Misha had predicted, a line of trucks stood outside the camp. Their tailgates were down, and the back ends yawned open. Without being told, Sol knew that he and Misha were about to be swallowed up. Further than that, he refused to speculate, even when he, the boy, and over a hundred inmates, selected for whatever the Nazis had dreamed up, stepped through the gates of Hell and into the waiting trucks.

Always in the past, the selections had meant a new work detail, at one of the Krupp factories perhaps, or a transfer to another camp. A worse camp, though it was hard to believe that such places existed. Still, he refused to theorize. He accepted the clothes that were flung at him, *real* clothes, held his arm out to be vaccinated, watched to see if anyone dropped dead from whatever was introduced into their veins, and climbed into the truck. With Misha's hand in his, he listened to tailgates slam shut, and jerked forward as the vehicle set out down the road.

No one spoke on the journey. They sat on the trucks' wooden seats, backs bent, forearms on thighs, and retreated into their own worlds, jouncing without complaint and staring at the metal floor's landscape of scraped paint. When the trucks halted, they spilled out. Prodded by guards, they clumped along a dusty, unpaved track toward a farmhouse that stood alone on a hill just beyond. Few of them looked up. Those who did, Sol among them, saw no Oranienburg lines of Jew-haters, no quarry, no shoe track. No one was bludgeoned or shot for faltering.

Around the fields, around the farmhouse, was the greatest miracle of all.

There was no wire.

No electrified, barbed, garroting wire, ready to be slipped for sport around the neck.

At the end of the dusty track they entered the huge farmhouse.

Holding firmly onto Misha's hand, Sol looked around him—at crumbling plaster walls and a floor which had been torn up in numerous places, revealing dirt below. The air within the house seemed preternaturally still and reeked of mildew. Clearly the place had been closed up for a long time.

Men coming in behind him forced him forward, away from the apparent safety of the first room into what looked more like a great hall than a farmer's quarters. His mind took in the impossible reality of a dozen crates marked with Red Cross stencils, knowing the guards had played such tricks before, replacing the precious cargo with body parts or human excrement.

A small murmuring began, but neither Sol nor Misha spoke. Then, with a suddenness that smacked of careful staging, an exceptionally tall, café-au-lait-colored man stepped into the room. He appeared from behind a mocha and cream curtain which hid an alcove that reminded Sol of the one at *Die Ziggarenkiste*. The shock of his appearance was as much due to the fact that he matched the curtain, as it was to its unexpectedness. Sol might have thought he had plunged into a vision, had it not been for the tugging he felt from the small hand that clutched his.

The man who stepped into the room was a marvelous sight. His color and stature gave him the bearing of a character out of the pages of *The Arabian Nights*. He was white-haired, and swathed in a white cotton shift. A mouselike creature crawled from his collar. It glanced around with huge eyes before retreating inside the shift.

The man smiled, a smile of reassurance and security that reached his eyes.

"I am wearing a *lamba*," he said. "My shy little friend is a lemur." He paused and smiled again. "And now you have had your first lesson about Madagascar. Welcome to your first stop on the road to my island."

"*Welcome*," the man called Mengele, the one in his vision, had said, Sol remembered. "*Welcome to the world of the dead.*"

And there was another, older memory, but no less haunting: *"Send all the Jews to Madagascar. Pen them like wild dogs, tame them, and use what assets and abilities they possess for the good of humanity."*

Walther Rathenau had told him that, Sol thought, but they were not the statesman's own words. The Foreign Minister had simply been repeating what Hitler and the National Socialists espoused, even then, in the days before the Führer was empowered. Sol had been a boy, the Great War less than four years past. Rathenau died, killed by an assassin's bomb, but the ugly idea— apparently born long before Hitler—had not.

The brown man stopped smiling. "Have you listened to your dreams, little sparrow?" he asked, looking directly at Solomon. "Have you learned from them?"

A chill tiptoed down Sol's spine. A gypsy woman had said almost the same thing to him once, long ago. And how did this man, apparently an African, know his childhood nickname? Was Erich behind this new madness?

"I am Bruqah," the African said, "a member of the first tribe to inhabit the island to which you are bound."

As he pulled the curtain fully aside, Solomon almost expected to see his father hanging by the neck. Instead, he saw two sagging shelves, filled with dozens of books. "Some I brought with me from my island," the man said, "others I find…found…in second-hand bookstores in Berlin." He lifted a rolled-up paper from the corner, glanced around as if assuring himself they were out of Nazi earshot, and said, "Maps, too. The Nazis have not yet burned all books. I wonder why they bother to burn books of the world when they wish to burn the world itself?"

He stepped forward and put a hand on Misha's head. "You are safe here, little one," he said to the boy. He looked at Sol, as if imploring him not to counter the lie. "Within the hour, the Nazis will order the Red Cross boxes opened."

Before Sol could say anything, the man stepped back into the alcove and was gone—doubtless, Sol thought, past some panel and into another room or into a passageway that led out of the building. Like going down into the cellar beneath the tobacco shop, where lay the sewer, and the rats, and Sol's memories.

Within the hour, the Red Cross boxes were opened. The inmates were instructed to eat their fill. They fell upon the food, but having been so long deprived, they could not eat much. Even the little they did consume made many of them retch.

Later, Bruqah returned.

Then began the first of many lectures, the African speaking to Sol in French—apparently more comfortable for him, despite his perfectly reasonable command of German—and listening intently as Sol sifted and interpreted for the others. Sol did not always fully understand what he heard, and had to ask Bruqah for explications. Occasionally, he was able to embellish with what he remembered from his own books, read so many years ago.

Madagascar lay, Bruqah and then Solomon related,

in the Indian Ocean, off Africa's southeast coast. The world's fourth largest island, it was an enigma beside which many of Africa's darkest secrets paled. Having broken away from the mainland a hundred million years ago, it developed a unique flora and fauna. Its northern rain forests, the world's densest, teemed with orchids and lemurs; the spiny deserts of the south were home to latex trees, whose sap caused blindness, and to harpoon burrs which tore flesh to ribbons. Until they were hunted to extinction about a thousand years ago, pygmy hippos roamed the land. There, too, stalked the giant, flightless Aepyornis—the elephant bird known as the *roc* in the Sinbad story—whose rare, semifossilized eggs, still found on occasion, were worth a fortune.

Perhaps even more startling than its plants and animals was the fact that the island, only two hundred and fifty miles from the mainland, had remained uninhabited until five hundred B.C. Even then, the settlers arrived not from Africa but from Java, three thousand miles to the east. Only later came the people of what were now Mozambique and Somalia, followed by Arabs and, finally—the last to add people on the island—waves of pirates, mostly British.

"Why Madagascar, Herr Professor?" a man asked on the third day.

The remark was a miracle, Sol thought, for the silence of the past days had been that of men who had lost the will to question. He hoped that the one question would trigger a barrage of others, but his hope was in vain. The hush that followed made him wonder if the others remained quiet because they had lost the will to question *anything*. Were they disinterested, or simply more interested in the question than the questioning?

"We Jews are to be given a homeland," Sol said, choosing not to argue about the man's means of address.

"He who gave us Sachsenhausen has had a change of heart?" the man said.

With a brisk movement of his fingers, Sol motioned everyone closer. As they scooted forward, it occurred to him how natural it felt for him to be before them in this manner. He had always been shy, but he felt no shyness now. Satisfaction warmed him.

"I think Hitler, our Führer," he raised his voice to make it easier for eavesdroppers or in the likely event that there was an informer among them, "wishes to exercise control," he had to restrain himself from saying *seize control*, "of the Indian Ocean's shipping lanes…not to mention helping the Italians maintain their presence in Ethiopia, the southern entrance to the Red Sea. Couple that with the larger picture. Would not world opinion side with a beneficent Führer more readily, a Führer who gave bedraggled Jews a place of their own? Who, truly, could object? The French control the island, but I have learned from Bruqah that the idea of sending Jews there *began* with them. The British have already blockaded us from emigrating to Palestine. The Arabs would surely think our presence in Madagascar less a burr than if we returned to Jerusalem. And the

South Africans, our nearest powerful neighbors, have welcomed Jewish settlement."

He watched the quiet faces.

"Then only the Malagasy might object," someone said, more wistfully than sarcastically.

"Yes." Solomon fought to keep the emotion from his voice as he looked at Bruqah. "Only the Malagasy."

Chapter Twenty-Seven

"I'll be waiting to hear every detail," Miriam told Erich.

He could not possibly know how profoundly she meant those words, she thought. Nor should he.

She modulated her voice carefully, making sure it contained no urgency. "Enjoy your moment. You deserve it."

"Shall I send your regards to Perón?"

"Do that." Pleased that his tone lacked any hint of the sardonic, she added, "You might even think about asking him to the estate for dinner. It wouldn't do you any harm to humor him."

A frown darkened Erich's features, but his annoyance was directed at the tie he had knotted and unknotted several times. "Do this for me, would you? I can't seem to get it right."

Relieved, she retied the knot. "Good luck," she said again, kissing him lightly. "Now go."

He put on his jacket. "I may even come to like that Perón of yours," he said. "Last time I saw him, I asked how he felt about the church. He said, 'The priest who serves best, serves dinner.'"

She laughed. He looked surprised and happy, as if he could not quite believe she might let him go without so much as a single invective about the Party. Her tongue never would be as sharp around Solomon, she thought as Erich left the room. Or would it?

Maybe Erich was right about marriage being purely a female-endorsed institution designed to annoy men. He had once asked her why women packed away romance with the wedding pictures, to be peeked at when they deigned—and then only for an instant.

As if romance had anything to do with *their* being together!

There had been moments, transient as the dream of a better tomorrow, when she had tried to believe the lie of love between them. But then the longing for Solomon returned, or her fears for him, or her guilt at living like this. There was nothing she wanted she could not have...except Solomon, and the freedom to be a Jew.

She stood at the window and watched the lights of Erich's car disappear as he drove off the estate. When she was reasonably certain he was not coming back for something he had forgotten, she finished dressing and went to the garage.

Konrad was already behind the wheel. When they got

to the Zoo Station, Werner Fink was pacing impatiently beneath the clock.

"Werner!" She kissed him hurriedly on the cheek. "Sorry I'm late. We only have a few minutes. I had to wait for Erich to leave." She looked at him more closely. His eyes spoke more than ever of hatred, and of a need for vengeance. She took hold of his arm. "What's wrong? Is it Sol?"

"I got word that my brother is dead. They said he signed a paper requesting castration. *Requesting!* My brother? They showed me the death certificate. It said, *"Adverse reaction to anaesthesia during voluntary surgery. Cause of death: Heart Failure."*

Miriam glanced at the station's clock. Eight. Thirty minutes from now Perón was due at the Reichschancellery. Time enough to hear about Solomon and about the underground, and to be a friend. She reached for Fink's hand.

"If I could blow up this whole country, I would!" he said.

To add one word was an exercise in redundancy, Miriam thought. Of the people in her life, only Erich did not fully comprehend the extent of her hatred for Germany.

"Come, I'll walk you to the car." Fink moved her through the people thronging the Zoo Station. "About Solomon—"

An iciness enveloped Miriam. What good was her planning and scheming if something had happened to Sol? She placed her free hand on her belly as if to reassure the unborn child.

Fink watched her and smiled sadly. "A new generation," he said. "Why do we do it, Miri? In a world like this, why does the human race keep propagating?"

They exited the station. She could see Konrad waiting for her across the street. "I am so terribly sorry about Hans," she said simply. "I wish there were something more I could say, or do—"

"There isn't, darling." He paused. "Look, forgive me for being so wrapped up in myself today. It's not your fault that those bastards—" He stopped. "You have been very patient with me, Miri. Let me tell you about Sol. I would not have kept you waiting had the news been anything but encouraging."

"Thank God!" Miriam let out her breath.

"When I heard about Hans, I went storming into the Bureau...in fact, the way I carried on, I can't really understand why they didn't arrest me at once. I suppose it's because I'm a public figure...one of their token gestures to the free world, at least for the moment." His tone was heavy with bitterness. "Anyway, while I was there, I asked about Solomon and they told me."

"That simple?" Miriam laughed. "I can't believe it! Erich insists he has tried everything. Poor man. Occasionally, on my better days and when he is attempting so pitifully hard to please me, I even succeed in feeling a little sorry for him. He appears to truly believe that I am deluded and that Sol is in Amsterdam."

"Maybe so." Fink sounded unconvinced. "The ways of the German bureaucracy are not to be questioned. Nevertheless, I tell you, that's exactly how it happened.

I asked—and I received. Sol and a contingent of other prisoners, excuse me—*free laborers!*—have been moved from Sachsenhausen to a holding area—"

So Perón had succeeded! Miriam felt a stab of guilt at having doubted him, tempered by annoyance that he hadn't managed to let her know. "Where? I want to see him!"

"Hold on, young lady. Not so fast. They haven't released him. They have the prisoners under heavy guard at an old, abandoned farm on the outskirts of Oranienburg. It would be far too dangerous for either one of us to go there, but I did send one of our people—a local farmer—to snoop around. The prisoners are being fed, bathed, and rested. He said it almost looks as if they're conducting some kind of school in the farmhouse. He saw Solomon—at least, the man thought it was Sol."

"How did he look?"

"How should he look? If I were you, I would prepare myself for a very different man than the one you knew." Fink glanced around. He appeared to see something that made him uneasy. "We don't have much longer," he said.

"Have our people found a new safe house?" Miriam asked. Since Sol's arrest and the loss of the sewer as a safe house, she had entered a new network. Bigger. More dangerous. Without the double blinds which, though safer, were more cumbersome. However, her role was smaller than before. She delivered messages from Werner to Konrad, who passed them on somewhere, to someone....

"Safe houses have become as difficult to find as a Nazi who can laugh at himself." Fink's grin held a little of his old wry humor.

"We must go," Konrad said, approaching them.

"Go, and God bless." Fink kissed her cheek. "I've told you everything I know. If I learn something new, I'll be in touch."

Before she could say anything more, he was gone.

"Where are you meeting with Colonel Perón?" Konrad asked, opening the car door for Miriam.

"We are to pick him up at the Hotel Adlon and drop him off near the Reichschancellery."

"And then?"

"The estate. Tonight is Erich's big night—and mine. I have to be rested when he gets home. My head needs to be clear."

"Aren't you pushing yourself a little too hard under the circumstances, Lady Miriam?"

"I'm not pushing myself hard enough!" She looked down at her belly. "Our lives are at stake!"

Juan Perón was waiting for them outside the Adlon. He was talking to a tall, café-au-lait man wearing a white caftan. In one hand the stranger held a polished, carved walking stick; in the other, a roll of ivory-colored paper.

Miriam opened the window.

The brown man stared at her and bowed as if to acknowledge that he knew her. He walked toward the car, his movements graceful and rhythmic, like a dancer moving to secret music in his head.

Both men slid onto the back seat, Perón first. She

moved over to the far side, fighting a combination of anger that her friend had allowed her to suffer for longer than was necessary and irritation at a stranger's presence. What she and Perón had to discuss was private, and not a little dangerous. Nor could the discussion be left for another time. What was he thinking of!

"This is Bruqah," the colonel said. "Bruqah...Miriam Rathenau Alois."

The man called Bruqah smiled and put out a brown hand. "So you are Miriam," he said. His voice was soft and husky, with that same trace of music she had sensed in his movements.

Despite her resentment of his being there, Miriam smiled at him. She turned to Perón. "Getting a little paunchy around the middle, aren't you, Domingo? Too many dumplings, I think."

"Domingo?" Bruqah sounded puzzled.

"My middle name." Perón eased himself into a more comfortable position.

"Where I come from, we do not have what you call middle names. We have given names and earned names, which are something like your nicknames."

"Where is it that you come from?" Miriam was fascinated by his ability to speak German without the guttural quality which most foreigners, and so many natives, imposed upon it.

"Bruqah is from Madagascar," Perón said, answering for him.

"I suppose the missionaries taught him German?"

"Missionaries taught that to save a soul, one loses life.

Not so good an arrangement, I think." As if he now saw the humor in what he had said seriously, he chuckled. "I learn your language at Lüderitz, in German South West Africa. Now I study at your university...where your colonel found me."

"You're studying German?" she asked.

"Souls of plants. What you call 'botany.'" He grinned, showing his teeth.

It was Perón's turn to chuckle. "I've never heard you voluntarily loquacious before, my friend." He looked at Miriam. "Nor have I forgotten your comment about my corporation. Are you not, perhaps, calling the kettle black?" He patted her stomach, then lifted her hand and kissed it. "Only joking, of course. You are as beautiful as ever."

"And you, Domingo, are a beautiful liar. You remember me thin and beautiful, and I try my best to preserve the illusion. The truth is, I'm fat and I'm clumsy—"

"And beautiful!" He lifted her hand and kissed it again.

"I feel fat and ugly. And tired." She fought to keep her rising panic out of her voice. Perón was studiously avoiding talk of Sol, perhaps because of Bruqah's presence, but more likely because she had been right about him in the first place. He enjoyed her company, which could have been reason enough for his agreement to try to help her and for the secret meeting and rendezvous. Sol's transfer to the farmhouse was probably a coincidence.

"Relax," Perón said. "I have not forgotten the reason

for this rendezvous, though I would prefer it were a romantic tryst."

"Can you tell me…?" She glanced at Bruqah.

Perón did not miss the implication. "He is part of the plan. Like Konrad, he is that rare creature—a trustworthy ally. Must be the Christian influence."

"I am Malagasy," Bruqah said, bristling. "We know of honor."

"The plan?" Miriam urged, determining that she would not let him know quite yet that she had already been informed about Sol's transfer to the farmhouse. "Tell me you have arranged everything, that Sol and the child and I are going to live happily ever after."

"Now you are asking me to play God," Perón said. "I have power, yes, but it is not absolute." He looked at her and smiled. "All right, my lovely and persistent Miriam. Let me tell you what I *have* been able to achieve. I spoke to Hitler and his cronies and planted my ideas…our ideas. They listened, closely if I may say so."

"And?"

"And, sweet Miriam—" He laughed at her impatience. "And my words have taken root. Solomon has been moved to a holding area—"

"I know. Werner told me."

He looked disappointed, like a child whose surprise had been spoiled.

"What else?" she asked insistently.

"I will tell you that my destination is Lüderitz. Yours is Nosy Mangabéy, a tiny island at the mouth of a bay on Madagascar's northeast coast. The roll of paper

Bruqah is holding is a series of topographical maps. I used your rationale to manipulate Solomon into the advance party. In fact, the others call him the Professor. Bruqah has been going to the farmhouse to teach him about Madagascar, and Solomon, in turn, teaches the others—"

"You saw Solomon?" They were approaching the area of the Reichschancellery, and there were so many questions she wanted to ask.

"There is no time left for conversation," Perón said. "I have not seen Solomon yet. I must not seem to be too enthusiastic. However, Bruqah tells me that Solomon, like all of the others, is thin, sad, but alive and functioning. Tonight Bruqah and I will show the maps to everyone concerned with this plan, including Erich and the Führer. Your Erich will be bringing home the details to you tonight—that is, provided the great German bureaucracy has not already changed its mind."

"But Juan—"

"Enough! You will have to wait for the rest...unless you wish to go to your other sources."

His voice reflected mild annoyance with her for having spoiled his dénouement, and much irritation with Hitler, whom he found to be a distasteful, officious little man invested with too much power. In Miriam's judgment, the Argentinean appreciated the Nazi Party but was not enamored with it; he did what he felt was right for Argentina and for himself. Clearly, he had political aspirations. Clearly, too, she would hear no more today until she heard it from Erich later tonight.

Not by any means for the first time in her life, she wondered why she attracted men with such volatile personalities. Javelin Men, as Erich called them, whose need for prowess outweighed their sensitivities no matter how hard they tried. Erich and Perón had that in common. They were the Magellans, the Vasco De Gamas and Columbuses, explorers because of a need to prove themselves to the world rather than simply because they were internally driven.

Sol's explorations were metaphysical and philosophical, though in their own way just as demanding. With him, however, *she* could be the volatile one, the balance between other-worldliness and pragmatism. She could hardly wait, she thought, to be that for him again, and for herself. Playing a part on the stage was one thing; playing it day and night, around the clock, was another.

CHAPTER TWENTY-EIGHT

Moonlight drenched the marble steps of the renovated Reichschancellery. Ascending them, Erich felt blessed by the light and wonderfully dwarfed by the building, its Doric columns lifting into shadows like sentries. He was Alexander, claiming his territory.

When he entered, a corporal took his hat, cloak, and gloves, bowed stiffly, and escorted him through huge doors into a hall tiled in aquamarine mosaic. In the next room, which was round and domed, stood other officers, clustered in groups. Most were SS, with whom he had little in common, among them Otto Hempel—who had dallied briefly at the Oranienburg labor camp in preparation for his present assignment at Sachsenhausen.

A demotion would have been more satisfying, he thought, acknowledging Hempel's greeting with a cursory nod. The man inevitably threatened his good spirits. But not tonight. Not when he expected to be the only one being honored with a double promotion. He must create an impression of strength and imperturbability.

The other officers were smoking nervously or sipping cognac brought by a woman whose hourglass shape drew many second glances. One golden cordial, in a thin-stemmed, tulip-shaped liqueur glass, remained on her tray. Erich took it. In the doorway of the great gallery, said to be twice the length of Versailles' Hall of Mirrors, after which it was modeled, he toasted himself.

The corporal opened the gallery doors to Adolph Hitler and a phalanx of functionaries. The Führer stood with Goebbels, Bormann, Hess, and Eichmann, the four framed in moonlight muted by the windows' deep niches. Standing slightly apart was Colonel Perón.

The assembly snapped to attention with an echoing clack of boot heels. Arms sprang to salutes. Feet squarely planted, eyes keened as though he were reviewing a parade, Erich joined them.

"Heil Hitler!"

At once he felt uncomfortable, as if he did not quite fit into his own skin. Just words, he reassured himself.

The Führer and his entourage returned the salute. His soldiers waited for a signal that would indicate his mood of the moment.

Eyes gleaming, cheeks puffed, Hitler gave them their cue.

"Glory to the Fatherland! We must promise obedience, industry, honesty, order, truthfulness... sacrifice!" Jerking his arm to his side, he clenched his hand into a tight fist and opened it, slowly, reluctantly, as though by doing so he relinquished some of his power over the gathering. "Gentlemen, let us dine."

He wheeled and walked up the hall; the order of functionaries reversed, the rest of the assembly following like migratory birds. Erich could detect a communal nervousness as they entered Hitler's living quarters which, to Erich's surprise, proved warm and inviting. The architect obviously had respected the apartment's Bismarckian past; he had kept the beamed ceiling and wainscoting. In contrast to the cold ostentation of the receiving areas, a fire burned in a fireplace graced with a Florentine Renaissance coat-of-arms, and leather-upholstered chairs the color of bittersweet chocolate completed a look of male domesticity.

Entering the dining room, Erich thought fleetingly, and not without regret, of his bachelor quarters above the Landswehr. He had given them up as a gesture to Miriam, though not at her request.

Civil servants and soldiers mingled without regard to rank, a violation of protocol Erich found distasteful. He watched the surge toward the food, laid out on a sideboard of palisander wood against the far wall. Oxtail soup—rich, brown, and gelatinous. Silesian Heaven casserole of dried fruit, pickled pork, and dumplings. A peach tart accompanied by Pilsner, and a Rhenish wine.

Past three glass doors that formed the opposite wall lay a garden with a startling profusion of roses.

"Beautiful roses, mein Führer," he heard someone say. "The new hybrid from Sachsenhausen?"

"Centurians," Hitler said. "Remarkable species."

As was his custom, Hitler waited until the company had almost finished the meal before he ate—his fear of being poisoned was well known. After picking at his meal, vegetables garnished with minced white radishes, he remonstrated about the decadent French infatuation with hors d'oeuvres, sauces, and pastries, and boasted how fasting, combined with a vegetarian diet, gave him strength.

Now he rose from his chair, glass lifted. "Power for the Fatherland! We must be rid of the flab that cost us the Great War."

"The flab and the Jews!" Bormann shouted as everyone rose.

"They are one and the same!" Hitler said. "The Jews are a people of excess, whose ideal is to gorge their bellies and wallets at the expense of good Germans." He tapped his glass of mineral water. "*This* represents what I seek for Germany. Purity!"

"*Prosit!*"

The doubt and horror that had lingered with him since his visit to Oranienburg settled on Erich's shoulders. Hitler demanded absolute commitment. Absolute purity. If he and his cronies decided the baby was, after all, half Jewish...the order to kill Achilles might be repeated—with a child. *His* child.

Erich refilled his glass, keeping his hand steady. The

Führer was the essence of the nation; he could have Erich assigned to guard Sachsenhausen convoys. After what he saw in Oranienburg, all else—even losing his dogs—would be a benediction in comparison. He had to believe the worst of what he'd heard about the camp, that it was a pesthole of disease, a place where human suffering was considered necessary for the larger scheme of the Reich.

The larger scheme! That was why he loved his dogs so much. They lacked understanding of man-made complexities—understood only generalized goodness and suffering.

Whatever his double promotion entailed, he vowed, fiddling with his linen serviette, he would refuse to be involved with hurting the Jews. He would not do anything that resembled his father's treachery toward Jacob Freund. Perhaps the past was not sacred; perhaps, as Hitler claimed, only the present counted. Nevertheless, he was not going to repeat his and his father's mistakes.

The small-talk became less reserved than before dinner, but he spoke only when spoken to. When Leni arrived to film the official events, he felt relieved that the evening was almost over.

Hitler clinked a knife against a glass. "Our army, the one the imperialist powers did not allow," he waited for the muffled laughter to cease, "continues to strengthen into the world's finest peace-keeping force. I have personally encouraged many promotions due to excellence. Some of those who have been promoted were invited tonight to sup at the table they serve."

He paused again for polite applause. "Would those being honored step forward."

The promotees formed a line, Erich among them. He felt as impatient and self-conscious as a boy awaiting Eucharist during Mass. When his turn came, Hitler shook his hand, took hold of his shoulders, and turned him toward the audience.

"The imperialists," Hitler said, "are afraid of shadows and of Germany's clear vision. They fear we wish to renew hostilities with France over Alsace-Lorraine, as if we would shed a single drop of German blood to gain control of the Alsatians who have switched sides so often they no longer know where their loyalties lie!"

Laughter followed. Glasses were lifted. "The only Alsatians the Fatherland wants are the shepherds raised by this young genius with canines. His army of dogs lives up to the heart and wisdom of our highest Aryan aspirations. For that, and for future services—the details of which not even he, as yet, knows—Alois has been accorded the rare honor of a double promotion, to full colonel."

The Führer applauded as the assembly rose to its feet. Swept up by Hitler's impassioned speaking, Erich felt excited. Yes! He could have it all! Miriam, his dogs, the glory that was due him!

As the applause died, however, a shroud fell into place. His doubts about the Party had been eroded too easily by the Führer's speech. His weakness embarrassed him.

After dinner, while officers formed amiable groups or

stepped into the garden for a smoke, Erich sat where he was, watching Hitler with Bormann, Hess, and Eichmann. Bormann was speaking earnestly, as if to counter the rumor that he took just a little too much pleasure in "arranging" the Führer's finances.

Perón joined them for a moment, then walked over toward Erich as Hitler and the other notables filed through a side door.

"The Führer wishes you to remain after the others leave," Perón said. "There's to be a meeting. You, Eichmann, Hempel, Riefenstahl." He ticked them off on his fingers.

"What is it all about, Juan—if I may call you Juan?"

Perón smiled. "You may call me anything you like." He left as abruptly as he had approached.

Trying not to dwell on the possibilities, Erich watched the diners disperse. Some congratulated him, offering platitudes about how a man's worth eventually surfaced and was recognized. Ultimately he found himself alone except for the steward's helpers clearing the tables. He ordered coffee from a waiter he knew to be a member of the SS and, forced to wait, allowed himself to dream.

Since his rank now equaled Perón's, the South American had to be part of Hitler's plan for Colonel Erich Weisser Alois. That could only mean one thing: Erich and his canine corps would help lead the Fascist revolution in South America. That would explain the double promotion. Any rank below Perón's would diminish the Germanic presence; any above would hint of imperialism, like Bismarck's error when, during the Great War, his envoys had tried to persuade Mexico to attack the United States.

Alois and Perón.

Everything fit, as if his life were part of a grand design shaped for this moment; his role in military intelligence, his guerrilla training under Otto Braun, his knowledge of Catholicism...all were essential for a German-Argentinean thrust through South America. He tried to recall which cities were where, and what strategy the South American generals, San Martín and Bolívar, had used. If only he'd studied harder at the *Gymnasium!* Too late to worry about that. He would act informed and responsive toward Hitler's and Perón's proposals tonight, then plunder the university's library in the morning and seek out the best Spanish tutor in Berlin. With the right incentive, he could learn—and face—anything.

Like the matter of Miriam.

Ironically, everywhere except in Germany she was a Jew. How would the South Americans react to her?

Cross that bridge later, he thought, imagining a Fascist conflagration with Hitler, Mussolini, Franco, and Degrelle in Europe; Hirohito in Japan; Chaing Kai-Shek with his Blueshirts in China; the German-American Bund Party in the United States; the recently disenfranchised Integralistas in Brazil. And the Argentineans.

Together they would burn the world clean of the Communist threat and the decadence of democracy.

Leading the troops, he would be the swordtip of a revolution, its fiery wedge!

The stewards exited, and he allowed himself a congratulatory smile.

"You look pleased with yourself, Herr Oberst," Colonel Perón said, reentering. "The Führer will be ready to see you," Perón glanced at his watch, "in fifteen minutes. The meeting will be brief. He is most weary."

"Be so kind as to give me an indication of the subject of this meeting," Erich said, forcing himself to keep his smile.

Clasping his hands behind his back, Perón looked thoughtful. "At my instigation, the Führer has arranged to give you and your dogs an opportunity to prove your worth. I am told you consider them the equal of any good German soldier."

Erich's smile broadened. "How is it we are to prove ourselves?"

"As part of a two-part operation." Perón sat down and lit a cigarette. "In brief, I wish to view a particular naval operation in the South Atlantic. You are to accompany me."

"And that operation is?"

"A military secret, even from you, Herr Oberst. Outside of the highest officials, only the captain of the *Altmark*, whom you shall meet in due time, knows those details. I can tell you that I will be with you as far as Lüderitz, a port on the west coast of Africa."

"I see," Erich said, but he felt a mounting confusion. He struggled to maintain his professional reserve.

"I told you that this is to be a two-part operation," Perón said. "The first, the one I am to view, is top secret."

"And the second?"

"You and your men and dogs, together with a contingent of SS and free laborers, will proceed to Madagascar. Yours will be the advance party for troops that will secure the island for the Reich."

Madagascar! Erich thought. A stroke of genius! The Italians had invaded and defeated Ethiopia, and now Germany would have Madagascar. With the Italian hotheads in control of the southern entrance to the Red Sea, Hitler had to make a similar move. Whoever held the island controlled the Indian Ocean. That meant control of oil.

The top secret operation Perón was to observe, Erich figured, must be an invasion, to help galvanize Perón's belief in the German cause by demonstrating how, with Germany's help, he could acquire not just his country but his continent!

"What is the timetable for the primary invasion?" Erich asked.

"If the invasion comes, it will come in good time."

"*If?*" Erich's excitement halted. "There are no immediate plans?"

Perón shook his head.

"Then why am I being sent to Madagascar?"

"As you're no doubt aware, Poland has become increasingly aggressive. Should the Poles be foolish enough to spill German blood, your Führer intends, as he says, to crush them like roaches. He knows, however, that the problems he will have to contend with after peace is restored will be staggering. Over three million Jews in Poland alone!" Perón paused, as if to allow the information to take hold. "The Führer is convinced that a foothold in Madagascar will give him a solution to the Jewish question. He wishes to transport all Jews there to form a country of their own."

"I'm being sent to some *remote* African island where I am to wait out the war with the *remote* possibility that *perhaps* Germany will use the objective?" Erich felt his temper rising.

"Calm down, Herr Oberst." Perón's eyes flashed a warning. "Let me attempt to explain. As you know, your Führer is determined that he must rid himself of the Jews. You may not, however, be aware that your government has been trying to work with the Zionists to arrange for secret convoys to Palestine. Those talks have broken down. The British have canceled all immigration approvals to Palestine and pressured Greece and Turkey not to accept Jews. They have sealed off the coast of Palestine with a flotilla of destroyers and intensive air reconnaissance. An alternative must be found."

The words peppered Erich's mind like shotgun pellets. Absurd!

"Hauptmann Eichmann favors resettling the Jews in a farming area near the Polish town of Nisko," Perón went on, "but Madagascar is not out of the question. If not Poland, then the island. The Poles apparently think the same thing, because two years ago they sent researchers there to see if Jews could be relocated in the island's Ankaizina region."

A nightmare. It could not be happening. Not to him.

"The idea's not new," Perón said. "Napoleon had such a plan, and Bonnet, the French Foreign Minister, recently made a similar suggestion. Here, Eichmann is the one who thought the thing through—in concert, naturally, with your Führer."

"Will we make war on Madagascar?" Erich asked wearily.

Goebbels joined them. "The Führer hopes to persuade France to cede us the island. After the indigenous population has been moved to the mainland, the Sicherheitspolizei will orchestrate the Jewish resettlement in non-German ships."

"Another camp," Erich muttered.

"A homeland," Perón said.

Erich looked up, amazed at the conviction in Perón's voice.

"You will have six months to get this program on its feet," Perón said. "Do that, and the Führer will scrap plans for resettlement in Poland and institute resettlement to Madagascar. You will ensure that the Jews *work*. Once the colony is established, production and trade will be managed by German-run organizations. There will ultimately be purely German and purely Jewish businesses. The merchant bank plus the issue and transfer bank will be German. The trading bank and production organization will be Jewish."

"I'm to stay in *Madagascar*, while Germany glorifies herself in Europe," Erich said in disbelief.

"The Führer will let Miriam accompany you,

assuming you both approve. Leni Riefenstahl—I believe you know her—will film all this for the Reich. She would like to include a sense of domesticity. I believe she is also planning to do a documentary on the Bushmen, and at least one other African film, so you will see a lot of her, as you will Otto Hempel."

"Hempel! Going too?"

Perón ignored the outburst. "The war with Poland, if it comes, is unlikely to last. France is too worried about Mussolini and Franco to risk a war with Germany. You will return here soon enough."

"What if the war drags on?"

"Then, Herr Oberst," Goebbels said, walking toward the door, "you wait—and enjoy the tropics."

Erich stood up and shoved his chair hard against the table. "So you have found a way to rid yourself of me and my dogs."

Goebbels did not turn around.

Breathing hard, Erich looked at Perón.

"This has nothing to do with Goebbels," Perón said, his smile not wavering, "though it is true that you do not exactly inspire his love. I myself have heard him say that your dogs stink like Jews."

CHAPTER TWENTY-NINE

Looking into Miriam's bedroom and watching her sleep, Erich decided he would never understand the female psyche. The last thing he had expected from her was enthusiasm about Madagascar. Anger, yes. Neutrality, perhaps. But open enthusiasm? Just when he had begun to accept Solomon as a permanent specter between them?

In the two weeks since the Reichschancellery, she had been almost excited—sorting, packing, asking questions about what she should or should not take in the single steamer trunk allotted her. Maybe they would have a real marriage someday after all, he thought. One that included lovemaking. Not just sex. Certainly not rape. Perhaps one day she would let go of the pain of her thighs digging into the rim of a metal bathtub—

He reached for the book Leni had sent him after the

meeting at the Reichschancellery. *The Memoirs of Mauritius Augustus, Count de Benyowsky.* Her accompanying note explained that, after her current projects were finished, she wanted to do a feature-length about the Count. She and her crew would film Erich's trip as far as Lüderitz, divert to do her Bushman shoot, and rejoin him to continue filming the Jews after their base camp was in place. Then—the project dearest to her heart, the Benyowsky movie. The Count, she wrote, bore startling similarities to a good friend of hers, recently promoted to colonel.

In the autobiography, Benyowsky liberally mixed fiction with fact, but the lies were so outrageously inventive that Erich found them amusing. He felt drawn to the Hungarian, an eighteenth-century aristocratic adventurer captured by the Russians during the Seven Years' War.

Escaping from a Siberian penal camp, Benyowsky and his fellow exiles had stolen two ships and eventually ended up in northeastern Madagascar. There they had encountered malaria, native unrest brought on by the jealousy of European traders competing for economic rights to the huge island, and humidity that could wilt even the strongest of men. Undaunted, he had borrowed an idea from the Americans, and with supplies and moral support from Benjamin Franklin had founded a colony and written the island's first Constitution, guaranteeing equal rights for all. The result was peace between the tribes.

As drums beat and nearly naked women danced beneath an African moon, thirty thousand warriors laid down their *assegais*—spears—and prostrated themselves at his feet. In gratitude, they proclaimed Benyowsky *Ampandzaka-bé*, Chief of Chiefs.

The memoirs had given Erich insights he could never have found in Goebbels' military documents. Madagascar began to fascinate him, especially after his five or six meetings with an island native named Bruqah, who was to be his guide and translator. The man was a fascinating dichotomy—knowledgeable, an excellent teacher, outwardly Westernized—yet in many ways that combination of mystic and pragmatist he had only seen before in Solomon.

Maybe Madagascar would give him a way to design for himself a place in history *and* to spit in the Führer's eye. What if he created a homeland for the Jews, not founded on ghetto or camp conditions, but on equal rights? A true homeland. He, Erich Alois Nobody, recipient of an empty double promotion and false promises. *That* would earn him Miriam's forgiveness...and maybe even God's.

Were it not for Otto Hempel going to Madagascar too—

He forced himself away from thoughts of that pig and indulged instead in a fantasy of dancing women and beating drums and thousands of grateful warriors laying down their dogwood spears to prostrate themselves at *his* feet—all the while chanting *Ampandzaka-bé*.

Like his flirtation with Leni, this too was a pleasant and harmless fabrication, he told himself, staring at Miriam, who turned awkwardly in her sleep.

"Bruqah!" she cried out.

He tried to remember when he had mentioned that name to her. Not that there had been any reason to avoid doing so; she would be meeting the Malagasy herself soon enough.

Miriam was again breathing regularly, sleeping more easily. Their bedroom's French doors were open, and a lightly humid breeze carried with it the intermittent barking of the dogs reacting to the full moon. Tonight, he thought, the grand house encapsulated him. For once it was an extension of himself...its stone his cells, its heritage *his* heart, and not only Miriam ex-Rathenau's. Tonight he could believe that the events of that cabaret night when he had first seen her—the night he had met Rathenau, and Miriam had danced upon his boyish desire—had been no accident of fate, but rather destiny, preparing him to claim the important things that had been Rathenau's.

He was finally master of this castle.

Rising quietly, he slipped into his smoking jacket and went downstairs, intent on quieting the dogs. When he opened the front door, he discovered a messenger about to knock.

"Heil Hitler!" The messenger clicked his heels together and saluted.

Erich returned the greeting, though without enthusiasm. "Must you come in the middle of the night? Can nothing in this country wait until morning?"

He glanced past the young man and, surprised to see a bicycle instead of a motorcycle in the driveway, realized this was not one of the usual messengers from headquarters. They were all beginning to look alike, these young Nazis, he told himself cynically. So blond and fervid.

"My apologies, Herr Oberst. I was told to deliver this package immediately." The messenger swung his knapsack off his back and pulled out a receipt book, pen, and a small box wrapped in butcher paper.

Erich signed and dated the proffered page. The messenger noted the time after checking his watch, stepped back, and again saluted. It irritated Erich, having to comply.

The young man lowered his arm. He looked at Erich expectantly.

"Well?" Erich asked. "What are you waiting for?"

"Are you—are you going to open it, sir?"

"Is it any of your business?"

The messenger suddenly looked flushed. "I'm sorry, sir. It's just that everyone at headquarters is talking about," he glanced around and lowered his voice, "the *project*, sir. It's damn exciting!"

"And you thought you could carry back another piece of gossip to fuel the fire," Erich said, looking at him sternly. "I'm afraid you will have to return empty-handed."

"Yes, sir. Forgive me, sir."

The young man turned and hurried toward his bike. Erich waited until Krayller had let him out the gate before he examined the box. He did not open it immediately but rather held back, checking its heft, as though it were a birthday or Christmas gift.

The butcher paper had no return name or address. He ripped if off and tossed it aside. The box proved to be likewise unmarked. As he opened it and pulled out a jar with a metallic-gold lid, a premonition of fear mixed with an urge to kill someone gripped him with such force that he almost dropped the jar. Then, gingerly, he held it up to the light.

Bile filled his throat. He placed a hand on his chest and sucked a short breath to keep from retching. There was no mistaking the contents—a set of purplish genitalia. Shaking, cursing his weak stomach, he set the jar down on the stoop.

An envelope the size of an invitation and embossed with fleur-de-lis lay in the bottom of the box. He tore it open.

Inside, neatly folded, he found a death certificate.

Solomon Isaac Freund, prisoner 37704. Adverse reaction to anesthesia during voluntary surgery. Cause of death: Heart Failure. 10 June 1939. Detained 1 January 1938, Stuttgart. Entry into camp system 3 January 1938, Marienbad. Relocated Sachsenhausen, 14 August 1938.

He refolded the paper slowly, stupefied by the enormity of the irony. For over a year the lies he had been telling Miriam had been the truth. Solomon, in Sachsenhausen...Hempel's camp! But how! When had he returned to Germany? And why Stuttgart!...something to do with Miriam's past? Had he contacted her? Did she know the truth?

He sat down and ransacked his mind, trying to recall if Miriam had acted strangely about the time Solomon returned, but it was too long ago, and her moods were so volatile anyway! Perhaps, he thought hopefully,

Solomon had been on his way *to* Berlin and was arrested before he ever contacted...

My God, what was he thinking! Solomon dead, that bastard Hempel surely somehow responsible, and he was hoping that...! To his horror, he found that he had unconsciously put a hand on the jar. He lurched away, then swiveled so his back was to the thing, and shuddered. Jesus, Mary and Joseph!

His mind sprang back to the paper. He shook as he fought to unfold it. There! He jabbed at the information as though to point it out to someone.

Designation: pink.

Pink! Solomon, arrested not as a Jew but as a queer! Surely there was some mistake!

His mind raced through memories as if through the narrow, chaotic streets of some medieval city, reason and feverish logic opening doors long battened down as though against a plague. For the first time in his life the past made sense to him.

That was why Solomon would wince whenever anyone made derogatory remarks about queers! Why he had to be goaded into buying that hot little whore with the banana-shaped tits, only to emerge afterward so repulsed with himself that he looked sick. *That* was why Miriam...

So that was her obsession with Solomon! Not because he was having her every night after they closed up shop, *but because he wouldn't.* Or—he had to cool down hysterical laughter bubbling up at the back of his brain—*or because Solomon couldn't.*

He thought about Miriam, that Christmas in the

apartment. Wanting him, not wanting him, seducing and denying, until he had no other choice but to take her by force. She probably had not spread her legs for anyone since returning to Berlin, since touring out of...Stuttgart.

Stuttgart!

Could it be possible that Solomon had returned to Germany not for Miriam, but for something buried in her past that he thought might resurrect the manhood he had never had?

Solomon Freund, a fucking queer! Erich looked at the jar with angry disgust. All that time Solomon had squired Miriam, claimed to be in love with her, when in reality he had desired....The thought made him ill.

Desired me.

That was why Solomon had not abandoned their friendship when Erich joined the Party...why Miriam seemed happy about Madagascar. It was not Erich Alois she hated, he decided, for though he had raped her— well, sort of raped—that union had given her what she wanted most. A child. And now...a chance to raise that child outside Nazi Germany. It all made sense.

He stood up. He would give her more than that chance, he vowed to himself. Once he had the colony established and in running order, then if she wanted to raise the boy as a Jew, he would consider it.

Ready to head back to the shepherds, he strode around to the kitchen, opened the lid of one of the garbage cans, and let the jar slip from between his fingers. Goodbye, *friend*, he thought, and slammed the lid down.

The dogs yelped and strained at their chains upon his approach. *Those* were real friends. You know who feeds you, he thought affectionately.

Taurus fought to lick his face when he squatted beside her. He hugged her neck so tightly that she had to lower her back and pull her head down to keep from choking. Her body rippled with power beneath the gold and black coat. She was more vicious since she had tasted blood, but that did not make him love her less. Nor did her dysplasia, especially since her performances requiring intelligence and not just physical prowess equaled or exceeded those of the other dogs—as if she had been created to remind him that a disability cannot defeat a true champion.

He stroked her head gently. Did he really have the right to subject her, or any of the dogs, to the long voyage and the tropics? Was he placing personal gain before the health of his troops? Madagascar's dampness was bound to affect Taurus' hip joint. Filled with fluid, it was edging from its socket. And what about brain fever? Dogs unaccustomed to tropical sun and humidity were highly susceptible.

Lantern glow interrupted his solitude. He squared his shoulders and stood up.

"Redwing," Siegfried Krayller said. His affenpinscher bared its teeth, as if grinning in recognition of Erich, who was its feeder, as he was for all the dogs.

"Comfort," Erich replied, completing the password exchange.

Krayller stooped to pat his terrier. "Sir?"

"Yes?"

"Will you be taking Grog with you?" The huge man's voice was heavy with emotion. "Rumor has it that I will not be going to Madagascar. Is Grog slated for a new trainer?"

"Rumors don't run an army. Brains and oil do." Erich looked down at the black monkey terrier. "I'm not positive who is going."

The trainer drew a distraught breath. Hitler himself had presented the little dog to the corps, a gesture Eva Braun had apparently inspired. At first Krayller had been insulted when Erich put the animal in his charge, but the dog proved quick and intelligent, with a sense of comedy that provided relief from the seriousness of the work with the shepherds.

"I will leave you now, sir." Krayller swept the light along the line of tethered dogs and began to walk off.

"Just a moment." Letting go of Taurus, Erich walked toward the far wall.

"Sir?"

"When I reach the back fence, let the dogs loose. Pull the pin and let them run with their chains attached."

"What?"

"You heard me."

"But, sir, the other trainers are asleep or in the city—sir!"

"Do as I say!"

Nearing the iron gate, Erich looked up at the sky, studded with stars. Along the horizon of chestnut trees, long feathery clouds shone silver and bright, and he thought of the dogsled that had taken Benyowsky across

Siberia. *Master of this castle. But who is really master of these grand, graceful animals?*

"I can't do this, sir." Krayller sounded plaintive as a child. "Unless the dogs are muzzled, without their trainers here they will tear each other apart, even if they don't wrap their chains around something and choke to death."

"You will do as I tell you."

"If you insist on doing this, sir, I must wash my hands of all responsibility for the consequences."

"That goes without saying. You are not my keeper."

On impulse Erich closed his eyes and lifted his arms, as if seeking affirmation from the clouds. Did his destiny, he wondered, like the Count's, lie in Madagascar? He could hear Krayller tinkering with the main pin designed to disconnect all the animals from their runs in case of fire or other emergency.

That's it, he thought. He would let his real friends decide his destiny. His only friends. Should they obey orders and attack him, he would refuse to take them to the tropics—assuming he lived through the attack—but if they disobeyed an immoral command and bounded to their feeder like children to a loving parent, he would set aside his fears for them. For then they would not be Nazi puppets but true German soldiers, capable of thinking for themselves.

Yes. He willed forth his resolve. Let the dogs decide.

They came bounding, barking and snarling, tongues and tail wagging with excitement. When they were near enough so that he could see their dark-velvet eyes in the moonlight, he issued an unspoken command:

Kill me!

For a moment the dogs kept charging. Then those in front slowed and parted, whining, their ears uplifted, some now looking backward as though listening to a secret signal.

Kill me! he commanded again as Taurus stormed past the others, no longer fast but her determination undiminished, eyes gleaming with fury. With a primeval rasping deep in her throat, she leaped.

And, even as he fell beneath her weight, she began to lick him.

CHAPTER THIRTY

He rolled with the dogs, feeling their panting and excitement as his own. When he and they were spent, he lay in the grass and looked at the clouds, physically and emotionally exhausted but happy. He thought about inventing lies for the clouds, images that he could not see but felt a more imaginative man might, then settled for reveling in their ordinariness. Clouds were clouds were clouds. He let his mind roam among them, inventing realities that fit the lies of his life and talking to himself as he so increasingly did. He played out the dialogue in his head, divorcing himself from his own responses as if he were an eavesdropper listening to two people speaking about him.

He remembered a conversation he had not had with Solomon, but should have. In his head, his friend asked about his relationship with the Party. Solomon had always seemed frightened to mention it, except as vituperous aside, as though sarcasm could safely shield him from his friend Erich Alois' potential enmity. From his quaint little lies, like the Amsterdam fairy tale? Quaint little lies in extenuating circumstances, such as Hitler's increasingly obvious intention to rule the world, if not the universe, that might make an officer in the Reich abandon a friend who was also a rival?

So Solomon was careful about asking Erich about the Nazis.

"My feelings toward Hitler?" Erich imagined himself answering. "They parallel my feelings about my father, who rants when there's an audience, but when it's just the two of us is afraid to lift his voice or his hand. Like the time at Pfaueninsel. There was a crowd around us when Achilles attacked the Reich's precious peacock, but when Hitler whispered to me to shoot her I heard fear in his voice behind that assurance and command. He was afraid of how he would look if I refused. So now I fight him my way, with every step and with every breath. I do it not only because of what he made me do, but also because he is a fool and a coward. A *hamster* who sells lies instead of other men's half-rotted produce. He has no honor. That's the one thing I cannot abide.

"And so I fight him, but without his knowing. It's dishonorable, I know that, Solomon, but what other avenue...*alley*, I should say, is open to me, given that kind of opponent?"

"You're not exactly the rebel type, Erich. Perhaps as a child, but you are fooling no one now, except maybe yourself."

"I'm a rebel against rebelliousness."

"And that's how you define Adolph Hitler—as a rebel?"

"As far as I am concerned, he has rebelled against all that is sacred."

"So now you claim to fight him. By wearing the uniform. That's hardly what one would call sabotage, or even espionage."

"When I was taking my Abwehr training at Tekel," Erich said, "there was a retarded boy—a man—whose only job was to clean the blackboards. Every day after classes he arrived with his bucket and rag. Always grinning.

"One day our instructor was using a projector, and because the classroom was small, he shone the projector against the board instead of a screen. The retarded man arrived early, who knows why. Oblivious to the lesson, he began erasing and washing the board. The instructor was livid, but just stood and watched.

"The retard reached the place where the picture was projected. A graph regarding troop movements, if I remember correctly. He kept erasing and washing, but naturally nothing came off. I was the first to stop laughing. That's how it is with Herr Hitler and myself. He's going to keep thinking he has all the answers, and I'm going to keep trying to erase the board."

He realized he was actually talking aloud, as though Solomon were among the clouds. *Fitting*, he thought.

Solomon with his head in the clouds, and me with my mind on theoretical physics, the only subject other than Imperial German history that I enjoyed at the *Gymnasium*. Well, those times are over now. School's out. For the whole country, it's out.

Thinking about school, about training, he experienced a pang of anxiety as he realized the dogs were no longer muffed against him. Then, relieved, he saw that they were sitting in a circle half a dozen meters away, perfectly equidistant from him and each other, each in its respective place. A zodiac, with Aquarius at twelve o'clock. He smiled at Taurus seated at five o'clock, her head regally lifted, ears back. He could sense her joy in the pride he felt for the dog team, but for the moment she was too ensconced in her role to acknowledge him as friend. In the affenpinscher's absence, he had become, for her, the center of the pack, the hub of the wheel of the zodiac.

That was the way they had been trained: the affenpinscher presided; the other dogs obeyed and guarded that central position.

Unlike with most guard dogs, trained to follow their handler's lead and to move against an enemy in a typical flanking pattern, he had built his corps to respond to one another, and to attack outward from the hub. That would best assure that headquarters remain inviolate, especially, as he hoped, if his main base were behind enemy lines.

In Madagascar, it occurred to him, he would always be behind enemy lines. All he need do was assume that the Malagasy were the enemy.

The whole damn island was in France's back pocket, wasn't it? What a prize the island would make if—when—war broke out in Europe: a median in the midst of Indian Ocean shipping lanes! Not that he would give Herr Hitler anything other than a bullet in his heart, but were he, Erich, to control Madagascar, what a hole card he would have.

He looked at the dogs, sitting like guards before a castle keep, barely blinking, seemingly so patient but, he knew, waiting with high anxiety for an order to begin whatever game he required. He mentally reached out to Taurus and felt the effort it took her merely to maintain an uplifted head. Her pain made his eyes water. How could he subject her to the rigors of the rain forest? She and the others were mentally ready—but was she physically capable? Were any of them?

"*Come*," he silently commanded Taurus. She glanced around at the other dogs as though confused at being singled out to break the formation, and at last left her post. "*Come all*," he ordered, and the rest followed, beginning with Cancer and continuing around the clock.

Taurus lifted her head once more. How she loved leading, Erich thought, feeling her happiness.

At the edge of the cobbled, crescent-shaped driveway the men had set up a dog pull. That Erich had not yet scheduled the event was due less to the dogs' condition than to indecision about how it should occur. Most of the trainers wanted a competition, dog against dog to see which could pull the most weight, while Erich found that motivation misdirected—more appropriate to humans than to animals. Teamwork was difficult enough to perfect among the dogs. Like prima ballerinas forced to become chorines, they held onto their individuality. His focus was on the finer details of unit cooperation. Still, the trainers had a point. If all of the dogs literally pulled together, how, they asked, might they assess the teams' weakest and strongest links?

The blocks of concrete sat on the sled like a pyramid awaiting ruin beneath wind and rain. It was time to move the thousand-kilo mountain.

Erich called to Aquarius. He could never feel the other dogs in the team as strongly as he could Taurus. Largest and most powerful of the Zodiac team, Aquarius was slow to respond, eyeing Taurus as if for confirmation or approval. That Taurus was clearly the leader among the shepherds despite her age and infirmities brought a slight smile to Erich's lips, though he tried his best to block the emotion lest Aquarius feel slighted and under- or overperform as a result.

He hooked Aquarius into the traces and mentally issued the command. Taurus and the other dogs looked on as Aquarius strained. The dog lurched, struggling, sliding back against its own efforts, claws scraping on the tarsprayed cobbles. On the second try, the mountain of concrete broke loose and began to move. The shepherd kept low, seeming to dig its claws into the tar as the mountain slid forward.

"Go! Erich commanded. "All the way across the drive. You can!"

The sled slid more easily as Aquarius' powerful shoulders hunched into the trial.

"*Yes!*" Erich cheered.

Aquarius reached the far side of the drive and entered the grass, digging up divots, belly almost touching the ground. Behind him, the sled touched the lawn.

"*Enough,*" Erich said. He patted the dog while the others looked on jealously, wanting his affection.

"Now you," he said aloud to Taurus, though even before he spoke she was moving in an excited circle. He pointed to the traces. She ambled over, the hitch in her hips almost imperceptible. "Good girl," he said. Her tail wagged in answer, and her happiness and determination beat against his mind like a frothy surf.

He unhitched Aquarius, still catching his breath, his chest heaving. Taurus waited patiently, almost seeming to distance herself from the insult of any form of leash, while Erich hooked her up. Aquarius shook himself and trotted back to take his post in the circle.

Erich knelt and held Taurus' head in his hands. Touching her that way gave him an odd sense of déjà vu: *lifting Miriam's chin and kissing her at the wedding.* The wedding was simple: Konnie, the trainers, a few Nazi functionaries as a matter of form. Hitler had been unable to attend but sent his good wishes. No family members or friends. She had none left who were not Jewish, and they were in Switzerland; as far as he was concerned, he had none—period.

Now that Sol was gone.

Had I known about his perversion, he would have been dead to me long before the goddamn jar arrived.

He gave Taurus a final pat, and stepped back. A breeze had come up, and for a moment the scent of roses and freshly mown lawns from the surrounding gardens assailed him. It felt good to be alive. He put the horror of the jar behind him.

"*I love you*," he told his dog.

As if sublimating her happiness into determination, rather than wag her tail she leaned into the task of pulling the pyramid back across the drive. Unlike Aquarius' surges to jump-start the weight, she strained forward without moving, her shoulders level with her hips, the forelegs taking the bulk of the load. It was, Erich knew, poor form, especially given the size of what she was expected to carry, but she seemed loathe to engage in tricks which, while effective, would render her less than regal.

Her entire body took on the look of a freeze-frame: jowl set, eyes bulging, shoulder muscles bunched beneath the skin. He could feel the dysplasia raging as he opened his mind to her misery, hoping the combined psyches would will her onward.

Pain sliced from one of his hips to the other with such force that it sent him staggering. His mind reeled with agony. It shot up his spine and clutched the base of his skull. Breath issued loudly through his lips. He tried to cry out her name but only gasped as the pain triggered a series of lightening seizures, shaking his body like minor aftershocks of an earthquake.

In the split seconds between its beginning and its end, there came an intense awareness of greenery around him. He was no longer at the estate that once had belonged to Miriam Rathenau and now was the property of the Nazi Party, as she herself was—officially. He was amid thigh-high grass beneath a white moon crimped into an otherwise ink-black sky like a notary punch. The night was hot, oppressive; oppressive, too, was the dark tangle that, surrounding him, seemed to press toward him as if to listen to another of his dialogues carried on in solitude. At the top of a gentle slope above him, a dozen dressed stones and totem sticks, all the height of a man, stood beneath the moon which backlit half a dozen dogs which walked upright, like men.

As instantly as it had come, the image vanished. Once again Taurus was before him, pulling with all her might but unable to move the mountain. Aquarius joined her, followed by Pisces, Virgo, Sagittarius with her clipped tail, Libra. Then all of them. Before Erich could object, they clamped their mouths upon the traces and, tugging backward as Taurus continued to pull, brought the pyramid scraping along the drive.

The satisfaction that flooded Erich washed the pain away, his and Taurus'. For the first time in months, he felt free of anxiety and dread, utterly at peace, without concerns or plans for what the dogs' teamwork would mean in the greater picture called Madagascar. This is the satisfaction, he decided, I would have known after lovemaking with Miriam, had not the Party turned her away from me. He assessed the loss without remorse or self-pity, no more emotionally involving than the clouds that were clouds.

CHAPTER THIRTY-ONE

A sound invaded Erich's consciousness, unmistakable and too familiar, coming from the direction of the west gate.

Few sounds in the universe approximated that of a round being chambered. There was about it a certainty of its own importance, like the hiss of a highly venomous snake. Someone or something *else* held the power of life and death, and the myth of immortality was briefly, however briefly, dispelled.

Erich's attention leapt toward the sound. What he saw commanded his full attention: Heinrich Wilhelm Krayller, who had dreamed of being a circus clown but whom fate and Hitler had conspired to make a clown in the Nazi circus, stood with his Karbiner 90 beneath the chin of Sachsenhausen's Deputy Commandant, finger on the trigger, face rigid with wrath.

Hempel's head was tilted back from the pressure of the muzzle. Though he clearly was attempting to maintain his military bearing, his eyes registered fear.

On the other side of the men, two other soldiers also faced off: Krayller's affenpinscher stood before and below the larger wolfhound, neither dog moving, both tight with fury, tails set like sticks.

"I'm going to kill you, you son of a bitch," Krayller said, his finger tightening on the trigger. Krayller, who would not harm so much as a fly unless the defense of his country or its women or children necessitated it, had murder in his eyes and held the power of God in his hands.

For a moment.

As suddenly, the power shifted. He dropped the carbine to the ground and clutched his throat, staggering backward into the affenpinscher, whose neck was being jostled between the wolfhound's jaws.

The terrier kicked ineffectually as it lay on its side, fighting with no more sound than a wind wafting through the linden trees that lined the Grünewald's streets. Then its rump flopped twice upon the driveway and the little dog lay paralyzed, chest rising and falling, eyes staring…and the shepherds charged.

Everything happened almost without sound, like a silent movie where only the tick, tick, tick of the turning metal wheel indicated that there was a mechanical helper that balanced the magic of film. Perhaps, Erich thought, the dogs sensed that there was no need for sound, that nothing but death would deter one like Sturmbannführer Otto Hempel, who bent effortlessly and lifted up the corporal's weapon. Without looking at Erich he said, "If your dogs so much as rub against me I'll kill your friend here." He moved the carbine toward the terrier. "I'll kill them both."

My friend? Erich reacted with surprise. Was that what he and the trainers had become? No. He would not countenance that, not after what had become of the only real *friend* he had ever known. Solomon *Freund.*

He called off the dogs.

They halted but refused to sit, as he commanded. Instead they moved nervously along an imaginary boundary drawn across the drive, anxious to finish what they had begun.

Corporal Krayller picked himself up, blood seeping through his fingers which still rested against his neck. He looked up at Hempel with terror and, Erich realized incredulously, a certain measure of awe.

"You sick bastard," Erich said to the Deputy Commandant.

"That I am, Herr Oberst," Hempel replied, casually checking the button of his sleeve. "Not only emotionally but actually. Points of fact, I might add, of which I am intensely proud."

Erich bent over Krayller and, despite the soldier's attempt to keep his hand over his throat, examined the wound.

"Not deep," Erich concluded. "He didn't cut the jugular."

"I am a surgeon in that regard," Hempel said. "Keep that in mind, Herr Oberst."

Relegating his anger to the back of his mind, Erich

lifted Krayller by the arm, the corporal cradling the affenpinscher. Krayller pointed toward Hempel, trying to tell Erich something, but the wound or perhaps his fear had momentarily taken away his ability to speak. Erich patted him on the shoulder and sent him trundling toward the first aid locker in the garage, the shepherds parting before him and the terrier, the guard of the hub of their team, with the respect one might accord royalty.

"You don't belong here," Erich told Hempel. "Neither you nor Goebbels, with his starlets and whores. But especially not you."

"I never liked this place anyway. I *rejoiced* when I was given Sachsenhausen. There, we know how to eradicate the stench of Jews." Hempel stooped to pat the wolfhound, who accepted the affection without returning it. "But where you or I live, or with whom we work or socialize, is not our decision to make. We are soldiers, are we not?"

"Only *you* would call yourself that."

"It seems, Herr Oberst, that others do not share your opinion, so it is best that you keep silent concerning your feelings about me." A slight, wry, almost seductive smile creased his lips. "As you already know, we will be working together, *closely* together, at least for the foreseeable future. Herr Reichsführer Himmler himself has placed me in charge of security on the Madagascar expedition. What you may not yet know is that my Boris," again he patted the wolfhound, "will be replacing that insult the bleeding corporal over there calls a dog."

The wolfhound, at the hub of the shepherds, Erich thought. My God. My God. It took every effort of his being not to protest. Hempel was awaiting that protest, would revel in it. And it would be futile. For an instant, he saw the jungle of Madagascar with startling clarity. In the distance, a dog howled. The moon, pale and heartless, felt like a cold hand upon his bare shoulder.

"Do you hate me because my friends are Jews?" Erich asked abruptly, unable to contain himself. "Or because I stayed away from you when I was in the Freikorps-Youth?"

"You would have enjoyed my…company."

"Did the other boys?" Erich asked angrily.

"Those who did not at first—learned to."

"You are…despicable."

"And you, Herr Oberst, are too close to our Führer."

Then Erich understood. The realization startled him, made his mouth dry. What had brought him such despair, such hatred of himself and of Hitler—the Führer's order to shoot Achilles—had caused others to assume a closeness they found threatening.

"We will never allow your dog into the Zodiac," he said.

The captain was stroking the wolfhound's head. In the two years Hempel had lived at the estate, Erich had never seen him show affection toward any animal. The transparent turnabout sickened him.

"I don't know whose boots you licked, but you can unlick them," Erich continued. "You have no place in my corps."

"Reichsführer Himmler might think otherwise," Hempel said.

"The Reichsführer might like to know about your little episodes with Goebbels' whores," Erich said. "You think Toy didn't tell me how you ordered her not to wash after Goebbels humped her? Out of his bed, down to your room…" He stuck his hands in his pockets and started away. "As you can tell, Herr Sturmbannführer," he said over his shoulder, "Toy gave me more than a smoking jacket before you relegated her to the docks."

He was past the garage before Hempel's voice, surprisingly articulate, buffeted him. "And I have the transfusion papers, Herr Oberst. They have sat on my desk for a year," he said. "Strange how I keep forgetting to send them to *Medizinalrat* Schmidt so your dear wife can be scheduled."

Erich continued walking, afraid that if he stopped and turned around his horror would be visible. All the favors he had called in to stop the transfusions…all for naught. Fool that he was, he had thought his own best efforts had halted the insanity.

"I will leave Boris chained here at the gate," Hempel called out after him. "Treat him well."

Erich walked around to the dog runs behind the mansion. The shepherds followed him, moving with a heaviness that told him that his mood of despair had transferred itself to them.

"Herr Oberst?" a sad voice called out to him from the bushes.

Krayller stepped into his line of sight. There was bloodied gauze wrapped around his throat and he held

Grog in his arms. "It will happen, won't it?" he said without preamble.

"I'm afraid so. We will find you…another place."

"I have no other place," the corporal said. "We both know that. It's back to the Wehrmacht for me…unless Hempel sees fit to have me court-martialed and shot." He appeared on the verge of tears as, with a hamhock-sized hand, he stroked the terrier's head. The affenpinscher tried to lick his wrist. "What stupidity, pointing my carbine at an officer!"

"You should have shot him," Erich said.

The corporal's gaze leapt up—surprised and hopeful.

"I would have helped you dispose of the body."

Krayller looked toward the west end of the estate. "But not now," he said. "It's too late."

Erich nodded. Yes, it was too late, he thought. Hempel would waste no time making arrangements for the implementation of the papers, should he not return to Sachsenhausen.

The corporal pulled up his massive chest and slowly released a breath. His shoulders sagged. Sorrow seemed to pervade his very being. His eyes were moist. "I can't leave Grog," he said. "And I won't fight in the trenches. Not for Hitler. Certainly not for the likes of Hempel." He eyed Erich's holstered pistol. "You might as well shoot me now."

"Such talk is foolishness, if not insanity," Erich said. "You can have my motorcycle," he told the corporal.

Krayller narrowed his eyes, not comprehending.

"It's yours," Erich said, "if you will do what *I* should do. What I *would* do, were I in your place. Take your dog and my cycle," he reached to pet the affenpinscher, who appeared to enjoy the attention and was, amazingly, none the worse for wear after the incident with the wolfhound, "and ride to Switzerland. Don't even think about looking back."

C HAPTER THIRTY-TWO

Misha and Sol were looking out of the window when the staff car pulled up to the end of the road. Pleshdimer, who was driving, stayed behind the wheel while the Sturmbannführer walked to the farmhouse.

"Bruqah said I would be safe here," Misha said.

"And so you have been," Solomon said. "But n even he could guarantee that it would last fore Besides, you don't know that he has come for you."

"Yes, I do," Misha said, looking around desperately as if for a hiding place. "The alcove," he said. "The one Bruqah uses. It must lead to the outside. I could run away."

"We are due to leave the farmhouse within twenty-four hours. Why risk being shot by one of the guards? That would not be wise." As if staying here and waiting for *him* is *wise*, Misha thought, but he stayed where he was.

The hours that followed were, at best, a blur. He was instructed to pack a small sea-bag with what clothing he had been given since his arrival at the farmhouse. Then he was escorted by the Sturmbannführer to the car. Pleshdimer was asleep and snoring in the back seat, a bottle of alcohol loosely in his hand.

Hempel placed Misha in the passenger seat and took the wheel. Misha was within easy reach of the man's groping fingers. In desperation, he thought about the list, going over and over it in his mind as the fingers pushed and pulled—

The next time he was actively in the present, he was lying on a bunk bed in a small cabin on board a ship. Hempel, who had apparently told Pleshdimer to wait outside, leaned against the wall and waited—his expression that mixture of love, lust, and hatred that Misha had come to know all too well.

Aware of what was expected of him, the boy removed his clothes, folded them, and piled them neatly on a small dresser that was built into the corner of the cabin. Then he lay down on the bunk.

Hempel drew two pairs of nylons from his pocket. He wrapped them around Misha's wrists and ankles and tied each one tightly to one of the metal posts that anchored the top bunk to his. At once Misha's hands and feet began to swell.

"A half hitch followed by a clove hitch," Hempel said, standing back to admire his handiwork. Having done that, he did *the thing* to Misha.

"I have a present for you," Hempel said afterward. For the moment, his lust was sated and his voice was almost disarmingly gentle.

Don't fall for it, Misha thought. Nothing has changed. He stared up at his own reflection, distorted in the sea-green metal of the upper bunk, and tried to obey Bruqah's instructions. "Think of yourself as a dolphin," the Malagasy had said. "Let his words and his acts wash over you like sea water." It had seemed like a wonderful idea at the time, but it didn't work now.

Not that Misha was surprised.

How could anyone be a dolphin if, as Bruqah claimed, they stood on their tails and chittered, and played tag around ships, and led lost sailors to safety through dangerous waters and sharks and everything. Besides, he didn't have a tail or fins, nor could he hold his breath for very long at all.

But he wished he could.

He wished he could hold his breath until he died.

"Get dressed," Hempel ordered, untying Misha's bonds.

Misha did as he was told. When he was fully dressed, Hempel held a package out to him. The boy looked down at the blue wrapping paper and the bow that littered the package like a tangle of curls.

"You must earn it, of course," Hempel said, pulling the package away. He was already breathing heavily again.

Misha lay back down. His gaze returned to the top bunk. Mechanically, he began to unbutton his trousers.

"Skip that part," Hempel ordered, putting a restraining hand over the boy's.

Misha shut his eyes.

"Don't close your eyes," Hempel said. "I would hate to have to order *him*," he nodded his head toward the closed door, "to slit your eyelids so that you will be forced to watch." He unsnapped his stiletto from the wrist attachment within his sleeve. "Have you ever seen someone with his eyelids cut off, Misha darling? Have you ever seen eyelids fried in a pan? They jump around like squid. It's quite fascinating to watch."

Misha said nothing, not even when, using the stiletto, Hempel flicked the buttons from Misha's shirt. He lowered his face and licked each nipple before cutting the shirt the rest of the way off and starting on Misha's trousers.

I am a dolphin, Misha thought. I am free as a dolphin.

Except he was not a dolphin.

He lay looking at his distorted face in the sea-green metal.

"Do you like what I do to you?" Hempel asked huskily. "Does it make you feel warm inside?" He put the package down on the bed and pressed both hands against the insides of Misha's groin, making the genitals mound up. "How do you want it tonight? How would you like me to do it to you?"

God help me, Misha thought, saying nothing.

If there is a God.

If there are dolphins.

"Tell me," Hempel insisted, "or must I cut you? I once

sliced off a boy's penis for less insolence than this. Is that what you want?"

Misha searched for words, but thought itself stopped as Hempel slid a finger inside him. He heard Hempel sigh. Even hating him as he did, he knew that the Hauptsturmführer was somewhere else, on a ship and a sea of which Misha had no part.

"How could any man want a woman, or even another man, when there is such tightness available," Hempel said. "Except you must talk to me..." his voice turned even huskier, "my love."

He rested the tip of the stiletto against Misha's testicles, and sat back. Fear and pain raced through the boy's every muscle, up his every nerve.

Hempel reached for the package, tipped it onto its side, and pulled the ribbon. The lid fell off, revealing white tissue paper. He reached inside and pulled out a black turtleneck sweater and a flat, smaller box, such as might hold a woman's bangle.

He shook out the sweater, held it in over the boy as if to see if it was the right size, and laid it aside. "Open it," he said, handing Misha the smaller box.

Diffidently, Misha did as he was told.

Inside the box, curled into a bed of cotton, lay a heavily jeweled dog collar.

"Beautiful, is it not?" Hempel removed it from the box and leaned down to kiss Misha. "Lift your head."

Again, Misha obeyed. Hempel fastened the collar around the boy's neck. "Fits perfectly," he said with satisfaction. He stood up. "Regretfully, I must leave you now, but I shall return in a matter of hours." He bent to stroke Misha's hair. "Rest. You will be a good boy while I'm gone, won't you?" He patted Misha's side. "We will talk when I return." He retied Misha's hands and put the stiletto, which had fallen onto the sheet, back against Misha's testicles. Then he adjusted his uniform, and opened the cabin door.

Pleshdimer entered as he left.

"If the knife falls, you know what to do," Hempel said.

The door had barely closed behind the Sturmbannführer before a new round of terror began for Misha. While Hempel was the sexual aggressor of the perverted two-man team, and as such caused physical pain, that was not his primary intent.

For Pleshdimer, however, the thrill lay in the causing of pain itself.

Now, dropping to the floor, surprisingly agile despite his heft, he knelt at the side of the bunk. With a flick of his finger, he knocked away the knife.

"Look at what you've done," he said, leaning over Misha. He stank horribly of cheap liquor and body odor. It was a point of honor with him never to bathe, lest, he said, the water wash away his man-smell. Women liked that, he said, and his daughters had liked it even better.

"It's not fair," he said seriously. His eyes, set like globules of white fat amid the oily corpulence of his cheeks, appeared to shine with genuine sorrow. "The Sturmbannführer won't let me touch you the way I wish to. The way you would like. The way I did with my own children, my daughters." He opened his arms, eyes closed in serenity.

Misha had heard the stories. Everyone had. The man was absolutely crazy. He pictured the Kapo's daughters, strung up in the barn like sausages. And for no reason that anyone could figure out, except that their father was just plain *bad*.

"You dropped the knife," Pleshdimer said. "You know what that means." Tucking an arm around Misha's calves, he drew up the boy's legs to his forehead, bending him nearly in half.

Misha closed his eyes again as the belt came down, buckle first. "How can you, a Jew, do this?" he cried out.

The belt slashed down harder. "I'm no more Jewish than God!"

Blood ran down Misha's buttocks, and he could feel the stranglehold of the collar around his neck. The small cabin closed in on him, and he wondered if this was what it felt like to be a dog in a kennel.

"You hear me, you little sonofabitch?" Pleshdimer shouted. "Just because I had some ancestor who humped some Jew cow once or twice—don't mean a thing!"

The Kapo was deep-down evil, Misha decided. But then so were lots of people. Like Hempel. Only after Hempel did what he wanted he felt guilty and made excuses and tried to do some sort-of nice things so other people would forget how really mean he was. The nice things seemed to make him feel better, at least for a while.

It was different with Pleshdimer.

The Kapo only felt good inside when he was hurting someone. He never cared what the world thought. Besides, no one ever tried to stop him from doing what he wanted, so why not go on doing it?

Pleshdimer untied the nylons from the boy's ankles and, to the boy's disappointment, stuffed the stockings into his pocket. He was clearly furious, and in a hurry to find Hempel and report that the boy needed disciplining. When the Kapo was angry, he often forgot things. Misha had hoped that this time he might forget the nylons. Or, better yet, the stiletto. Maybe he will forget to retie my legs, he thought.

Maybe when the knife is mine I will learn how to be bad.

He felt red-hot fury rise inside him and added something to the list. Sooner or later, he would get away. When they got to Madagascar, maybe. And when that happened, he would find a knife and kill Pleshdimer, and he would not feel guilty.

He would feel free and beautiful, like a dolphin.

CHAPTER THIRTY-THREE

Fog hung like used cheesecloth around Kiel's Hochwaldt Wharf, and smelled as bad. Erich frowned with disgust as he stuck his head out of the window of his touring car and peered up at the gray ship. *Altmark*, she proclaimed in meter-high letters.

Her construction, the proud captain, Heinrich Dau, had told him, was a masterpiece of deceit. To the unwary, she seemed just another old steamer. In reality she was well built and less than a year old. Every centimeter of her 178-meter length and twenty-two-meter beam was designed to maximize space while minimizing bulk. Her 11,000-ton gross had a loading capacity of 14,000 tons, and her four nine-cylinder M.A.N. diesel engines were capable of twenty-one knots.

Most impressive, or so Dau would have him believe.

With his lack of naval experience, what Erich heard meant little to him. She looked about as interesting to him as a used-up whore.

Stevedores, their knitted caps pulled low against the dampness, moved silently around the wharf, their carts piled with boxes to be loaded onto the ship. Light from the large triangular docklamps reflected off puddles and off the harbor's rainbowed oil slicks, but none of it looked inviting.

A panel truck drew up. Cameramen piled out, complaining of the chill and the odor of rotting fish, and clowning as if preparing to film a comedy and not the loading of camp Jews onto a military transport. They quickly turned the dreary dock into a complex of lights and tripods.

Fools! Erich thought. Or were they?

They worshipped Movietone News, others bowed before Hitler. Both were dictators invading the privacy of their idolaters. Soon he would be rid of all propagandists. He would feel whole again. He and Miriam and the baby—especially the baby—deserved more than the Führer's empty assurances that manhood and statehood went hand in hand with the Fatherland.

"Stay!" he commanded Taurus, and stepped from the car.

A cameraman, pulling equipment along on a cart, followed him to the ship. As they started up the gangway, the ship's stack blasted as if in greeting. Erich pulled back his shoulders, not for the cameras or the petty officer piping him aboard, but for himself.

Captain Dau, small and wiry, and apparently nonplused by the camera, rambled forward to meet him. A graying beard poorly hid a weak chin, but his face, wrinkled and weathered, was not a stupid face, and his eyes were cold and shrewd.

Erich returned the greeting respectfully. He would spend a long time confined with the old man; it would not do to antagonize him, a Nazi hard-liner. Dau's military exploits had been legendary for a quarter of a century. It was said he would flee a fight only if the Seekriegsführung—the Naval High Command in Berlin—would allow him to reengage the enemy as soon as possible.

"You two ready for us up there?" Leni Riefenstahl called out from below. "I want you shaking hands."

"Ready for our 'historic first meeting'?" Erich asked Dau.

The old man reluctantly put out his hand. "In my day such foolishness would have been rewarded with a trip to the Front."

"Miriam will be here shortly," Leni yelled.

Erich waved in acknowledgment.

"A few more takes, with the boy in the picture," Leni shouted.

"Boy? What boy?"

Leni pointed to Erich's left, to a pale young boy in a black turtleneck pullover.

"Come on over here," Erich said, wondering whose idea it had been to include a child on the journey. Judging by the look on Dau's face, the boy was certainly no relative of his. "What is your name, son?" he asked, lifting the boy onto the rail, and balancing him with one arm.

"I am Misha," the boy said.

"And to whom do you belong?"

"Haupt...the Jews...myself—"

"Never mind. We'll figure it out later. For now, put your arm around my neck and hold on tight."

Leni smiled and gave him the high sign.

After two takes of what was actually their fourth meeting, they were spared further attention by the arrival of twelve army trucks. Erich released the boy, leaned his forearms on a rail and watched a squad of soldiers emerge from the first. Placing themselves well out of camera range, they raised their rifles to their shoulders, and waited.

One at a time, bucking like unbroken steeds, the trucks' engines were killed. Now their lights winked out. Escort guards, weaponless in deference to the audiences who would view the film, climbed from passenger seats and strode around the trucks to pull the pins on the tailgates, which came clanging down.

The cameras whirred.

A dog and trainer jumped from each of the remaining trucks. Only Krayller was missing, having accepted reassignment along with the affenpinscher—and contrary to Erich's advice—to a military pool.

"Escorts," Leni explained into her microphone. "We must make sure the one hundred and forty-four boarding Jews are safe from Jewish traitors who might seek to sabotage our Führer's grand experiment."

Erich looked over at Hempel, who stood near two trucks that had arrived earlier, carrying the forty guards he had selected for the mission. *If anyone is likely to sabotage this experiment, it's that sonofabitch,* Erich thought. *And that damned orderly of his, Wasj Pleshdimer. What a beauty! The man was rancid as a month-old fish.*

Pleshdimer. Hempel. He repeated their names angrily under his breath. Sometimes he agreed with the worst of Hitler's methods. The *Altmark* was scheduled to reach Madagascar in forty-two days. If either of them so much as spoke harshly to his dogs or his men, he would plant their severed heads on the landing beach.

"Let the Jews out before we run out of film!" Leni shouted at Hempel. "Idiots!" she said to her chief cameraman, without worrying about being overheard. "The whole trip better not be so disorganized."

Pleshdimer started toward her, but Hempel put a restraining hand on his arm. "Let them out," Hempel ordered.

The inmates, wearing clogs, spotless trousers, light jackets and caps, climbed from the trucks. In accordance with Goebbels' instructions, nothing about the boarding was to appear involuntary; it was to look like an orderly emigration, not a chaotic exile. Each man carried a satchel, one side inscribed with a swastika, the other with the Star of David. They looked like determined workers undertaking an important mission for the good of all European Jewry.

"Thanks to the generosity of our great leader, these Jewish volunteers are being resettled on the African island of Madagascar," Leni said, playing the dual role of overvoice and director. "It is our Führer's desire that they live there in peace and that others of their kind follow to make their homes along the island's balmy shores—a paradise of curious lemurs and colorful orchids. These men will work the very soil which scholars believe may have been the original site of ancient Lemuria, the remnant of a sunken continent known as Gondwanaland."

Pushing away the memory of Sachsenhausen's walking cadavers, Erich surveyed the living cargo. They looked passably healthy after a month's sequestering and proper meals, but even at this distance he sensed their anxiety.

"Keep in mind," Captain Dau said, "that if one Jew causes trouble at sea, the lot of them go overboard." He thumped his meerschaum pipe against the rail. "Into the water, all of them."

"You are in command—at sea."

A wistful smile played around Dau's mouth, softening its hard edges. "The sea has her own criteria concerning necessity. I remember when…"

Erich blocked out Dau's words. For all the captain's military mien, he was like most old men; he sought an audience for his stories.

As Dau rambled on, Erich watched the line of Jews thread on board. Most, he had been told, possessed specialized skills that would be useful in Madagascar. One, for example, was supposed to be a scholar who spoke fluent French and had been schooled for the past two weeks on Madagascar's customs and culture. He might prove invaluable if Bruqah, who was black, after all, and thus prone to laziness, took off when they reached the island.

Invaluable…or would the scholar remind him of Solomon? Erich gritted his teeth. He had no business feeling guilty about Solomon's death. He had, after all, helped him get to Amsterdam. If the stupid queer was so brainless as to come back, why should *he* give a damn?

"…Is that not so?"

"Is what not so!" Erich said abruptly, momentarily forgetting his resolution to treat the old man with respect.

"I suggest that in the future you listen when I speak, Herr Oberst. You might learn something."

"I might, indeed." Erich had not intended the words to sound sarcastic.

"Do not underestimate me, Herr Oberst." Dau sucked at his empty pipe, shook it once, and placed it in his vest pocket. "I saw more action in the Great War than you could dream of. Now I have brought this ship back from helping Franco against the Republicans. I know my purpose in life, and how to wield the power the Seekriegsführung places in my hands." Erich could see a burning, icy patriotism in the man's eyes. "Your little vacation southeast of Africa is not my primary mission. Interfere with the real reason the *Altmark* sails, and I will shoot you for treason as easily as I'd squash a Jew or a June bug."

Clearing his throat, Dau excused himself and stalked toward his cabin, leaving Erich to swear under his breath as he lit a cheroot.

"Notice the man about to board the *Altmark*," the overvoice said. "He is bearing a jeweled scroll, known to the Jews as the Torah, a word which, strangely enough, also means 'an African antelope.' This Torah is alive in a different way, for it contains the entire body of Jewish religious literature. It is a gift from our Führer to the new Jews of Madagascar."

Curious, Erich leaned over the rail. He had seen a Torah only once, at Sol's bar mitzvah—covered in white satin and encrusted with jewels and gold braiding.

Head bent, the man carrying the scroll made his way slowly up the gangway. The skin on the hands that held the scroll was dried and wrinkled. Short hair emerged from his scalp like bristles on an old porcupine, and blackened, misshapen toes stuck out of the end of his clogs.

Suddenly, as if sensing Erich's gaze upon him, the man stopped walking and looked up. The other Jews, on their way to the open steel hatch that led to the holds, flowed around him like a stream around a rock, but still the man did not move.

"Hello, old friend," the prisoner said quietly.

Erich stared into a face so shrunken the eyes looked like big shooter's marbles.

"Do you truly not know me? Or do you not wish to?"

"Solomon?" The word emerged as a whispered plea.

As the man continued walking toward him, Erich gaped in disbelief. A rush of anger and anxiety made his skin tingle. "But I thought you were…"

"In Amsterdam?" Now abreast of Erich, Solomon stopped and looked at Erich's uniform. "You know what the English say about the best laid plans, Herr Oberst. I'm one of the chosen, I'm told, despite my appearance." There was a hint of the old Solomon, with his wry acknowledgment of the inappropriateness of things. "They even offered me the option of sharing quarters with Bruqah."

"Take the offer."

Alive! Erich thought. Alive! Hempel had faked the death certificate! He reached out a shaking hand as if to take Solomon's, then pulled back. What if he were diseased! What if Hempel had not faked *all* the information? Erich glanced at Solomon's clothing, searching for a pink triangle. The clothing was without special identification.

"Angst and hatred are contagious," Solomon said quietly. "Suffering is not. I prefer to be in the hold with the others." He adjusted the weight of the Torah and placed a hand on Erich's shoulder. "We have lived in sewers before, you and I."

A hefty sailor, sensing trouble, stepped from the rail and raised a fist. Grateful for the chance to reassert authority, Erich held up a hand to warn the sailor away. "The free laborer lost his balance, is all." He glanced down at the camera crew, hoping the filming had stopped. He had to be careful not to cross the fine line between acceptable behavior and favoritism.

"I thought you were being threatened, sir," the sailor said.

"Thank you, but there really is no problem." Erich could feel Solomon staring at him. "This man and I are old...knew each other as children. When he came on board and saw me at the rail, he became emotional and lost his footing."

He turned to face Solomon, wanting to say something more, but all he could see was Solomon's back as his friend followed the other Jews down through the hatch.

CHAPTER THIRTY-FOUR

The Rathenau limo pulled up at the end of the tarmac. Barely able to think or feel after seeing Sol, Erich returned to the rail. Bruqah climbed from the car and watched Perón help Miriam out.

A cameraman closed in.

"No!" Erich raced down the gangway, stuck a hand over the lens.

The cameraman blanched and backed away.

"Be reasonable, Erich," Leni said. "The story of Miriam Alois, stalwart German wife accompanying her husband on so arduous a journey despite her pregnancy, will make them cry with happiness out there. We can't bypass such an opportunity. Bruqah is much too colorful a character to pass up, and Perón would not forgive me if I did not get him on camera!"

"Then wait!" Erich replied brusquely. He ran toward

Miriam. "How are you feeling?" he asked, still too affected by his encounter with a live Solomon to think clearly.

"Are the...free laborers on board yet?" She was making an effort to keep her voice light, but her unmistakable earnestness set him further on edge. "You saw them?"

"Yes. I, I saw." He was no better at sounding casual than she.

Miriam placed a hand on her belly as if troubled by its weight. "Get me on board, Erich. You know how I hate these films!"

He straightened up. "*Mach schnell*, Leni—or turn the cameras off!"

"Camera one!" Leni shouted.

"Ready."

"Camera two!"

"Ready."

"Sound!" There was a slight pause while a microphone attached to a long beam was rolled over to the limousine. "Sound!" she repeated, when it was in place.

"Testing," the sound man said. "Say something please, Frau—"

"What would you like—"

"That's enough. Ready with the sound."

"Most of you watching this film have seen Frau Alois before," Leni began, loudly enough to compensate for the whirring of the cameras and the clacking of the metal reels. "You know she is bearing the child of Oberst Erich Alois."

Erich watched Miriam compose her features. He knew what an effort of will this was taking, and he could not but admire her fortitude. This was the girl who'd won his heart that night in Kaverne. The inveterate performer. Not the other Miriam, the one whose attachment to Solomon made him doubt himself. Here were the traits he wanted passed on to his son. How could he bring himself to tell her that Solomon was aboard, and spoil everything?

She had taken the news of Solomon's death very hard. The death certificate must be a mistake, she had insisted. Knowing what he did about Solomon's perversion, he had found himself genuinely pitying of Miriam rather than being jealous of Solomon. He did not tell her about the jar, though he did send a corporal to check the camp's files—he could not bring himself to face the place in person. Besides, the risk was not worth it. He was likely to attack Hempel. Kill him, even. Ridding the world of that slime would probably mean a firing squad for him, and incarceration for Miriam.

The corporal reported back that prisoner **37704's** papers were in order, and eventually Miriam had stopped grieving, at least openly. Perón had been a big help with her, though it irritated Erich to have him sniffing around so much, and that strange Malagasy, Bruqah, had also seemed a calming influence.

And now what to tell her! If she found out about his Amsterdam lie, she would keep on equating him with the rest of the Nazis, regardless of what miracle he might perform building the Madagascar colony...or what love he might show her and their child. So, what if she did not find out…what if Solomon died en route to the island? The world would be better off without another cock-sucking queer, wouldn't it?

Erich shuddered at the idea that he was capable of such thoughts—and yet—

"Cut!"

He had missed the rest of Leni's spiel. No matter. The only important thing was to get Miriam to the cabin so she could rest. He did not want to take risks with the child.

"Bruqah! Herr *Oberst* Perón! Please be good enough to escort Miriam on board."

He trotted to his car to get Taurus. By the time he went up the gangway, through several hatchways, and into the cabin that was to be home for the voyage, Miriam's escorts had left. She lay on the cramped lower bunk, looking around the tiny room which, Erich knew, was no match for the one she'd had on her return trip from America with her uncle. They had traveled in luxury aboard the *Titanic*'s sister ship, the RMS *Olympic*. This was a metal cell smelling of diesel and thrumming from the engines.

He sat down on a metal pull-down seat opposite her, Taurus at his feet. "You must rest."

"Yes, sir." She saluted. "Herr Oberst!"

Telling himself she was teasing him, he rose and opened the cabin hatchway. Later, he decided. He would tell her the truth later, when she was rested. In fact, there was really no reason the whole thing could not wait until they reached Madagascar. Miriam would be spending most of the voyage in the cabin; Solomon would be in the hold. She would not see the Jews until they debarked, and the chances of her finding out that he'd known from the start that Sol was alive and among them—

Yes, he thought. That would be best for everyone. He clanged the cabin door shut behind him, exited the cabin area, and led Taurus across the deck. His heart was beating rapidly, and he was having difficulty concentrating. Just how much did Solomon know, and how much Miriam? Should he interrogate Solomon? He could hardly ask him about his sexual preferences; killing him would be easier than that. Besides, it made too much sense not to be true.

He would not question Solomon yet, he decided. Whether he had gone specifically to Stuttgart or had been arrested on his way to Berlin was irrelevant. He had never made it back to Miriam, that was clear. She was a fine performer, but not *that* good. She might delude an audience, but not the man she lived with...not over the long term.

Lifting Taurus into his arms, he climbed down through a hatch and into the windlass house, where the other dogs were kenneled. Ten of the other eleven shepherds, seeing their feeder, began to whimper and whine and pace. Hempel's wolfhound ignored him; Aquarius, apparently disturbed by being penned inside a room, lay listlessly in his cage.

Holding Taurus by her leash, Erich stood in the middle of the room and looked at the cages with wonder and satisfaction. A master could be deformed or diseased, yet you would still love him, he thought, feeling closer to the dogs than usual. What he had once felt for his parents, even what he felt for Miriam, paled by comparison. All else was superficial. Ephemeral. Surely no other friendship could rival this loyalty and devotion.

He took down an army folding stool from a nail near the huge green refrigerator which stretched across the other end of the windlass house. Sitting down before Taurus' cage, he released the dog and opened the door. He patted her squarish head.

She wagged her tail, eyes keen and dark and mirroring the light as she pressed her muzzle against Erich's thighs. He scratched behind her ears; she nuzzled closer, murmuring deep in her throat.

He ran his hand down her back, reveling in the stiff, silky coat. As he rubbed her hindquarters, her foot thumped the floor spasmodically. She looked dismayed, as if she had no idea where the sound came from.

From the corner of his eye Erich saw movement among the other dogs, but when he stopped stroking Taurus and looked around, the dogs seemed still— almost docile. Grinning, he bent and hugged his favorite. He glanced uneasily at the others, expecting the usual jealousy when a feeder paid attention to one and not the others.

The dogs appeared strangely quieted by the scene; they lay chewing their cage wire, a look of insensate ease in their eyes.

He went to give Taurus a final scratch—and then he saw the movement again. He scratched Taurus vigorously. Her leg began to thump, and all but Hempel's elegant wolfhound took up the movement, thumping their legs like a line of chorines.

Erich stopped scratching Taurus. The feet stopped moving.

He tried it a third time, a fourth. Each time was the same. At first it was merely amusing. He lifted Taurus' head and stroked the animal's throat, and again watched the others. They ceased to chew the cage wire and raised their heads, eyes brightening as though in enjoyment.

So that's how Zodiac works, he thought. I communicate my instructions to Taurus, and she passes them on to the other dogs.

The other trainers were simply that: trainers; Taurus did the rest. She was the hub of the emotional wheel, the leader of the pack. No matter if the response were purely imitative, or if a true empathy existed among the twelve shepherds—she was the catalyst for the unit. The leader. Without her, his dogs were rabble, as a crowd without a leader was a mob.

He gripped the animal's head and held it close, thanking her for the lesson he had just been taught. Shutting his eyes, he saw a beach studded with Nazi skulls, like the icons of Easter Island, and beyond it, a homeland. He would be the catalyst that made the seemingly impossible happen; he would leave a legacy for Miriam and Solomon and the other Jews, one that would earn him forgiveness.

And admiration.

CHAPTER THIRTY-FIVE

For Sol, the close, dark confines of the *Altmark*'s hold were like a sewer inhabited by a giant, sweating, sentient amoeba made up of men's bodies. Each time a body crawled to the open fifty-five-gallon drum that passed as a toilet, the amoeba changed shape. When the hatchway's circular handle spun and the door creaked open on its huge hinges, it tensed with fear. When the opened door meant only that it was time for those nearest the door to transport the sacks of drum slops up the ladder or bring down jerry cans of soup, water, and bread, the mass breathed a sigh of relief.

As with the other sewer, the darkness destroyed any accurate sense of time. Try by whatever ingenious methods they invented, the inmates could not gauge how much time elapsed between each opening of the hatch, nor was there any pattern to when the jerry cans could be acquired.

Not knowing, the inmates invented fictions and served them up in the darkness like succulent dinners. Those who had gone up to dump the slops overboard or to pick up the cans from the kitchen reported sighting cliffs through the fog or the sun setting starboard. This led to speculation and storytelling, both of which helped pass the time. Once, a man returned to report that the ladder had thirty-nine steps, as in the American spy film. Even those who had seen the film listened like eager children to its retelling.

To all this Solomon made no contribution, not because he was miserable but because he preferred to spend the time in introspection. Avoiding thoughts of the present or future for fear of sinking into despair, he reviewed the fragments of his past, with the thought that nothing happened without purpose. First he concentrated on language: Jacob Freund's homespun philosophy, Beadle Cohen's scholarship, Walther Rathenau's eloquence.

Then, knees drawn up and eyes closed, he let himself drift into happy familial memories. His father behind the cigar counter. *Mutti* and Recha after a recital, taking down the Passover dishes. Miriam waltzing with him, holding him, kissing his eyelids.

When he slept, his unconscious extrapolated from his memories. His dreams were, for the most part, such as all men dreamed. He took pleasure in their substance, finding even the occasional nightmare tolerable because it was based in a reality he could track down and understand. He began to experiment, deliberately turning his thoughts to events in his past and challenging his mind to make of them whatever interesting dream-fiction it could.

To a small degree, he succeeded.

Once, having dredged up what facts and memories he recalled about the Berlin zoo, he dreamed of taking Miriam there. His muse created pastel images worthy of Watteau or Renoir. She in ruffles and lace on a warm, hazy day; he in flannel trousers, his straw hat set at a carefully careless angle. Arm in arm, they strolled between the cages. Lilacs were in bloom. He plucked a white sprig and tucked it in her chignon.

"*Wenn der weisse Flieder, wieder blüht,*" she whispered.

Hoping to repeat the dream, the next time he was ready to sleep he again dipped into his memories of the zoo. This time his muse placed her next to the monkey section. She wore a drab brown raincoat. The sky was slate-gray. A lemur similar to the one he had seen at the zoo as a boy pushed its long ebony arm through its cage bars and, screeching "*Indri! Indri!* Behold!" dug its nails into the side of Miriam's neck.

Sol awakened to a pounding headache and to cobalt-blue light. Trying to ward off a vision so close after a nightmare, he pressed his palms against his temples, but succeeded only in increasing the ferocity of the pain in his head—

—*a girl of about eight fights against thin ropes that bind her, naked, to a carved wooden post almost twice her height. She runs her fingers along its chipped designs.*

Perhaps thirty other intricately carved posts are grouped behind her, each topped with the skull of an ox. In the background, beyond a flickering fire, stand monoliths and menhirs that evoke Stonehenge.

"This is no dream." The voice comes from the girl, but her lips do not move. "Your father is gone and you stand in *aloala*, the shadow of death. This *valavato* was built by the Antakarana as a dwelling for restless souls whom they sought to honor and console with sacrifices.

"*Human* sacrifices, Jehuda?" This time the girl's lips move, the voice frightened, girlish…hers. "Are you to be my *alo* when the Nazis sacrifice me to their god? Are you to mediate between my family and my ancestors?"

"You have no family left and they have no god but Hitler." Tough, older, masculine, the voice comes from somewhere inside her.

"Father said the Antakarana believe in Zanahary, the Creator, and in Andiamanitra, the Fragrant One," she tells the voice.

"The Antakarana are gone; dog-men now own the *valavato*."

"Does that mean that I am not to be sacrificed?"

"It means I believe you will be given a choice between torture or staying alive in the dog-men's service. You will need all the strength and hope you can gather, Deborah."

"*You* chose life!" the girl shouts. "*You* chose to survive no matter what the cost to your soul—or to mine!"

"To choose survival was a sin only because I did so out of fear," the inner voice answers.

"Will you help me overcome my fear, Jehuda?"

Laughter floats among the stones. "I cannot help you," the voice answers. "This is the time for your gift to me."

The girl strains at the ropes. "Help me!" she calls. "I'm over here!"

Here, her voice echoes against the stones. *Here*—

Solomon awoke to tumbling sensations. He did not know the girl or understand the vision, but from Bruqah's lessons he recognized the totems, fashioned to celebrate the death of an island nobleman, someone whose social standing also warranted the water buffalo horns that guarded the burial area.

"Madagascar." He let the word roll from his mouth. It echoed behind his residual headache like the obscure music of a calliope. *Mad-a-gas-car.* He said it again, louder; it seemed to hang in the darkness like a banner.

"Why a homeland there?" someone asked.

"Why not?"

True to tradition, Solomon answered the question with a question. There was laughter in recognition of the rhetoric.

As silence resettled, Solomon could sense each man mull the word, allowing it to absorb strength and texture, like moist terra cotta under the touch of a blind child.

"Madagascar," someone said.

Leaning against the hold's metal wall, Sol relaxed into the familiarity of his old haunting-ground, darkness, and took comfort in it. Like the Jews after their Babylonian exile, like Moses' followers, the prisoners must come to terms with another Diaspora, he thought. Like those other times, the end was in God's hands, but daily survival was in their own. Meanwhile, he was ready, at last, to think of the present—about Erich; and Misha, now Otto Hempel's cabin boy; and Miriam. At the farmhouse, Colonel Perón had told him she was well. And pregnant.

Whose child! he had wanted to ask. Mine or Erich's? Instead he chided himself. *Why should it matter?* "At Sachsenhausen there are more learned men than I," he had said to Perón. "Ones far more deserving of being given a second chance at life."

"Thank Miriam's obsession with getting you out. She talked me into engineering this. You may not be able to thank her in person until you arrive in Madagascar—"

"Miriam is going?"

"Miriam and Erich. But how could you have known? Your old friend is in charge of the expedition."

Later, Bruqah also brought word of her; they had even managed to exchange a few notes, cryptic and hopeful—

A man across the hold shouted in his sleep. What kinds of nightmares, Sol wondered, haunted him? Did he dream of people he would never see again, and times he would never relive? Did Miriam? How he longed to hold her—

Patience, he told himself. You are alive, she is alive, and you are headed in the same direction. The rest is up to God, *mazel*, and our inventiveness.

To calm himself he let his mind roam over his lessons in the Kabbalah. How happy the times had been when he and Beadle Cohen explored the cosmos and the eternal!

"*Nothing* is random," the beadle had told him. "Before the beginning of time, when light had not erupted from its shell and our universe was minuscule, then—*then!*—chance ruled the cosmos. And God was that universe. *Everything*, opposite of nothing, is not random, and *everything* is now the universe. Therefore, the cosmos as we know it is no longer minuscule—and this cosmos is also God."

The discussion had ended there, only to be taken up again a week later, when Sol had had a chance to try to understand what the beadle was saying:

"We are the mind of God or, more exactly, a single thought in the mind of God. The universe will continue to expand while this thought continues, and when the thought dwindles and dies, the universe will again contract to that tiny *nothingness*, and randomness will again prevail. The process of the beginning, expansion, and death of the cosmos may take a hundred billion years, yet all that time is but one thought in the mind of God."

"So *everything* is God," Sol remembered saying. "Everything, and nothing."

Many Gentiles, the beadle explained, limited God through their belief that man existed in His image. Jews conceded only that the soul of man might exist in God's image. Still, he said, there was a time when man was one with God, and true ecstasy lay in knowing that we contained in our hearts a microscopic memory of that unity.

Sol thought about that now, as he had then. It led, as always, to a reexamination of *ayin*.

According to the beadle, God directed *everything*,

while *nothing* by definition could not be directed—there was nothing to direct. Humankind was the mind of God or, more exactly, an anomaly in the mind of God. God was the universe, which meant the universe was itself sentient. When He ceased to think that thought, the universe would contract and, at least as we knew it, cease to exist.

The correlation excited Sol as much now as it had the first time he had come to that conclusion. He felt a need to talk. Since he could not expect the others to be interested in the complexities of chaos versus order, he spoke to them of his meeting with Walther Rathenau and of how he had walked with pride in the Foreign Minister's shadow. He spoke of the Adlon, and of the assassination. Later, urged on by the others, he warmed to other tales: lunch in Luna Park, the morning Recha tried a cigar, the smell of potato pancakes, evenings on an astrakhan rug strewn with tinsel and pine needles. At first, he spoke only of Berlin and of his own experiences, but increasingly he found himself digressing into the Talmud and the Kabbalah. The more he talked, the more his voice, whose timbre had so embarrassed him in his teens, took on a power that enthralled his listeners, and the more he found he could comfort the others with his rich images.

"What does it really mean, this Madagascar business?" a voice asked, after Sol had finished repeating a Talmudic parable about a wanderer who had to learn to obey the unfamiliar laws of a strange land into which he had stumbled.

"I don't know. Perhaps a chance at freedom?"

"How will we break free of our Nazi captors?" another asked.

"Only God and fear are masters of men," Sol said with as much conviction as he could muster.

"We have no chance against their guns or their dogs."

"Chance is random, as at some points in time the universe is," Sol said, hoping his listeners would at least recognize the concept. "Unity must be our weapon. Only therein lies hope."

When no one responded, he felt lonely, set apart, as if his academic skills were somehow less valuable or manly than their physical ones. Few of the others were educated men, as if Hempel or Erich Alois, or whoever had done the selecting, had deliberately ignored other men of scholarship. He alone among them had attended a university. Each possessed specialized training of some sort, but their thoughts and responses were couched within the confines of job skills and religion rather than academe. They could all read and write, Sol thought proudly—surely no other culture could boast of such universal literacy—but the Nazis had obviously decided they had little need for men of gown and mortarboard. Or perhaps the Nazis were as afraid of scholarship, and other Jewish assets and abilities, as they were respectful and fearful of the mantic arts.

If Hitler were not a maniac, Sol reasoned, he was either stupid or possessed by his own dybbuk, in whom was vested the conscience of past German guilt...a guilt deepened by the terror and shame of the Great War. The Führer could own the world if he chose to ransom those Jewish assets and abilities, use them to his own ends, use such men and women as those who inhabited visions.

"Please, *Reb*," the man next to Sol whispered insistently. "Give me your blessing."

"I am not a rabbi," Sol said.

"You speak like a rabbi, and you have chosen to be our teacher. Are not all rabbis teachers?"

"Yes. But not all teachers are rabbis," Sol answered.

"Bless me, Reb," the man repeated.

Sol placed his hands over the man's head, and in his heart he felt the sadness of the man's soul. Though he told himself that such intimate knowledge came out of comradeship, he knew better. In some part of his being, he had always known better.

"I am Goldman," the man said. "Pray for me. Teach me. Teach all of us."

During the voyage, Solomon had resisted names and identities; he had wanted no more attachments like Hans Hannes and Misha Czisça—one dead, the other…

"I will tell you all what the beadle taught me." He lifted his voice. "More than that, I cannot do."

The lessons began in earnest. Mostly they dealt with emotional and spiritual survival. The voice and confidence of the teacher in him surfaced; passages and parables filtered through and began to flow. The world of action, the world of human existence, had two parts, he explained: the physical, where natural law and material things prevailed; and the spiritual world of ideas and ideals.

In language reduced to its simplest form, he described

the existence of the world of angels, the world of formation or feeling according to the Zorah. The human soul, living as it did in the world of action, was multisided, capable of distinguishing between good and evil and equally capable of failure and backsliding. In contrast, the angel was unchanging, its existence fixed within the qualitative limits it had been granted upon its creation.

"Then an angel has no chance at self-betterment," someone said.

"That's right," Sol answered, pleased with his student. "On the other hand, humankind can better the angels."

Sensing that he was on the verge of passing on the beginnings of understanding, he continued with growing fervor. "We are the fathers and mothers, and midwives of the angels. Each sacred act we perform, each spiritual transformation we create, is part of an angelic essence." He let that settle in. "The angels we create must live in our world, the world of action, but they can influence the higher worlds, especially that of formation. In that manner, we can reach out for the Divine and, in a sense, direct it."

He paused to feel the effect of his words.

"I have heard that angels sometimes come down from the higher realms," a pleasant voice said from across the hold. "Also that a prophet or seer or holy man, sometimes even an ordinary person, can be visited by angels from the higher worlds."

"So it is said," Sol replied.

"Then I think you must have received such a visitor."

Whispered assent became clearly voiced approval and, finally, applause. Sol received the accolades in shocked silence. Was it possible? Had the visions from which he had tried so hard to divorce himself not been ones of evil, but rather keys to a higher kingdom beyond his understanding or interpretation?

"I—" he began, knowing a response was expected.

From far to his left came the clanking of metal. Light leapt into the room as the hatchway was thrown open by two guards with carbines at ready arms.

Lifting his hands to shield himself from the glare, Sol waited for his eyes to make the adjustment. At the bottom of the ladder well, crammed into the small space, were forms he assumed to be other guards.

"If they try to harm us, we must fight—with bare hands, if necessary," someone whispered.

"No more hells like Sachsenhausen," another answered.

A tall figure shouldered its way between the guards and blocked the opening. The amoeba tensed.

"Topside!" Otto Hempel bellowed. "Everyone!"

Wondering what new torture had been devised for them, Solomon followed the others up the ladder. The shock of emerging into the brilliance of a red-orange sun sent him reeling. His body felt weaker after disuse than it ever had during the ardors of camp life, and the sun, glaring at him like the eye of flame at the end of a black tunnel, blinded him completely. Panicked, he shut his eyes and tried breathing deeply of the salty air. He choked on the humidity and opened his eyes.

His peripheral vision offered nothing.

By looking straight ahead, he was able to distinguish shapes. At first they were surrounded by bright haloes that dulled any detail he might otherwise have made out. As the auras dissipated, he grew more frightened. Those objects and colors he could see were etched almost too clearly. The gray of the ship, the whites and browns of the Nazis' uniforms, the compressed emotion glowering in the officers' eyes. They took on the clarity of a still-life seen through a keyhole.

His eyes had become a camera lens, able to see only the point of immediate focus; his vision was confined to a small circle. Beyond that, everything was black.

Just because I have eye problems is no reason to assume my eyesight has deteriorated permanently, Sol told himself, trying to arrest his panic. More than likely, all the others confined to the hold were having similar problems adjusting to the bright light.

Holding onto the shoulders of the man in front of him, he raised himself onto the balls of his feet and squinted at the horizon. The freighter was outside a small bay. He could make out land of some sort, a gently sloping brown breast spotted with greenery and with shapes that were either buildings or huge rocks. He tried to visualize the map of Africa he had studied briefly at school and again at the farmhouse. There were two fairly major ports of call for ships en route to the Cape of Good Hope: Walvis Bay, a British enclave; and Lüderitz, a German port of call. Both were in South West Africa.

He concentrated on the gathering assemblage of Nazi guards and sailors. The sailors stood to his right; the

guards, some with dogs heeled at their sides, stood at
attention at the rail in front of the contingent of Jews.

"Heil Hitler!"

Hempel's voice. As everyone responded, Sol turned
his head to place the scene more in the center of the
tube of his vision. The pederast stood on the bridge,
to Erich's right. Ascending the flight of steps that led
to the bridge was a spry, bearded naval captain. Once
on the bridge, he began to speak.

"Two days ago we received a wireless message from
the Seekriegsführung." He held up a sheaf of papers.
"It seems the Führer has given orders to the Wehrmacht
to repel the Polish aggressors. As a result, we have
changed course to avoid official shipping lanes and to
prepare for a call to duty."

He cleared his throat and stood with stiff military
bearing, eyeing his crew. After a theatrical pause, he
went on speaking slowly and deliberately, hammering
home each word.

"This morning, September 2, 1939, will be
remembered in history as the day England and France
declared war on the German Reich—a decision they
came to regret."

Again he paused. "Now, let me acquaint you with the
primary task the Führer has allocated to the *Altmark*."

So this was it, Sol thought. War—and a homeland
for the Jews in Madagascar. Now all that was left to
confirm the accuracy of his visions was for the Führer
to hold a place in the homeland hostage against the
use of Jewish assets and abilities to help him win the
war.

C HAPTER THIRTY-SIX

"Though we shall not have the privilege of entering actively into the fight," the captain continued, "the task the Führer has selected for us is indispensable, and we should feel honored. We are to act as the floating supply base for a German battleship destined to turn these seas into a graveyard for the enemy."

Standing rigidly, Erich felt rather than saw Hempel move up behind him. "The crates Fräulein Riefensthal filmed for the witless Red Cross?" Hempel whispered sarcastically, "did you really believe they contained farming equipment? The Führer would never waste cargo space on Jews! The supplies are for the battleship *Graf Spee*. Hear me? The *Spee!*" Then he added, "Except for my Storch, Herr Oberst. The plane's in the hold, all right, disassembled and waiting, but only *for me*."

In angry panic Erich clenched his fists at his sides but did not turn around. Hempel, the subordinate officer, made privy to top-secret information, while he, in charge of the land operation, was told almost nothing! He had been biding his time, waiting for an opportunity to confront Hempel about the "death certificate." He would have to wait a little longer.

"And as for you scum!" Glaring, Dau pointed down at the Jews. "I would love an excuse to throw you all overboard!"

"The Führer might not like that!" one of the Jews called out.

Hands dexterously sliding along the rail to support his weight, Hempel flew down the stairs and bounded across the deck. Even without the added momentum he was a force to be reckoned with; his fist connected with the closest Jewish jaw, and the man crumpled.

Grinning, Pleshdimer separated himself from the other guards. Hempel nodded; the Kapo lifted the inmate and pitched him overboard.

The cold water of the Atlantic brought the man around, and he screamed for help.

"For God's sake, have someone throw him a line!" Perón said huskily, beside Erich.

Erich fought the urge to give the order. Pleshdimer stood between the men and the rail, a serene smile on his lips, and Erich was sure the Kapo would kill anyone who obeyed, regardless of the consequences. Life had no meaning for him. Murdered his whole family, someone had said, and hung them up like sausages.

Are you any better, standing here, Herr Oberst? he asked himself.

When we reach Mangabéy, he thought, I will be in charge. Then I will do something about the guards' sadism...and about Otto Hempel. There would be no punishment without a trial in *his* homeland. No more deceit.

He searched for Solomon, but was unable to distinguish him in the press of inmates huddled together in shock. His gaze swept Bruqah's and the sailors' faces, some of which were white as their starched uniforms. Not murderers either, yet they too did nothing. He was thankful that he had confined Miriam to their cabin, telling her that Dau did not want her on deck during muster, but in reality not wanting to risk her seeing Solomon. At least she was not witness to everyone's moral inertia.

The Kapo grinned, showing his teeth, then spat into his hands, wiped them on his pants, and returned to the ranks.

In the water, the prisoner was still screaming.

Leni Riefenstahl stepped toward the bridge. "Someone do something," she said. "Your little melodrama bores me."

Otto Hempel walked casually to the rail, drew his revolver, and fired two shots into the sea. The man in the water went silent.

Dau turned toward Perón. "I apologize for this disturbance, but as military attaché in the embassy of our Italian friends, you must surely understand the value of discipline."

Lifting the megaphone, the captain again addressed the men. "We are outside the port of Lüderitz. We will wait here for the *Graf Spee* to arrive. Captain Langdorff and the rest of the *Spee* officers may wish to inspect our ship. Should that occur, Fräulein Riefenstahl will film the event. It is therefore imperative that the *Altmark* be clean."

His glance sought out Hempel's. "Proceed."

The major snapped heels together and saluted. "Shower detail!"

Erich noticed Leni gesture to her crew to stop filming as four barefoot sailors in rolled-up pants and striped undershirts stepped from the shadows beneath the bridge. Each held a fire-hose nozzle.

"Jews strip! Everyone else out of the way!" Dau commanded.

Once the Jews were isolated, valve wheels squealed, and water roared at them from the twisting hoses. Arms flailing, they fell before the onslaught; water tore at skin, splashing off it into the sunlight and creating a rainbow water-dance that lasted until they all lay on the deck in a tangled heap of arms and legs.

"Shut off the water! Free laborers, on your feet!"

Soon, very soon, Erich promised himself, he would teach Dau and Hempel that "free laborer" did not describe slaves but rather men who labored in freedom for their own good and that of their community.

"Jews—prepare yourselves for shaving! Head and groin!" Dau boomed through the megaphone. "There will be no lice aboard my ship. You will return with buckets, brooms, and rags. Every centimeter of this ship will shine...and if so much as a rivet is ruined, the sharks will feed on that saboteur's hands. Heil Hitler!"

"SIEG HEIL! SIEG HEIL! SIEG HEIL!"

Chapter Thirty-Seven

Erich looked tanned, vigorous...young, Solomon thought, looking down at his own nakedness as he stood in line waiting to be shaved. The surge of hope that touched him in the hold was gone, a delusion of the darkness. Being thrown overboard seemed suddenly not so terrible a fate.

"Next!"

Sol stepped forward and stood at attention. The ship's doctor had selected three Jews with barbering experience to do the shaving. Sol stared straight ahead and tried not to think about the man on the stool who was lathering his groin, turning the penis to the left and right, scraping the razor along the skin.

The doctor looked up from his clipboard and extended a hand toward Sol. "Tyrolt," the doctor said, introducing himself. "You must be the linguist I've heard about."

Shocked, unused to courtesy unless it preceded a beating, Sol hesitated. Dare he respond? Dare he *not* respond? "Freund. Solomon Freund," he said finally, purposely not saying his camp number and trying to forget the man working at his groin as he shook the doctor's hand.

"Relax. And—don't worry. They cannot force me to cut off your family jewels." Tyrolt put a gentle hand on the barber's shoulder, and smiled at Solomon. "Freund? *Friend*. Perhaps we will be. Friends, I mean."

"I am a Jew," Sol said simply.

"And I am a doctor." Tyrolt checked his list again. "Says here you are to go back to the hold while the rest of your friends swab the ship." He looked at Solomon carefully. "Is there a reason for such preferential treatment?"

"I was not aware I had been singled out, *Medizinalrat*."

"Tyrolt will do nicely, thank you. Is that clear?" The doctor's warm smile belied the arch to his voice.

"Yes, Herr…Tyrolt."

"Others may command this ship and its cargo but I am in charge of the health of those on board. You need exercise and sunshine and air. Is that understood?" Before Solomon could open his mouth to reply, the doctor added, "You will report to the galley. Tell one of the cooks that I said you are to be given duty outside."

He patted Solomon on the shoulder, then moved

down along the line of Jews, talking quietly, offering encouragement and checking eyes, ears, and teeth, and leaving Solomon to wonder if the doctor truly possessed compassion or was merely deranged.

An hour later, about to hoist the last of five huge garbage cans onto his shoulder to dump it aft, he was still considering Tyrolt's response. The doctor should be warned that his aberration was dangerous, Sol thought, scooping congealed grease from the bottom of the fourth can. Removing the thick elastic cord that secured the lid, he sloughed off the grease into the fifth can, the last one he would have to dump, after which he must shine all five with steel wool. Not that he minded; the labor was satisfying after the confines of the hold.

Potato peelings lay atop sodden newspaper. Sol watched a seagull hovering overhead; gourmet dining really was in the eye, or stomach, of the beholder. Then a sound like the whimpering of a puppy drew him to his knees. He squinted into a small metal alcove behind the cans, where oily rags and other flammables were kept until disposal, and made out a small figure pressed into a fetal ball.

"Herr Freund."

"Misha! What on earth!"

"Help me, Herr Freund! Throw me overboard! I tried to jump, but I got scared. The sea looks so deep. But I can't go back in there. To him. I...*can't!*"

He began to sob, dangerously loudly.

"Hush, Mishele. Let me think."

Heart aching for the child, Sol stared across the sea,

to the coastline. *Could it be possible?* A can containing the boy might drift that far, or maybe Misha could float part way, then climb out and swim. Sol lifted the lid of the can and, filled with desperate hope, buried his arms elbow-deep into peelings and newspapers and grease. There was enough cushion there to protect the boy—

He stopped dreaming. The sea was deceptive. What looked like a couple of kilometers was likely to be twenty or more. Even if he could figure out the tide, the currents might carry the boy farther out to sea instead of toward shore.

"Action Stations!" a voice crackled from loudspeakers.

Sol shoved Misha back into the darkness. "Stay down!"

Activity aboard the *Altmark* turned feverish. Naval officers ran to and from the bridge, ordering seamen to carry or collect various items. Two sailors climbed aboard from their painter's platform against the hull, where they had been busy changing *Altmark* to *Sogne*.

"Ship ahoy!" said the loudspeaker. "Smoke north-northwest!"

Solomon clung to his garbage can, using his body to shield Misha from sight, as seamen rushed to the rail, bumping past him. Officers sprinted to the bridge.

The engines thrummed and shuddered; exhaust from flues filled the air with diesel stench as the *Sogne* retreated, charging and lifting, blinding sparklers of sunlight dancing across the waves.

"If it's a British cruiser those Beefeaters will sink us sure if they find out what's in our holds," one sailor told another as he loaded his carbine and checked the safety.

"We should be arming the Jews," his companion said. "It's their goddamn war, after all."

"They would turn against us in a minute."

The flag of Norway was run up. Solomon peered toward the horizon in the hope of seeing the pursuing vessel. He could make out a column of smoke: a warship, silhouetted by the sun.

If the ship following them were British, would the English rescue them? Beneath their airs and dress of tolerance, were they or any other race less prejudiced than the Germans?

How long could he and Misha hang onto the can and tread water if the captain threw the prisoners into the sea?

A light from the silhouetted ship blinked rhythmically.

"Morse code," a sailor said. "Gustav...Sophie."

"Gustav Sophie!" the loudspeaker screeched.

The officers on the bridge began to applaud, and understanding dawned on the enlisted men. Jumping up and down, cheering, they watched their signalman blink back confirmation. Some of them rushed inside the ship's superstructure and emerged with cameras.

Gustav Sophie. The *Graf Spee!*

The pocket battleship approached with amazing speed. Sol could see it clearly in the center of his tunnel vision. Slashes of gray and green camouflaged its upperworks and turrets and false bow wave; its gun tower was massive and, above the bridge, the war mast stood bulked like an automaton. Beyond the powerful superstructure stood a crane, and above the funnel a catapult. Doubtless beneath the tarps lay a reconnaissance seaplane, which the crane could pluck from the water after a mission.

The *Sogne*'s boats were lowered in a series of splashes. Metal clattered, and sailors swung down with the agility of gymnasts to wait as cargo cable and the head of a six-inch oil line were snaked down. The first boat, carrying Erich, took off toward the *Spee*.

Feeling relatively safe from scrutiny, Sol moved the cans aside and stooped to see Misha. "I can't do it, Mishele. I…just can't." He struggled to keep his voice from cracking with hurt. "It's too dangerous. Right around the corner is a door that leads inside. I'll tell you when it's safe to go back."

Misha looked up at him, eyes brimming with tears. "Kill me, Herr Freund. Kill me and *then* throw me overboard."

"Hush now," Sol whispered, thankful that he had heard voices directly above him and had to stop talking. He looked up. Dau stood on the bridge, watching Perón and Bruqah, Miriam between them, walk toward Solomon. She had one arm resting on the sleeve of Perón's green uniform, the other holding the Malagasy's cloth-draped arm as he moved along using his constant companion, his carved lily-wood walking stick. She wore a crisp white seersucker dress and a floppy matching sunhat, and was chatting as amiably as a Tiergarten stroller.

How beautiful she was, despite the swollen belly that had transformed her balls-of-the-feet dancer's walk into the slightly awkward one typical of pregnancy, Sol thought. His heart did a schoolboy somersault.

As if she had heard it, Miriam stopped walking. Tilting her head at a coquettish angle, she laughed sweetly, lifted the edge of her hat, and observed the man dumping slops.

CHAPTER THIRTY-EIGHT

Calling upon every last reserve of inner strength she could garner, Miriam avoided Sol's gaze. If she looked into his eyes, she would have to embrace him, and she dared not do that. Not now, not here…no matter how long she had waited.

"Oh, Domingo, Bruqah, look," she said. They would surely know that her performance was directed at Dau, she thought, glancing quickly up at the silver-haired man on the bridge. "A Jew doing an honest day's work! How amusing! I'm going to talk to him."

She moved forward and touched Sol's shoulder. He jerked away and slammed the can-lid shut.

"Tsk! Testy, aren't we," she said, giving a bravura performance.

"Let the man be." Perón distanced himself from her as if to show his disapproval, and raised his voice.

"Have you not punished him enough?" Bruqah looked at her, nodded as if to tell her he understood, and left.

"You are so rigid sometimes, Domingo." She pouted, holding onto the rail. "Do I know you, Jew? Tell me your number!"

"My camp number, Frau—?"

"I would hardly be asking for your telephone number!"

"Come along, please. This is foolishness," Perón said.

She glowered at him darkly and, ignoring his admonition, opened and raised the camera that hung by a cord from her gloved wrist. "Let me get his picture. His head reminds me of a doll I played barbershop with as a child." Finger on the camera's button, she looked straight at Solomon. "Say your number!"

"Three seven seven zero four."

Midway through the number, she snapped the picture, then looked down at his forearm. "Three seven seven zero four," she repeated. "Looks like *Hölle*— Hell—upside-down." She laughed delightedly. "Someone must have singled you out for special treatment! I must inform my husband that there is a Jew named 'Hell' on board. It will amuse him. Tell me, did you request that number?"

"Request?" He laughed bitterly. "The number belonged to the last prisoner who—who passed away before I entered the camp."

"A special number," she said. "You must be a special person."

"I am a Jew."

"Nothing else?"

"Nothing important."

Perón tugged gently at Miriam's elbow. "They are waiting for me on the *Spee*. Allow me to escort you to your cabin."

"I am quite able to find my own way back," she said arrogantly. "I may look like an elephant, but I do not need a trainer. I have been cooped up there long enough."

He opened his mouth as if to protest, but she cut him short. "I can assure you, I'll not fall overboard," she said, her voice rising, "though perhaps I'll amuse myself by having this *special* prisoner thrown to the fishes."

After trying a final time to convince her, Perón gave in. She rewarded him with a smile and a "Heil Hitler!" He looked up at Hempel. "Ready to escort me, Captain?" he called out.

"Right away," Dau answered, and disappeared off the bridge.

Perón went on his way, stopping only once to look back.

"Forgive me. It was necessary," Miriam said under her breath. "Are you well, Solomon? You look terrible. Oh God, I've waited so long for this moment, and now I don't know what to say except that you must trust me and you must live. You must!"

"That sounds like one of Erich's ultimatums." His voice sounded flat. "I too have waited, Miriam. And for what? This?"

"I have kept you alive, Solomon. It wasn't easy for me, either. You're aboard this ship because of me."

"I know."

"I have not betrayed you, Solomon," she said quietly. "The child—"

She clutched his wrist. "We have very little time. The charade Perón and I played out is worth a few minutes, no more. Once we reach Madagascar, we'll find a way—"

"We?" Solomon looked at her belly. "You, me, and the child? And Erich? Whose child is it, Miri?"

Her eyes held his for a long time before she looked down. When she finally spoke, the words sounded empty—rehearsed—even to her. "You were the one who told me to go to Erich. I am his, at least for now." She gripped his wrist more tightly. "I have to go."

She glanced around anxiously, then kissed her fingertips and touched them to his lips. "I thought I heard Hempel's voice." She looked terrified. "The man's an animal. The way he treats Misha..." Her tears broke and flowed freely. "The boy is being brutalized, Solomon. When he wakes up, when he lies down, in the shower, with the dog sometimes." She tried not to sob, but could not help herself. She pulled a handkerchief from her sleeve. "He begged me to throw him into the sea, and let it swallow him."

Solomon straightened up and took a deep breath. "Hempel's been abusing him for a long time."

"What can I do to help him!"

"Probably nothing."

The sound of a motor broke the stillness. Miriam looked down to see a boat crossing from the *Spee*. It was carrying Erich and several other officers. "I must go before Erich sees me," she said. "He claims you're dead. Maybe he even thinks so himself. It's all so terribly complicated! That day they took you away, I thought my world had ended." She stopped. "A few days before we sailed, Erich showed me a death certificate. God knows where he got it, but his grief seemed genuine, Sol, it truly did. If it hadn't been for Domingo to set me straight...."

"He knows," Sol said quietly. "He knows I'm alive. The day we sailed, he saw me coming on board, carrying the Torah. We spoke."

And he never said a word to me, Miriam thought. Erich's lies suddenly took on a new dimension that made her head swim. He thought she believed that Solomon was dead, and he was going to leave it that way. What did he intend to do, she wondered, throw Sol overboard before they reached Madagascar? Have him quietly murdered? Or had he simply not been able to face me with the news?

"I don't understand. Why hasn't he told you? What difference would it make?" Sol asked.

"None, I suppose," she said softly. "Or maybe it would. Maybe it would make all the difference in the world."

CHAPTER THIRTY-NINE

Much as Erich had longed for the feel of solid ground beneath his feet, his return to terra firma was less than satisfying. It had taken him several days to find his sea legs; now, to everyone's amusement except his own, he swayed like an old sea dog.

More disappointing still was the fact that Lüderitz was little more than a village. The town, whose sands he had imagined littered with diamonds, was cloudy with copper dust that turned the faces around him into golden-red masks and lined his scalp with grit.

It did, however, have a bar. There, surrounded by bullflies and curious Negroes in rags and peppercorn hair, he, Perón, and Leni listened to Bruqah talk about Lüderitz—and about Africans.

"Is it always so hot?" Erich batted at an insect on his neck.

"This the cool season, Herr Oberst." Bruqah downed a warm beer shandy in three gulps and raised his walking stick for another. "You think it is bad here? Wait for Madagascar!" He grinned. "The rain pour, you pray for sun. Humidity she come, you pray for rain." He laughed and gulped the beer.

Not only was the heat oppressive, Erich thought, but there were such a *lot* of Blacks! They made him uneasy. Compared to them, Bruqah looked brown, almost bronze. He was glad he was packing his Walther, gladder yet he had not allowed Miriam to come along.

In contrast to Perón and himself, Leni looked annoyingly fresh, as young as she had more than ten years ago in her mountaineering-movie phase. He had seen her in *The White Hell of Pitz Palu*, among others, and had found her far more attractive than the mountains, the real subjects of the film. When the mountaineers had conquered peaks, he had imagined himself conquering Leni...just as he had promised himself he would do with Miriam Rathenau.

So far he had not done too well on either count.

"When I live here, natives they call me Tsama-Melon." Bruqah cupped a hand on each side of his mouth. "'Hey Tsama, hey you come help me plant!' they call. In Madagascar I plant travelers' trees. They always have water for thirsty people. Because of that, they call me Tsama. These people here are Herrero, mostly. The Bushmen, they live beyond the sandveld. Nine maybe ten month they go without water." His lips were chapped from the days out at sea. When he grinned, blood showed in the cracks. "Only tsama melon juice, is all." He indicated with forefinger and thumb. "So life, she is precious to Bushmen. Precious, like *this*." He poured a drop of beer onto his hand, and held it out.

A tall, sinewy-muscled Black who had been staring at Erich put a hand on Bruqah's shoulder. Bending, he whispered in the Malagasy's ear. Bruqah nodded, and the man stepped back.

Erich feigned disinterest.

"What did *he* want?" Perón asked irritably, but quietly.

Bruqah leaned across the table toward Erich. "I tell you, Herr Oberst, if you promise you don't go fly off the stove." Apparently not expecting Erich to answer, Bruqah said, "This man and the others...they want to see your hand."

"It's none of their goddamn business." Erich spoke without emotion. As was his habit, he held his right hand over his left.

"They think your hand is magic."

Erich moved both hands off the table without revealing his dead fingers and unsnapped the holster strap of his pistol. Fear and anger displaced curiosity in the faces around him.

Leni touched his forearm. "They mean no harm." She flashed him a look that said, *Stay calm. For me.*

He slid his left hand beneath his leg and snapped his right fingers for another beer. Another infantile female contradiction, he thought. She would be more impressed if he controlled himself than if he sent the bunch of them hurrying outside so there could be some peace and privacy inside. Women relied on men for protection, then condemned them for taking a stand against a possible threat.

The Blacks drew together. Some were murmuring. Suddenly, everyone was quiet. Erich followed the tallest one's gaze outside.

A bare-breasted woman with enormous buttocks came padding down the dirt street. A crowd of followers seemed to be encouraging her to do something.

Leni stood up and trained her camera on the woman, who raised her arms, heavy with bracelets, over her head.

Fingers interlocked, the woman began a slow, shuffling dance, weaving in and out of the lacy shadows of an acacia tree. A gray-haired Black threw a smoldering stick onto the ground; others added twigs and small branches...the beginnings of a fire.

Without looking away from her camera, Leni felt for her camera bag, opened it, and handed Erich various pieces of equipment. He wiped off the table with his sleeve before setting them down.

"Herreros and Bushmen don't usually dance together," Leni said with excitement.

"Here in Lüderitz, oh yes," Bruqah said. "When German people take this country, the Herreros flee into the Kalahari. Many died—no water. Five and fifty thousand out of seventy thousand. Bushmen helped many survivors. So they be friends here, now."

The crowd around the woman began to clap and sway. The woman, her head uptilted and only the whites of her eyes visible, stamped her feet against the dust. She was chanting softly. Her huge buttocks jiggled beneath her loincloth, and dust puffed around her.

"*Janha Janha Jan-ha!*" the crowd chanted. She snaked her hands over her breasts, neck, face. Her fingers gripped her peppercorn hair, released it, started again; breasts, neck, face, hair....

Linking arms, the crowd started moving in a circle, clockwise first, counterclockwise, clockwise....

Leni crouched as if on a battlefield, and scurried close, jabbing and feinting with the camera as she tried to snap pictures between legs.

"What's happening?" Erich attempted to follow her as she wormed her way through the growing crowd, but she was too agile. The press of spectators quickly filled up the empty space she had created. He tried to peer over everyone but couldn't see a thing. Wrinkling his nose at the Negroid stench, he pushed his way after her, his hands together like a wedge.

One Black looked down at Erich's hand and anxiously leaned away to let him by. Soon the others were nudging each other, intent on letting him through without their touching the mangled hand. About time it came in handy for something, he thought, easing his way through the crowd.

The tall, very black Herreros gave way to an inner group—tiny brown Bushmen with thick, flattened noses and small perforated gourd-rattles around their calves.

Four Bushmen, imitating young gazelles by holding *gemsbok* horns against their foreheads, jumped through the inner ring and into the center of the circle.

Gyrating, they approached the woman and retreated, approached and retreated. Pelvises pulsing and shoulders rolling, they yowled and grunted and gesticulated to the moaning of the other Bushmen and the pounding hands and feet of the Herreros, who rushed from the outer edges of the crowd to the inner circle to throw imaginary spears at the dancers.

"Watubai na! Ha! Watubai na!"

Her breasts bouncing as she rolled her head, the woman in the center patted herself as if she were cooling flames breaking through her flesh. She made a nasal sound and clicked her tongue.

Leni repeated the sounds. Without taking her eyes off the woman, she motioned Erich to hurry forward.

"What is it!" Erich shouted above the noise of the dancers as he pushed his way toward her. The Bushmen were more difficult to get through despite their smaller size. His hand did not seem to trouble them.

Leni drew a word in the dust: *n/um*. "I think that's what she's saying! The slash represents the tongue click." Her eyes shining with excitement, Leni pronounced the term, clicking her tongue in the middle of the word. "It's a fire-hot power they claim boils up from their bellies," she said as she stood up, nearly having to shout for him to hear her. "Fills their heads like steam. Helps them talk with the gods and perform healings. *Kai*-healing, it's called."

"Crazy," Perón said, having reached them.

"To you, perhaps, but not to them! Try to watch with an open mind and then tell me how crazy it is."

From the direction of the sand spit that formed

JANET BERLINER AND GEORGE GUTHRIDGE

Lüderitz's western end, there emerged two men carrying a ratty stretcher. On it lay a small naked boy. The crowd parted and the bearers passed between the Herreros and the inner ring of Bushmen, who threw dried crushed leaves mixed with dust onto the prostrate figure. While the Herreros continued their spear-throwing motions, the Bushmen in the middle of the circle leapt high into the air and fell on their knees, twitching and trembling and rolling their eyes upward, their chanting more rhythmic now except for the occasional wail that rose into the branches of the acacia tree like the cry of an exotic bird.

Erich edged forward to look more closely at the patient. The boy was a classic case of malnutrition: his belly distended, arms and legs thin as sticks, face so gaunt it seemed all eyes.

"*Kai!*" the woman screamed, toppling to her knees. "*Kai!*"

"KAI MEANS..." Leni started to yell in Erich's ear. Abruptly everyone was quiet. "...pain. Now watch."

"You appear to know a lot about them," Perón commented.

"A director can't film unless she knows *what* to film."

The woman wrapped her arms around herself and tilted toward the flames, beside which the stretcher bearers had laid down the boy. Her nose and forehead were among the embers. When she lifted her head, smoke plumed from her hair. Her face was unscathed.

"It's not possible," Erich said weakly as the woman crawled toward the boy and laid her hands gently on his cheeks. "Some kind of trick."

The stretcher was withdrawn. The woman lay beside the boy, her arms around his shoulders and his head cradled against her chest; she began groaning and wailing. Her limbs jerked uncontrollably. Four squatting male dancers surrounded her. One massaged her with dust. The second rubbed sweat from his armpits onto her body, while the third dipped into a small tortoise shell held by the fourth and rubbed herbs into her scalp.

When they stepped away, a hush came over the crowd. The circle tightened.

"She's near death," Leni whispered. "The others are trying to bring her back from the spirit world."

All of this time there had been no sign of life in the boy. Now Erich could see tears emerging from the outside corners of the child's eyes and rolling down the sides of his face.

The woman opened her eyes and raised her head. Leaning over the boy, she scraped his cheeks with her fingernails—a cat sharpening its nails against a piece of bark. She was purring softly, her trembling less violent, like a woman after lovemaking.

The boy's head moved slowly from side to side. When it was stilled, his mouth opened and Erich saw something twitch inside. One of the male dancers seized it and, with a milking motion, drew it slowly from between the boy's lips.

Erich's stomach turned over as he watched a two-meter-long worm emerge from the boy's mouth.

"Tapeworm." Leni kept snapping the shutter.

"Sleight of hand!" Erich insisted.

"Believe what you want."

The four males drew knives from sheaths attached to their legs and hacked at the worm, cutting it into a hundred pieces. The crowd began to depart. Two women, one elderly and one in her late teens, lifted the boy to his feet. With their help, he walked away.

The male dancers collected the pieces of tapeworm and, crossing the street, pitched them into the harbor. One of the men returned to kick apart the small fire. Lifting a stick on which a flame continued to burn, he glanced at the woman. Her hips bucked once and she lay still, one arm crooked beneath her cheek, the other stretched out above her head. She appeared at first to be asleep; but apparently sensing the man's presence, she opened her eyes and looked up at him.

"*Hamba Gashle,*" she said.

"*Salamba Gashle,*" he answered, and wandered off, leaving her where she lay.

"What did they say to each other?" Erich asked Leni.

"*Hamba Gashle,*" Bruqah said, coming between them. "Go softly." He gave Erich a tolerant smile. "*Salamba Gashle.*" He took a swig of beer. "Return softly."

"What about the woman?" Erich asked. "Are they just going to leave her there?"

"She might as well rest there as anywhere."

Erich checked his watch. "I'd better get back to the ship pretty soon."

"Then it is time to begin our farewells. You take care of that young Frau of yours," Perón said amiably, lifting his beer bottle as though in a toast. "If you two need to get off that island, *ever*, you know what to do."

Erich settled back in the chair. The ship, and Miriam,

could wait. He glanced at the line of dirt along the nape of Leni's neck and wondered why it added to her attractiveness. He wished she were going on to Madagascar now, instead of weeks, maybe months, from now. And Perón. Erich hated to see him depart, too, though he was uncertain if he genuinely liked the Argentinean or whether it was a matter of Perón being an ally in a ship filled with enemies.

Perón would accompany Leni as far as Windhoek, help her and her crew hire the native guides and rent the trucks they would need for the Kalahari, then board the train for Walvis Bay, where a Spanish freighter waited to take him to Buenos Aires.

One last beer, Erich decided, and he would call for the tender to take him back to the ship. He tipped his chair back slightly against the stucco wall. Evening was coming on quickly. The acacia's shadows lengthened, ribbing the street like the scarifications he had seen on some of the Negro faces. Cicadas began to shrill.

"The Bushmen believe the moon is hollow, and that's where their souls go when they die," Leni said, her camera pointed toward the darkening sky. "What a wonderful sense of eternity, to feel that on desert nights you can reach up and touch Heaven."

Erich glanced up. "If what I saw today was an indication of Heaven, I'd rather live in Hell." He sucked at the beer and looked at Perón. "That spectacle reminded me of Luna Park."

"What we witnessed was hardly what I would call an amusement," Leni said. She turned to Perón. "What would you call it?"

A heated discussion ensued, about Left and Right wing politics, as it inevitably did when those two got together. Not wishing to get involved, Erich shut his eyes. The cooler temperature relaxed him, and he found the sounds of the insects strangely satisfying. He thought about a girl he had kissed at Berlin's Luna Park. That same girl, a woman now and waiting in his cabin aboard ship, had grown all too quiet of late. He had almost welcomed her outburst this morning, when he told her that he would not allow her ashore.

A warm hand touched his cheek, moved down his neck, and returned to caress his forehead and massage his closed eyes.

"I'll miss you, Leni," he said softly, and kissed her palm.

She ran her fingertips over his nose and up and over his left ear. The gesture was more playful and exploring than erotic, filling him with a drowsy comfort rather than with urgency. He felt no need to open his eyes or lift his arms to embrace her. His mind slid with the ease of an otter through a wealth of memories and pleasant imaginings. He saw a white moon, large as he remembered his first wafer at Eucharist to have been, and beneath its brilliance a heavily mustached man in parka and mittens, standing with outstretched arms on a bald mountaintop. Below, as far as the eye could see, was jungle.

Benyowsky, he heard his subconscious say. He opened his eyes.

The Negress healer was huddled before him. She

reached up to his chin, wiped away his sweat, licked her fingers. *"Kamadwa."*

He lurched off the chair and grabbed it to fend her off as he might a circus tiger. A camera flash flared, and for an instant he experienced red blindness. When the color cleared, he saw Leni, who was frantically changing bulbs.

"Kamadwa!" The woman inched toward Erich and made a crabbing motion with her outstretched hand. *"Kamadwa mastna ha!"*

"Get away from me!"

"Calm yourself, Herr Oberst Germantownman," Bruqah said. "She wants to drink your sweat only. She says she has seen your soul." Now he looked at Erich meaningfully. "A jackal's soul, she says."

CHAPTER FORTY

The *Sogne* bellowed her position, plowing through the Cape's gray night and storming sea. A foghorn sounded as if in answer.

Jackal, Erich thought, clinging to a handle on the wall of the darkened bridge. *You're goddamn right.*

He had been drinking heavily since Lüderitz, but he had always been a heavy drinker. However, unlike his papa, the sullen-drunk, *he* could handle it. When he got tight, he became...he tried to think for a moment. *Logical.* That was it. He would sit straight as an arrow on a stool and be Goddamn Logical. He might reel when he attempted to walk, but as long as he stayed in one place he was Goddamn Logical. Some of his best thinking had come at such times.

Javelin Man, Jungle Man, Jackal Man...Goddamn Logical Man. The foghorn seemed to sound it out. Fuck

Hitler and Hempel and Papa and Dau. He was Goddamn Logical.

"She's closing, sir," a seaman said as he shut the bridge's sliding door, muffling only slightly the bellowing of the foghorn and the shrieking of the wind. "Bearing south-southwest at twenty knots, as near as I can tell." The seaman shook the water off his listening-horn and set it down in the corner. It looked more like a megaphone than a listening device. One more thing to announce Jackal Man to the world, Erich thought.

"As near as you can tell?" Dau removed his pipe from his mouth and lifted a brow.

"Bearing south-southwest and twenty knots, sir."

Dau smiled wryly, replaced the pipe, and flicked on a tiny light above the maps, which were covered with plastic and fastened down with gold screws. Sweat gleamed on his forehead. "Hold steady," he told the seaman at the helm. "We must appear to be just another freighter fighting a storm."

"Yes, sir."

Clinging to the rail that bordered the instrument panel inside the darkened bridge, Erich looked over Dau's shoulder. The nautical maps meant little to him, but the oncoming ship, its horn increasingly loud despite the closed door, was an obvious danger. Almost certainly British. A destroyer of the *Hipper* class, the seaman had guessed.

Erich turned to stare again through the spray-washed windows at the windswept seas. I am not afraid, he assured himself. I am not drunk. I am Javelin Man. I am Jackal Man. I am Jungle Man. I am Goddamn

Logical. Just seasick, is all. And…tense. It is logical to be tense in such a situation. Goddamn logical. How effective was a soldier, after all, without a little tension?

The scene outside was mesmerizing. Froth spilled across the decks with the ferocity of boarding pirates as the bow disappeared beneath the ocean. As the ship reared again, water cascaded off her sides to the dancing accompaniment of St. Elmo's Fire—balls of static electricity that glowed inside the fog and along the edges of the sea. Despite the transfer of supplies at Lüderitz, the *Sogne* remained heavy with oil and provisions for the *Graf Spee* and for the landing at Nosy Mangabéy. The weight slowed them down, yet did nothing to stabilize the ship against the storm that had the *Sogne* pitching like a canoe.

The seaman again opened the door and stuck the listening-horn outside.

"It's the Jews in the hold," Dau told Erich, having to nearly shout to be heard. "I *knew* they'd bring us ill luck. You must ready your guards to lighten the ship."

"The Jews caused the storm?" Erich struggled to keep from laughing. "Aren't you according them too much power?"

"Every major power that's tolerated them since the Diaspora has been destroyed."

"Coincidence."

Dau shook his head. "History's no more random than the sea."

"I understand that storms like this are common off the Cape."

"So is calm. I've stood at Agulhas…" Dau sucked

thoughtfully on his unlit pipe. "The southern tip of Africa isn't the Cape of Good Hope, you know. It's Cape Agulhas." He tapped his forefinger against the map. "That's where the Indian meets the Atlantic. I have been there on calm days when there is a perfectly straight line of foam between the two oceans, all the way to the horizon. Uncanny. Makes a man believe in God."

He put his hand on the map. "Care to see where God held the world while He shaped it? Here is the imprint of His thumb." With his pipe stem Dau pointed toward where his own left thumb was, in the gap separating Java and western Australia. "Here, between Burma and India, see the index finger? And here," he indicated the Arabian Sea and the coast of Somalia, "is the impression of His other fingers." He poked Erich gently in the chest with the pipe stem, and smiled. "An old sea dog's musings."

"Instructions, sir," the seaman asked, shutting the door.

"Maintain course." Dau turned to Erich, his face hardened. "Have the Jews shackled and brought topside, Herr Oberst."

They go overboard over my dead body, Erich thought, but instead of arguing—Goddamn Illogical to argue with an asshole like that—he went below, staggering toward the stairs that led to the maze of corridors and the hold. Slamming against the walls, he lurched up the hall and down the steps, until he found his way to the windlass room.

The trainers were there, seated cross-legged on the

JANET BERLINER AND GEORGE GUTHRIDGE

floor like a bunch of Indians from an American cowboy film, holding or grooming their charges. The dogs lifted their heads when Erich entered, but other than cursory glances the trainers paid him little heed.

To keep from falling down in front of them, he held onto the handrail, which ran around the room like a ballet barre, but pretended to hold it nonchalantly, as if he did not need its assistance, even in the storm. At his feet, Müller vomited into his puke bucket and went back to ministering to Aquarius, apparently not giving his own seasickness a second thought.

The atmosphere was sullen, sullen as Papa at his sherry. At first Erich could not understand why, or why they continued to ignore him. Then it came to him: all of the trainers had been there during the worst of the storm, tending to their animals. All except Krayller, of course. And him. The only dogs' cages not open were Taurus' and the wolfhound's. Maybe he *had* been drinking a little too much, thanks to that goddamn Dau, always beckoning him to the bridge. Except Dau had not called him up there this time. Or had he?

Erich couldn't quite remember.

He unlatched Taurus' door. She slowly padded out, and lay down again. He sat beside her and maneuvered her head across his lap. Borrowing a rag from Fermi, the little wire-haired trainer he had nicknamed after the Italian physicist, he removed the lid from the water bucket, dipped the rag, and began washing her. Her coat was stiff with vomit.

His own stomach clenched. He wanted desperately to throw up, and, with equal desperation, wanted not to do so in front of the men. It was the usual problem: if he opened his mind to the dog, he would feel her joy…and pain; if the dog were in pain, he had difficulty keeping his mind closed.

"The wolfhound's trainer hasn't been here?" he asked, as usual avoiding using either the man's or the dog's name. He had been forced to allow them into the unit, but he refused to *absorb* them into it. They would remain outsiders until he could rid himself of them.

"Franz comes down fairly often," one of the trainers mumbled.

"Franz? I thought the trainer was—"

"It is the corpsman," another said. "He's the only one of those bastards you can trust. Sturmbannführer Hempel's *man*," the trainer seemed to choke on the word, "hardly ever shows his face around here."

Erich looked at the wolfhound, so sick its muzzle lay in a puddle of bile, and felt like shuddering. Keep your mind closed, he told himself, remembering suddenly what had brought him down here.

He patted Taurus, who responded to the affection by attempting to lick his hand, then he stood up, this time unashamedly holding onto the rail. "Zodiac," he said.

The men continued their grooming.

"Zodiac," he repeated, with greater emphasis. One by one they looked up at him, their faces registering shock that he was serious about the command.

"*Now?*" Holten-Pflug asked, his face so white that even seasickness could not account for the pallor.

"Impossible…sir," Fermi said. "The dogs are too sick."

Perhaps, Erich thought, he had trained his trainers

too well. The need to question orders, if the dogs' welfare were at stake, had been a top priority with him, though such preaching had gone against everything he had been taught—if not everything upon which the entire German army and the very character of the country was built.

Dau's earlier words, though, overrode all other considerations: *You must ready your guards to lighten the ship. Have the Jews shackled and brought topside.*

The order, not meant to be questioned, was insanity. They were *his* goddamn Jews, and no goddamn sea captain with barnacles for brains was going to tell him what to do with them.

"Not a complete Zodiac," he told the men, backing off from his original intention. "You go outside the door. I'll see if the dogs take their respective positions."

Reluctantly, the trainers patted their charges, rose to their feet, and filed out.

He would not, Erich decided, use Zodiac unless Dau pushed him to the wall regarding the Jews-overboard issue. He had no intention of obeying that order; it was merely a matter of how far he would go in disobeying it. Zodiac protected, insured him against Dau. The strategy divided a field of battle into a clock, with each of the twelve shepherds securing the position respective to its name. The wolfhound, occupying what had been Grog the affenpinscher's position, was the hub, the center of the wheel.

If he thought of the ship as that wheel, the dogs could attack its various parts should Dau insist on carrying out his insane order regarding the Jews. Or, Erich decided, he could call only the bridge the wheel—appropriate, after all—and have the shepherds attack there. *If* they were not too sick to respond at all.

There was only one way he could balance the illness. He must open his mind to them. Not just to Taurus, whose lead they would follow. To all of them. Given the situation, they would need the emotional wherewithal he could provide.

He was Jackal Man. He was one of them.

He gripped the rail and opened his mind, sending out what strength he had left. The dogs resisted. Pathetic, he thought. Pathetic. Like even the best of soldiers under the best of conditions, they needed kick-starting; a kick in the butt.

The dogs stood and shook themselves, as if determined to throw off the seasickness. Erich's stomach roiled. His mind pitched harder than the ship.

Rather than moving to their positions on the imaginary clock, the dogs remained in the middle of the room, close to one another as if for comfort, looking back at the cages.

Erich concentrated harder, so hard that it was all he could do to maintain his grip on the rail.

The dogs, Taurus among them, turned their heads and looked at the cages as if for guidance.

No, not cages, Erich realized. *Cage.*

They were watching the wolfhound, which had gained its feet.

Erich recognized his error. The dogs were waiting for a signal. They followed Taurus' lead—absorbed Erich's commands through her. But the unit operated as a unit first, single-minded in its purpose, and the hub was its center, its headquarters. A spoken command went to the unit's center; a mental command went to Taurus—and likewise to the unit's center. Grog, by far the smallest of the dogs, had had final approval of all human commands, but had been loyal almost to a fault, forever happy to please.

The wolfhound had loyalty to none but itself.

The realization, combined with the dogs' seasickness, so wrenched Erich that he lost his grip and collapsed against the wall. Pain shot through his shoulder socket.

The door opened.

"You're not to—" Erich started to say to whichever trainer dared enter before the exercise was over, but it was Otto Hempel who stepped inside.

"Captain Dau sent me down to see how you're progressing with the Jews," he said. "I had some of my men start bringing the cargo out into the ladder well, for easier shackling." He smiled slyly. "Not that you wouldn't have done it yourself."

Erich crowded by Hempel and, shoving past the trainers who were waiting to return to the dogs, went hand-over-hand along the corridor rail. The light from the nearest ladder revealed Jews huddled in the well, looking up as if both wanting to climb and petrified to do so. He squinted down against the dimness, but could not see Solomon.

He's watching me, Erich thought. Wishing me dead.

"At your call, my boys will come down and get

started," Hempel said. "But you must give the order. Technically, they're still your Jews."

Throw them into the sea? Throw Solomon into the sea? If Dau gave the command, would he have any choice but to carry it out? Without the dogs' help, any resistance on his part could mean his own execution.

The intercom crackled.

"We have passed muster as a Norwegian vessel headed for Mozambique to exchange lumber for sisal and bauxite. Due to the storm, there will be no boarding. That is all."

"We shouldn't need an excuse to kill Jews," Hempel muttered as the trainers entered the windlass room.

Hempel shut the door and spun the handle, then turned and seized Erich by the lapels, shoving him against the wall. "When the *Spee* was here I saw your wife above decks, trafficking with your Jew friend. A *man* would throw him overboard."

Erich's mind was racing so fast that he had to fight to keep his anger directed wholly toward Hempel. *Miriam...and Solomon. And she had said...nothing.* "You're asking for a court martial," he blurted out.

"Am I? I don't think so. Save your threats for someone you can scare. I've nothing to fear from the likes of you...*Oberst.*" He almost spat the word. "But don't worry. I won't report you—yet. Not until I have what *I* want." With another shove, he let go of Erich. "I intend to run my own show, with my boys, once we reach the island. Get used to the idea, or I'll have Dau notify the Seekriegsführung about you."

Erich tightened his left hand. His dead, stiffened

fingers, shoved through an eye, would be as lethal as a dagger.

"*A man would throw him overboard....*"

Hempel's words echoed Erich's basest thoughts.

Laughing caustically, Hempel turned on his heel and walked toward the bridge. Filled with guilt, Erich followed him. Sailors and officers stood shoulder to shoulder before the starboard window, hands cupped against breath-frosted glass as they watched the British destroyer pass. Even with its outline broken by the fog, it loomed large, a gray behemoth closing on him with the relentlessness of a predator.

Chuckling, some of the seamen told him how the destroyer had signaled them to be careful of the *Spee*, adding that, being from a neutral country, the *Sogne* would probably not be a target.

Their joviality made him feel all the more isolated. They were together, and he on the outside, set apart because of Miriam and Solomon, and his own stinking conscience. The thought of his weaknesses made him feel as if he were suffocating. What power did he have over anyone as long as he was on Dau's ship! Hempel was Dau's kind of man. *He* was not. Never would be.

He looked up again at the oncoming destroyer and was filled with dread as though she were a premonition from God, for suddenly he was certain of the depth of Miriam's deceit. No proof except the weakness in his gut. Their...child. *His boy.* He felt sick to his stomach.

On impulse he shouldered open the door to the flying bridge. The storm whipped his head and shoulders.

"Close that!" Dau bellowed.

Salt spray beat against Erich's cheeks and clothes. Slipping and sliding, he stepped out and lunged toward the rail. Around him, balls of St. Elmo's fire jittered and danced like phantoms.

Dau opened the door. "Get in here, God damn you!"

Erich shook his head. The gesture was enough to send him off-balance. He fell to his knees and slid toward the rail, conscious of the ship's creakings and clankings and the howl of the wind. One arm looped through the rail, he fought against the waves that sluiced up from below bridge and washed over him.

Dau shut the door.

The destroyer was now directly opposite the *Sogne*. The thought of its power roared in Erich's blood and head. She sounded her stacks in mournful greeting. He shivered with cold and fearful delight as a sliver of moon broke through the clouds and played across her camouflage, revealing her war mast and guns.

And her name. *Glowworm.*

That goddamn music box! No wonder Miriam listened to it so much. Because all this time…she *knew!*…

The ship began to fade behind the fog. Trying to see, Erich batted at the spheres of St. Elmo's fire, now less than a meter from his face. A fiery edge of the sphere brushed the rail, and an electrical shock surged through him. Surf and froth slammed against the bridge. His feet went out from under him and he slid helplessly toward the stairs that led to the main deck.

His head smashed against metal. He heard a crack but felt nothing. His head was pounding, and his hold on consciousness as tenuous as his grip on the slippery deck. He tried to stand up, reeled, felt something seize his brain with a force he had not known since his two grand mal episodes during childhood. Teeth chattering, he tumbled onto his knees and into blackness....

The lights in the cabin were bright, Dr. Tyrolt's stethoscope cold against Erich's naked chest. Erich pushed the instrument away and shielded his eyes. He had dreamed that he was centered in the bright lights of Leni's cameras.

And what strange images had haunted him, he thought, closing his eyes. He could remember crawling from Caligari's cabinet and into a jungle twisted with lianas and tendriled with mists reeking of fishflies. Tree frogs croaked, and parrots and magpies cawed. A flush of orchids bloomed beneath the dense green canopy; their beauty mocked him, and something seemed to wish his death—a black form that came toward him, leaping from tree to tree, closing quickly. Trumpeting. Wailing. Sending him fighting for purchase on the mud and moss. He dropped to all fours and crawled wildly, not caring which way the tangle turned him as long as it was away from the black manform's caterwauling. Then he was crouching, naked and on all fours, on a cone-shaped hill blackened by fire. Heeled near him on the blackened breast were his dogs. Night had fallen, and the jungle below was a green-and-silver sea. In the light of a melting moon, chameleons and frilled geckos skittered across his flesh, their rust-red eyes ogling him, their tongues darting out to taste the sweat that meandered down the sides of his nose....

He blinked several times, arched his back against the tremendous fatigue that suffused him, and looked around Tyrolt's cabin. The door was open. In the corner, Bruqah strummed his *vahila*. He plucked one of the fifteen strings and a soft sound, amplified by the *vahila*'s resonating bamboo tube, floated through the room.

"Doctor Tyrolt!"

"I am here," Tyrolt answered from the passageway. "We have all been very worried about you."

"My head is killing me. Is there any reason why he must play his goddamn music at this particular moment?" Erich pointed at Bruqah.

"We thought it might soothe you," Tyrolt said, entering the cabin.

Bruqah pointed an elegant finger at his own forehead and smiled. His wrinkles deepened. "You bruised your bejesus pretty bad, Herr Oberst!"

Moaning, Erich felt the lump on his head. He lay back down and stared at the upper bunk.

"Take it easy." Tyrolt placed a weather-hardened hand on Erich's chest.

"I'm fine. Just a little dizzy."

"You took quite a beating. Whatever possessed you to go out there, anyway?"

Erich blinked but did not answer. He looked toward the porthole. It was still dark outside. Black and dark.

Chapter forty-one

Miriam glanced out of her cabin porthole, the binoculars Juan had given her within easy reach. In the background, the last slowed-down notes of Paul Lincke tinkled on her music box, working its magic. To her disappointment, the storm was abating. She had enjoyed the increased motion of the ship and the sense of danger—a change from the boredom that had set in since Leni and Juan disembarked. The HMS *Glowworm* had long since vanished. The coincidence neither escaped nor surprised her, not that she wanted to interpret its meaning. Life had a way of proving to her that coincidence was a synonym for serendipity.

The cabin door opened; she snapped shut the music box.

"I brought you a patient, Miriam," Dr. Tyrolt said as he helped Erich to her bunk. "He went out on the bridge without permission, and took a nasty fall. He should be fine, though. Call if you need help."

"A little childish to go out there, wasn't it?" she asked in a tight, controlled voice. "You might have drowned."

"My devoted little wife. Would you have shed a tear if I had drowned?"

I wish you had, Miriam thought, watching him stretch out his foot and kick the door shut as Tyrolt exited.

Erich ducked his head to clear the upper bunk and rose unsteadily to his feet. He put his hands on her shoulders and turned her to face him. "I believe we have some talking to do."

His touch was gentle, but something in his eyes warned her that she was in trouble. Whatever had driven him out onto the deck in the storm had not been pleasant; instinct told her that it had something to do with her.

"You should rest." She forced herself not to back away.

"You should rest," he mimicked. "Sweet mother-to-be Miriam Alois, epitome of caring and virtue! But we know that's not the real Miriam, don't we! We know the *real* Miriam Alois is all subterfuge and lies! How long have you been lying to me, Miriam?"

She tried to pull away. "You're hurting me, Erich! Let go!"

"How long have you been lying to me, Miriam?" He tightened his grip. "How goddamn long! Lying about that queer!"

"*You're* talking to *me* about lying? You must be

joking!" she yelled, letting go of her carefully maintained controls. She visualized Erich dead, killed by her pity and loathing. She should have killed him with the wine bottle when she had the chance, that day at the flat, instead of thinking better of it. How stupid to believe that he might help her—help Solomon—unless he could profit by it.

"You want me to tell you that Sol is a homosexual? You really want to believe that, don't you? And that I stayed with you out of love and never loved Solomon. Well, I won't. I won't!"

Damn him. He could convince himself of almost anything, like that night...believing that, under the circumstances, she had wanted to give him a wine massage!

Before she could speak, Erich's face went white, then flamed to red. "You and Hempel!" he shouted. "Toying with me! Lying to me!"

And Juan, she thought, as Erich raised his hand. With a deliberate motion, he hit her across the face. She was unprepared for the force of the blow.

"Erich—" She sank to the floor and leaned against the cabin wall.

"Get up!" He raised his hand as if to hit her again. Instead, he walked over to the porthole and stood with his back to her, absent-mindedly cracking his knuckles, but otherwise silent.

With effort, she rolled onto her hip, too hurt to speak.

"Tell me the truth about us," he said without turning around.

"You want me to make it easy for you?" she said at last, sure now that he would not hit her again. "You want me to admit that I've lied to you? About Solomon? About the baby?"

"Your guilt is your affair," he said quietly. He sighed, and let his shoulders slump. "I'm only interested in my own guilt in this. That's why I'm going to do things *my* way once we reach Madagascar. Hempel may try to sabotage the project. Every success will be his, each failure mine. I must confound him." He made a fist. "Beat him at this game. Confound them all."

"And Solomon? What of him?"

"The only hope you have for your safety, and that of the child, is to stay with me."

Pain seized her and she clutched her belly as the ship rolled. "My God! See what your brutality's done? The baby's coming!" She clawed at the smock as though tearing it off might relieve the pain. "God, please. Not here. Not now!"

"I'll get the doctor."

"Promise you won't harm Solomon!"

He looked at her with a scorn he had in the past reserved only for the likes of Hempel. "I won't kill him, if that's what you mean. I wouldn't think of it. I'm going to let him get as close to you as he can, and then," his eyes brightened, "and then I'm going to take you away from him. Forever. I can live with the fact that you don't love me. I can live with a marriage of convenience. The only thing I can't live with is being made a fool of!"

"If you don't keep your word, I'll tell them—"

He leaned down, grabbed her wrist, and twisted. "Tell them what!"

"That I was…" She stopped to allow another wave of pain to pass. "That I was already married to a fellow Jew when you…when you…'saved' me!"

He swung at her again, the back of his hand coming toward her cheek, and abruptly withdrew. "I'll find Tyrolt," he said coldly.

Almost as suddenly as they had started, the pains were gone. In a few days, four or five at most, they would be anchored in Antongil Bay. The baby would not be born on board, after all. She put a hand on her belly; the child kicked, harder than usual—as if it were trying to voice its objections to what had just happened. She felt a surge of love. Funny, she thought, the myriad shapes and forms love can take. She would give her life for Sol, yet if he ever laid a hand on her the way Erich had done, she would leave without a backward glance. And there would be no forgiveness. Yet she knew she would, eventually, forgive Erich, who had raped her, lied to her, beaten her.

Why?

Because, it occurred to her, she did not love him— but pitied him for his weakness. Because he did not have her, and never would.

And the child's father?

Thanks to the Christmas rape, she did not know which man that was, and she was tired of wondering about it. Better to think of something else, like the fact that, in a few days, it would be the start of the Jewish New Year. *Rosh Hashana*. Normally a time of forgiveness, of celebration, hope, prayer, thanksgiving.

Normally.

Nothing about her life was normal. She had never felt more abandoned. The burden of pretense had been a heavy one; its removal should have been sufficient compensation for her loneliness. It wasn't. There was too much still unresolved.

She returned to the porthole, her watching post, and stared into the fog. The storm was diminishing. She could no longer hear the wind. The next few days would be long, and even lonelier than before. She had read everything on board, including all of Erich's books about Madagascar, except the one he kept locked in the brass-hinged sea trunk. She missed Perón's company, especially since she respected him so completely. How very much he had done for her...for *them*—she, Solomon, Erich, the baby. She even missed Leni, Nazi or not, for her dry sense of humor and interest in the world of dance.

But Juan and Leni were gone, and she was left with her own company and Bruqah's. During the next few days he brought in her meals, massaged her aching back, and spoke of all manner of things in a fascinating mix of innocence and wisdom, as if infant and sage had conspired to occupy the same body. Erich continued sleeping in the cabin, but their uneasy truce did not include conversation. He crept into his bunk late at night, when he was sure she would be asleep, and was gone before daylight. On the few occasions she had awakened before he left, she turned awkwardly to face the wall—and remained silent.

Today, convinced they must be closing in on their destination, she had spoken to him—pleasant words, despite her need to scream; words that eased their truce a little.

The cabin door opened. She turned, smiling; she expected to see Bruqah.

It was Erich. He avoided her eyes. "We've dropped anchor. Get ready to leave ship. Bruqah will help you."

He left the cabin and she returned to the porthole. The usual fog had shrouded the sea since dawn. As she stood there, it began to lift. An orange sun shone through a halo of clouds, highlighting a green saddle of hills, thick with vegetation and laced with mist, as if a trillion caterpillars had woven a webbed shawl to protect the slopes from the morning. Along the shoreline, she could make out wavelets shuddering against a mangrove-flat whose red, scalloped edge was overhung with interlocking roots and veils of moss.

A light knock at the cabin door claimed her attention. "Come in, Bruqah," she called, knowing Erich would not have returned. "Is that Nosy Mangabéy?" she asked, without turning around. "That small island at the mouth of the bay?"

"Yes, Lady Miri...." He sounded as if there were more he wanted to say, but his voice trailed off. His hands, normally so relaxed, were clenched into fists at his sides.

"What's wrong, Bruqah?" Miriam asked.

After several moments, he mumbled, "They're back, Lady Miri."

"Who's back?" She was growing impatient with his

reticence. When he shook his head, obviously reluctant to answer, she took hold of his wrists and looked at him insistently. "Who? Tell me why you're suddenly afraid. Who has come back to that little island?"

With a finger that was quivering slightly, Bruqah pointed to the island. "There is smoke rising from the first hill, Lady Miri."

Another interval of quiet.

"The ghosts," he said finally. "They have returned. They have come back to the island where the dead dream."

CHAPTER FORTY-TWO

Misha started the day with a sense of purpose. He was going to search for a gun. He had no idea how to shoot one, but he could learn. He had seen Sachsenhausen guards shoot them—shoot *people* with them—often enough. If they could do it, he could, too. He had to, that was all there was to it, because if he could kill some of the bad people on his thought-list, everything would come into balance, or even be weighted to the good.

He pictured the ledger sheet. At the top of the bad side of the list were Pleshdimer and Hempel, who appeared over and over, once for every time they did something bad. He had done the same thing on the good side, like putting in each birthday separately and not just lumping them under 'birthdays.'

Fair was fair, so there was also one Hempel entry on

the good side. Hempel had been nicer to Misha since the escape from the stateroom at Lüderitz. In his relief that the boy had not fallen overboard, the Sturmbannführer had given him the run of the ship.

He took full advantage of the concession, exploring the ship from one end to the other, but staying out of trouble and out of everyone's way, especially Hempel's, because nicer did not mean nice. He had not stopped doing *the thing*, just decreased its frequency.

Come nightfall, Misha had to go back to more of the same.

As the sun sank lower, each pitch of the ship became a clock, ticking him closer to confinement and pain; each toss made him remember the mental tally sheet.

On the one side were the good people of his life: Papa, Hans Hannes, Solomon Freund, Fräulein Miriam. The other side was filled with hunger and pain, with the Nazi men breaking into the apartment, and, over and over again, Pleshdimer and the strap, and Hempel doing *the thing*.

Free for the day, Misha found his way into the cargo hold where the military equipment was stored. He sensed that there were guns in the metal and wooden boxes that were stacked within the hold, but his attempts to open them proved futile.

Behind the stacked boxes was an airplane. Its wings had been removed and wired to its sides, along with two long floats. There was also a tank, not much larger than one of the armored cars that sometimes roamed the streets of Berlin. Tarps only partially covered them.

He climbed on both, wishing, exploring. The tank had a machine-gun in front.

"Rat-a-tat-tat," he yelled, imagining himself sighting down the weapon and firing bursts as Hempel, Pleshdimer, and the other Nazis charged toward him, falling like the dominoes Papa had taught him how to stack in long rows.

When he tired of his solitary game, Misha made his way on deck. To his surprise, the ship had anchored and, in the distance, he could see land. Could it be Madagascar, he wondered?

He stood at the rail and looked down. He could see movement in the water, dark shadows which he took to be sharks.

Setting aside all thought of swimming to shore, he wandered to the windlass room. He hid in the shadows, watching the soldiers come and go. He recognized some of them as dog trainers, yet he could tell by their uniforms that they were real soldiers. What a wonder that would be, he thought, carrying a gun and commanding a powerful animal! Would anyone dare hurt him again? Would he even need a tally list? He liked the trainers, and had thought about putting them on the good side of his ledger, especially after the one Colonel Alois called Fermi let him into the hold to pet the dogs. Once he even fed them, under the trainers' watchful eyes.

He leaned out of the shadows and tugged at Fermi, who was the last to pass by him. "Could I visit the dogs?" he asked.

"Sorry, Misha. I don't have time to take you down right now," Fermi said.

"I could go in by myself."

"Never, ever go near the animals alone," Fermi warned. "They might chomp you in half."

The dogs were better now, he said, except for Aquarius, who was still terribly seasick, and Taurus, who had a fire in her hip.

"Why don't you put out the fire?" Misha asked, imagining smoke and flame.

Fermi laughed, and tousled his hair. As the trainer walked away down the corridor, Misha thought about putting him separately on the good side of the tally sheet, and the dogs, too.

Noticing that Fermi had failed to rotate the door handle behind him, Misha crept from his hiding place by the ladder well that led to the hold. He put a shoulder against the door and shoved. It clanged open against the wall.

All but three dogs—the two sick ones and Boris, the wolfhound—came to the front of their cages, trying to thrust their noses through the wire. He went to the cages, pretending he was passing in review, much as he and the other inmates had done back in Sachsenhausen whenever Hempel had wanted, the other men said, to be admired. He kept his hands carefully at his sides.

Several dogs wagged their tales. "Don't be fooled by the tails," Fermi had told him. "Means nothing, with these dogs. We taught them that trick. Wag and bite, wag and bite."

The wolfhound perked up its ears, but did not look

at him. It stood and shook itself, gazing toward the left wall. Misha had lain awake often enough at night, listening to the creaks and groans of the ship, and to the scurrying of rats and roaches in the hollow walls. He supposed that to be what the dog was doing.

The dog whined and pranced as much as the cage would allow, increasingly nervous and agitated. Maybe it's the island that's making him nervous, Misha thought, remembering what Bruqah had told them at the farmhouse about dead spirits on the island, and how animals could hear them. Maybe that *was* Madagascar he had seen out there.

As if they had been triggered by the wolfhound's nervousness, the other dogs—all but Aquarius and Taurus—followed Boris' example. Their nervousness transferred itself to Misha, who began to think that he, too, was sensing something very strange and mysterious outside the ship.

"Good boy," he told the wolfhound, and released the latch. The dog instantly pushed open the cage door and, ignoring him, dashed toward the eastern wall, where he stood whimpering.

Is that how Major Hempel feels about me when I ignore him? Misha wondered. He fell to his knees and, heart pounding from the sense of danger, put his arms around the dog's thick, warm neck. The animal did not resist, so intent was it on the wall. Did the dog not realize there was a door, at the opposite side of the room?

As if it had heard him, the wolfhound shook itself free and went to the door.

"No," Misha said softly, crawling after him. "You can't go. Whatever it is you want, you have to stay here with me."

He stood up, took hold of the dog's collar, and walked the animal back and forth. The wolfhound appeared to relish the pacing, as if it partially relieved his anxiety. The other dogs watched, whimpering. "Good boy," Misha kept saying. "Good, good boy. Just like me."

We are friends now, Misha decided. He scratched the dog behind the ear. The wolfhound pressed its head forward in pleasure.

Then Misha heard footsteps in the corridor. The dog looked toward the east wall, whined deep in its throat, and let itself be maneuvered into the cage without resistance.

After relatching the cage, Misha secreted himself behind some crates of dog food. He would watch the trainers carefully from now on, he decided. He would learn how they handled the dogs. These dogs were special, Fermi had told him. Smart, tough, trained to kill.

With your help, Misha thought, eyeing the silver-blue tag that said "Boris" on the cage door and fingering the collar around his own neck, the bad side of the list will grow shorter.

Chapter Forty-Three

"We have stopped moving forward," Solomon said. "They will be coming for us."

He sensed Goldman turn toward him in the dark of the hold.

"Moving. Not moving. What difference does it make?" Goldman said. "No one has been down here for days. They have probably decided to let us die in our own filth."

No one had been allowed abovedecks since Lüderitz. The storm had turned the hold into a hell-hole, and the question of whether or not they would die of disease before they reached Madagascar was never far from anybody's mind. Guards had brought food of sorts and drinking water, but the prisoners had none to spare for cleaning themselves or the floor, which was slick with a sour combination of vomit and the swill that had sloshed from the latrine-drum during the ship's relentless pitching and tossing.

In this last part of the journey, he made no attempt to stop himself from thinking about Miriam and the child she carried. He thought about their lovemaking in the cabaret and convinced himself that out of that had come the child. No matter what, he knew he would love the child, as he would always love Miriam.

And Erich.

Though with Erich, the love was tainted. Veiled in the confusion of wanting to hate him.

Finally, on this day when the ship's movement stopped, he thought about this so-called homeland. Berlin, the only home he knew, would never be his home again; now Jerusalem was the only homeland he wanted, not this ersatz place called Nosy Mangabéy which Hitler and Hempel and, more than likely Erich, would turn into another camp or, at best, a ghetto.

What, he asked himself, had he really learned, on this long journey from boyhood to manhood? That he could see into the lives of strangers, and not into his own, and that the only constant in life was change?

If that was all, was it enough? Would he ever understand why the German people needed to suck at the breast of the beast of riot, the beast that was the manifestation of their guilt?

Nothing, he told himself again, happens for no reason. In some lifetime, if not this one, then another, he would learn the meaning of all that had passed...of the dybbuk, and the voices, the cruelties and the joys.

"Put your hands on my head," Lucius Goldman said

to him, in a voice filled with fear. "Bless me before I die. Speak my name among the angels."

"I'll be sure to do that," Sol replied, though he wanted to suggest that no self-respecting angel would enter the *Sogne*'s hold.

As Sol reached for Goldman, the door was flung open. Sturmbannführer Otto Hempel, standing in the doorway, smacked his billyclub against his palm. "Deckside! On the double! Move, you swine!"

Sol watched his fellow prisoners squeeze toward the door, all but the one next to him.

"Bless me by name, *shakkid*," his friend said urgently.

Shakkid? I am no teacher, Sol thought, let alone a great one. I have too much learning yet to do.

Goldman gripped Sol's arm. "Tell the angels the farmer from Juterbourg planted well, even though this is what he reaped!"

"The Nazis did not bring us all this way to kill us."

"Ha! Isn't that what life is all about? The child learning to walk so he can reach the grave? You go along. I will stay here."

"You will not!" Sol said under his breath, taking Goldman's arm and pulling him to his feet.

Unresisting as a child, Lucius Goldman allowed himself to be led up the ladder's thirty-nine steps. Together they emerged, tottering, from the ladder well and joined the Jews who were struggling to form ranks on the steaming deck, Misha among them. Seeing him, alive if not well, Sol said a quick prayer of thanks and dispelled the image of the boy jumping overboard.

"You're all going into the boats!" Hempel shouted.

"You would be rowing if we thought you wouldn't row in circles."

Shading his eyes, Sol squinted toward an orange sunrise broken by low clouds. Looking down at the glassy aquamarine sea, he watched a sea-cow bob a welcome to the newest Jewish exodus. After the dark of the hold, he was surprised and pleased at how clearly he could see the mammal. It played in the corridor of his vision, cavorting around as if the *Sogne* were its bathtub toy.

He saw hills beyond, lush with greenery, seated beneath a plume of smoke. But something felt wrong.

Pushing away encroaching panic, he focused on the shore. Gnarled roots lay curled like giant sleeping snakes. He could see them clearly. Too clearly. As if centered in a telescope lens.

He could see nothing else. What little had been left of his peripheral vision the last time he was in the light was gone.

"Move!" Hempel pushed him. "Think we have all day? You're to get in the lead boat with that Rathenau bitch." Raising his voice, he said, "Eight Jews in the lead boat. You other swine into the dinghies, and count yourselves lucky you don't have to swim with the sharks. Welcome to your home sweet home!"

Hempel kicked Solomon in the small of the back. Sol stumbled and went down, fighting to suck air into his lungs. He was vaguely aware of Hempel nudging him with a boot toe and of hands helping him to his feet.

"I'm all right." Sol shoved away the hands that reached to help him. "Look after yourselves."

He found his way onto the Jacob's ladder, took two hurried steps down the ropes, and stopped. Dangling, unable to move up and afraid to look down, he thought of Erich hanging in the sewer.

"Have a problem, Jew?" Kapo Pleshdimer's voice floated up from below. "Afraid of heights? Jump and I'll catch you."

Clutching the rope ladder with both hands, Sol lowered himself.

"Do you hold your seasons dear, Solomon Freund? Is this your season of madness?"

He missed his footing, sprawled headlong into the lifeboat assigned as a tender to carry them ashore...

And looked up to see Miriam's face, ghastly pale in the center of his tunnel vision. He crawled painfully toward her.

"So much as breathe hard, Jew, and I'll see to it the dogs tear out your throat." Pleshdimer grinned amiably and, stepping over Solomon, settled himself on the seat. Leaning down until he was close enough for Sol to smell his rancid breath, the Kapo opened his mouth and clicked a fingernail against his upper and lower front teeth. "What flesh the dogs don't rip away, I will."

Sol brought his feet up beneath himself and lay still. Miriam turned toward the sea, her back toward Bruqah, who was massaging the back of her neck with long brown fingers. "I don't know what I would do without you," she said to him. "Thank you, my friend."

He rose and, stepping across, lifted Sol's elbow. "Lady Miri says—come."

"I want him right where he is." Pleshdimer pushed

the man away and spat in Miriam's direction, then jabbed Sol with a foot.

Bruqah steadied himself. "Herr Oberst Germantownman say—"

The Kapo drew himself aside and allowed Solomon to be helped to his feet and led forward. "Go to hell!"

"No—go to Hell-*ville*!" Bruqah laughed heartily and slapped his thigh as if at a private joke. Leaning close to Sol, he whispered, "Hell-ville Britishman town—northwest side of Ma'gascar, on Nosy Bé!"

"Wherever it is, I wish you'd go there and stop babbling," one of the sailors said. He picked up his oar and patted Sol on the butt as if the Jew were a recalcitrant child.

Pleshdimer and the other sailors roared with laughter. "Come on, come on, let's go!" The Kapo motioned like an orchestra leader.

The boat pulled through the water. Swaying, Bruqah helped Sol onto the seat next to Miriam and placed himself at their feet.

"*Shana Tova*, Solomon," Miriam said. "Happy New Year." She looked down at the brown man. "Again I have reason to thank you, Bruqah."

"*Help me, Bruqah! I don't want to die!*"

That phrase again! Involuntarily, as when he had been a child in the sewer, Sol clamped his hands over his ears. "Help me, Bruqah," he whispered. Tentatively, as if touching her would restore his sense of reality, he placed his hand on Miriam's blanket-wrapped shoulder.

"*Shana Tova?* Is it really—"

"A few more days."

"Are you well?" He avoided the traditional, hopeful response of *Next year in Jerusalem*. Trembling, he wiped a trickle of sweat from her temple.

She put her hand to her face where Solomon had touched it. "If it weren't for the baby, I'd be dead. We'd both be dead."

"What?"

"There is hope for us," she said. "Erich is determined to turn Nosy Mangabéy into a settlement...a homeland." She lowered her head. "No matter what happens, we must stay alive. For the sake of our child."

"*Our* child?"

"Biologically? God knows. But you are my husband in His sight. This is our child."

Solomon sat in silence as the boat moved shoreward. He watched the saddle of hills loom larger and higher, and was almost grateful that his head ached with so many questions; it relieved his physical pain. Could the child really be his? What was his connection with this man Bruqah? And what of the island ahead? Was survival possible there? For him, Miriam, the child, the other Jews?

"Antongil Bay," Bruqah said, letting a hand dangle in the water. "More fish here than rays in the sun! Good shark, too."

He stared thoughtfully across the water. When at last he looked at Sol, his eyes were glazed, their expression hard. "Nosy Mangabéy not a good place, I think. Full of the dead."

Solomon looked up at the approaching jungle. The strengthening sun was burning off the mists; they rose from the interior like smoke from the nostrils of dragons, curling from roots and branches and tall, pale, skeletal tree trunks. The closer the boat drew to the wall of greenery, the louder came screeching and cawing from the jungle. Fruit bats hung from branches like dark linen, as undisturbed by the gulls and paradise flycatchers that wheeled in and out of the mists as they were by the approaching humans.

The boat scraped to a halt against the rocky shore. Miriam put her head briefly on Sol's shoulder, and Bruqah leaned forward, shielding them both with his body.

"During the storm, after Erich found out that I knew you were alive, he...he beat me." She was crying softly, her arms around Sol's neck in open defiance of what Pleshdimer or anyone else might do. "We came so close to a life together, you and I."

"We will find it yet." Sol turned to the Malagasy. "Help her, Bruqah," he said, paraphrasing the words from his vision.

"Yes. And you," Bruqah said. "I will help you, too."

Epilogue

nosy Mangabéy
september 1939

Sitting on the damp sand, Sol watched the lifeboats
and launches travel back and forth from the *Altmark*
to shore. Some brought only men; others carried
equipment and supplies loaded by Jews, crew members,
and the freighter's cranes. Knowing the German
military, there was doubtless some order about the
landing, but to Sol it seemed chaotic. He wondered
cynically if Abwehr manuals contained explicit
instructions for hacking a path through a rain forest.

One of the first boats brought Hempel, who strode
from the water with the wolfhound and Misha in tow,
and his truncheon firmly in hand. Erich brought up the
rear, stepping from his boat with the air of a

conquistador, head uplifted and eyes surveying the surrounding jungle as if he half expected natives to come rushing out and throw themselves at his feet with offerings of gold. Behind him, two Jews carried Taurus, strapped on a hospital stretcher.

"We're going to have to cut a path to the top of the hill," Erich announced. He looked at Hempel. "Bruqah is to be given a machete. After you've supplied your men, give the Jews the rest of the machetes."

"The Jews?" Hempel asked. "Is that wise?"

"Are you questioning my decision?" Erich's voice was dangerously quiet. "Take one squad and lead the way. Use Bruqah to guide you," he went on, having apparently decided to drop the matter of Hempel's insubordination. "Freund, stay with them and take care of the woman. Pleshdimer, you and Taurus bring up the rear." He raised his voice. "We are going up that hill." He pointed toward the jungle. "There will be no relaxation of discipline. For the sake of every Jewish life here, I will say this once, and once only. You are to use the machetes to create a path. Look as if you see them as weapons, make one movement that smells of an attempt to escape, and we will shoot half of you Jews and let the dogs finish the rest. Now move it!"

Without so much as a glance at Miriam or Solomon, he turned his back to them and waited to be obeyed. Hempel, obviously furious, strode toward the ridge of trees, his ever-present companions trotting behind.

Bruqah watched without comment or movement.

"Do you not fear them?" Sol asked.

"Pah!" Bruqah spat onto the wet earth.

"Does anything frighten you?"

Bruqah threw his head back and laughed uproariously. "You ask questions like a small child." He helped Miriam to her feet. "What Bruqah fears you cannot understand. Not yet."

"Tell me."

"Bruqah only fears things of man and not of man," he said softly, all trace of laughter gone. "Come, Solly."

Sol caught himself smiling. No one had called him that since he left his mother in Amsterdam. Seeing his smile, Miriam returned it with one of her own. He saw a glimpse of the young girl he had once known and felt a transient stab of hope as they entered the jungle.

Sunlight gave way to the dark and dankness of the rain forest. Sol's physical discomfort was increased tenfold by his inability to see more than a couple of meters ahead. A high-pitched chittering spoke of living creatures disturbed by the human intruders, and around him, pinpoints of lights flickered on and off, as if the forest were peopled by a million glowworms. Were it not for the water that hung in the air and covered him with a film of sweat, and the mold and moss that enveloped everything like a possessive lover, he might have been in the Black Forest.

Abruptly, the chittering stopped. A raucous sawing began, then a series of deafening squeals which rose to a crescendo and shook the bamboo and ferns into responding. Leaves rustled and dripped and snapped back, ignoring his swinging machete. When he looked behind him, the forest seemed to have regenerated. He could hear the others, Jews and soldiers alike, fighting their way through the heavy undergrowth. The air was hot, damp, and heavy.

Ha-haai! Ha-haai!

Soft and shrill and mournful, the cry echoed through the forest, its sound so chilling it made Solomon's teeth ache.

He lifted his machete. Behind him, he heard the unnerving, metallic snaps of safeties being flicked off as, again and again, the sound came, piercing through the branches overhead.

A guard, panicked by the unfamiliar sound, opened fire.

Ha-haai! Ha-haai!

"Eeee-vil!" Arms raised, Bruqah followed the sounds with a shaking finger.

"Probably a harmless monkey," Hempel said contemptuously. "Stop acting like a bunch of children."

"There are no monkeys in Nosy Mangabéy," Bruqah said in a low voice, the veins pulsating in his neck as he strained to see up into the jungle canopy. "Not in all Madagascar."

"What was it?" Solomon asked.

"*H'aye-aye.*" Bruqah turned away from them and moved through the tangle of ferns and vines, parting the foliage with his walking stick and his machete. In an instant he had disappeared.

"Come back here!" Hempel shouted.

Bruqah returned, clutching his head, wailing and spinning as if he were performing a ritual dance. Gripping his face, ogling the newcomers to the forest, was a red-and-gold striped iguana the length of his arm.

"Do something, one of you!" Grabbing Sol's machete, Miriam chopped wildly at the bush ahead of her. She collapsed, crying, as Bruqah reeled toward her.

"For Christ's sake!" Hempel shouldered past Solomon. He tore the giant lizard from Bruqah and, holding it upside-down and squirming, cracked its back and threw it to his wolfhound. Pleshdimer, crouched at the dog's side, looked up and grinned as the dog ripped the animal apart.

"Whatever's amusing you," Hempel said, "you might remember that one of these days you'll be glad to dine on that same meat."

"Are you all right, Bruqah?" Miriam asked in a small voice.

"I'm all right, Lady Miri." Bruqah signaled Solomon to come closer. "That thing." He stepped aside for a moment to allow Hempel and his machete crew to work past them. "*Liguaan*, like you," he told Sol. "He eyes the future while he eyes the past."

"How do you know…?" Sol stopped. He would examine the meaning of Bruqah's words later. Right now Miriam needed his attention. He helped her to her feet. She looked exhausted, he thought. He wanted to pick her up and carry her, but he was too debilitated; even with Bruqah's help it was all he could do to half-drag her along.

The climb grew steeper, the forest more dense. Layers of branches crisscrossed overhead, creating the effect of several stories of latticework. Because of the humidity and the lack of sunlight, the accumulation of leaves underfoot was slick. Millipedes and beetles ran over their legs, stickers jabbed their arms, wet ferns, rough as a cat's tongue, stuck to the sides of their faces. Looking for ballast, they found themselves grabbing onto the yellow pitcher plants that seemed to flourish in the forest despite the weak light. When they did, a sticky, syrupy substance erupted, bringing armies of flies and ants and mosquitoes against which there was no defense.

Sol slapped at his neck and looked at his hand. On it lay a mosquito the size of an average fly. Well, he thought, at least it would feed with equal pleasure on Nazi and Jew. "Look at this thing," he said. "It's big enough to shoot. We'll probably all need quinine, which doubtless our Nazi friends have brought along. For the time being, we had better do what they say."

The four of them resumed their climb. Eventually they found themselves in a boggy meadow, darkened by overstory. Only the lack of incline, the larger expanse of clear flat ground between trees, and the fact that those who had gone ahead of them were gathered together at the far end of the clearing, gave them any sense that they had crested the hill and exited the forest. Near them, leaning against a tree, was Hempel. "Wait here," he told Pleshdimer. "Shoot anyone who gives you trouble. I'm going to see what's beyond those trees."

Taking Misha and the wolfhound with him, he strode through the long grasses at the boundary of the jungle. A great sadness took hold of Sol. He must communicate with the boy, he thought, watching an animal wander into the clearing. It was followed by two more. They were oxlike creatures, humped and sporting enormous dewlaps, huge ears, and curved horns.

"Zebu," Bruqah said as several dogs jumped up, growling.

"*Zebulun*," Sol said aloud. "Jacob's tenth son. Father of the tribe of Israel. What might he have thought of this place?"

Pleshdimer lifted his rifle.

"No shoot," Bruqah called out. "Zebu are valuable."

Pleshdimer hesitated, then swung the rifle across his back and took off in a waddling run toward the animals, waving his arms and yelling. He chased the zebu from the clearing.

Unable to see anything peripheral to the center of his vision, Sol moved his head from side to side to examine his new environment. Judging by the charred snags partially sunken in the marsh and by the singularly large count of dead trees, there were times of the year when there was relief from the wetness that hovered around them like a living entity. At the far side, beneath a tanghin tree and standing on uneven stumps that elevated it a meter off the ground, he could see a lopsided, thatched shack made of mud and wattle and pandamus palm fronds.

"Man who lives there carries storm in she heart," Bruqah said.

Sol turned to look at him. "Is he one of your people?"

Bruqah shook his head vehemently. "He is Zana-Malata. He can live only within she own self. Same for me. My people, Vazimba, are a tribe no longer. We are like the traveler's tree. We nourish those who need us."

Miriam looked down the west side of the hill through a break in the foliage. She pointed toward the island's smaller hill. "This island can't be more than five kilometers square," she said to Sol. "One of Erich's books called it 'two hills and an apron of rain forest.'"

Bruqah opened his arms as if to encompass the sun that had broken into the clearing. "Once before, this island drowned in blood. Bruqah died."

"You mean your ancestors…"

"I mean Bruqah," he said quietly. "You know little, Solly. But you will learn…next time the island drowns in blood."

Sol watched a ground squirrel poke a berry into its mouth, masticating with absolute concentration. The human intruders were of no concern, the food its universe. A deep envy overwhelmed him. How dare it be wiser than he, to know such single-mindedness of purpose? He must learn survival from this animal, and from all of the others here.

The trainers sat at the opposite side of the clearing, holding their dogs, which strained to investigate the new territory.

Erich strode out of the undergrowth and stopped beside them. He let his gaze rest on the lopsided shack. "Will he come back?" he asked Bruqah of the absentee landlord.

"In time, maybe. Days…years."

The mouse-lemur Bruqah had placed at the nape of his neck shifted position. It clung to his hair, its sad, dark eyes too large for so tiny a head.

"Zana-Malata lives alone, like me." His lips turned up, teeth showing, in a hard smile. "Zana-Malata nourish no one. They have no friends. We Vazimba have also walked alone these many years."

"The original Vazimba came from Java," Miriam offered. "They were Madagascar's first inhabitants."

"And Zana-Malata—the last Malagasy race," Bruqah said. A hard look had risen into his eyes. "We are the beginning and the end, he and me."

"You know him?" Erich asked.

"For too long." As if to end the discussion, Bruqah reached to one side, plucked a fig from a tree, and handed it to Miriam along with a piece of wild ginger.

"Atten-hut!" Pleshdimer snapped, stepping into the clearing. Everyone stiffened visibly.

"Where's Hempel?" Erich asked, walking over to Pleshdimer, who shrugged.

Ha-haai! Ha-haai!

Like spectators at a stadium, heads turned in unison to look in the direction of the sound, Erich's among them.

The cry came again, this time followed by the body of a creature that looked like a cross between a flying squirrel and the lemurs Sol had seen illustrated in the books about Madagascar. With the grace of a trapeze artist, the animal leapt from the overstory and landed on a beech branch entwined with liana the size of a man's arm. Slowly, almost insolently, the creature raised its plumed tail.

As if he had carefully timed his reappearance for maximum dramatic effect, Hempel stepped from the trees into the clearing and lifted his Mann. Misha seized the opportunity and scuttled toward the closest group of people. The wolfhound hunkered down in the tall grasses and waited.

Ha-haai! Ha-haai!

The major smiled a tight-lipped smile and clicked off the safety catch.

"H'*aye-aye* have finger of death," Bruqah said.

Ha-haai! Ha-haai!

Sol stared at the coppery fur-ball. Its enormous, sad-looking eyes seemed to stare back at him with human intelligence. Its tail was wrapped around the liana and its skeletal fingers gripped the branch.

"Don't shoot," Erich ordered, apparently fascinated by the creature.

Hempel did not immediately lower the Mann. The aye-aye, with almost human understanding, lifted its left hand into the air and pointed at Hempel. It had a thumb and three fingers, the middle one of which extended beyond the other two—fleshless as the finger of a corpse long dead.

Bruqah stood in hushed awe. The mouse-lemur on his shoulder squeaked and burrowed down, but the Malagasy did not appear to notice. He stood perfectly still, his usually placid features rigid with fear.

Commanding his wolfhound to stay, Hempel strode toward Bruqah. "Shut your mouth, or I'll gladly kill you instead."

Something made Sol look back at the aye-aye. Its hand was still raised, its long bony finger extended toward the wolfhound, which had risen to its feet in defiance of Hempel's orders.

Back arched, growling, the dog turned to face the trees.

Into the silence there came a muffled roar, like the distant thunder of an approaching storm, followed by another. Clearer this time. Closer. Accompanied by the pounding of heavy hooves through the underbrush and a blur of movement, a massive boar, head lowered, burst from the bush. In a lightning movement that defied the creature's lumbering bulk, it lifted the wolfhound high into the air and held it up there, a bloody trophy impaled upon one curved horn. Lowering its head once more, it shook off the dog's body, and raised its foot. A shot rang out. The boar looked up, snorted, shook itself, and trotted back into the forest.

Hempel walked over to his dog and nudged it with a boot. Like statuary imbued with life, the rest of the stunned watchers returned to movement. The shepherds, growling, tugged at their leashes, and the aye-aye, its business apparently finished, leapt back into the overstory.

"Dead?" Erich strode over to where Hempel stood, gun in hand, and looked down at the wolfhound. Even at a distance, Sol could see that it was a bloody heap of fur and torn flesh.

"Might as well be," Hempel said. "Fat lot of good he'll be to me now."

"Shoot him."

Erich issued the order without raising his voice, yet

loudly and firmly enough to be heard over the shepherds.

Hempel turned to face him. "Who the hell are you to order me to shoot my dog?"

"I am the commanding officer of this operation."

Hempel paused, raised his gun, and released the safety. "For now," he said.

If he could have shot Erich instead, he would have, Sol thought, watching the unfolding tableau. Miriam had told him about Achilles, whom Hitler had ordered Erich to shoot. He wondered if Pfaueninsel torchlights flickered, now, within Erich's brain.

But Erich was not looking at the wolfhound, or at Hempel. He was staring at a bare-chested, sinewy black man who had stepped from the shack into the clearing. The man was clothed in a ragged loincloth, the color of which matched the red that peppered his curly white hair. As he stood there, surveying the newcomers to his domain, two animals with red fur and feline faces joined him, their muzzles twitching.

This puts the *Theater des Westens* to shame, Sol thought, as the shepherds started up their insane barking again.

"The dogs do not care for the fossas," Bruqah said quietly. "They will like them even less as time passes."

Hempel swiveled around on the balls of his feet. He pointed the Mann at the newcomer. Judging by the look on his face, it would not take much to make him use it.

Sol turned his attention to the black man. Simply looking at him was a challenge. Where his nose and mouth should have been, there was a gaping pink hole.

The hand he held up to Erich in mock greeting was eaten away like the flesh of a leper. Dangling from his fingers like an offering was a large wriggling worm.

Seeing that he had Erich's attention, the man tilted his head. With some innate sense of drama, he waited just long enough to allow Erich's horror to peak. Then his tongue emerged to envelope the worm and draw it down into his throat.

"Pisces, no!"

Pulling free of his master, who was apparently too caught up in the spectacle to hold firmly to his leash, one of the dogs bounded at the black man.

The fossas wasted no time. Whirling around, they darted into the underbrush. Reacting almost as fast, the man leapt toward his hut and scrambled beneath it. The dog leapt after him, frenziedly digging his way under the structure. From underneath the hut came a mewling conciliatory cry, and the faceless creature crawled out on his elbows. Swiveling on his stomach, the muscles on his lean back glistening with sweat, he reached underneath the structure and drew out the dog by the collar. The dog lay passively where he left it, inert, defeated, head hanging limply.

The man stood up. The hole that had once been his mouth turned upward in a ghoulish imitation of a smile. Placing his hands on his hips, he bowed slightly as if acknowledging his victory. Sol heard Taurus, who was still lightly bound to the stretcher, whimpering softly. Two dogs immobilized and one dead and they had just arrived, he thought.

"Let the dogs go!" Erich commanded. "All of them!"

Snarling, the shepherds leapt forward. Terrified guards and prisoners found their feet and their voices, and from the encircling forest varicolored birds lifted into startled flight. The screams of lemurs joined with the softly insistent shrill of an aye-aye hidden in the trees.

The dogs never reached their victim.

When they were close enough so he could surely feel their heated breath, the Zana-Malata crouched and patted the earth.

Sol watched in disbelief as the animals stopped in their tracks and, in unison and panting heavily, crawled on their bellies to huddle like house pets around the man's feet.

"Bruqah!" Erich turned and shouted, "What the hell! What *is* that…*thing!*"

"Zana-Malata!" Bruqah yelled back, stabbing the ground with his walking stick as he hurried after the others.

"Leper?"

"Syphilitic." Bruqah gripped his crotch for emphasis.

Ignoring the ruckus, the Zana-Malata made his way across the clearing toward Hempel, who moved toward him.

Motioning to the major to follow, the Zana-Malata bent down and gathered the wolfhound in his arms. Seemingly without effort, he lifted the dog and carried it to the shack. Hempel started forward, then paused half way there.

At the doorway the Zana-Malata set down the animal, turned and, with the same sense of drama, lifted his arms into the air and held them there. Then he turned and ambled into the shack, pulling the dog in after him, leaving Sol to wonder if the heat had already affected his brain and caused him to imagine the whole thing.

Pistol in hand, Erich burst past Hempel and the dogs. They jumped to their feet. He leapt the shack's steps and slapped past the zebu hide door, only to reemerge moments later. For a split second he went rigid. His hand shot out as if seeking support, and his head snapped up.

"M-must have gone out a back way."

He waved the gun, and Sol waited for him to order dogs and trainers, perhaps the guards as well, into the surrounding rain forest to search for the black man and the wolfhound. Instead, he stumbled down the steps. "F-forget th-them, f-for now," he stammered.

Sol had not heard Erich stammer in fifteen years. He watched with concern, worried that the lightning seizure—over the moment it occurred—might have had a greater effect on Erich than usual.

"W-we'll deal with that bastard later," Erich told his troops. Confidence was returning to his face and voice, and his stammering was already less pronounced. "We have a camp to build. We must always—*always*—keep that primary mission in mind."

Moving with an easy grace despite the heat and the soggy earth, Erich turned to look at the inhabitants of his empire.

"Though I…I'm a man of action rather than words," he began, "I feel I should remind you why you are here and what our plans are for you. Two hundred years ago, this island was a base for British pirates. Later, it belonged to the French. Now, it is the F-Fatherland's turn. The camp we set up here is only a beginning. Eventually, we will also p-penetrate the mainland. Shiploads of other Jews will follow you here. This is your new homeland." He looked at Solomon. "Your Jerusalem—"

Sol stopped listening. Erich's benign dictatorship was pathetic. Even if he meant what he said, Hempel would never allow it. Their hope for survival lay in his recovering his wits and his strength. He recalled what Emanuel and Margabrook and the woman, Lise, had said to him as he dangled from the noose at the camp:

"You must live....You have not yet fulfilled your destiny."

"Survival, Solomon! Therein lies your duty! There are things to be done that only you can do."

"Only God has the right to order the universe."

God and not Hitler!

The madman must be stopped in Madagascar. That was the grand design of the visions. There would be no penning up of Jewish assets and abilities here.

"That awful man...this place! I can't make it," Miriam whispered, clutching her belly and rocking back and forth. "I hurt, Solomon."

Stooping beside her, Bruqah put his hand on her stomach and tilted his head as if he were listening to something. "Your baby will come soon, Lady Miri," he said, standing up. "You must rest."

Sol took Miriam's hands in his and placed them on her belly. "We will get out of this somehow," he said.

"But we need to learn the terrain first, and gain strength."

"You speak wisely," Bruqah said. "When time comes, I help."

"What will you call the…our…child?" Sol asked.

"Erich, if it's a boy," Miriam told him. "I'll have no choice. A girl? It is a girl, Sol. I know it."

"What name would you choose for our daughter?"

"I would call her—"

"She will be Deborah."

"Yes," Miriam said. "Deborah the prophetess and judge."

Sol gripped her shoulders. "And Deborah the fighter and survivor." A wellspring of hope he had long since thought dry flooded his being. "There will be a next year in Jerusalem," he said.

He would have gone on speaking, but a sound behind the twisted roots that fringed the clearing like the legs of a giant spider commanded his attention. Bruqah moved toward it. He parted the brush with his walking stick.

"Lemur, maybe." He stared into the foliage. "Or—"

"Bruqah calls this place 'the island where the dead dream,'" Miriam said. "He thinks it is peopled by ghosts."

"Think?" Bruqah said. "You know the child. Bruqah knows this land." As Sol had done, he looked at Miriam's belly. "Maybe you will chase away the ghosts, you and Solly and the baby. There are surely reasons why you are here."

Because he knew there was a reason for everything, Sol nodded. When he knew what those reasons were, he thought wryly, life would begin to make sense.

Maybe.

END OF BOOK TWO

Afterword

Prior to World War II, Madagascar was relatively uninhabited. That, together with its being situated south of the oil-rich lands of the Red Sea and close to the British shipping lanes between India and South Africa, brought it to Hitler's attention. In early 1938, he instructed Eichman to collect material about the island for a "foreign-policy solution" to the "Jewish question."

The idea of expelling Europe's Jews to Madagascar, then a French colony, did not begin with the Nazis; the proposal goes back at least as far as Napoleon, who favored it. Between the World Wars, the idea was championed by Britain's Henry Hamilton Beamish and Arnold Leese, and in the Netherlands by Egon van Winghene. The Joint Distribution Committee of the

U.S. House of Representatives also toyed with the notion of resettling the Jews to Madagascar.

In 1937, the Poles, who wished to encourage the emigration of large numbers of Jews, received permission from the French to send a three-man investigative commission—two of whom were Jews—to Madagascar to explore the possibility of just such resettlement. In Berlin, the idea was greeted enthusiastically, especially by Heinrich Himmler, who wrote, "However cruel and tragic each individual case may be, this method is still the best, if one rejects the Bolshevik method of physical extermination of a people out of inner conviction as un-German and impossible."

Confident that Warsaw would quickly fall once Poland was invaded, in spring of 1939 Himmler called upon the S.S. and the Seekreigsführung—the Naval High Command—to test the waters of the Indian Ocean regarding what had become known as the "Madagascar Plan." There were more than seven million Jews in Poland; Czechoslovakia, annexed in 1937, had over four million; Austria, annexed in '36, three million; and Germany itself, five million. The numbers were growing beyond comprehension. *And had not the Führer promised to resolve the Jewish menace?*

The Madagascar Plan is one of numerous elements in the novel that are based on reality:

The cigar shop existed in what, until recently, was East Berlin. The owner—upon whom Solomon Freund's father, Jacob, was modeled in *Child of the Light*—was Janet Berliner's grandfather.

Leni Riefenstahl eventually produced her book on the Bushmen. Her film about the 1936 Olympics is considered by some to have been, despite its propaganda, the finest documentary ever produced about athletics.

Sachsenhausen and Oranienburg are for the most part accurately described. Flower beds were created in many parts of the camp, and prisoners' blood was sometimes used for fertilizer; the shoe track is also accurately described. The fictional Doctor Schmidt is a composite of two male doctors who performed medical experiments at the camp. Tabun was a nerve gas developed by the Nazis in 1937.

The existence of the Cushitic Falasha Jews is a matter of public record. That a subsect of the Falashas consisted of refugees from Elephantine, Egypt, is conjecture on the authors' part, but is possible. When the Elephantine Jews were driven out of the Egyptian military post and never seen again, they fled southeast—to what is now Ethiopia and the Sudan.

The material concerning the atom bomb is also a matter of public record. In reality, however, Lise Meitner fled her native Austria and went to Sweden, where she and Otto Hahn exchanged love letters and probably scientific notes. A mistake in calculations that resulted in the Germans continuing to use heavy water instead of graphite as a neutron moderator, and the fact that the Nazis' fear of "Jewish science" caused them to fractionalize instead of concentrate research efforts, were the main reasons Germany did not develop the bomb. Professor Heisenberg, the leading player in the German race to create the bomb, did play Bach fugues in the Haigerloch *Schlosskirke*, where his laboratory was set up.

The meeting of the *Altmark* and the *Graf Spee* is accurately described. The *Spee* was scuttled by its crew in Montevideo, Uruguay, after a raging battle with British ships. Captain Langdorff committed suicide. The *Altmark* (renamed the *Sogne*) was boarded by British marines in a daring raid near Norway. The British seamen-prisoners she housed (taken from the *Spee*) were released. The day after WWII ended, Captain Dau committed suicide. As of now, the authors have been unable to find out what happened to Doctor Tyrolt. The *Glowworm*, which very likely was in the South Atlantic during the time alluded to in the novel, was sunk after its captain bravely used the ship to ram and thus destroy Germany's *Hipper*.

Nosy Mangabé (to help the reader with pronunciation, the island is spelled *Mangabéy* in the novel) is a real island in the mouth of Madagascar's Antongil Bay. Mauritius Augustus Benyowsky built a bamboo hospital on the island during the late eighteenth century. Daniel Defoe studied the island as background to his writings, and the English pirate Captain Avery used it as a stronghold. Today, the island is the world's only official refuge for the aye-aye, a lemur that, according to Malagasy belief, can cause people's deaths simply by pointing at them. The area is also the source of numerous rare gems, including apatite, found nowhere else in the world.

Finally, readers may be interested to know that Madagascar's rain forest is the densest, the most definitive, and the fastest declining rain forest in the world.

Biography

In 1935, Janet Berliner's parents fled Berlin to escape the Nazi terror. In 1961, Janet left her native South Africa in protest against apartheid. After living and teaching in New York, she moved to San Francisco's Bay Area; started her own business as an editorial consultant, lecturer, and writer; and wrote *Rite of the Dragon*, which got her banned from South Africa. She now lives and works in Las Vegas.

Aside from more than twenty-five short stories, fifteen of them in the last year-and-a-half, Janet is the co-creator and coeditor of such projects as *Peter S. Beagle's Immortal Unicorn* and *David Copperfield's Tales of the Impossible* (HarperPrism, Fall '95). She co-created Peter S. Beagle's *Unicorn Sonata* (Turner Publishing, Fall '96), and recently completed work on *The Michael Crichton Companion* for Ballantine Books. Among her current projects are two Caribbean-based television shows.

In 1982 George Guthridge accepted a teaching position in a Siberian-Yupik Eskimo village on a stormswept island in the Bering Sea, in a school so troubled it was under threat of closure. Two years later his students made educational history by winning two national academic championships in one year—a feat that resulted in his being named one of 78 top educators in the nation. Essays on his teaching techniques have been included in such books as *SuperLearning 2000*.

As a writer, he has authored or coauthored four novels, including the acclaimed Holocaust novel *Child of the Light* (with Janet Berliner) and the Western *Bloodletter* (Northwest Books, 1994). "The Quiet"—one of over 50 short stories he has sold to major markets—was a finalist for the prestigious Nebula and Hugo awards. He currently teaches English and Eskimo education at the University of Alaska Fairbanks, Bristol Bay.

Children
of the Dusk

janet berliner and george guthridge

The following is an excerpt from
children of the dusk,
the forthcoming final volume in the
Madagascar Manifesto Trilogy.

Nosy Mangabéy

Grasshoppers blackened the moon.

The Malagasy laughed delightedly and pointed what was left of his fist at the predawn sky. Abandoning his guardianship of the limestone crypt, he shrugged off the ragged clay-colored loincloth. By the fading light of the stars, of glowworms, and of the last embers of the coconut husk fire, he began a sinuous dance of triumph. He moved around the moss and ivy covered totems that dotted the area, carelessly swatting at the mosquitoes and the rain flies that heralded a tropical rain. When he tired of the dance, he removed a liana from one of the totems, wove it into a garland, and placed it on top of his grisly red and salt-and-pepper head like a crown.

He ran his misshapen fingers down the totem. Miniature zebu horns topped an arabesque of curling leaves and carved lemurs balanced on one another's backs, looking outward with huge, whorled eyes.

The grasshoppers moved away from the huge egg yolk tropical moon, away from the Zana-Malata who grinned a toothless grin. *"Minihana!"* he shrieked. "Eat!" He opened the gaping pink hole where his nose and mouth should have been, pushed his tongue outward in the manner of an iguana, and drew a stream of glowworms into his throat.

He exhaled a burst of fire and chuckled at his own cleverness. Soon, he thought, it would be time for *lambda*, the dressing of the dead, and only he knew who waited inside the crypt. He and the tree frogs and the glowworms. Meanwhile, he could wait. Here, in isolation, time meant nothing to him—any more than it did to those who were buried in the *valavato*.

He moved around the moss- and ivy- covered totems that dotted the area. At his feet, a *Dô* snake slithered away, carrying with it the soul of one of the dead who haunted the burial ground. Behind him, five short, black men, eyes painted with white and black tar circles, bodies pulsating with a luminous white substance, appeared out of the rim of trees, cavorted a moment, and disappeared.

As if it, too, knew that changes were imminent, the rain forest chorus stopped. When only the bats sang *a cappella* in the damp tropical air, the fox-lynxes raised their long faces to watch him. The aye-ayes and the larger lemurs fled, the oxlike zebu sauntered down the hill, bells clanking hollowly and dewlaps swaying beneath their chins.

The Zana-Malata stayed where he was, listening to the voices of the dead. Chief of all he surveyed, he stared down at the crescent coral reef three hundred feet below the burial ground. On the horizon, his keen eyes discerned the lights of a ship moving toward him. He glanced at the moon hanging over the horizon.

It was beginning. The ghosts were returning to Nosy Mangabéy, his island where the dead dreamed.

•

In no mood to encounter anyone, Erich skirted the

meadow and the Zana-Malata's hut by taking a trail through the jungle on the steeper, northwest side of the saddle formed by the island's two hills.

He began to climb.

After about half an hour, his interest gave way to fatigue as his calves and thighs started to feel the strain of the climb. If this was to become his hill, his refuge from the problems of Hempel and Miriam and the Jews, there would have to be a wider path. And, he thought wryly, he had better rid himself of the thirty-one-year-old city-boy weakness that had developed in his muscles since the demands of rank and family had curtailed his daily workouts. He would take Miriam's advice, he decided, ignoring the spirit in which it had been given. He would fashion himself a javelin and use that and daily walks up this hill to get into shape.

He put his arm back, took several long strides which carried him through the last of the trees and onto the top of the hill, and threw an imaginary javelin. The action felt good.

Very good indeed.

He leaned against a heavily sculpted totem and saw that there were more than two dozen of them, each bearing the skull of an ox. At the crest of the hill stood a stone menhir—what looked like a three-sided rock house dug into the hillside. The roof was a huge stone slab overgrown with moss. At the northwest corner stood a larger totem. It, too, bore the skull of an ox, this time crowned with a woven liana garland.

He examined it up close. He could make out miniature zebu horns, curling leaves, carved lemurs standing on top of one another's backs and looking outward with enormous eyes.

He put out his hand to touch the totem, and quickly withdrew it as the thought occurred to him that the syphilitic had probably forged the path and woven the garland. Automatically, he turned full circle to make sure that the hideous black man wasn't standing somewhere watching him. Assured that he was alone, he forced himself to relax.

He had only been on the island for two days, yet he felt oddly at home.

If only...

He looked down at the area he had chosen for the base camp. The encampment, was roughly the size of a soccer field. The far corner had been set aside for the Jews, some of whom were still at work emplacing the tall posts of an eastern sentry tower. Others, barehanded, strung barbed concertina wire across the fences they had just completed. As for electrifying the fences—which Hempel was trying to insist upon—there were other, more urgent uses for the generator when they got it up and running. First and foremost, it had to be used for lighting the compound at night, and for pumping water into the water tank if the rain couldn't keep it full.

Yes, Erich thought, he could be happy here, if only Taurus were not taking the climate so hard, and if only he could avoid conflict between his trainers and Hempel's men, and the major's syphilitic friend, and...

Putting the question of Miriam and Solomon aside to examine later, along with his assessment of Hempel's true motives in accepting this assignment, he looked across the meadow at the trainers, exercising their animals while Taurus lay helpless in the medical tent.

Maybe he could use the seaplane for escape once it was ready. Take the dogs and the baby, and let the rest rot. From what Perón had told him, Buenos Aires seethed with women beside whom Miriam was a dishrag.

Yet despite his desire to leave, the island seemed to speak to him in tongues he understood. It was his, in a way the Rathenau estate could never have been.

Bruqah ran his hand from the mouselemur's head to its tail, causing the tiny animal to shudder with apparent joy. "We Malagash measure our worth by our cows, but we allow them to kill the land that is our mother... and theirs."

"We Germans measure our worth by—what, Erich?" Miriam said in an ugly tone, looking at the butchered zebu with undisguised disgust. An apparent wave of pain, reflected in her face, passed over her. "By our... our scientific accomplishments?" Her breaths began to saw. "Or our industrial efficiency." She shot Erich an angry glance. "Or by our capacity for killing."

"You weren't always this harsh, Miriam," Erich said, his voice trailing off. He stared past them, as though something held him motionless. Neither was it a sight that gave Bruqah pleasure.

At the edge of the rain forest stood the Zana-Malata, holding up the head of Hempel's huge wolfhound. Bruqah watched Erich carefully. He saw him glance from the dog to Hempel and back. Rather than revulsion, the colonel's face held an expression of anticipation and something tantamount to envy. He wants the major's head on a stick, and the sooner the better, Bruqah thought.

"I wasn't always hard and you weren't always a Nazi," Miriam said.

The words were barely out of her mouth when her eyes rolled backward and her knees buckled. Bruqah stepped forward, but Erich was closer to her. He caught her as she collapsed. She winced and, clutching her belly, doubled over in pain.

"I am ashamed to be part of the human race," she said in a whisper. She looked at Bruqah, and the animal wrapped around his neck. "Small wonder you hold lemurs in higher esteem than man." Glaring at Erich, she straightened up and pulled free of him.

"Concerning some men," Bruqah said, "I could not agree more."

Rapidly, the sun heated up and crawled under the wing. Misha stood up and brushed himself off. Pretty soon, he figured, Hempel would come to the plane for his morning inspection. What better time than now to do what he had sworn to do and kill the major? As far as Misha could tell, no one would miss Hempel, except maybe the Zana-Malata and Pleshdimer. Herr Alois would be happy, especially after yesterday. So would Miriam and Solomon. Maybe Bruqah would too, though it was hard to tell what he cared about.

His mind made up, Misha looked around for a weapon. The stones near the mangrove roots were either too little or too heavy. A stick, he decided. If he kept one hidden and at hand, he could plunge it into the major's black heart.

He picked up several sticks and tested them by stabbing them into the sand. The first two broke; the third bent into a bow.

Too tricky, he decided. If he chose the wrong stick, he'd end up not doing the job properly. He was going to have to find something more sophisticated. Something that couldn't miss, like a gun, or Pleshdimer's knife.

He found some shade under the second wing, lay down again, and looked up at the morning sky. He could see a raincloud approaching rapidly, bringing with it the day's first cloudburst. He didn't mind, in fact he rather enjoyed the momentary coolness that the sudden showers brought in their wake. But a gust of wind diverted the cloud, and it dropped its weather just to the right of him, onto the water.

With no other cloud in sight to distract him, he turned his thoughts to his list. He had neglected it of late because, truth to tell, it had grown a little confusing—what with Hempel racking up points on the plus side just by leaving him alone. That the major deserved to die hadn't changed, only the urgency of it.

The same was not true of Wasj Pleshdimer.

In his mind's eye, Misha walked through multiple possibilities: death by knife—too much fat to work through; by bullet—same problem; by fire—now there was something to contemplate. Better yet, he would set fire to the Zana-Malata's hut while the two of them were asleep. That way the fat Kapo and the syphilitic could fry together, like the grasshoppers on the fence yesterday—

"You think you can hide from me?"

Misha jumped at the sound of the Kapo's voice, so alive for someone who, in Misha's imaginings, was at that very moment being reduced to ashes. Not only was he very much alive, he held Taurus by a leash which he slung over one of the plane's struts.

Knotting it firmly, he knelt down and leaned over Misha, his face so close and his breath so acrid that it alone made the boy sick. Misha turned his head to avoid the stench.

With one hand, Pleshdimer turned Misha's face back toward him; with the other he gripped Misha's crotch and twisted.

•

Miriam allowed Sol to cover her head with his arm as the bats wheeled down to feast. Though she knew they had not come to hurt her, this was hardly her idea of a day at the Tiergarten.

She closed her eyes.

When she opened them, her fear having given way to

curiosity, she saw that the grasshoppers were still feeding on the grasses, oblivious or uncaring that they in turn were being eaten.

"I'm all right now, Sol," she said.

He removed his arm from her head and started to rise. As if on signal, the insects took flight. The flurry, followed by the bats again taking wing, nearly bowled him over. He sat down hard on the ground.

Miriam chuckled. "I don't mean to laugh at you, Sol," she said, "but this is all too crazy for words. What else can one do but laugh?"

When the last of the bats had flitted away into the shadows, she turned over and sat up. She felt amazingly calm as Bruqah helped her to her feet.

"I suppose you're going to tell me those were the spirits of the dead on this island where the dead dream," Miriam said, her voice almost jocular.

"Perhaps," he replied, "they were *messengers* from the dead."

She shook her head in exasperation and brushed herself off. Bruqah took hold of her wrists.

"You are bonded to the child you carry, Lady Miri," he said seriously. "Bruqah is bonded to this land." His eyes searched hers. "Maybe you chase away ghosts, you and Solly and the baby. But do not think the grasshoppers they come by—how do you call it—by coincident. Nothing happen by accident here."

Sol nodded, and Miriam felt the echo of her own earlier musings. Maybe Solomon was right. Perhaps there *was* a reason for everything, and if so, perhaps this insanity *would* eventually make sense.

But all of that notwithstanding, right now it was not reason that she sought. What she really wanted was a hot bath, a loofah to scrub away some of her weariness, and a real bed with a real mattress.

All of which, she thought, labeled her—and not Solomon—as the ultimate dreamer.

•

Solomon sprawled across the matted grass and listened as a nocturnal lemur, not yet settled after its night of roaming, took up the melody of the rain forest. Its voice sounded shrill and lonely—though Sol was sure his perception was colored by Bruqah's explanation that nocturnal lemurs tended to be solitary animals, while those that prowled by daylight were social and sounded quite different from their night brothers.

Far to the left, another lemur answered, its caw piercing the drone of the cicadas. There followed the tinkle of a music box playing "Glowworm."

"*Glühwürmchen, Glühwürmchen, Glimmre, Glimmre,*" Sol sang quietly. No matter what else happened in his life, he would never be able to hear that music without replaying the first time he had seen Miriam. The first time Erich had seen her. The night they had both fallen in love with the beautiful and charming fifteen-year-old niece of Walther Rathenau as she performed at the *KAVERNE,* the nightclub her wealthy, society grandmother opened next door to the Freund-Weisser tobacco shop.

How extraordinarily beautiful she had been, Sol thought. Not that she was any less beautiful now; just older, wearier.

He blinked open his eyes and sat up to find the canvas-covered area around him filled with activity. He realized his reverie had been deeper and longer than he'd supposed. Squinting in the direction of the music, he saw Bruqah, *vahila* in hand, seated cross-legged in the path that ran between the Jewish sleeping area and the main fence.

The Malagasy listened intently to the music box, then plucked out a reasonable rendition.

"Must you?" someone asked.

"Maybe some of us enjoy the music," a different voice said. "Close your ears if you do not wish to hear it."

Sol scrutinized the *vahila* player. Bruqah was so engrossed in his attempt to imitate the music that he scarcely looked up from the strings except to stare disconcertingly at the box and try another chord. After a dozen measures, he frowned and shut the box lid. He reached beneath his *lamba*, removed a small ring-tailed lemur from next to his stomach, and tucked the box in its place. Squinting toward the dogs, who were pacing and yapping nervously, he patted the lemur on its rump to shoo it toward the fence. It went hesitantly, constantly looking back, like a raccoon loathe to give up food found at a campsite. At the fence it lifted its tail and, as if aware that the shepherds were chained, sauntered with a diffident air between the wires.

"A gift for you, Rabbi." Bruqah's voice was low and emotional as he emerged from the latticework shadows cast by the sleeping area fence.

Sol glanced furtively to see if the guard was watching. He was. The man shifted nervously from one foot to the other.

"If it is not important, may *do* snakes slide from my ancestors' eyes!" Bruqah said, passing his hand across Sol's and leaving something metallic in Sol's palm. The shape was familiar, but he dared not look down, for fear the guard would come running.

"It was in the box of music," Bruqah whispered. "Lady Miriam say it yours. Germantownman would love to possess it, I think."

Suddenly the shape made sense. Sol passed his thumb

across the object, his mind immediately atumble with painful memories.

Papa's Iron Cross.

"That's an Iron Cross," he whispered. He took the medal from Bruqah, wiped the mud from both sides, and ran a fingertip down it. He could feel the inscription on the back, etched into the base of the clasp pin so lightly that the casual observer would miss it.

He remembered how Jacob Freund had gone over the original engraving, cutting deep into the metal for fear someone might attempt to delete it.

Solomon seized Bruqah's wrist and wrenched the Malagasy closer. "Where did you get this!"

"Germantownman take it from music box drawer. He say 'This was my father's.' Lady Miri say he lie."

"Erich told you this was his?" The depth of Erich's self-deceit made Solomon feel weak.

"This belongs to me," he said quietly.

The cold muzzle of a rifle touched the nape of Solomon's neck. "Move, or I'll kill you." The guard walked in a semi-circle, faced him, and jammed the barrel into his gut.

Along the perimeter of the fence, lemurs watched, eyes huge as eternal questions.

coming january 1997

the powerful
conclusion to
*The Madagascar
Manifesto*

children of the dusk

written by Janet Berliner and George Guthridge

WW 12122
ISBN
1-56504-932-2
$5.99 US
$7.99 CAN

It is friend against friend.

Follow the final journey of Solomon, Miriam, and Erich
as they enter the foreboding African rain forests of
Madagascar. In the breathless conclusion of *the
Madagascar Manifesto* trilogy, Jews begin building their
homeland—and plotting their freedom—under the
watchful eyes of their Nazi captors. Meanwhile, Solomon
and Erich face each other as friend and foe in a delicate
battle of psychology, ideology, and love.

ASK FOR IT AT YOUR FAVORITE BOOKSELLER.

Also from White Wolf Publishing:

The

Psalms

of

Herod

THE PSALMS OF HEROD

A NOVEL

Esther M. Friesner

Written

by

Esther

Friesner

Dark Fantasy
ISBN
1-56504-916-0
$5.99 US
$7.99 CAN

"There are a lot of delightful and unique twists to this book.... Friesner obviously has a lot of things to say, about religion and sex, spirituality and birth control, women and men, and this book provides her with and excellent forum in which to say them."
—Locus

"Friesner is likely to acquire a new group of fans with this new SF novel... totally unlike anything she's written previously.... A formidable novel.
—Science Fiction Chronicle

In the wake of an eco-catastrophe, civilization has risen once again in a form at once familiar and horrific.

A woman's place is to submit; to obey. A woman's place is to surrender her newborn for exposure on a hillside if the child is flawed in any way, even if it is born the wrong sex. A woman's place is not to decide these things.

Becca of Wiserways Stead knows this is the way, but in her heart, she cannot accept it. Becca's desire for change forces her to confront these dark traditions—but will the secret she carries be miracle enough to redeem a world?

Yes! Please send me

☐ *The Psalms of Herod*
>   *ISBN 1-56504-916-0*
>   *$5.99 US/$7.99 CAN*

For Visa/Mastercard and Discover card orders, call
1-800-454-WOLF

White Wolf Publishing
Attn: Ordering Department
780 Park North Boulevard
Suite 100
Atlanta, Georgia 30021

Please add US $1.50 for shipping and handling for the first book
and .40 for each book thereafter. No cash, stamps or C.O.D.s. All orders
shipped within 6 weeks via postal service book rate. Canadian orders
require US $2.00 extra postage.

*Name*_____

*Address*_____

City _____ *State* _____ *Zip Code* _____

*I have enclosed US$*_____*in payment. Payment*
must accompany all orders.

☐ *Please send a free catalog.*